Daughter of Destiny

# Daughter of Destiny

Erica Brown

**CANELO**

First published in the United Kingdom in 2005 by Orion Publishing Group Ltd.

This edition published in the United Kingdom in 2018 by

Canelo Digital Publishing Limited
57 Shepherds Lane
Beaconsfield, Bucks HP9 2DU
United Kingdom

A CIP catalogue record for this book is available from the British Library.

Print ISBN 978 1 78863 125 9
Ebook ISBN 978 1 78863 045 0

Look for more great books at www.canelo.co

Printed and bound in Great Britain by Clays Ltd, Elcograf S.p.A.

# Chapter One

## BARBADOS

'As the eldest son, I have the right to be first!'

Sending his chair crashing to the veranda floor, Emmanuel Strong staggered drunkenly to his feet and banged the table with both fists.

Opposite him, his back to the trees and the moon, Otis Strong belched, broke wind and shook his head. 'Shame on you, brother; married with two children and contemplating adultery.'

'He needs more practice,' exclaimed Jeb, the youngest, and laughed until the tears rolled down his face. It seemed outrageously funny to him.

The brothers were alike in looks, tall and square-shouldered with golden hair erring towards red and blue eyes that could be as bright as May or cold as December. They were all young, wild to varying degrees, but Emmanuel was the eldest and the dominant male in a pack of young lions. Otis was more lightly built than his older brother, whom he tried to emulate, though being second eldest was second best.

Jeb was last in line with regard to inheriting the immense wealth of the Strong family, so felt no need either to compete with or to respect Emmanuel. In fact he took immense pleasure in mocking his inflated self-esteem. Even now a smile curled his mouth, almost as though he were daring his brother to turn his words into action.

Emmanuel avoided matching Jeb's challenging look, and concentrated his attention on Otis, whom he'd always regarded as overly sensitive. Now he looked at him as if he were a complete fool. 'My wife's not in Barbados,' he snapped. 'I am, and a man has needs.'

Otis grinned hesitantly. 'That's got nothing to do with it. You didn't throw the first six. Whoever throws the first six, usually—'

'Neither did you,' Emmanuel interrupted, his voice and countenance surly with drink.

They both looked to where Jeb sprawled in a chair, grinning. 'To the victor...' he slurred and waved one hand like the conductor of an imaginary orchestra. 'And I will do my best...'

Gripping the table for support, he rose unsteadily, almost falling back into his chair as his knees buckled. Always the easygoing one, he laughed at his own ineptitude. 'I don't know that I'll be able, but the prospect of bedding that pretty little mulatto will no doubt encourage Peter the Pistle to rise to the occasion!'

Emmanuel Strong grinned and patted his crotch. 'No matter if you can't manage. I'm sure my own willing member can make up for your shortcomings.'

All three laughed as young men do, when fired up with an over-indulgence of Barbadian rum and the prospect of unfettered sex.

'Then let's to it!' Otis, the middle brother, who was never wild until he'd drunk a few glasses of rum, sent both glasses and bottles crashing to the floor as he reached for a brass bell and rang it vigorously, not stopping until Caradoc, a squat-faced Yuraba appeared, his walnut-coloured skin almost matching his uniform. Butlers, brown suits and gold braid had been unknown in West Africa, the place of his birth, but there had been slave trading, and, as a child, he had been bundled on to a ship along with the tusks of dead elephants. Africa was only a memory. Barbados had sometimes been a nightmare.

At first glance, Caradoc's expression was like that of a goat, placid and unexciting. But if the brothers had been sober they would have seen the contempt in his eyes as he asked them what they wanted.

'Viola!' cried Emmanuel, smacking his hands down on the table, his features sharply accentuated by the candles in front of him. 'I want...' He exchanged knowing sneers with his brothers before correcting himself. '*We* want Viola. Fetch her.'

'Not here,' slurred Otis, slicking his long fair hair back behind his ears. Sweat glistened on his high forehead reflecting light from the overhead candelabra. 'And not in the slave quarters either. It stinks. Let's have some comfort. No doubt the bitch will want some too. It's only right if there's three of us.'

A sudden draught disturbed the candle flames. Spirals of black smoke curled up to Emmanuel's face making it seem demonic. His eyes glittered. 'My room, Caradoc. Take her to my room.'

Otis backed down. Even when he was sober, Otis always did when Emmanuel gave orders, mostly because he sounded and looked so much like their father, Sir Samson Strong, who always expected to be obeyed.

The smiling Jeb shook his head. 'No. It stinks of brandy and old farts.'

Emmanuel glared. Unlike Otis who regretted being second son and tried desperately to please both his father and his brother, Jeb was the youngest and would always be overlooked. Therefore, disagreeing with them had become something of a habit.

A deep cleft appeared in Emmanuel's chin as he clenched his jaw, stood straight and clasped his hands behind his back. As the eldest son, he'd been groomed to take over the running of the business and was proud of the fact. Jeb had never been impressed, yet nevertheless, Emmanuel always strived to show him he was as ruthless and powerful as his father. Well he'd damn well impress him now! 'Supreme comfort; Father's bedroom,' he said with obvious relish, his eyes glowing with pride.

Otis smiled nervously, then pushed his hair back from his face, holding on to the sweaty strands as he contemplated the enormity of what Emmanuel suggested and the possible consequences. 'Oh, lord!' he muttered, and chewed his bottom lip until the blood ran.

Jeb, his face pink with drink, had a merry twinkle in his eyes and his smile was almost a smirk. 'You're not the master yet, brother. Take care.'

Emmanuel was incensed. 'Do you not believe I would do it, brother?'

Jeb raised his eyebrows, his cheeks round and shiny. 'You would violate the holy of holies, my brother?'

Emmanuel scowled. 'You mock me!'

Jeb laughed and shook his head. 'No. I dare you.'

Otis attempted to say something, but Emmanuel, angered by Jeb's scorn, fetched him a hefty whack that sent him sprawling to the floor.

'I'm going to be richer and more powerful than my father, damn you! You just see if I'm not!'

He took the stopper off a quarter-full decanter, tipped it up so some of it trickled down his chin, then wiped his mouth on his sleeve.

'Fetch the girl!' Emmanuel aimed a kick at Caradoc but missed. 'Well, get going, man!'

'And bring more rum,' Otis shouted after him.

Emmanuel threw him a withering gaze.

'We've none left,' Otis explained apologetically.

Jeb laughed quietly into his sleeve. What a disparate trio they were. Emmanuel had a need to compete with their father, but didn't even know it, and second son Otis would always consider himself to be second best, although he was a better man than Emmanuel. And me? thought Jeb. I'm like a pig's tail, pink and curly and stuck on at the end.

He laughed loudly and the sound was infectious. Soon, the others were laughing too, though they hadn't a clue why.

Their laughter followed the butler as he headed into the house and the back stairs that led up to the attic where the female house slaves slept three to a mattress and twelve to a room. He tried not to care about what was about to happen. Hadn't he seen it many times before? Leadenly, he dragged his legs up the winding staircase. There was no door at the top. The stairs spilled directly into the attic.

Little air came through the small windows set into the steep slopes of the mansard roof, a style more suited to the climate of Bath than Barbados. The moment Caradoc approached the room sweat broke out on his face and neck, and trickled into his braided collar. During the day the roof had conducted the heat of the sun. Like a bread oven just after baking, the heat remained, made stale by the sweat of many bodies lying naked and glistening upon the straw-filled mattresses.

Reluctant to enter, he stayed by the stairs and called her. 'Viola!'

Aware that the young masters had been drinking and apprehensive about what was to come, all the women were awake but lying still, waiting to see which of them would be called upon to provide the entertainment. A communal sigh seemed to fall over the room as most of the bodies relaxed. Only one body stiffened.

'Just Viola,' Caradoc added.

Sure now of their rest, sleep came easily for some after a fourteen-hour day of cleaning, cooking and laundering. Others raised their heads and looked to where Viola was rising from her rude bed, their expressions a mix of sympathy and relief.

Viola started to pull a white cotton nightgown over her head.

'That won't be necessary,' said Caradoc, pained that he had to say it but experienced in these things.

The girl looked at him, her eyes blazing. He'd expected her expression to be one of pleading, and was surprised. All the same, he shook his head and murmured, 'I'm sorry.'

Letting the nightgown fall to the ground and holding her head high, she followed him down the narrow staircase, welcoming the cooler air on her body as they got closer to the ground.

He told her to wait outside the door that led to the cellar. Wine, rum and a few kegs of sherry were stored there, the latter, along with flour, tea, fine clothes and fancies, brought over with the supplies from Bristol every three months or so. Although far from home, Rivermead House was as well stocked as Marstone Court, the Strong estate near the City of Bristol.

At last Caradoc emerged with a bottle of dark green glass, its neck narrow and its base balloon-shaped. 'Follow me,' he said without looking at her, steeling himself to cope, though it was her ordeal not his. Unlike other women and girls summoned like this, Viola showed no fear; in fact, something seemed to tick in her eyes. He felt she was measuring him up and, despite his stoic exterior, could read his thoughts.

There's nothing I can do, he told himself, nothing at all. He was just a slave, had been for most of his life, and would probably remain so. Thinking of what little life he had left triggered a deeply felt anger, an anger that had lain dormant for years.

Are you not a man? he asked himself. He'd heard that saying often of late, the confident chants of the abolitionists, unafraid in the face of men like Samson Strong.

*Are you not a man?*

In name, he *was* a man. But in deed? A eunuch, he thought. It was a word he remembered in tales passed from slave to slave, generation to generation. He'd heard of eunuchs in North African harems, there to protect the women, but not able to love them as a man should; just slaves, men whose penises and testicles had been cut off before puberty, now able only to pee through straws. That's how he was feeling now, like a eunuch, incapable of being anything but a slave.

Head bowed, Caradoc took Viola back up the wide staircase, where oak balustrades had been painted to look like stone, along to the wide mahogany door where light from the room within seeped on to the first-floor landing.

He knocked, entered and placed the bottle of rum onto a large satinwood chiffonier the young men's grandfather had brought out from England.

The room fell to silence. Emmanuel Strong stood behind a settee. Without taking his eyes off the naked Viola, he unfastened the mother-of-pearl buttons on his waistcoat.

Otis Strong was sprawled on the settee, smoking a large cigar, determined to emulate his elder brother. His eyes flickered as he gazed through the smoke. Viola stood in the doorway, looking incredibly desirable and without the slightest sign of fear. Otis gulped. She was not what he'd expected.

Jeb had already passed out. He was slumped in a chair, his head back and one leg crooked over the arm. He was snoring loudly.

Emmanuel Strong lay down on the bed, his head resting on his hand. He patted the woven cotton coverlet. 'Over here, my dear. Tonight I will make you a woman.'

Viola cocked her head. 'Are you sure you can make me a woman? Are you yourself yet a man?'

Emmanuel was transfixed. Otis coughed on cigar smoke, unable to tear his gaze away from the girl. Biting at the lip he'd chewed earlier, he waited fearfully to see what Emmanuel would do. He didn't like backchat from anyone, and this young woman was looking at Emmanuel as if he were the slave and she were the mistress.

Emmanuel stared at her, his expression alternating between delight and disdain.

The girl was unperturbed. Folding her arms across her chest, she said petulantly, 'Well? Are you going to keep me waiting all night?'

Caradoc closed the door behind him. Muffled by the thickness of the rich, warm mahogany, he listened, wishing he had the courage of his forebears who had hunted and fought their way from desert to coast on the continent of Africa.

'Are you a man or a mouse, you lazy, good fer nothin' black-assed...' he muttered to himself, then stopped suddenly as if something of the greatest importance had fallen on to his feet and pinned him to the spot. 'The old folks wouldna put up wiv this.'

Misty images of his ancestors flooded his mind and a terrible redness rose like dust before his eyes. He saw feet, many, many feet, tramping in time to a fast-beating drum. He saw shields, spears and felt the bloodlust of battle. Suddenly he was a warrior, just as his father had been, a man willing to fight and die – until he remembered how old he was.

'No, no, no!' He shook his head despondently, wrinkles rippling across his face then receding as he remembered other customs, other ways of vengeance.

He waited outside the room for his chance. It was two or three hours before all became quiet and Viola emerged.

He'd expected to see her upset as he had others. Instead, she frowned at him. 'What you doin' here?'

He looked her over and sniffed. 'You smells of them. Looks sweaty shiny too.'

'Might 'ave got more than their smell,' she said and patted her belly.

Caradoc was confused. Women were usually weeping after being called down to 'entertain' the white men. But Viola had a strange look in her eyes and seemed to welcome the fact that one of them might have made her pregnant. Women were unpredictable. It was up to men to be proud.

He raised a finger to his mouth and stealthily, so very stealthily, crept into the room.

Puzzled and unabashed by her nudity, Viola followed and watched, as Caradoc bent over the eldest brother, and spat into his face.

'What you doin'?'

'Sshh,' he hissed. 'Old African way of showing contempt while the enemy's sleepin'. When he wakes, he'll see the smug look in my eyes. An' he won't know why he feels uneasy. He won't know that I insulted his spirit as he slept.'

'You don't need to do this for me. I can take care of meself,' Viola said.

'Shhh!' he said again and someone stirred.

Viola backed towards the door as Caradoc bent over Otis.

Placing each hand on the chair arms, he braced himself so his face was only inches from that of Otis.

Behind him, Jeb Strong blinked the bleariness from his eyes, saw a dark figure bending menacingly over his brother, and leapt to his feet. Before Caradoc could move, before anyone could explain, Jeb grabbed a silver candlestick and brought it crashing down on the butler's skull. Buckling from the waist, Caradoc slid down over Otis's legs and on to the floor.

'My God! He was going to kill me,' Otis screamed as he awoke. His eyes were wide with horror.

Blood spurted from the butler's head, trickling blackly into his collar and quickly staining the rich pile of the pale green carpet.

Viola shook her head, her accusing stare meeting the eyes of Jeb Strong. 'No, he weren't. He was spitting in yer face, insulting yer spirit while you slept. What else could an old man do?'

Jeb stared down at the dead butler and let the candlestick fall to the floor. 'Oh my God! He was going to kill you,' he mumbled as he took in the enormity of what he'd done.

White-faced, he gazed at his brother in disbelief. 'He was going to kill you,' he repeated, felt sick and rushed to the window.

Otis staggered to his feet. Legs shaking under him, he wove his way across the room and shook his sleeping elder brother. 'Emmanuel! Jeb's killed Caradoc. Do something, Emmanuel. Do something, for God's sake!'

Emmanuel opened his eyes and started before the close proximity of his brother's face.

'And in our father's bedroom!' Otis proclaimed in a shocked, hushed voice.

Emmanuel hated being disturbed from sleep, and his face showed his displeasure. Expression unreadable, he got up from the bed, and pushed his brother aside.

With hardly a glance at the deceased, his gaze fixed on the naked Viola. 'Get back to where you belong,' he shouted angrily.

Otis pleaded. 'What shall we do?'

Emmanuel glared at Viola. 'Get rid of her. She's a witness.'

Wiping traces of bile from his mouth, Jeb shivered with fear, his face still as stone. 'What are you saying?' he asked without any trace of the usual sarcasm he reserved especially for his pompous brother.

Emmanuel looked at him sidelong. 'Sell her. Do anything.' He sprang to the door, laid himself against it, and fixed a cold look on the girl. 'Anything. We have to.'

'That's murder,' said Viola, her voice calm yet forceful.

Emmanuel tried to assess why she showed no fear. He'd been in card games with such people; Samson Strong had that same look when he was doing business. They all had one thing in common. Each of them had ulterior plans and had fixed their own agenda.

Jeb remained silent.

Otis was stunned, choosing to fix his gaze on Viola rather than on the dead man. Viola saw his interest, draped herself over the chair at his side and rested her chin on her hand.

'No need to sell me or do anythin' to my mind.' She shrugged a shoulder at the dead Caradoc. 'He tried to poke me on your papa's bed. You was passin' by and heard a helluva hootin' and hollerin' – me screamin' an' that. Ain't that fer the best?'

Emmanuel burst out laughing. 'Clever girl. Everyone knows black men are like animals when it comes to fornication.'

Swaying from side to side, as if she could hear a tune no one else could, she smiled as if she agreed, as if she had no intention of taking advantage of their own lust and the present situation.

Jeb, who up until now had seemed in a shocked stupor, wailed to high heaven as he slid to his knees and clasped his hands in prayer. 'Oh my God! Forgive me! Forgive me!'

Emmanuel frowned at the sight. 'For God's sake, pull yourself together.' He nodded at Otis. 'Get him to his feet. His behaviour unnerves me.'

Otis struggled with a wailing Jeb. Emmanuel's attention returned to Viola. 'For what price?' he asked in measured tones.

Viola thrust her pretty little chin that bit higher.

'I don't want to be a slave any more – I want to be a lady.'

Emmanuel glanced at his brothers. Jeb was still distraught, begging God's forgiveness and resisting Otis's attempts to get him off his knees, not that Otis was putting in much of an effort. His gaze kept sliding back to Viola. He still wanted her – badly.

Emmanuel smiled. 'Then a lady you shall be, my dear, though one slightly spoilt in the making.'

Sir Samson and Lady Strong arrived from England five days later, their arrival coinciding with the advent of Otis's twenty-first birthday. This was to be a one-off occasion, father and sons inspecting the cane fields, the threshing mills, the cooperage and transport to ship's hold. Following this, each son would be allocated his part in the family business. One son would go home with their parents with a view to reviewing the shipping side of the business. The other two would stay on the plantations and learn about growing sugar and the management of labour.

Tea was being served out on the veranda when the subject was aired. Sir Samson and Lady Strong had been told that Jeb had killed their butler to protect a maid.

'Obviously Jeb has to go back to Bristol,' muttered Sir Samson, his fine white hair fluttering like a cotton cloud around his gleaming pate. 'I had thought of leaving him here, but after this bit of nonsense...'

'Sugar?' asked his wife.

'Of course!' he snapped.

'I meant how many,' she said, her smile never faltering.

'Three, naturally!'

'Remember your gout, dear. The doctor said—'

'A quack! They're all quacks!'

At that precise moment a brightly coloured butterfly landed on his bandaged foot. Displeased by its presence, he swiped at it with his walking stick – and clipped his toe.

'Damn and bloody blast it!'

'Here's your tea, dear.'

'Damn the tea!'

Lady Amelia Strong rose from her chair, her smile undiminished. The pinkness of her cheeks matched the tiny rosebuds that patterned her dress of palest pistachio green. 'Business talk is one thing, my dearest. Blaspheming is another matter entirely.' With her head in the air and a swish of silk, she went into the house.

Otis's eyes strayed between father and elder brother. Jeb seemed not to notice her leaving. He was still thoughtful, staring at the floor as if it were interesting. Emmanuel's gaze remained fixed on his father, the man he most admired.

Sir Samson nodded at his eldest son as if sensing and appreciating his admiration. 'Now she's gone, you can tell me more about this other matter.' He grinned broadly as he remembered younger times when he hadn't had gout and had picked his women with as much delight as a child choosing a sugar mouse. 'Sly old dog, that Caradoc. 'Pon my word, I never knew the man had it in him? 'Pon my word, indeed!' He chuckled salaciously. 'Was she pretty?'

Emmanuel looked to both his brothers, but each seemed preoccupied, one with guilt and one with thoughts of love. It was up to him to reply.

'She's very pretty.' He omitted her name, but went on to explain matters further, along the lines that Viola herself had suggested.

''Pon my word,' Sir Samson repeated, shaking his head, his fleshly jowls wobbling against his high collar. 'The sly old fox!'

'Yes, indeed, Father,' said Emmanuel, his palms damp with nerves. He almost sighed with relief that his father had believed the story so easily, but he should have known better. His relief was short-lived.

Sir Samson's walking stick connected with Emmanuel's shin. 'That's the truth for the law, my son. Now let's have the real truth for me!'

Gritting his teeth, Emmanuel considered assuring his father that he was telling the truth, then saw the flint-hard eyes, the iron jaw. So he told the truth and watched for his father's reaction.

At first his frown was like an overhang in a granite quarry, solid shadows over his eyes. But slowly his expression changed. Sir Samson began to laugh, his face running with sweat and bags of loose fat creasing into folds around his eyes. 'Stallions!' he exclaimed. 'Fiery young stallions, just like I was in my day.'

Reassured by his father's exuberance, Emmanuel relaxed and began to laugh with him. Otis too joined in. Only Jeb remained unmoved.

Sir Samson slapped the back of his eldest son, causing Emmanuel's heart to leap in his chest. He was surely favoured, the eldest son and heir to a fortune.

'Like father like son,' Sir Samson said. 'So, who was this midnight nymph that you took to my bed?'

Confidence renewed, Emmanuel almost shouted her name. 'Viola,' he said and laughingly added, 'She wants to be a lady – in exchange for her silence.'

'Does she now!' said Sir Samson, his voice laced with a mix of sarcasm and cruelty. 'In exchange for her silence, she'll have the whip across her back – or I shall sell her, ship her off to the Carolinas where she can do no harm to this family. Lady indeed! There's no chance of that—'

'Detail, my dear Samson. Detail.' Lady Amelia, who had obviously been listening among the shadows of the house, swept back out on to the veranda and stood between her husband and his eldest son. 'As usual, my dear, you have no idea of the detail in this delicate little drama. You can't sell the girl, and neither can you have her whipped. You promised her father.'

'Eh?' Sir Samson looked nonplussed.

His wife's smile was undiminished as she towered over him. The fringes of her silk shawl fell like a waterfall from beneath her folded arms.

'Viola is Captain Desmond's daughter that he got on Magdalene. Her mother might be a slave, and so is Viola, but with stipulations. Captain Desmond is one of your best captains and you promised him you'd look after her properly. That means no whipping and no selling on.'

Sir Samson glared at his wife, then at his sons. 'But that means I have to adhere to the bargain that these young puppies made with her,' he exclaimed in amazement.

Lady Amelia's lips parted in an amused smile. 'My, my. A moment ago your sons were stallions. Now they've become puppies.' She pushed past Emmanuel and fondled the head of her youngest son. For the first time that day, she turned a smile-free face on her husband. 'Either that, my dear husband, or one of our young stallions could end up on the gallows.'

Emmanuel sprang to his feet. 'They couldn't hang him. He could say it was self-defence. He thought Caradoc was attacking Otis.'

Lady Samson looked at him coldly. 'You may be willing to take a chance on that. As his mother, I will not allow it.' Jeb remained as silently withdrawn as he had done since that evening. His mother nestled his head beneath her breasts, her fingers running through his hair. She looked down at him. 'Prison would be bad enough, but look at him. He's riddled with guilt. He'll tell them he did it in cold blood purely to save his soul.'

For a while, time seemed suspended in silence. Only the sound of insects and the crying of seabirds disturbed the warm evening. It was Otis who finally spoke.

'She's a lovely looking young woman,' he said and surprised everyone. It wasn't like him to express his feelings, especially in front of his parents. 'I think I could be fond of her,' he said.

Lady Samson raised her eyebrows and looked from her son to her husband. 'I take it that this is the time when respectable women should leave the room.'

No one responded.

'I see,' she said and, for the second time that day, she left them to cogitate.

The men guarded their conversation until sure they were alone. Sir Samson looked to Otis. 'I trust we're talking about setting her up apart from the family, not moving the wench into the house?'

'Well...' Otis began in his usual nervous fashion.

'He does,' said Emmanuel.

Otis shot him a grateful smile.

Sir Samson turned his attention to his youngest son and frowned. His other sons had come through this easily enough, although of course they were not the perpetrators of the killing. That responsibility lay on Jeb's shoulders.

He said, 'Under the circumstances, it's best that Otis stays here in Barbados as manager of the estate.' He smiled. 'In time we'll get him a wife, but no doubt he will not be lonely.'

Otis smiled warmly and Emmanuel laughed.

With the help of his stick, Sir Samson struggled to his feet. 'Back to England for both of us,' he said to Emmanuel, and looked pleased at the prospect. Turning to Jeb, he said, 'I had planned for both you and Otis to stay here. I now think it's best that you accompany your brother and me back to England. There's the shipping side of the business—'

'The clergy!'

Jeb had hardly spoken for days so the sound and sharpness of his voice took them all by surprise. 'I've decided to join the clergy,' he repeated.

His father looked fit to burst. 'Nonsense!'

Emmanuel was astounded. 'You're mad!'

Jeb shook his head. 'I have to do penance for my sin. It's only right.'

'Right? Right?' Sir Samson began to splutter, his face reddening as he fought for breath. Finally, he got his coughing under control. Pointing his quivering stick at his youngest son, he said, 'You'll regret it, my son. You have all this!'

Jeb ran his eyes over the rich green fields, the toiling slaves, and the sea beyond. Behind him was the stunning opulence of Rivermead House, though its construction and furnishings were nothing when compared to Marstone Court.

'I've been walking and thinking a lot just lately. I walked down to the harbour and I saw children around the Bridgetown docks, starving they were and dressed in rags. There's sugar growing all around, but not for the likes of them. I want to do something about it.'

Sir Samson guffawed as though it were the funniest joke in the world. 'Well, you can't. You're going back to Bristol. That'll scupper that little plan, my son!'

Jeb shrugged, his expression completely calm. 'Barbados or Bristol. It makes no difference. There are street urchins in every city.'

Sir Samson scowled. 'You'll regret it, my boy! Mark my words.'

Unseen by her husband, Lady Strong watched from the shadows beyond the doorway. She smiled and there was a look of pride on her face. Jeb saw her, and knew his mother understood. He'd been born into wealth and administered to since birth. In recompense for what he had done, he would administer to the disadvantaged for the rest of his days.

'You're a fool,' muttered Emmanuel.

'And you're the eldest son,' Jeb said with a smile. 'You have to follow in our father's footsteps, but I can do as I please.'

Their father interrupted. 'Manny,' he said, his face shining with the pride of a man who knows his son is exactly as he wants him to be, a perfect copy of himself, 'not going to disappoint me and join a monastery, are you?' He laughed loudly.

Emmanuel clicked his fingers at the new butler, whose hands shook as he filled four glasses to the brim with dark, Barbadian rum. 'No, Father.' He raised his glass. 'I promise to follow in your footsteps – only I shall take bigger strides!'

Father and son laughed together.

Hating to be left out, Otis laughed too, pleased to remain in Barbados with sole responsibility for the plantation, and to be regarded enough of a man to take a mistress.

Only Jeb remained silent, his eyes locking in mute understanding with those of his mother. Perhaps she knew that he woke in a sweat in the middle of the night, unable to move and crying for something lost. The slaves believed that dreams were portents of things to come. He hoped they were wrong and that retribution would not fall on his or the heads of those he loved.

## Chapter Two

'I am truly blessed,' the Reverend Jeb Strong said to his wife Miriam on their wedding day.

He repeated that statement frequently over the next eleven years on the birth of their six daughters and one son. Life was good, and Jeb had come to believe that God had forgiven him for killing Caradoc. He often preached from the pulpit that God forgave the wickedest sinner so long as they truly repented. Spending his life in the service of God and of those less fortunate than himself, he believed, would be his enduring act of penitence. All the same, he got down on his knees every night and prayed that his happiness would continue, that the dreaded retribution would never come.

Unfortunately, it did.

It had been raining for weeks. Jeb's children – Jasper, Patience, Piety, Charity, Ruth, Rachel and Leah – pressed their faces against the rain-lashed windows, desperate for the chance to get out.

'They're like parrots in a cage,' Miriam Strong said.

'Now, where are you parrots hoping to fly?' Jeb asked his children.

'India,' said Piety.

'Jerusalem,' Charity countered.

Jeb shook his head, his eyes rolling as if all patience with his children was at an end, which was far from the truth. Jeb was a patient man.

'And where do you want to fly?' Jeb asked his son, Jasper, who was eight years old and not as strong a lad as he'd like him to be.

'The South Seas,' lisped Jasper, his voice full of wonder. 'But I'd like to sail the South Seas, not fly over them. I like the water. And I like ships.'

Jeb shook his head again. 'Sorry. No India, no Jerusalem and no South Seas. But how about Marstone Court on Sunday? It's your cousin Horatia's birthday and we're invited to tea. Nelson will be there too.'

Just as he'd expected, the idea of getting out of the house and the city, and into the country with the prospect of a good tea, was enough to lift their spirits – and send them off in search of bread and jam.

'So will Emmanuel's new wife, no doubt,' muttered Miriam who, although she thought it only right and proper that Emmanuel's two children by his first marriage should have a new mother, did not approve of his choice.

'I know she's young...' Jeb began, giving her a disparaging look. It wasn't like Miriam to dislike anyone.

'That's not the point,' Miriam interrupted. 'Verity may well warm his bed, but her heart's cold, especially where Horatia and Nelson are concerned. If only Marguerite hadn't caught smallpox...'

'God's will,' murmured Jeb, and said a silent prayer for his sister-in-law's soul and also for his parents, who had drowned in a Caribbean hurricane.

'Amen,' Miriam said with a heavy sigh.

–

On the day of Horatia's birthday, thin clouds still hid the sun, but the rain had stopped. Once the children were together at Marstone Court, they were accompanied outside by their nurse whose real name was Gertie but was called Peters, as every other nurse had been.

Peters was being courted by one of the footmen, who followed them out of the house. Some but not all of the children took advantage of her lack of attention and headed across the park – quietly past a small gathering of red deer they'd always been told not to disturb – over a stile and down to the water meadows.

The river had broken its banks only a few days before and the meadow was partially submerged. Daring, despite his delicate appearance, Jasper chose to climb a stout oak. Some of its branches dipped into the floodwater, which swirled across' the meadow in a raging torrent.

The girls attempted the lower branches, except Horatia, who considered herself too grown-up for that. But she didn't like being left out.

'Come down, all of you, or you won't come to my birthday party.'

The girls, mindful of getting their party dresses snagged on sharp twigs, got down. Much to Horatia's annoyance, Jasper stayed put.

'Jasper, if you don't come down, you can't come to my party.'

Jasper did his best not to show he cared about going to his cousin's party and swung his legs nonchalantly from either side of a branch some twelve feet or more off the ground. 'I don't want to go to your tiresome party, Horatia Strong!'

Careful so as not to slip, Jasper drew his legs up on to the branch and slowly stood up, gripping branches for support. Sharp twigs scratched at his brown velvet suit, an outfit he'd willingly see ripped to shreds. 'I can see the sea,' he shouted, tossing his corn-coloured hair and pointing into the distance.

'That's not the sea. It's the river, you stupid boy,' said Horatia. 'It's just wider than usual.'

'I'm hungry. Can we go now?' her brother Nelson whined, tugging at her sleeve.

Leah, Jasper's youngest sister, was jumping in and out of a puddle. One of her older sisters, Ruth, pulled her out. 'Come on, Leah. We have to get back to the house before Patience and the others eat all the cake.'

Rachel, the last of the three sisters to accompany Jasper, Horatia and Nelson into the water meadow, began bounding back up over the grass.

'Are you coming, Jasper?' she shouted over her shoulder.

'No,' he shouted back. 'I'm going to run away to sea.'

'He's always telling Father that,' said Rachel in a weary tone.

Horatia folded her arms and looked up at him. 'You wouldn't dare go away to sea. Besides, you've got a bad chest.'

'I would,' he replied. 'I shall climb masts every day. I'm a good climber. Just watch me.'

Nelson and Horatia strained their necks looking up, as Jasper climbed higher and higher.

Without taking her eyes off him, Horatia shook her head. 'You are so stupid, Jasper. I hope Boney the Bogeyman gets you! Come on, everyone! Back to the house.'

Jasper took no notice. His gaze was fixed on the flooded river as it wound its way towards the Avon Gorge and the sea beyond. 'I'm going to run away to sea,' he said softly, as a stray log bumped into the trunk of the tree before the water tugged it away.

By the time he got down, the others were gone and the light was dying. He ran back up the water meadow alone, jumping hillocks of coarse grass and reaching out for mayflies before they darted out of his way.

As he re-entered the park, he looked round for the herd of red deer that had been there earlier but was disappointed. The girls had scared them away, he decided. They were probably giggling too loud and should know better.

Light from Marstone Court fell out in great oblongs upon the terrace that ran along between the main entrance and the orangery.

Cupping his hands, Jasper pressed his face against the windows of the ballroom where his red-faced Uncle Emmanuel was standing next to a painting, pointing at it with one hand, and waving a full glass in the other. His mouth was opening and shutting, but Jasper couldn't hear what he was saying. The room was packed. It seemed as though the whole household, right down to the scullery maids and the stable lads, had been summoned.

Everyone inside seemed to be listening, even the children, which seemed stupid to him as the feast was in the other room. Avoiding having to listen to his uncle seemed a good idea. He would creep in and sample the cakes and jellies before anyone else. He decided to sneak out through the stable yard and into the dining room through the passageway that the servants sometimes used when they were leaving for their day off.

Running as swiftly and silently as possible, he darted across the swept cobbles. The door was heavy, but he managed to heave it open. It was dark inside and smelt of dampness, leather and cabbage. And it was so quiet and far blacker than he'd expected, and he'd never liked the dark. Heart beating fast, he tiptoed along the passageway. Halfway along he stopped. A muffled but regular thudding sounded off to his left. The shy glimmer of a candle or lantern ebbed from beneath a door. Curious to discover the source of the light, he opened it, looked down a flight of cold stone steps and froze to the spot.

A man, a very ugly man, looked up at him. The body of a red deer lay on the steps. Its eyes were glassy and staring, and its tongue lolled from its mouth.

Jasper remembered what Horatia had said.

Boney the Bogeyman! Boney who'd fought the Russians, Boney who'd marched over half the world, fighting and killing men, women and children.

He'd heard stories about him, read of his crimes in cheap penny sheets. Though they said he was dead now, the penny sheets thought otherwise. And here he was, having killed a deer! And Jasper was smaller than a deer...

Before Boney could grab him, Jasper turned and ran. The ballroom where everyone was gathered perhaps? Or the kitchens? Someone must be around! He ran towards the dining room where he had meant to sample the birthday cake and all the other delights and tugged at the door that divided the old passageway from the new one that led into the main house. It didn't budge.

Jasper ran back towards Boney – who was coming at him with a *knife*. Terrified, he side-stepped and ran up the narrow staircase that led to the top of the house and the servants' quarters.

By the time he'd climbed to the top, he was breathless and his chest pained, enough to bend him double. He'd seen no one since leaving the stable yard except the man in the cellar. Although everyone had been summoned to the ballroom, he'd still expected to bump into a maid or a boot boy.

His pursuer's earthy sweatiness followed him like a rancid fog. He could hear his breathing, almost as loud as his own, which now came in short, sharp gasps.

'Stay there, boy. I won't 'urt you.' The voice was accompanied by the tramp of heavy boots. The man was tiring, but so was Jasper.

He ran as swiftly and silently as he could along the top corridor, trying each door he passed, but each of them was locked. Eventually he found one that wasn't and pushed it open. It looked as if it hadn't been entered in years. Cobwebs hung from the ceiling and dust covered the floor.

He'd thought to find a cupboard to hide in, or perhaps even someone to save him from the man with the knife. Frantic with fear, his gaze travelled to the fireplace. It was bigger than most in this part of the house and hadn't been used in a long while. Bits of dry mortar and soot littered the grate. The iron flap that was bolted across the flue when it wasn't in use, hung down, unbolted at the back.

Jasper bent under the mantelpiece and looked up. He could see no light at the top, but could make out gaps in the mortar where he could easily get a foothold. After closing the heavy metal flue plate behind him, he climbed up into the darkness. The pain in his chest increased as he breathed in the sooty, stale air. To make matters worse, smoke seeped from the main chimney through gaps in the brickwork. Breath rasping in his ever-tightening chest, he climbed higher into the narrower part of the flue and jammed himself there, safe from Boney, warm and steadily sinking into unconsciousness.

–

'The last time we saw him, he was sitting up a tree.'

Horatia's words echoed in Jeb's mind as he stared at the swirling waters, his arm lying protectively around his wife's back.

'She told him Boney the Bogeyman would get him,' whimpered Rachel, her eyes red from crying. 'He's frightened of Boney.'

Horatia was too frightened to glare, but felt she had to justify herself. 'He knows Boney's dead. He knows we beat him at Waterloo. He must do! That's why he wasn't frightened. That's why he stayed.'

On seeing her words made no difference to what people were doing, she burst into tears.

Emmanuel patted his brother's back. 'There's nothing you can do here, Jeb. The tide's high, the river's swollen. He's gone.'

The men from the estate had spent two days wading through the flood-water, probing with sticks, diving into the deeper and more dangerous waters, but had found nothing. There was normally a forty-foot difference between high and low tide. Following the heavy rain, the tidal range had increased, the ebbing waters sucking trees, carts and animals from swollen eddies.

Jeb felt colder than he ever had in his life. He squeezed his eyes shut, but the tears still came. He'd promised himself that, for Miriam's sake, he would not cry. But he couldn't help it. They cried together.

At last he threw his head back and looked up at the sky. 'Why did this happen, God?'

It was Miriam who comforted him. 'There must be a reason,' she said to him. 'God does everything for a reason.'

They still had six daughters and each other. They were still a family.

–

Miriam never presented Jeb with any more children. They both consoled themselves feeding the street urchins they found along Bristol's waterfront and enrolling some in their training ship moored next to the Hole in the Wall tavern in the centre of the city.

He wasn't sure when the dreams started. There was a blue-eyed boy, thin and ragged and shiny with sugar. In his dream he took hold of his hand, turned away, then turned back and the boy was a man. He told Miriam about it.

'Perhaps he's a replacement for the one we lost,' she said. 'A gift from God.'

Sugar from the Strong plantations was landed at Redcliffe Wharf and from there was taken by barge to one of the many sugar refineries in the city. Starving people were attracted by the sugar, though only the most desperate got past Reuben Trout, the night watchman.

'There's one out there,' Trout whispered when Jeb arrived at the warehouse around nine one night.

'Good work,' Jeb whispered back.

His breath turned to steam as he peered through the darkness, the light from his lantern flickering over piled casks and sweet-smelling hogsheads. Suddenly, he saw movement, a shadow still, then running.

'Trout! Get him, man!'

Trout lumbered after the shadow and pounced. 'Got ya!' Grabbing the boy by his filthy rags, he sneered as he spat through the gap in his teeth and slammed the boy against a bank of barrels hard enough to break bones. 'Now, what you bin up to?'

'Nothing!' The boy's tone was defiant.

Jeb Strong held his lantern a little higher to see what manner of street urchin it was. The light picked out eyes sunk deeply into dark sockets and cheekbones that looked in danger of piercing the skin. Jeb gritted his teeth. Almost dead, he thought, and swallowed back the lump that rose like bile in his chest. There were plenty of skinny children in Bristol. Scrawny ragamuffins were almost as numerous as the rats that gnawed the barrels and sucked the molasses out through the thinned wood. Starvation had made most of them thieves. With sugar at more than £2 per hogshead on the open market, it paid to roll a barrel away when no one was looking, smash it in some dark corner and half fill a sack before running off. Rogues looking to turn a profit thronged the dockside taverns from the Hole in the Wall to the Shakespeare, from the Welsh Back to Redcliffe Wharf; there was always a market for contraband.

Something shone around the boy's mouth and Jeb knew it wasn't frost. It was cold enough, but not late enough. By the time the frost formed, well before the clocks and bells of the city's many churches struck twelve, he'd be off home, in the bosom of his family and sitting snugly before a roaring fire with a plate of muffins on his lap and a glass of toddy warmed with a red hot poker.

Self-consciously, the boy licked his lips.

Jeb Strong was not a hard man and prided himself on being fair. He kept an open mind as he asked, 'What's that around your mouth, boy?'

Trout shook the boy as vigorously as he might shake the dust from a dirt-laden mat and the boy flopped like one, his thin white arms hanging like bare sticks from torn sleeves. 'Go on. Answer the Reverend gentleman.'

The boy's eyes rolled in his head as though they, like him, would escape if they could. Lively eyes, thought Jeb, the only bit of life in his skin-stretched face.

'Sugar,' said the boy.

'Bin stealing the sugar, you little toe-rag?' shouted Trout, pulling the boy up by his ragged clothes so that his bare, dirty toes hardly touched the ground.

'Easy on the boy, Trout.' Jeb shot him a warning look. The man was a bully but the docks and dark alleys of the city were no place for those of a more temperate disposition and his knowledge of the grimmer side of the city mostly paid dividends. Reuben Trout was sometimes employed to keep rough seamen in order, and that certainly took some doing. But this was no sailor full of rum and stinking of the confines of a sea-going barque. Shaking the lad too roughly was likely to kill him or at least send his bones bursting through his skin. There was no flesh to stop it, that was for sure.

'I licked the outside of the barrels,' the boy said, his tone still defiant despite the fact that Trout was almost strangling him. 'See? Got the splinters to prove it.' He poked out his tongue. Jeb winced. It was speckled with blood.

Trout cuffed his ear. 'Less of your cheek, lad.'

'Whoa!' Jeb raised a warning hand. He had half a mind to slap it against Trout's dumb, ugly head. 'The lad's telling the truth.' He raised the lantern so that its meagre glow picked out the shining traces of raw muscavado that had crystallized on the outside of the stout hogshead barrels.

He traced the light back on the boy's pathetically thin face and thought of his own six daughters all safely tucked up in bed at home. His heart lurched in his chest as the light from the lantern fell on the boy's face. The sugar made it shine, just like the boy in his dreams.

'Where do you live, son?'

The boy shrugged and cocked his head. 'Wherever.'

'What's your name?'

'Tom.'

'Tom what?'

There was a blank look on the boy's face.

Jeb tried again. 'What was your father's name?'

The boy shrugged again.

Jeb sighed. 'Have you got a mother?'

'Yes.'

'Where does she live?'

The boy wiped his nose on what was left of his sleeve. 'Anywhere.'

'She must live somewhere. Where does she sleep?'

'In doorways.'

'What about food? What does she live on?'

'Gin.'

Jeb sighed. He'd heard it all before. 'How does she get the money for that?'

The boy paused as if afraid or unwilling to tell. At last he shivered, rubbed at his freezing arms and glared defiantly, as though his intention was to spit in Jeb's face or gob on his shiny black shoes.

'Men give it to her after she bin with them in the dark for a bit.' He said it almost accusingly and not without a trace of bitterness.

Jeb sighed and nodded at Reuben Trout. 'Let's give this lad a bit of leg up in life, shall we, Trout?'

The night watchman's dark, bushy eyebrows almost obliterated his eyes as he frowned. 'If that's what you want, squire, though if you ask me, he'd be best chucked in the river. I could do it if you wanted me to.'

'No frightening the lad, Trout,' said Jeb Strong in a calm and careful voice. After placing the lamp on a handy capstan, he took his arms out of his coat, pulled the sleeves into order, and patted the black wool almost lovingly before draping it over the boy's shoulders. 'Come along, lad. Let's see what we can do for you. Do you like ships?'

Defiance was replaced by a wariness borne of both curiosity and fear. The boy, Tom, huddled into the warm coat and looked up at the one and only benefactor ever to have entered his life. 'Yes.'

'Ever thought about going away to sea, Tom?'

'Sometimes.'

'Right. Then it's off to the Merchant Seamen's Apprenticeship School. Ever heard of it?'

'No.'

'That's fine. They haven't heard of you either. It's time you both met.'

—

Tom was apprehensive and his feet ached to run, but the man called Trout had a firm grip on his collar. The other man, obviously a gentleman and some kind of clergyman judging by his clothes, held the lantern as they traversed the dark lanes around the city docks where there were no decent streetlights and the air was filled with the reek of the river and the dampness of unused cellars.

The cobbles were icy cold and slippery underfoot. The men's shoes slid occasionally, but Tom and his bare feet were hardened to it, his toes curling over the uneven surface with careless efficiency. Once the temperature had dropped to the point where the frost formed dazzling patterns on windows, he wouldn't feel them at all.

Tom was used to discomfort, to being hungry and cold. He was used to being neglected and cursed. Kindness was therefore alien and although he instinctively felt this man was genuine, he'd heard nasty stories from other boys with no one to look after them and no one to care. He had to be sure.

'Sir? Where we going?'

The man was stout, but his stride was long. He still held the lantern, the flickering flame lighting their way.

'To my house, Tom, the house of Jebediah Strong, for that is who I am.'

Tom couldn't remember the last time he'd had a roof of any kind over his head, but he was wary. The street stories about the bad habits of wealthy men kept popping into his mind. Wriggling free was not an option; Trout held him too tightly.

They left the ships and the river behind them. The temperature rose a little and the winter wind swung round to the north. Snow began to fall. By the time they came to a brick-built house, flakes the size of sparrow's wings beat on their backs as Jeb Strong fumbled the key into the lock. Tom looked up in amazement at the imposing building. A whole street full of people could live in a house like this. Surely it couldn't be the home of just one man? It was almost like a castle, though castles didn't have a canopy above the door like this house – at least he didn't think so. It was shaped like a seashell, and captured Tom's imagination.

Jeb Strong pushed him gently but firmly into the house, then turned to the man called Trout and thrust a coin into his hand.

'For your trouble, Trout. I'll bid you goodnight.'

The door closed on the bitter cold darkness, and Tom found himself in a world he had only seen through windows when the night was dark and candles and burning coals glowed from within. Just looking through those windows had made him feel warmer, which was more than the meagre rags that clothed his body could do.

As Jeb Strong shook the snow from his hat, Tom took in his surroundings. Black and white floor tiles made him think of playing hopscotch. A staircase wound upwards from a lion's head newel post to a galleried landing where the light from a candelabrum shone on mahogany doors.

Eyes wide with wonder, Tom rubbed his arms while his stomach rumbled at the smell of cooked food. Someone had eaten earlier that evening and the aroma lingered, even here in the hall.

The interior of the house was like a dream. Tom kept rubbing his arms, needing to feel his cold flesh so he knew this was real, that he wouldn't wake up suddenly in some cold doorway or stinking privy – anywhere out of the snow. Not entirely convinced, he took in all the details just in case it vanished.

Against one wall was a fine table and, beside it, an armchair with cabriole legs and pale gold upholstery. The tick of a floor-standing clock measured the passing of time, though it seemed slower than his beating heart.

Tom jumped as the clock struck eleven.

Jeb Strong placed a hand on his shoulder and he jumped again.

'No need to fear, boy,' said the cleric on seeing the sudden suspicion in the boy's eyes. 'It's just a clock.'

Tom headed for the door, suddenly disbelieving and wary of Jeb Strong's true purpose for bringing him here. Some men preferred boys to women. His friends in the street gangs had told him that. A number of them had got so hungry they had acquiesced to the demands of such men and had told him what sort of things they'd been forced to do. A house that specialized in such things had even taken one of the boys in, but Tom would rather starve.

Jeb Strong folded his hands before him and shook his head. 'You are free to go if you wish. Believe me, Tom, I mean you no harm.'

Tom reached for the door, meaning to run into the darkness and face the familiar cold and hunger, even though his belly was rumbling and his flesh was frozen. The sound of footsteps running lightly along the galleried landing followed by a female voice made him pause.

'Is that you, Jeb?'

Jeb smiled and winked at Tom. 'My wife asks an unnecessary question if ever there was,' he said, then upturned his face to the landing and said more loudly, 'And whom else would you be expecting at this time of night, my dear? Do you keep secrets from me?'

The woman giggled. A long shadow thrown by the candlelight preceded her before she appeared wearing a pale blue brocade dressing gown over a lace-trimmed cotton nightdress, her hair covered by a large muslin cap. She rested her hands on the balustrade and looked down at them. In the light from the candelabra, her eyes looked bright and merry.

'I have a friend with me,' Jeb added, and Tom fancied that both the man's voice and his overall demeanour had softened and warmed in the presence of his wife.

Her voice was like singing. Tom was spellbound. 'Another lost and lonely boy? Goodness, my dear, however many are there?'

Jeb ruffled Tom's filthy hair. 'Too many and all in need of help, but with the Lord's help we'll do what we can.'

'Amen,' said Mrs Strong.

'Amen,' echoed her husband, then added, 'What have you got for young Tom to eat?'

She pressed a finger to her dimpled chin and her merry eyes turned thoughtful. 'Well, to start with, Cook made lamb stew for our dinner tonight. I'm sure there's plenty left in the kitchen along with bread, butter and milk. Ample enough for a growing boy, I think.'

Swiftly businesslike, she began to trip down the stairs, her voluminous attire floating out behind her like a blue cloud.

More sounds came from further along the landing. Tom looked up. Mr and Mrs Strong exchanged knowing glances.

'They should be in bed,' said Jeb Strong.

'They're young and curious, like we once were,' his wife said.

Scurrying along like large mice, a host of little girls appeared, ranging in size and age from three to thirteen or so. They all wore white cotton nightdresses and had healthy pink faces that looked newly woken from sleep. Wobbly knobs of rag-tied hair bounced all over their heads as they followed their mother down the stairs.

'My daughters,' Jeb explained proudly as they all gathered round him, arms entwined.

Tom gazed at them wide-eyed. If he'd ever had that sort of treatment from anyone, he didn't remember it. Mostly he remembered being alone in the cold while some ugly stranger grunted and groaned above his mother on the small bed they'd shared between them in the distant past when they'd at least had a roof over their heads. And he'd been warned to be silent, as if he wasn't there; a nobody who had had to survive as best he could.

Later, as Tom devoured the food set before him, six pairs of eyes watched silently, the smaller ones only just managing to peer above the table.

'Tomorrow he enrols in the Merchant Seamen's Apprenticeship School,' the Reverend Strong declared to his children as though it were an event of historic importance. The eyes of the little girls seemed to grow larger. The truth of the matter was that it was Jeb Strong himself who had set up the school for destitute boys and he was immensely proud of his achievement.

A maid lately roused from her bed followed Mrs Strong into the kitchen, which now seemed full of people, warmth and an irrepressible determination to dispense Christian goodness. Both Mrs Strong and the maid carried various items of clothing dangling over their arms.

'These used to belong to my son Jasper. They're quite clean,' said Mrs Strong, measuring a coat across Tom's back as he tore at the bread and spooned the stew into his mouth. He barely acknowledged their presence. Clothes that would keep him warm would be welcome, but nothing could beat hot food. The last time he'd eaten a hot meal was when one of his pals had found a cat run over by a cart. They'd skinned it, skewered a stick through the length of its body and cooked it over a driftwood fire. It had tasted good to a hungry boy, but nothing like this.

'Will I be fed at this school?' he asked Mrs Strong as she tucked him into bed.

Mrs Strong blinked back her tears and brushed her hand over his hair. 'Of course you will, child.'

Later she told her husband what he had said.

'Poor boy,' he responded. 'It is a shame he's had such a bad start in life for I'm convinced he has a quick mind.' His voice trailed away. Thoughtfully he sat on the side of the bed and slipped off his shoes.

Miriam Strong looked at him sadly. 'You're thinking about Jasper.'

Jeb sighed, took off his wig and scratched his head. 'His face turned shiny in the light from the lantern, just like the boy in my dream.'

Miriam threw up her hands in delight. 'I knew there was something! I could see it in your eyes.'

She came round to her husband's side of their big, oak bed, knelt at his feet and cradled his face in her hands. 'God's sent us a replacement. That's what the dream meant. Can you possibly doubt it?'

Jeb slowly raised his head until his gaze met hers. 'Do you really think so, Miriam?'

Miriam kissed him gently on the mouth. 'Do our best by him, and he could be a living memorial to Jasper's memory.'

Jeb smiled and nodded sadly. 'God moves in mysterious ways. There's always a purpose. And if it's God's will then so be it.' He squeezed his wife's hand. 'You've the last word on the matter, Miriam. Is it really God's will and would Jasper agree?'

She smiled at him, clutched his hand with both of hers and dragged him with her on to his knees. 'Let us pray, husband, and perhaps by morning we shall know for sure.'

Next day at the quayside, Tom felt small. He knew he was thin though quite tall, but the size of the ship Jeb Strong took him to made him feel tiny.

The *Miriam Strong* was strongly curved from prow to stern, though the gold, red and blue paint around the tight windows of what had once been the captain's cabin and officers' quarters was faded and peeling in places.

Her main mast seemed to touch the sky, and the fore and aft masts' lesser height and cross spars were like supplicants to its majesty.

Tom was a wharf rat, a street urchin familiar with the city centre quays and the ships that berthed there. He'd seen barques, brigantines, trows and packets, but none had been quite as splendid as the *Miriam Strong*. He eyed her with interest, then frowned. Something was wrong.

Jeb saw his expression. 'What's wrong, lad?'

Tom chewed over whether to mention the matter but decided he would. 'She's got no figurehead.'

'Ah!' Jeb exclaimed. He sounded as if he'd been found out doing something he shouldn't.

'Why?'

Jeb looked downriver to where the tower of St Mary Redcliffe church cast its shadow over the water.

'I'll tell you someday,' he said. By the tone of his voice, Tom could tell the subject was closed.

'I thought I was going to school before going to sea,' said Tom with sudden wariness. He'd heard about gangs in years gone by who had pressed men and boys into service before the mast, though Jeb Strong didn't look as though he belonged to a gang. He was a clergyman after all, though you could never be too sure of the motives of rich men.

Jeb Strong smiled, his chin doubling and trebling above his clerical collar. 'This *is* the school, Tom, where you will live and learn all that Captain Gooding and this ship can teach you. And don't think the *Miriam Strong* is just a rotting old tub. This ship has not been to sea for many a long year, though she's seen plenty of action in her time. She's fought in some very famous battles.'

'Don't sound like a man-of-war to me with a name like that,' said Tom.

'I named her after my wife.' Jeb grinned in a wicked way, not at all in keeping with a man of the cloth. 'There's many a tale this ship could tell, Tom, and she's had more than one name. Trust me when I say she's a ship to be proud of, a ship that generations henceforth will remember with affection and wonder.'

Tom looked as though he almost believed him then returned his gaze to the spot on the prow where her figurehead should be.

'So what was her other name then?'

Jeb winked. 'Not for you to know, lad. One day maybe, when it doesn't matter who knows and those that would be concerned about how I got her are dead and gone, that's when you will know, Tom.'

But Tom was no longer listening. He was looking towards the Hole in the Wall, a waterside inn where rough men gathered to drink and do business out of sight of the customs men. A woman was screaming and a man was swinging her around by her hair, slamming her body against the wall of the age-old building.

'Ma!' shouted Tom.

Like a skinny hound, he was off, running towards the pair, shouting then launching himself at the man, his head thudding into an unprotected midriff.

At first the man was surprised. He let go of the woman, his prime objective now to protect his own body rather than abuse hers. But he recovered quickly, his brawny arms making light work of lifting the boy above his head and making as if to slam him down on the pavement.

'Henry!' shouted Jeb. He rushed towards the mêlée, sure in the knowledge that Captain Henry Gooding, master and teacher on the *Miriam Strong*, was right behind him and with all the confidence of a man of strong muscle rather than wide girth, his black frock coat flapping like the wings of a bat behind him. Waving his walking cane, he shouted, 'Put that boy down, my good man!'

The brute looked surprised that someone was giving him an order. On seeing that Jeb was no waterside bully, surprise turned to a sneer, until Captain Gooding, a man of over six foot, put in an appearance. He had a massive beard and his hair was plaited into short pigtails all over his head.

'Want his neck broke, Reverend?' Gooding's voice was surprisingly high, not at all suited to the size and density of his frame.

Jeb looked undecided. Captain Gooding advanced menacingly. His shadow fell over the man and Tom was quickly released.

Tom immediately went to the woman, who was lying against the wall, groaning and shaking her head from side to side.

He knelt down at her side. 'Ma, are you all right?'

She looked at him blearily as if she didn't know him, or was waiting for her vision to clear. Once it did, she began to groan louder. 'I ain't got nothing for you, Tom. I told you to get out of my bloody sight! What you doing 'ere?'

Tom straightened suddenly as though he'd thought something over very carefully and had now come to a decision. 'I'm going to sea, Ma. I'm going to go to school on that boat. The gentleman there said I could.'

Jeb stood silently, curious as to what response Tom's mother would give. She looked at her son with tired eyes from beneath a thatch of tangled hair that had once been dark brown, but was now peppered with grey.

'Best thing for you,' she said wearily. 'I can do without you hanging around my skirts.'

The brute who had thrown her against the wall found his confidence returning, although his bravado had diminished.

'Come on, woman. You owe me a shilling's worth, and there's more than one dark doorway in this street.'

Tom helped his mother to her feet. Jeb sensed the bond between mother and son. Whatever she was, Tom loved her. And for just a moment, he thought he had seen a flicker of affection in her eyes.

'Go on with yer fancy gentleman, Tom,' she suddenly exclaimed, brushing him aside before waddling off to her client's side. 'I got a job to do, ain't I, darling?'

'I'll look after you when I'm a proper seaman,' Tom shouted after her. He heard her laugh and the man's deeper, baritone join in as they sauntered off. 'I mean it,' he said more quietly.

It was the last time Tom saw his mother alive. One week later her body was fished from the river. Her throat had been cut and she was naked. Jeb took Tom to identify her although he said he didn't have to. Jeb also took care of the funeral arrangements rather than have her buried in a pauper's grave.

'Now he's got no one,' Miriam said to Jeb two weeks after the funeral.

Jeb patted her hand. 'I think he's got us now, Miriam.'

'Good,' she said, brushed the back of her hand across her eyes and went back to her sewing.

Together they told Tom about their decision.

'We lost our son Jasper some years ago, but we never once doubted that God had taken him for a reason. We think you are that reason, Tom. We believe God sent you to be our son in his place.'

Tom was amazed, but wondered if his luck could change yet again. 'What if your son Jasper comes back? Will you throw me out on the street?'

Jeb Strong reached for his wife's hand and smiled at her as he squeezed it. He shook his head. 'He won't be back. We believe he drowned, and the waters took his body out to sea. It was God's will. You've no surname, Tom, so what say you that I give you mine?'

Tom fell silent, his eyes downcast. At last he said, 'Do I get to stay at the school, on the ship?'

Jeb nodded, unable to stop smiling each time he looked into Tom's eyes. They were so like Jasper's, blue and honest. 'Yes. If you want to.'

Tom thought about it for a moment. 'S'pose I can't argue with God.'

Miriam clapped her hands. 'Praise be!'

Jeb could see by the look on Tom's face that the boy had something else to say. At last it came out. Tom's deep blue eyes looked up into his, the dark lashes seeming to intensify their liquidity rather than making them larger. He swallowed nervously and cocked his head a bit like a bantam just before a fight. 'Just so's you know – I won't ever forget me mother, even though she was a whore and met a sticky end.'

Jeb winced. The boy spoke so matter-of-factly, and yet he sensed the turbulent emotions running just beneath the surface. He didn't want to think what the boy might have had to witness. 'I understand, Tom. You'll never forget your mother, and we'll never forget our son.'

He nodded at his wife and they took his hands and led him to another room that had obviously once been Jasper's. The bed was made and the curtains were drawn, just as if the boy was about to go to bed.

A hoop and a hobbyhorse were propped up in the corner. There was a top on the floor, books, a wooden boat with sails and a regiment of red-coated soldiers lined up in battle against their green-jacketed opponents. The only sign of mourning was a strip of black cloth hanging around a portrait.

Tom looked up at the painting.

'Tom, meet Jasper,' said Miriam Strong.

The boy that looked back at him was probably a little younger than Tom was now. Strikingly blue eyes, similar to Tom's own, smiled out of the painting. Jasper had crisply ginger hair; Tom's was dark. Jasper held a toy with both hands, a mounted knight on a painted horse, the cross of St George emblazoned on his chest.

'My son,' said Jeb, and Tom wasn't quite sure whether he was referring to the boy in the portrait or him.

'He was wearing those clothes the day he left,' said Miriam Strong. She sounded regretful, as if she wished she'd been there to see him off, as if he'd merely gone off on a trip to relatives or friends.

And took his toy with him? thought Tom. It didn't look to be among those in the room.

'So, do you want to be Tom Strong?' asked the Reverend Strong in a kindly voice.

Tom thought carefully before answering. Even though his mother was dead, he was fiercely proud. Begging for a name was something he'd never stoop to. But Jeb was offering and he seemed a good man.

'It's as good a name as any,' he said.

—

Forgetting the bloated face of his mother wasn't easy, but living and learning on board the *Miriam Strong* helped Tom enormously. He enjoyed the lessons on seamanship. He even liked learning how to read and write and became so far ahead of the other boys that Jeb Strong took him home on occasion to join his daughters with their tutor. Gradually, he became part of the family and Jeb told him so. Only when he first accompanied them to Marstone Court, the home of Sir Emmanuel Strong, Jeb's brother, and his family, did he feel otherwise.

While the adults congregated in the dining room and dined on wine-rich pheasant, wild duck, fat geese and a broad saddle of beef, the children were fed boiled mutton, semolina and bread and butter up in the nursery.

The nursery was on the fourth floor and was furnished to be of service rather than to impress like the rest of the house. The windows were small, and the walls were painted a dull mushroom colour that did nothing to lift the gloom and compensate for the lack of light.

Nelson Strong, Sir Emmanuel's son, took to Tom immediately, which caused his sister Horatia to scowl. It seemed to Tom that she considered her brother to be her property and hers alone.

'Do you have a pony?' Nelson asked brightly.

Tom shook his head, but wished he could say yes. He so wanted to fit in.

Nelson made a face. 'Neither do I. I hate riding and shooting and things like that. I like theatre, nice clothes and looking handsome. Do you like poetry?'

Tom was unsure, though disinclined to admit it. 'Yes.'

Nelson reclined in his chair like a Regency dandy, his older female cousins in rapt attention and hanging on to his every word. Leah, Ruth and Rachel sat like puppies at his feet. 'Do recite some for me.'

Tom scratched his head as he thought about it, then recited the only poetry he knew, the first lines of a sea shanty he'd heard sailors singing as they fell out of the dockside taverns along St Augustine's Quay.

*Oh, Betsy is a buxom wench, she's tasty and she's willing,*
*And she'll do anything you want, if you've got just a shilling,*
*So hoist 'em up, me pretty girl, oh get em down, me darling,*
*For I'm a-sailing shortly now, and you'll not get a farthing.*

Charity, Piety and Patience, Jeb's eldest daughters, threw their hands over their mouths, to stifle their giggles. Ruth, Rachel and the very youngest, Leah, not quite understanding the sentiments, grinned hesitantly, Leah eventually clapping her hands in childish delight.

Nelson beamed. 'Not exactly Richard Brinsley Sheridan, but very entertaining.'

The only one who did not laugh was Horatia, Nelson's older sister. They were very alike, both golden-haired and blue-eyed, though Nelson was but a weaker imitation of his sister, like a reflection in foggy glass. Horatia glared hard at her brother who suddenly looked ashamed of liking the rude ditty.

Horatia was angry. 'Shut up, all of you!'

Her voice was like the crack of doom. The children fell into silence. Nelson seemed to shrink in his chair, his semolina spoon slipping silently into his dish.

Tom had been wary of Horatia from the moment they'd arrived. Although he'd bowed to her and said good afternoon, she had not responded, but had looked him up and down as if he were still in rags and wore no shoes. Only when everyone else was out of earshot, did she whisper, 'You're wearing a dead boy's clothes.'

He'd felt himself colour, and was only glad that no one else heard what she'd said.

The Reverend Strong's daughters sat like stones in their chairs as Horatia's eyes raked over them, her look far too disdainful for a child of her age. Her gaze finally settled on Tom, just as he'd expected it would. 'You don't belong here. And we have no wish to hear your dirty dockside songs from your dirty mouth and the dirty place you first came from.'

Tom clenched his jaw and resisted the urge to hit her. After all, she was a girl and Jeb's niece.

Horatia held herself like an adult, a haughty look on her face and her blue eyes hardening to suit her mood. Everyone stayed silent and still, afraid to move lest her stony look fell on them.

She said, 'You're a brute of a boy. Do you know that? You're not our kind at all.'

For the Reverend Strong's sake, Tom had no wish to rock the boat. Without returning her gaze, he went on eating, sure that in time she would tire of her game and leave him alone to torture someone else.

'Well, brute, aren't you going to say anything?'

Tom carried on eating and would have continued to do so, but Horatia made the mistake of saying the worst thing possible.

'Your mother was a whore, and you never had a father. There's a word for a child like you—'

Tom let fly his bowl.

Horatia herself sat dumb and immobile as dribbles of semolina trickled down her face and into her open mouth. A deep hush fell.

Then, Leah began to giggle. Gradually, each of her sisters began to giggle too. Tom showed no emotion, but kept his eyes fixed on Horatia's face. Nelson merely stared into his lap, a wry grin flickering over his lips. As the giggles grew into loud laughter, Horatia's stone features cracked with rage. She opened her mouth wide, threw back her head and screamed, 'Nanny Peters!'

The scream soared on the air. The sound of footsteps ascending the stairs quickened and a small figure in a dark dress with a white apron and mop cap dashed to her darling Horatia's side.

'Oh, my poor dear!' the nurse exclaimed.

Of course, the whole story came out. Tom knew he was in for a birching. The Reverend Strong wouldn't let him get away with reciting rude verses in the presence of young ladies and behaving as he did towards Horatia.

Tom was summoned to the library at Marstone Court where the Reverend Strong waited, a bundle of birch twigs in his right hand. He sighed and shook his head at Tom. 'I have to do this, boy, though I don't want to. You do realize that, don't you?'

Tom nodded. 'Yes, sir.'

At the crook of the Reverend Strong's finger, he made his way to the corner where he was standing behind a big green chair.

'Pull down your breeches and bend over the chair, boy.'

Feeling less than contrite, Tom did as he was told. The chair's leather was cold against his belly. As the birch swished through the air on the first stroke, he felt the air grow colder. Although his backside warmed under the birch, a draught blowing in from somewhere lessened its intensity. The windows were closed, and then he realized he hadn't shut the door properly. As the sixth and last stroke rose and fell, he glanced over his shoulder. Through the narrow gap he saw a figure and knew it was Horatia.

He knew she'd be enjoying this. She'd deliberately insulted him. Although Jeb wielded the birch, she was the one really beating him, showing him her power and he hated her for it.

Outside the door, Horatia bit her lip guiltily. Absorbed in what was going on, she didn't notice Nelson approaching until he spoke to her.

'What are you doing?' he asked in a loud voice that made her jump.

Embarrassed at being caught watching, she pushed past him, her nose in the air.

Undeterred and intrigued by her behaviour, Nelson danced along at her side, skipped across in front of her, laughing and singing, 'Horatia has a sweetheart, Horatia has a sweetheart.'

At the end of the hall, Horatia stopped dead and slapped his face. 'Shut up! Shut up! Shut up!'

Although his face stung, Nelson grinned. 'You like that boy Tom. I know you do. He's a boy and you're a girl, and—'

His sister's cheeks flushed pink as she snapped, 'That's a stupid statement, Nelson. I know what I am. I don't need you to tell me. And what would you know about such things anyway? You know nothing. Nothing at all!'

Now it was Nelson's turn to be embarrassed because he didn't know that much, only the way the maid giggled after one of the stable lads had whispered in her ear. But he wouldn't be put down.

'One day I'll know all there is to know. Father will tell me,' he said emphatically. 'Father knows everything.'

## Chapter Three

Over the years, Nelson learned a little more about men and women, thanks to an obliging housemaid who didn't mind a handsome young lad sneaking a quick grope on the stairs.

It was in the autumn of 1832 when he was ordered to accompany his father to Bath for the weekend on what he presumed to be a business meeting. He'd attended others, but never in Bath.

'Why do I have to go?' he asked, as their carriage clattered over the gravelled drive through the park.

'Because you're seventeen. It's time,' said Emmanuel purposefully.

Nelson smiled to himself. So his father thought he was still a virgin. Best to humour the old man.

They went to the house in Green Park where Nelson was introduced to a certain Madame Sybil. She had a pink nose, a plunging neckline and wore enough gold to sink a battleship.

'Tonight you become a man, my son,' his father said, accompanying his comment with a hefty slap on Nelson's back.

A high-cheeked Chinese girl with sleek black hair and a small rosebud mouth showed them into a ground-floor salon. Nelson's attitude changed in an instant. She was the most exotic woman he'd ever seen.

'I have to paint her,' he said to his father.

Emmanuel looked at him in disbelief. 'You're not here to paint a girl, son. You're here to poke one!'

Madame Sybil paraded a number of her girls in front of the seated Nelson. He stared at them all. Blonde, brunette, redhead and colours in between, they were all lovely, but his mind was fixed on the Chinese girl who had let them in.

'Her,' he said and pointed.

'Lucy Lee, *mon cher*.' Madame Sybil raised her eyebrows in his father's direction.

His father nodded. 'If that's the boy's fantasy, then let him have her.'

Madame Sybil was unusually pensive. Emmanuel misinterpreted the reason and dug into his waistcoat pocket. 'You want money? Then I'll give you more money. Just see that my son gets what he wants.'

The pensive look disappeared as Madame Sybil poked the golden guineas into her copious cleavage. 'Then he shall have Lucy Lee and all the fantasies he requires.'

Nelson was mesmerized by the smiling Chinese girl and, although he'd had some experience with the maids, he felt immensely nervous. He never took his eyes off her as she led him by the hand to a room on the first-floor landing.

He hesitated as they stopped at a door.

'You are nervous?' she asked.

He nodded, his mouth too dry for words.

Lucy Lee smiled. 'I have something for you that will calm your soul.'

Taking a small, round box from inside the bosom of her robe, she took off the lid, dipped her finger into the contents and dabbed it on his tongue.

Nelson gulped it down.

Lucy Lee smiled. 'Dragon powder will also give you courage.'

He didn't know what it was she gave him, but its effect was meteoric. His nervousness melted away as he entered the most splendid of rooms. Red walls, red carpet, red curtains and a bedspread of red silk embroidered with a writhing dragon. The dragon took his eye.

'That's an amazing beast,' he said in breathless admiration and was sure he could see it moving, its jaws opening and closing and its tail lashing from one side of the bed to the other.

'So is this,' said Lucy Lee, her tiny hand closing over the hardness at the front of his trousers.

Her body was as smooth as the silk. She moved like the dragon that decorated the bedspread, curving her spine so that her breasts and belly teased, withdrew, then pressed against his body. At times it felt as though they were flying on the dragon's back, the world misty and vague beneath them.

When it was over, he slept. His father collected him in the morning, his expression a mix of pride and satisfaction.

'I felt like I was flying,' Nelson said blearily, as the coachman bundled him into the carriage. 'She gave me something. It was better than brandy.'

'Opium,' said his father. 'Unlike brandy, it calms the blood. I hear it yields good profits. Maybe I should expand to the East and trade in opium as well as maintaining our sugar interests to the West.' He nodded thoughtfully. 'I may enquire.'

Nelson closed his eyes, not surprised that his father's thoughts had turned to trade. Wealth was wonderful, but Lucy Lee was still in his mind and her smell lingered on his clothes.

He came back on many occasions after that and each time he tasted a little of the dragon powder. Nothing was beyond his reach, not sex and certainly not painting. In fact he saw colours, shapes and scenes as he'd never seen them before.

Unknown to his father, he persuaded Lucy to sit for him, every sitting ending with them making love on the silken bedspread, sometimes just once.

Their time together lasted until Lucy Lee ran away with a Spanish acrobat.

'How could she?' Nelson wailed when Madame Sybil told him. 'I wanted to paint another portrait of her.'

'This time with her clothes on?' said Madame Sybil raising her finely plucked eyebrows that helped take attention away from the pitted redness of her nose.

Nelson laid his head back against the wall and closed his eyes. He was sweating like a horse, perspiration running down his back and beading his forehead. It was Lucy Lee's fault, he told himself, wrapping his arms around himself as he started to shiver.

'You choose another girl,' said Madame Sybil. 'I only charge you half price. *Oui?*'

Still with his eyes closed, Nelson said, 'Do you have any more Chinese girls?'

'No.'

He shook his head. Lucy Lee had been the most exotic thing to enter his life. Every other woman he would ever meet would have to match up to her. They would have to be unique, dark-haired and slender.

Madame Sybil seemed to understand. 'You want something a little different?'

He nodded, biting his bottom lip as he fought to overcome the wave of nausea curdling his stomach.

'You keep in touch,' she said, tapping his chest with the tip of her ivory fan. 'I find you something. I promise. I always find you something.'

'And the dragon powder,' he blurted. 'Can you get that for me too?'

She looked at him sadly and sighed. 'There is an apothecary on the corner of Trenchard Street. You can buy it there. It is not expensive. Even the poorest of mothers buy it for their babies.'

—

A ball was held on Nelson's twenty-first birthday, partly to celebrate his engagement to his cousin Adelaide Tillingham, and partly because he was about to depart to see Uncle Otis in Barbados and get to know more about the sugar trade.

Both the ball and his impending departure to Barbados were welcome; the same could not be said about the engagement to Adelaide, which had been agreed in principle even before he'd met the girl. He had not protested. His sister Horatia had told him it didn't matter whether he was married or not. He was a man. Marriage would not impair his lifestyle in any way whatsoever.

'Unlike me,' Horatia had grimaced, having just had another argument with her father over the fact that she was twenty-three years old and still not married. 'I can't say that I'm at variance with loving and honouring a husband as stated in the marriage service, but I might find obeying rather more difficult.'

Nelson laughed. 'You're outrageous!'

'And you're a wastrel – though you hide it well.'

'And you're beautiful.'

'And you're handsome – though I would say that, wouldn't I? We look so alike.'

For the ball, Horatia Strong wore a blue silk dress that shimmered when she moved. Silver and white feathers fluttered in her hair, and blonde ringlets framed her face. Whereas all the other young girls at the ball were pink-cheeked from dancing and blushing at the attention of young men, Horatia was listening with interest to the conversation of men in their forties, fifties and above.

Through a haze of cigar smoke, her father watched, sighed and shook his head.

'She should be circulating with young men, not talking with old ones,' muttered his wife, Verity, whom he'd married following the death of Horatia and Nelson's mother. As bevies of beautiful women floated and danced around them, she held on to his arm tightly, as if afraid he might escape.

Emmanuel was as concerned as she was that Horatia showed little interest in young men. She much preferred older ones who talked of plantations, the price of sugar, insurance costs and shipping manifests.

'She'll marry when she's ready,' he said in a confident manner, though he didn't feel it. I'll damn well make her, he thought to himself, but blanched at the prospect. She was strong-willed. He would have trouble persuading her.

He studied the men with whom she was talking. Now which of them would be the best marriage prospect with a view to expanding the Strong fortune? How about Stephenson, a widower and a millionaire with substantial interests in cocoa and copper? Or Josiah Benson, a banker and wealthy merchant? At present he was standing closest to Horatia, seemingly hanging on to her every word.

Emmanuel believed in using every means at his disposal to build a business empire. His children were part of those means – Horatia and Nelson, plus the four children Verity had presented. They were all usable capital.

He looked again at Horatia, but she had gone.

'Did you see where Horatia went?' he asked Verity, almost hopeful that she'd sneaked outside with a suitable – even an unsuitable – and lustful young man.

'The last I saw of her, she was holding Josiah Benson in thrall. Perhaps she's with him.'

Emmanuel grunted approvingly. Josiah Benson had his finger in a lot of pies. He'd be a welcome addition to the family.

Horatia was not with Benson but out on the terrace, strolling arm in arm with her brother Nelson. She waved her fan in front of her face, glad to breathe the fresh air rather than the fug inside.

'He won't be pleased,' Nelson was saying. 'He's probably looking for you right now before your honour is compromised.'

Horatia laughed. 'Of course he won't. He'll be hoping that I've finally favoured some callow youth with acne and a large fortune.'

Nelson raised his eyebrows. 'Not favouring him too much, I hope.'

Her expression echoed his own. 'And compromise my honour? My dear Nelson, a woman is supposed to be untouched on her wedding night, guided in what to do by her husband.'

'Who will, of course, be well versed in what has to be done,' Nelson responded.

Horatia slammed her fan shut. 'I wish I'd been born a man.'

Nelson adopted an expression of mock horror. 'Heavens, no! That would make you heir apparent and me second son.'

'And able to follow your own star – painter, poet or general cad.'

Nelson grinned. 'The prospect's enticing. Perhaps we should change places.'

'I wish we could, my dear brother,' she said, adopting a more serious tone that instantly reminded him of his father.

'I take it none of these young men excites you?'

Horatia stopped pacing the terrace with him, let go his arm and took a deep breath that was full of exasperation, anger and longing. 'Business excites me. Making money excites me.'

'You have your own money left to you by Mother, and good advice from Josiah Benson, so I hear.'

Benson advised them both on the matter of the stocks and shares left to them by their mother. Horatia's face brightened at the mention of it, but she held her smile in check.

'He no longer advises me.'

Nelson looked taken aback.

'*I* advise *him*,' she said with obvious pride. 'I was beginning to find his advice too retrospective. I told him I felt that a new century required new ideas so we should look out for any opportunity arising in new industries or innovative inventions. So far my judgement has proved better than his. But it isn't enough. I will never be like the simpering little rosebuds standing around that ballroom. A smart uniform or a fine pair of whiskers will never enthrall me!'

The steady creak of small wheels turning beneath a heavy weight signalled the arrival of Uncle Jeb. Tom had arrived home from the sea and was pushing him in his wheelchair.

Tom's tanned complexion was accentuated by the whiteness of his crisp cravat and the dark blue of his evening suit. His dark hair was tied back with a velvet ribbon at the nape of his neck; a slightly old-fashioned style, and mainly favoured at sea, but it suited him. Horatia's expression softened and her smile – obviously for Tom rather than her uncle – lit up her face.

Jebediah Strong was not the man he used to be. His health had deteriorated considerably following the death of his wife and three of his daughters. Emmanuel had insisted he move in to Marstone Court with Ruth, Rachel and Leah, his three remaining daughters. All three had left to marry, a fact that was still a thorn in Horatia's side. Her father never stopped reminding her of it.

'All married,' Emmanuel had shouted at his spinster daughter. 'So why aren't you?'

'Because I'm too much like my father,' she'd retorted.

Jeb was slumped to one side in his chair. He still managed to speak, though his words were slurred and spit bubbled from the corner of his mouth.

'Not dancing, my dear?'

'I haven't met the right partner,' she said, her eyes bright as she smiled at Tom.

Tom bent over Jeb to wipe the dribble from his mouth.

Horatia watched then said, 'Let's place Uncle Jeb so he can look into the ballroom and see the dancing. Would you like that, Uncle Jeb?' Though her offer was aimed at her uncle, her gaze was fixed on Tom.

Seeking his approval – and his affection, thought Nelson.

'Yes,' he slurred.

Tom looked apprehensive as she edged to his side. Between them they pushed the wheelchair closer to the large windows of the ballroom, Horatia's fingers grazing those of Tom.

'Do you like that, Uncle Jeb?' Horatia asked cheerfully, as if touching Tom was purely accidental.

'Yes,' he slurred again.

Bending over her uncle, Horatia looked up at Tom as she said, 'I think it would be nice if Tom and I danced for you. What do you think, Tom?'

Tom seemed to take a deep breath. 'If that's what Jeb wants.'

Horatia stood expectantly.

Jeb seemed to nod, though with his debilitating affliction it was hard to tell. Tom offered Horatia his arm.

'My sister always gets what she wants,' said Nelson, as he and Jeb watched them take the floor.

'Her father won't like it,' said Jeb, his words seeming to drown in his throat.

'No fortune, no profit,' murmured Nelson. They were all pawns in his father's great game and, as such, they had been trained to play their parts. Horatia had been educated to be a lady, to speak French, to draw, to hold polite conversation and to look beautiful. She was a valuable asset her father would use to best advantage – if she let him.

Jeb struggled for control of his mouth before managing to say, 'Off soon?'

'Yes,' said Nelson. 'Next Wednesday on the early morning tide.'

Jeb struggled again. 'You're... looking... forward to it?'

'Exotic places... hmm... yes, I think so,' he said thoughtfully.

Jeb made a rattling sound as he fought to speak. Eventually he said, 'Rrrr... egards to Otis.'

'Of course. I hear Barbados is beautiful,' said Nelson. 'If that is so, then I shall paint it.'

'Beau... ti... ful.' Nelson did not notice the faraway look in his uncle's eyes and the tear that rolled slowly down his cheek.

Inside the brightly lit ballroom where the buzz of conversation mixed with the clink of cut glass and silver cutlery, Emmanuel Strong stood alone. Through a blur of colour and energy amongst a rainbow of silks, evening suits and uniforms, Horatia and Tom whirled around the dance floor. Horatia was gazing up into Tom's eyes in a way that worried him. He did his best to reassure himself. After all, they'd known each other from childhood and Tom, he decided, knew his place. All the same, he thought, looking around him for one particular face, one particular presence that exuded money, it wouldn't hurt to hedge one's bets.

'Josiah!' he exclaimed, slapping the broad back of the richest banker in the city, noting the good clothes, stocky build and healthily pink complexion. 'I've been wanting to have a word with you, my boy.'

Benson allowed himself to be led into a colonnade where the lighting was less bright. Emmanuel noticed his gaze kept straying to the dance floor every time Horatia swept by in the arms of Tom Strong.

Emmanuel seemed to be looking too, though in actuality he was studying Josiah Benson, evaluating just how far he would go in order to gain his daughter's hand. The man was besotted, that much was obvious.

'I understand you've been advising my daughter with regard to the monies settled on her by her mother,' said Emmanuel. 'How long did it take before she was advising you?'

Josiah jerked his gaze away from the dance floor. Emmanuel assessed his expression as one of embarrassment, but he recovered quickly.

'She has a fine mind.'

'And a fine body.'

Josiah flinched at such forthrightness.

Emmanuel twirled the thick Carabino cigar he had specially made in Havana and brought over on his ships in boxes of two dozen, forty boxes at a time.

'Women are like fish,' Emmanuel continued. 'You have to keep them interested before you reel them in. In that regard, you have to give them every assistance, no matter how devious the means, until you become a habit, a confidante they cannot live without. Do you understand me, Benson?'

He could almost feel Benson's amazement through the thick cigar smoke that circled his head.

'You favour my suit?'

'So much so that I will assist you in any way I can. I know that money is no object, but in order for my daughter to achieve her business aims – and for you to bask in her gratitude and, one hopes, her affection – you may need something or someone else.'

He didn't need to look at Josiah to see his stunned rapture.

'I'm most grateful.'

And so you should be, thought Emmanuel. The prospect of melding a sugar fortune with that of a banker was mutually attractive. In the meantime he could not possibly allow a relationship to develop between Horatia and Tom. He'd keep an eye on them. That was easy enough at Marstone Court, but in the city...

As the music changed, he saw Tom trying to leave the dance floor and Horatia pulling him back. Josiah made his excuses; Emmanuel nodded his affirmation, and watched as Tom eased himself away from Horatia and Josiah Benson took his place. Her smile seemed brittle and her eyes, he noted, followed Tom from the floor.

At the end of the evening, noisy toasts were made to Nelson's health and a good voyage to Barbados. Emmanuel didn't bother to join in. Good luck, *bon voyage* and safe journey had been repeated over and over again that evening. His son had been born into privilege. One day he'd inherit a fortune. That was good luck enough so far as Emmanuel was concerned, and anyway, his thoughts were elsewhere.

There was no doubting what he had to do. The situation was too dangerous to ignore. He couldn't possibly contemplate his daughter's fortune falling into the hands of a guttersnipe. Even in the city it would be wise to have Tom watched, he decided, preferably by someone who would not be noticed among the quays and inns and warehouses, the places Tom frequented and knew best. He remembered the name of a man they'd used years ago who'd been diligent in action and areas where the Strongs could not possibly be seen. Trout was his name. Reuben Trout.

# Chapter Four

The sun was setting in Barbados, thin grey clouds drifting like torn lace against a rose pink sky.

'One hundred and eighty-one, one hundred and eighty-two, one hundred and eighty-three, one hundred and eighty-four...'

Dark-haired and grey-eyed, Blanche Bianca, Viola's daughter, was running barefoot along the shoreline, dodging surf as it tumbled on to the sand. 'One hundred and eighty-five, one hundred and eighty-six...' she counted to the beat of her stride; the wind was in her hair and the hem of her dress clung wet around her ankles.

The beach formed a lingering spit from the edge of the immense plantation owned by the Strong family, back along to the tangled copse that bordered the house she shared with her mother. Every evening she ran close to the water's edge, not stopping until she'd counted to three hundred. At that point she was over the boundary into the Rivermead plantation where she would stop, take a deep breath, then turn and run all the way back again.

A cool stream tumbling from hills in the island's interior dissected the beach at the perimeter of the Strong estate. The water tinkled like bells over exposed rocks and tangled tree roots. Officially, this was private property, a fact that Blanche habitually ignored. Lengthening her stride, she cleared the stream, her long brown legs kicking spouts of dry sand behind her. 'Two hundred and fifty,' she exclaimed on landing.

Tinged pink by the setting sun, the sand was warm and dry beneath her toes as she emerged from the cover of palm trees and ran onwards, her stride slowing when she saw that the beach was not empty as it usually was. An artist's easel stood uneasily on three spindly legs. A stool and a jumble of boxes, jars and brushes anchored the corner of a blanket spread out on the sand.

Her counting faltered. 'Two hundred... and seventy-five...' she said, breathless now as she came to a stop.

She looked all around her, the evening breeze tossing wisps of dark hair around her face. Someone from Rivermead had left this here. No one else could have afforded the boxed paints, the sable brushes, the rosewood palette. Whoever it was had also left the work in progress. Blanche couldn't resist taking a peek at the painting.

Stepping on to the blanket, she held her hair back from her face and got close, then even closer as she fell in love with the beauty of the work. It was of the sea at evening, spangled pink by the setting sun, palms in silhouette against an orange sky. Although beautiful sunset had never seemed so bright to her as on this canvas. It was as though the artist had captured reality and improved upon it, as though he were seeing something no one else could see.

So where was this maestro?

She looked towards the cane fields, the trees and the plantation house beyond. When she looked along the beach and towards the sea she saw the pile of clothes, then the head bobbing about in the waves, a raised hand waving to her.

Remembering this was private property, she sprang on to her toes, meaning to run back the way she had come.

She heard a male voice shout, 'Hoy! Don't go!'

She stopped and reconsidered. Will he shoot me for trespassing? She smiled at her foolishness. The man in the sea was at a distinct disadvantage. He was not dressed and armed only with paintbrushes and a rich imagination.

He was obviously one of the Strong family, she decided, or perhaps a guest. Who else could afford time to paint? Who else would be swimming off this beach? They owned this as they owned many things.

She stood closer to the layered bundle of clothes that lay just beyond the reach of the surf and watched as he came to shore, his shoulders then bare torso slowly rising out of the green sea.

He paused. 'Do you mind turning your back?'

He had a handsome face, a straight nose and an easy smile.

She folded her arms. 'Why should I?'

At first he seemed to seriously consider the question before his smile travelled to his eyes.

'Then stay there,' he said blithely, and slowly, very slowly, he started forward again, his body inching slowly into sight with every step he took.

Blanche held his gaze. She could see he was daring her to stay there, to see him emerge from the sea completely naked. He expected her to run. Most women would.

Head held high, she stood her ground.

Hairless, his body gleamed like soft gold and he kept smiling, smiling all the time, willing her to drop her eyes, to see he wore nothing, nothing at all.

He shook his head and smiled, water trickling down his body. 'I could paint you,' he said as he reached down for his breeches.

Blanche kept up her defiance. 'I might not want you to.' She lied and watched, fascinated, as strands of blond hair fell forward and droplets of water made pinholes in the sand.

He glanced up at her as he pulled on his breeches. His eyes were as blue as the willow pattern on Chinese porcelain – deep blue and shiny, bright against white. Blanche felt something light and alien flutter in her heart.

'I think you should be a painting,' he said. 'I could make you beautiful.'

The fluttering did not die, though the defiance returned. Blanche was speechless. 'You could make me beautiful? Are you saying I'm ugly?' She wanted him to say no.

He grinned and Blanche felt her face reddening. Damn the man! She'd promised herself she wouldn't blush, be bashful or run away. Now he was making her want to do all those things.

His head gradually appeared through the neck of his shirt and his bare torso disappeared. He was still smiling when he eventually emerged. 'Have you seen my painting?'

'No!'

'I saw you looking.'

'Are you calling me a liar?'

'Yes. A long-legged one with the most fetching eyes I've ever seen in my life. I *have* to paint them!'

She'd never had anyone wanting to paint her before, let alone saying she had fetching eyes and long legs. 'You shouldn't have been looking.'

He picked up his shoes and headed for her and his easel. 'At your eyes?' His look was querulous as well as amused.

'At my legs!'

He laughed and she found herself wanting to stroke his hair back from his forehead and caress the tight muscles that cinched in his belly.

Suddenly, he pounced on the painting sitting on the easel, and gripped it tightly between his hands. Frowning, he said, 'Is this really evening? Is this really a thing of beauty?'

Blanche eyed the painting with him. 'It is beautiful. Every evening in Barbados is like that.'

She jumped as he gripped the framework more tightly, brought up his knee and cracked the painting in two. It made a snapping sound, like a pistol shot.

'Not beautiful enough,' he said, grimacing as he stooped and rummaged among a stack of other canvases, some bigger and some smaller than the one he'd just destroyed.

'This, this and this,' he shouted, flinging the paintings out over the sand. 'I want none of them. They're not beautiful enough.'

'No!' Blanche shouted, as he flung every painting into the air. She ran after them and retrieved as many as she could. 'They're lovely,' she said.

There were sunsets framed by palm trees and ruined sugar mills standing sentinel on the hills, their crumbling domes black against the sky. She gathered all of them up and piled them where they'd been before.

'I'll use that one,' he said, snatching a medium-sized painting from her hands. 'Now sit down there.' He pointed to a rock that spiked the sand.

'I'm usually home by eight,' she told him, but allowed him to push her down until she was sitting on the rock. 'I run for the same time, over the same distance every night. They'll come looking if I'm late.' They wouldn't, but it made her feel safer to say so.

But he wasn't listening. He'd begun painting over a hilltop scene, went on to wipe the brush, grab a sketch pad and charcoal, made her sit down when she tried to get up, altered the angle of her shoulder, her head and the way her sleeve fell off her shoulder. Then he lightly brushed the black beauty spot that sat beneath her right eye and looked deeply into her eyes. 'What's your name, girl?'

She gulped before answering. 'Blanche Bianca.'

'Blanche,' he said as if by repeating the name it was instantly committed to memory. 'In future, you will present yourself on this rock every night—'

'But my mother might not—'

'Your mother will do as she's told. If she protests, tell her that Nelson Strong, son of Sir Emmanuel Strong, requires your presence each and every night that he is in Barbados.'

He talked as he painted her, telling her about Marstone Court, the splendid house he lived in back in England that was surrounded by over two hundred acres of parkland and close to the City of Bristol. He told her of the city's sights, especially the Old Vic in King Street where the great Mrs Siddons had played alongside David Garrick, the Shakespeare Inn where Defoe was supposed to have met his inspiration for Robinson Crusoe. 'It's mostly used by smugglers and thieves nowadays,' he told her. 'The types that would sell their mothers for a tot of rum or a bag of sugar.'

Blanche swallowed the urge to point out that the Strong family had sold slaves before abolition, sometimes splitting mothers from children. Nelson Strong intrigued her and, for now, he could say anything and she'd agree with him.

'There,' he said at last. 'The preliminary sketch is done. Present yourself tomorrow, please,' he said without looking at her.

Blanche rose achingly from the rock. 'I'm so stiff,' she said, arching her back as she raised her arms above her head.

She caught him looking at her. Their eyes seemed to lock even when he said, 'Being an artist's model is not so easy as people think. Would you like me to rub your back?'

She smiled at him sidelong and turned her back, reaching behind and pulling her hair to one side thus exposing the naked expanse of back above the neckline of her dress.

His breath was warm upon the nape of her neck. His touch was soft, his fingers instinctively seeking and unlocking the tension in her back.

With long, firm strokes, he ran his fingers down her spine, over her shoulder blades and on to her arms.

The rate of his breathing seemed to increase as his palms circled her neck, his fingers tracing patterns up into her hair.

She expected the kiss and prepared for it. When it came it sent a shiver down her spine, which radiated all over her body.

'I have to go,' she said, springing away from him.

'Wait!' he shouted, and reached out to grab her. But she was already running, her long legs covering the ground as she headed for the trees and the spring of fresh water.

'Make sure you're here tomorrow,' he shouted after her.

Without breaking stride, she waved in acknowledgement.

'Three hundred and two... no... two hundred and seventy...'

It was no good. She couldn't possibly concentrate on counting. The blue eyes, the blond hair and the naked, gleaming torso burned in her mind.

Melville – her uncle, who also kept house for Blanche and her mother – was already serving dinner when she got back.

Viola threw her a searching look. 'Where you been?'

Tossing her hair back over her shoulders, Blanche took her place at the table. 'Running,' she answered without looking at her mother.

Viola arched an eyebrow. 'Who you been running with?'

Blanche laughed. 'The wind and the sea. They never caught me though.'

When she got to the beach the next evening, Nelson was sitting in front of his easel, his brush making concentrated strokes over a green background around a white space that vaguely resembled a human figure.

'How many paces tonight?' he asked her without turning round.

Blanche slowed to a walk. 'How did you know I count my paces?'

She fancied he was grinning, though she couldn't see his face. 'I heard you last night. I do the same when I swim. One hundred strokes out into the bay, and one hundred back in again. It helps you concentrate, don't you think?'

He turned, his brush balanced between finger and thumb. The striking colour of his eyes took her aback. So did the way he smiled, the whiteness of his teeth against the sun-kissed gleam of his skin. Most white men didn't like the sun colouring their skin. Obviously Nelson didn't care.

Tonight he recited poetry while she sat as he wished her to, hair in wild disarray around her bare shoulders, the sleeves of her dress pulled down a little more than they had been the day before. His hand habitually brushed against her bare skin, causing her to notice the difference in colour: his light tan; and hers closer to coffee infused with cream.

Again, on the pretence of massaging her shoulders and back, he kissed the nape of her neck, his hands lulling her into trusting abandonment.

He stroked her cheeks, brushed at the dark mole beneath her right eye, then apologized. 'It deceives me into believing it a speck of dirt.'

His voice was soft against her ear. She shivered when he stroked it, tracing each fold and curve and finally kissing her lobe, then her cheek, turning her head to face him and kissing her lips.

She was late again that night. Later still the night after and the one after that.

Dinner was missed regularly, and her mother's looks were becoming more suspicious, her comments more searching.

'Who is he?' her mother asked, nearly two weeks after Blanche first encountered Nelson on the beach. Blanche merely laughed and said, 'The Man in the Moon.'

She got away with it, skipping away to bed and lying there, dreaming of him as she gazed at the moon's reflection on the glassy sea.

The painting was not proceeding well, mainly because Blanche was spending more time lying in Nelson's arms on the warm sand than posing on the rock.

It was a matter of time before they slept too long. Frogs clinging to the exposed roots of the nutmeg trees sang their nocturnal chorus. The surf pounded the shore. Blanche and Nelson heard nothing. Ticklish at first, then more vigorous, Blanche felt something pulling her hair.

She tried to raise her head, but something held her down. 'Get it out!'

Nelson roused himself. 'What's the matter?' he asked groggily.

'Someone's pulling my hair.'

She tried to rise again. Nelson held her down. 'Wait!'

She lay flat as he untangled a large crab from her hair.

'There,' he said, flinging the creature on to the sand where it promptly righted itself and scuttled off towards the sea.

Blanche sprang to her feet, brushing the sand from her body before pulling her dress back over her head.

'It's late,' she exclaimed, noticing the height of the moon and stars in relation to the sea. She knew every one of those constellations and where they should be in relation to the time. She was late. Very late.

They kissed, for the last time in Barbados as it turned out, but they weren't to know that, nor the circumstances in which they'd meet again.

'Goodbye,' Blanche called before bounding over the stream and along her part of the beach.

'Goodbye,' he called after her. 'I'll see you—'

The rest of his words were drowned out as a large wave broke fiercely on the shore.

A solitary light burned in the long, low house that Blanche shared with her mother and two old servants who were also relatives.

Stepping softly, Blanche made her way on to the veranda and reached for the door. It squeaked and she cursed her Uncle Melville for not oiling it. Much as she might want to escape any confrontation tonight, she doubted she'd make it and she was right.

Her mother was reading beside the plain funnel of an oil lamp, its blue flame flickering. She looked up when Blanche entered and closed the book.

'So where you been all this time? And don't tell me runnin'!'

Blanche considered lying. She'd never wanted to admit Nelson's existence. She enjoyed having a secret world and another life away from home. But the time had come and there was no reason not to tell the truth.

'I'm in love,' she cried and flung her arms around her mother's neck as she fell to her knees beside her chair.

Viola eyed her knowingly in the dim light and laughed. 'I should have known, you little minx. So who's this beau I should have horse-whipped for keepin' my little girl out so late?'

Blanche smiled up at her. 'He's beautiful. I met him rising out of the sea.'

Viola frowned. 'A merman?'

'No. A Strong man. Nelson Strong. He's the son of Sir Emmanuel Strong. Is that respectable enough for you?' Blanche exclaimed, almost laughing up into her mother's face.

Her mother's response was not as expected. A dull, drawn look made her face seem suddenly longer. She pursed her lips and all joy left her eyes.

'No!' The word echoed around the room, bounced off the well-polished furniture and seemed to dance around the ceiling.

Blanche flinched. 'Didn't you hear what I said, Ma. He's Nelson Strong. If you can bed Otis Strong, why can't I bed his nephew?'

It was so fast. Her cheek stung from the swift slap of her mother's hand. 'I'm your mother, child! Respect me and respect my wishes. You are not to see that young man again. Do you understand?'

Blanche stared up into her mother's face, her palm still flat against her throbbing cheek.

'No, I don't understand. I'm a Strong too, aren't I? That's what everyone says.'

'Says what?'

'That Otis is my father. He's always treated me like a daughter. You said so yourself.'

Viola's cheeks jiggled as if she were chewing the matter over. 'That don't mean that you're getting involved with the Strongs. It's best you don't.'

'I want to, and I will.'

Viola shook her head. 'No!'

Blanche's plans to thwart her mother's wishes proved futile. She was locked in her room at times, and never let out of sight in others.

'When can I come out?' she screamed from the other side of the door.

'When the time's right,' her mother answered.

'Why?' she asked time and time again. 'Why?'

Viola never answered. Blanche felt she was never going to be let out of the house alone again, especially not to run along her beloved beach.

–

Nelson gripped the rail of the *Lizzy Brady* and took a deep breath of salt air. Sailors high in the rigging released more sail, which fell with a crack as they filled with wind. He didn't flinch when a stray sheet barely missed his head, but kept his eyes fixed on the view.

Bridgetown huddled on the horizon like the colourful wooden bricks he'd played with as a child. He picked up his sketchpad and charcoal, began scraping a few abstract lines, but found he couldn't concentrate.

A shadow suddenly fell between him and the parting scene.

'Sorry to be leaving the place, sir?' asked the ship's captain, a stout man with huge whiskers named Tucker.

Nelson flung the pad and charcoal down. 'A fine place.' He said it through gritted teeth. Creative people hate being interrupted. Of course, he couldn't expect a simple sea captain to know that, not this one anyway.

Nelson gripped the side rail again, his fingers making movements like a pianist trying to find the right tune. The captain assumed he knew the reason for the young man's agitation.

'Hot climes make the blood run hot, sir, especially in women, so I'm told, them of a certain disposition.'

'Is that so, Captain?' Nelson snapped. He wanted the man to go away so he could sketch Barbados before it sank beyond the horizon. The passion he needed to involve his imagination or accentuate his insight was presently absent. It was almost as if he'd left it behind on the island with Blanche and her coffee-coloured body.

Sensing Nelson's reluctance to talk, Captain Tucker nodded courteously before moving away. He considered himself a man of the world and reckoned he knew a lovesick fool when he saw one. Nelson Strong wanted to stay; he could tell that by the tone of his voice and the look in his eyes. A wench was the problem no doubt. He certainly wouldn't be the first or the last to go home alone with an ache in his heart and an itch in his pants.

Nelson couldn't settle to sketching. Poetry wasn't an option either. For the moment, his muse had left him.

Tucking his sketchpad under his arm and throwing his charcoal overboard, he made his way down to his cabin, a cramped but private domain where his muse could be recalled after drinking a little wine, lightly sprinkled with dragon powder.

## Chapter Five

On the evening she was finally released from her room, Blanche ran faster to the beach than she'd ever ran before, her counting forgotten and her heart thudding against her ribs.

A warm breeze was blowing in off the sea. In the distance a ship in full sail sat on the horizon, dipping slightly before it finally disappeared.

The beach was deserted. The frogs were silent and only the insects attempted to compete with the pounding of the surf.

'Where is he?' Blanche asked her mother when she got back to the house.

'Gone,' answered Viola.

She stood querulous and confused. Did that mean gone from River-mead, perhaps into Bridgetown? For the moment Blanche resisted asking, in case questions about Nelson Strong landed her locked in her room again.

'I'm going into Bridgetown. Shopping to do. Dinner to prepare,' said Viola, her words minimal but descriptive enough.

'That's nice,' said Blanche, aching to go into Bridgetown too, but unwilling to arouse suspicion.

'You can come.'

'I'll get my parasol.' And she tried not to run.

All along the harbourside in Bridgetown, the stench of dried animal excrement, sweating bodies, overipe fruit and fish sizzling on ramshackle braziers, was sweetened with the sticky smell of sugar, and the thicker pungency of fermenting molasses on its way to becoming rum and the remnants to *dunder*, the cheaper and lethal rum of the islanders.

Melville was playing coachman today, his brownness in stark contrast to his snow-white wig and an old-fashioned jabot of tiered frills falling from a tight band around his neck. A tri-cornered hat worn at a jaunty angle shaded his determined look as he urged the matching greys through the crowd that surged around Viola's carriage as if she were royalty.

'Nice dress,' said a banana-seller, eyeing the empire-style lilac-sprigged muslin Viola was wearing. 'Did Dodie May make it for you?'

Viola, splendid in a straw bonnet trimmed with silk violets, turned contemptuous eyes on the woman. 'Certainly not! It's a Paris fashion. I likes to stay in fashion like they does in Europe. You'rn all ignorant of fashion. Just watch me, and you'll learn all about it.'

It was a lie. Dodie May had indeed made the dress from a pattern that was now almost twenty years old and falling to pieces.

A grey-whiskered white man, a lone pale face in a sea of cheerful brown, doffed his hat in greeting. 'If you're such a follower of fashion, how come you ain't got your horses' tails *fashionably* docked, *Lady* Viola?'

'They got to keep the flies off their bits. I wouldn't like no flies crawling over my private bits. Drive me crazy.'

The carriage stopped again as the crowd pressed more thickly ahead of them. Traders of all sorts took advantage and pressed forward with their wares.

'Bananas? Fresh guava? Pineapples?'

'Rum! Sweet dreams for a penny.'

'Odd jobs, dig the ground, pick the fruit, mend yer front gate.'

Blanche glanced at her mother, saw that her face was glistening and that she looked paler than she normally did. She was about to ask if anything was wrong, when a man dragging a sad-looking sheep behind him stopped the carriage.

'Fresh mutton, lady? Fresh mutton? You want, lady? You want?'

He grinned boldly, thick lips stretched over yellow teeth. Like anyone who'd worked among the sharp leaves of the sugar cane, his face, body and limbs were covered with scars and he smelled of stale rum.

Viola seemed to recover and began to bargain.

Back to her old self, thought Blanche, and hid behind her parasol. Who cared about food? Who cared about drink? Where was Nelson? Without him, Barbados reverted to what it really was: bustling, bright and brashly commercial. Today was no exception. Many sloops, barques and brigantines were tied at anchor. Small boys swung from the hefty hawsers looped around the drumheads of stout wooden capstans and dropped from there into the water, dripping as they climbed out, only to repeat the exercise over and over again.

Viola was saying, 'I ain't paying no three shillings for a scrawny creature like that. Two shillings and no more.'

The man pleaded. 'Three shillings. I have a family. I must put food on the table.'

'You got a sheep. Put that on the table 'stead of selling it to me.' The carriage springs squeaked in protest as Viola settled back in her seat. 'I tell you what. You butcher that scrawny creature for me and get it to my place right away and you can have your three shillings.'

'Three shillings! Yes, lady, right away!'

'Hell! I didn't mean that quick,' gasped Viola.

Blanche came out from behind her parasol.

Sunlight flashed on sharp steel. A swift slash from right to left and blood surged from the sheep's throat.

Smelling almost metallic in the hot sun, the blood steamed on to the ground, welcomed by screaming seagulls and the furtive licks of carrion dogs that were kicked and stoned for their trouble.

Viola folded her arm across her belly, her face drained of colour. 'Get going, Melville. I don't feel too well.'

Blanche opened her mouth to ask what was the matter.

Her mother patted her hand. 'It's all right. I'm all right.'

The carriage jolted forward, the mass of humanity dividing like water before the high-stepping hooves.

More ships lined the quay, men seeming no bigger than ants, climbing up masts, along spars, checking ropes and sails, necessary tasks before re-crossing the broad Atlantic. Brown bodies, gleaming with sweat, moved like a many-legged alligator up and down the gangplanks of ships, casks of sugar and rum on their shoulders.

Blanche took her mother at her word, presumed everything was fine and scanned the crowd looking for Nelson.

'He's gone back to England,' her mother said suddenly. Blanche felt her mother's dark brown eyes on her, perhaps trying to ascertain just how upset she was. 'I don't understand—'

'I went to see Otis. We both felt it was for the best.'

'I can't believe it.'

'You'll get over it. There are some good prospects in Barbados, if only you'd just look.'

Blanche thought of the beach, the paintings, the surf beating the shore and the warmth of Nelson's arms, his lips upon her skin. 'I don't want a prospect! I want Nelson.'

'Well, you can't have Nelson. He's a Strong. He could never have married you.'

'Is it because we're cousins?'

Blanche saw her mother flinch. 'No! Not really...'

Blanche slumped back in the carriage seat, distraught. 'I won't marry anyone except Nelson.'

'Then you'll not marry at all.'

'Then I'll be like you, a mistress.'

She'd fully expected another slap, but her mother seemed suddenly tired as she shook her head and said, 'There's no security in being a kept woman. Be a wife. There's respect and security in that. This is a man's world. The best a woman can be is a wife.'

'You have security.'

'But I don't have respect, which means being respectable. I could never give you that because I've never been a wife. So you must give it to your children, and to do that you must have a husband.'

'Otis Strong wouldn't marry you!' Blanche snapped the name like a turtle about to take a bite out of something far larger than itself.

'He couldn't marry me, but he's always taken care of me.' Her mother's eyes met her searching gaze.

All her life Blanche had wanted Otis Strong to claim her as his daughter, but he never had, even though his pale, English wife had given him no heirs.

'I love Nelson.'

'Love someone else.'

Blanche slumped back against the warm leather of the carriage seat. 'I'll write to him. I'm good at writing. I like teaching it too.'

'So I notice,' said Viola. 'You bin teaching Melville's grandchildren to write their own names and suchlike, and look what that's led to!'

Viola pointed at the wooden door of a disused counting house. Scrawled on it with a chalky yellow stone was one word: Samson. Blanche smiled. 'He's very good at writing.'

'I can believe it,' said Viola as they passed a tumbledown tin hut where barrels were stored. 'It's all down to practice!'

Samson. Samson. Samson. His name was everywhere and the enterprising young lad had also written it in what looked like the hot, black stuff that shipbuilders used with rope to caulk ships and boats.

'But it's got him a place at the school,' remarked Melville from the front of the carriage.

Blanche sensed Melville's pride and her own mother's resentment. Reading and writing was something her mother had never been taught and had never needed.

'People ain't never satisfied,' Viola grumbled. Lines furrowed her brow and the vibrant voice lapsed into silence.

'I mean it,' said Blanche suddenly. 'I will write to him!'

Her mother said nothing, her face immovable.

Blanche persisted. 'I have his address. I *will* write to him!'

'I suppose so.'

'You won't mind?'

Her mother shrugged.

'We *could* have married. Wouldn't that have been possible?'

Her mother smiled as she shook her head and gently touched her daughter's cheek. 'No. He's not for you. He'll have an English bride.'

Blanche sat with folded arms, the handle of her parasol tucked into the crook of her arm, studying her toes in preference to the sea, the unending fields or the verdant greenness of the centre of the island where fluffy white clouds seemed to sit like hats on the hills.

Melville did all the talking for the rest of the journey, his conversation instigated by Blanche's mention of schooling.

The afternoon was warm and the dusty road that wound between fields of high-growing cane was hard-packed mud, sticky in the rainy season, but dusty at this time of year. The smell of frangipani blossoming in the heat mixed with the salt smell from the sea and the sweetness of the smoke from the curing house chimneys.

Blanche remembered Nelson's paintings of the neglected sugar building on the island. He'd made Barbados more colourful with the flick of a paintbrush and the touch of his lips. Without him she saw only shabbiness, smelled only decay and the stale sweat of tired men.

'I'll never forget him,' she said resolutely.

Her mother didn't answer.

'I won't,' she said more vehemently, harbouring a childish determination to cause an argument.

At first she presumed the warm afternoon had sent her mother asleep. When she looked, her arm was resting, on the side of the carriage and her head had flopped forward on to that.

'Ma!' she said, and nudged her mother's arm. She tried again. 'Ma?'

Her mother groaned and her head lolled forward on to her chest. Then she crumpled to the floor.

'Stop!' Blanche screamed.

Melville pulled the horses to an instant halt and looked over his shoulder.

'She's sick,' shouted Blanche.

Melville got down from his perch and came back to investigate.

'Her belly's big,' he said matter-of-factly, pointing at her mother's stomach.

Round-eyed, Blanche looked too. Why hadn't she noticed it before? The seam of high-waisted dresses came just below the breasts. A big belly was easily hidden.

'We need a doctor perhaps,' said Blanche.

'Or a midwife,' said Melville.

Blanche did not meet his gaze. It was too much of a shock to believe that her mother might be pregnant.

'I'll get Miss Pinkerty,' said Melville.

Blanche let him take charge, convinced that her mother would be all right. Lots of women her mother's age got pregnant; though it seemed strange after all these years. But the only man she ever saw was Otis Strong... and everyone knew his wife couldn't give him children. But Viola could.

Blanche seethed with anger. Otis Strong had to face up to his responsibilities and she would make sure he did. In the past she would never have dared knock at his door. But if he wanted to be left alone, then he should have left her mother alone or married her, and he should never have dared send Nelson away.

Once her mother was in bed and Miss Pinkerty sent for, Blanche took one of the matching greys from the stable.

'That's a tired horse,' remarked Melville. 'Where you going?'

Blanche mounted astride. Sidesaddle was a skill she'd never quite mastered.

'Rivermead. I won't be long.'

Digging her heels into the grey's side, she cantered off along the dirt track that joined the road to Rivermead.

At the Strongs' house men were hoeing around flowering shrubs and young boys were sweeping dead leaves. They looked up, as Blanche cantered down the winding drive between carefully planted bushes, each spot chosen to throw shade over the drive.

A servant in brown and yellow livery held her horse as she dismounted. 'I want to see Mr Otis Strong,' she said in the most imperious voice she could muster, though her stomach churned with nerves.

The servant looked her up and down as though trying to reach a decision.

'He don't see coloureds.'

Blanche felt the blood rushing to her cheeks. 'Well, he's damn well going to see me!'

With that, she flounced up the steps. Just as she reached the top, a set of glazed French doors swung open. A tall woman in a striped dress and a large bonnet stepped out into the sunshine carrying a trug. Her eyes were like marbles; their colour something between brown and hazel and set into a floury-white complexion. Her dress was like a large bell and swung slightly as she moved, so different to the high-waisted dress of pale yellow muslin that Blanche wore.

It was obvious from the start that the woman knew who she was. Her mouth was set poker straight, and her eyes bored into Blanche as if she were of no more worth than the sheep her mother had bought that morning.

She plucked up all her courage. 'I want to see Otis.'

Mistress Strong stood absolutely still, raised her eyebrows contemptuously but said nothing.

'My mother's having a baby. It's his responsibility.'

The woman's cheeks quivered as if she were swallowing her shock. Suddenly there was a scream and the trug came flying past Blanche's head. She ducked, the trug missed her, and she saw Otis's wife running off into the house, still screaming hysterically and calling for her husband.

The servant told her to go. 'He ain't going to be pleased.'

'I'll stay,' she said.

The servant judged that he'd lose any argument, so left her alone but he told her that someone had gone to fetch his master from the fields he was currently inspecting.

It was an hour or so before Otis Strong came riding in astride a striking chestnut.

He stared down at her, swallowed and seemed almost nervous in her presence. He was also strangely pale, had dark rings beneath his eyes and a stoic look, as if he were half expecting the news she brought.

After a groom had taken his horse and was well out of ear-shot, he asked what she wanted.

'It's my mother. I think she's having a baby.'

He showed no emotion as he said, 'She's not having a child.'

Blanche prepared herself to argue, glaring at him with fire in her eyes. 'Look, her belly's big and she's feeling ill. I've never seen my mother looking like this, so don't tell me that she's not having a child.'

For a man of such power, he seemed oddly silent, as though not wanting to say anything else. 'She's not having a baby. Go home.' He turned away.

His attitude angered her more than she could bear. She rushed up behind him, grabbed his arm so that he had to face her.

'How can you say that?'

She saw that his eyes were moist and for one solitary moment, she was sure he was on the verge of crying. He looked at her then towards the house where his wife had resumed her screaming.

'My wife is a little highly strung,' he said. 'I have to go to her.'

The tears were for his wife!

The sight of his turned back was unbearable. There was so much she wanted to ask him, but she had promised her mother – long ago – that she wouldn't. But at least she could ask him about Nelson.

She followed him as far as the wide veranda that ran along the front of the house.

'Why am I not good enough to join your family? I want to know why Nelson has been sent home. We love each other!' She held her head high. He'd never told her he'd loved her, but she assumed he did. 'I want to know,' she said again.

Otis shook his head and wouldn't meet her eyes. 'He's not for you.'

Briefly, they looked at each other before he gave a servant orders to help her remount and be seen off the premises.

Blanche was dumbstruck. It no longer seemed of any importance whether this man was her father. She hated him. He would never acknowledge her, just as he would never acknowledge the fact that her mother was having a baby. He was hard-hearted and a coward.

Before going home, she went one last time to the beach. Tying the horse to a tree, she stepped on to the warm sand just at the spot where the stream marked the boundary of Rivermead. Taking off her shoes, she forded the cool waters, not running this time, but merely striding to the spot where she'd last lain with Nelson.

It seemed desolate now, empty of everything that had once been. All the evenings were gone.

The sun had sunk into the sea and left a purple sky by the time she got back home. To her surprise, Miss Pinkerty's donkey and cart were still there and Uncle Melville was sitting on the porch steps, holding his head in his hands.

Instinctively aware that something was wrong, she slid down from her mount.

'Is it born?' she asked.

Her heart sank when she saw the tears squeezing out from between Melville's fingers. 'She's dying,' he said lamely, a trail of spittle running from the side of his mouth.

Open-mouthed and feeling terribly cold, Blanche entered the house, knowing that she wouldn't welcome what she was about to be told.

Her footsteps seemed to echo off the stone corridor as she made her way to her mother's bedroom.

Miss Pinkerty, her turbaned head as high as a steeple, was singing soft and low as she held her mother's hand.

Blanche approached the bed hesitantly, afraid to look around the room in case she saw a bloodied bundle of what might have been a life.

'Is the baby not coming?' She directed her question at Miss Pinkerty, whose eyes were like brown moons beneath thick eyebrows.

'There ain't no baby, child. That's a cancer she got there. Somethin' that won't stop growin'.'

Blanche glanced at the small phial beside the candles on the bedside table. Even before she asked the question, she knew with chilling certainty what the answer was likely to be.

'Will the medicine make her better?'

Miss Pinkerty shook her head. 'Laudanum – opium mixed with a little rum. It will take the pain away, but it won't cure her, child.'

Fear clutched at Blanche's heart. Her mother couldn't die. It wasn't possible.

'What about if you give her more of it? Won't that work?' she asked.

Miss Pinkerty shook her head. 'Just wine and moondust,' she said. 'It will take you to paradise and back again, but take you to hell if you're not careful.'

Blanche sank on the opposite side of the bed to Miss Pinkerty and reached for her mother's hand.

Just before midnight, Viola's eyes blinked open.

'You're going to get better,' said Blanche, smiling at her mother as if she were telling the truth, her eyes moist with tears.

Her mother shook her head. 'I'm dying, Blanche.'

Blanche shook her head. 'No. No, of course you're not.'

Viola's lips were dry, and her breathing shallow. The sound of fluttering wings drew Blanche's attention to the candle burning at the side of the bed. Mesmerised by the light, a brown-winged moth dived carelessly into the flame and perished. By the time she looked back at her mother, she'd gone too.

–

The funeral passed in a blur. Otis Strong paid for everything, but did not attend. Blanche leaned for support on the arm of her uncle.

'Why didn't he come?' she asked Uncle Melville after it was all over.

Melville shrugged. 'He couldn't I s'pose.' As always, he seemed disinclined to talk about Otis.

Blanche hung her head. Her mother was dead and her father refused to acknowledge her. All she had left was Uncle Melville and a clutch of relatives scattered around the island.

A sea breeze was blowing straight into her mother's bedroom when word came from a solicitor in Bridgetown that she was to attend a meeting with regard to the settling of her mother's estate.

'What do they mean by that?' she asked no one in particular as she looked down at the letter.

Before leaving the room, she looked round at the pale colours, the patchwork counterpane, the hairbrushes, perfumes and creams sitting neatly before an oval mirror on cherub supports. It was her mother's smell she would miss, that hint of spice mixed with a heady perfume that arrived from England once a year. It was contained in a stout bottle of dark blue glass with a silver stopper attached to the bottle by a fine silver chain. She picked it up, pulled out the stopper and sniffed. The smell was comforting, so much so, that when she went to see the solicitor, she wrapped the bottle in a lace-trimmed handkerchief, pushed it to the bottom of her purse and took it with her. So long as she had that bottle, her mother would never be too far away.

The solicitor's office was stone built and had started life as a counting house, a place in which past plantation owners had once done business. As Bridgetown had grown, planters had set up counting houses and crushing mills closer to the fields, the former so they could keep a better eye on things, the latter because the cane had to be crushed immediately after being cut before its moisture was sucked up by the Caribbean sun.

Otis Strong was there, standing at the window with his back to the room.

'Everything reverts to the Strong estate,' began the solicitor, a refined gentleman with a thin face and an old-fashioned wig that sat askew on his meagre head.

He seemed nervous, constantly deferring to the broad-shouldered figure silently looking out of the open window. Not once did he acknowledge her.

Hardly listening, Blanche sat very still in her pale green day dress with matching bonnet, her net-gloved hands folded primly on her lap. Her gaze remained fixed on the man at the window. She so wanted him to look at her and to like her, to declare that she was his daughter and to embrace her with the love and affection a father should give his child.

If only this was a dream, she thought, and closed her eyes as she waited for the solicitor to finish rustling his papers and get on with whatever it was he had to do. It was a vain hope, but she found herself wishing that when she reopened her eyes she would be laid against crisp linen pillows in her own bedroom and this little man and his musty office would have disappeared.

'Miss Bianca?'

The solicitor's voice was as thin as his body and pierced her thoughts like a bodkin.

'Are you all right?'

She blinked. The musty office and the little man were still there. So was Otis Strong, his shadow falling on to the dusty floorboards like a cloud across the sun. He chose that moment to speak. 'Get on with it, Morgan. I haven't got all day.'

Angry and grief-stricken, Blanche couldn't help herself. 'No! Of course not. Your wife's waiting for you at home, glad my mother's dead. So, what are you to do with me? What does your *wife* want you to do with me? If it wasn't for abolition, she'd have got you to sell us on by now, wouldn't she? Both me and my mother!'

Otis Strong's broad shoulders stiffened as though he were holding himself back.

He wants to hit me, she thought, and didn't care if he did.

But he remained looking out of the window. 'Your mother had every comfort,' he said, his voice seeming to rumble like distant thunder.

Blanche thought of the brightness of the company at her mother's house, the men and women who had danced and sang on the lawn, where frangipanis shed their ice-white blossom and filled the air with a scent reminiscent of almonds.

'As I said, everything reverts to the Strong estate, including the house—'

'But what about me? Where do I go?' she asked.

It was the only home she'd ever known. The house and garden were set on a hill with glorious views towards a wine-dark sea in one direction. In the other, fields of pale green sugar cane rolled away to the hills. The cane was tall and hid the toilers; men and women with cut faces, their hands bleeding and made tough by immersion in buckets of urine.

The solicitor cleared his throat. 'Now Miss Bianca,' he began. He was not used to dealing with feisty young women. He'd expected compliance, humility bred into her ancestors over years of subjugation. But then, her grandfather was a sea captain her great grandmother an actress, he thought, so it was only natural. But he was a nervous man by nature, so felt and looked agitated.

Blanche sprang from her seat, the flimsy muslin of her dress clinging to her bosom and hips as she joined the man at the window. She fixed her eyes on the nerve that twitched beneath Otis Strong's right eye.

'What am I to you? Tell me, please?'

'Just a girl.'

'And my mother? What was she to you?'

His mouth seemed to quiver for a moment, as if he were remembering a moment, a touch or a kiss. His answer surprised her. 'A lady to whom my family owed a great debt and, because of that, I have made arrangements for you.'

Hope sprang in her breast. 'Will I live with you?'

'Certainly not!' He almost sounded frightened.

Somehow, she'd hoped he'd accept her because her mother was dead. She'd thought his wife might, eventually too. On reflection, it was a vain hope. She was nothing to either of them.

'Then what else is there for me?'

Otis Strong kept his eyes on the scene outside the window, the street, the buildings and the Caribbean beyond.

'Get on with it, Morgan.' He said it evenly, almost coldly, and without a sideways glance at her.

The solicitor sat like a dried twig behind his great mahogany desk, an obvious cast-off from one of the plantation houses on the island. He squeaked, 'As you have not yet attained the age of majority and because you have no fortune of your own, Letters of Bonding have been authorized. You are to set sail for Bristol where the Strong family have made arrangements to provide for you in the household of Sir Emmanuel Strong, brother of Mr Otis Strong.'

Blanche's mouth dropped open. 'I'm going to England?' She could barely contain her surprise, let alone her excitement.

'To stay at my brother's house in Bristol,' said Otis without turning round.

Blanche was ecstatic. Bristol was where the sugar and molasses went to, where it was refined and sold. And Nelson was there! Was that the reason he was sending her? Had Nelson mentioned how much they cared for each other and insisted she join him?

Unable to contain her excitement, Blanche almost laid her hand on Otis Strong's arm in gratefulness for what he was doing. At the last moment she held back, sensing that he did not want it.

She decided to play the demurely grateful young lady.

'I'm sorry, Mr Strong,' she said. 'I know that whatever you've arranged for me is for my own good.'

She saw Otis Strong's eyelids flicker briefly as if he'd been suddenly reminded of a painful memory.

'The *Ianthe* sails in three days. Betsy and Melville, your servants, have been advised.'

Although the prospect of travel and seeing Nelson again excited her beyond belief, she did have a care as to what happened to her servants who were also related on her mother's side. 'What will happen to them? What will happen to the house?'

The solicitor glanced at Otis Strong as if seeking guidance. None was forthcoming. He swallowed before taking the initiative.

'The house will be boarded up. The servants will be re-employed on the Strong plantation.'

A terrible thought occurred to her. 'Not in the cane fields! They're too old.'

The strong voice of Otis Strong boomed through the office. 'They will join my household.'

She was greatly relieved. Cutting cane was a job for young men. Even then they were burned out after seven years of it, their hands, faces and bodies a mass of healed scars and hard skin. The cane was as sharp as the knives to cut it down.

'There is just one proviso,' squeaked the solicitor, 'and that is you never mention any connection between your mother and Mr Strong to anyone at Marstone Court.'

Under Blanche's demanding gaze, he looked embarrassed, cleared his throat and added, 'Should you mention that Mr Strong is anything other than a philanthropic patron, should you state the existence of any intimate relationship between your mother and Mr Strong, your servants' lot will deteriorate considerably.'

She was aware of him rambling on as she digested the facts. In one brief moment, she had imagined herself arriving at Marstone Court as the daughter of Otis Strong. Obviously he was not recognizing her as such, and she dared not voice her views on the matter for the sake of Melville and Betsy.

The solicitor was saying, 'Marstone Court is the home of the Strong family. It is situated in the County of Somersetshire, yet close to the city of Bristol.'

'I know.' Of course she did. Nelson had told her so, and the thought of seeing him again lifted her spirits.

'Do you agree to this?' the solicitor asked.

She nodded. 'Yes. Yes, I agree.'

When she got back to the white house with its tin roof and shady veranda, Betsy, the housekeeper, who had patchy skin like a piebald horse and breasts that curved over her apron waistband, was already packing a brass-bound wooden sea chest with most of Blanche's clothes.

'I've been given instructions to pack your things in your grandfather's chest,' she explained guiltily, as Blanche swept into the room, her eyes flickering between Betsy and the chest. 'You have to go, they told me.' She looked crestfallen and worried, then surprised when Blanche flung her bonnet on to the bed and waltzed around the room. 'I'm going to England to live with the Strongs in a big house with lovely carriages and horses, and I'll go to beautiful balls and dance until dawn.'

Betsy eyed her with a mix of disbelief and tenderness. 'England ain't Barbados. There ain't no sun, so I hear, and 'cos of that everyone's got skin as white as fish meat.'

'They're always white!'

'No, they ain't! Out here they're pink. The sun puts some colour in 'em.'

'I'll take them some sunshine.' Blanche thrust her face towards a mirror with cut-glass edging that her mother said had come from France. Blanche was paler than her mother, though dark in the same way that some Spanish are dark, with pale freckles over her nose and the distinctive mole beneath one eye.

Betsy fastened the trunk with an air of finality and adopted the sort of expression she usually did when Blanche was about to get a lecture. She said, 'You know that Blanche means white, don't you, child? Betsy's eyes held a warning. 'Just 'cos you're named white don't make you white. Just you remember that.'

'I'm going to Bristol, Betsy. I'll see Nelson and all the places he told me about.'

'They goin' to keep you like a daughter?' asked an incredulous Betsy.

'Something like that. Because I'm young I'm going to be bonded.'

Betsy's eyebrows shot up. 'What does that mean? Ain't that like being a servant?'

'Of course not! It's to protect me,' said Blanche, choosing to think it was a good thing rather than let it cloud her excitement of seeing Nelson again.

Betsy frowned, afraid to voice what she thought being bonded meant. In her heart of hearts she had a worrying suspicion that it wasn't much better than being a slave.

The scepticism in Betsy's expression remained. Turning her head, she spat at a bug-eyed beetle crawling up the frame of the open window. It hit the insect hard, hurling it back out into the vinery that straggled in riotous splendour up the iron trelliswork around the windows.

'They're Strongs,' she said disdainfully. 'They only care about sugar. You'd do well to remember that.'

## Chapter Six

'The sins of the fathers are returning to haunt us.' Jeb Strong's voice crackled with each painful breath and his eyes rolled as his head fell to one side.

Emmanuel barely controlled his anger. 'You and Otis went behind my back. You should have told me.'

'Would you have agreed?'

Emmanuel avoided answering. 'What's done is done.'

Jeb tried to study his brother's expression as he took a light from a candle with a long taper. The moment was fleeting. Emmanuel went back to pacing the room, studying the familiar family portraits, the Delft china on the mantelpiece, the French clock, the view from the window. Anything but look at me, thought Jeb, who was sitting in the specially adapted carver chair that had wheels fixed to its legs.

Emmanuel hated sickness.

Jeb was adamant. 'It is our Christian duty to take this child in. She has no one else, and our brother's wife certainly won't take her into her household. Perhaps it might have been different if she'd not been barren.'

Emmanuel held back a curtain so he could look more easily out of the window across the sprawling parkland that surrounded Marstone Court. He'd not failed in his duty to his family, taking Jeb in after he became ill, but sometimes he regretted it. Jeb was like a living, breathing conscience.

He sighed, smoke spouting from his nostrils. 'She'll suit as a nurse. It's all we can do.'

'Except atone,' said Jeb.

Emmanuel was adamant. 'I feel no guilt. Why should I? Otis took it upon himself to look after the child and her mother. I'll take on that responsibility purely out of respect for him. I understand his predicament.'

Unseen by his brother, Jeb tried to shake his head, though he'd been warned not to on account of the fluid seeping from one side of his body to the other. 'You didn't murder anyone. I deserve to be in this chair, but I just hope that God forgives me eventually.'

Emmanuel looked flustered. Jeb made God sound like a real person, not as outlined with thunderous prayers and moral sermons preached from the pulpit.

'I will abide by the promise you gave Otis.'

'He loved her,' Jeb said simply and a faraway look came to his eyes. His words became strangled as the fluid in his lungs began to choke him.

Emmanuel started for the door. 'You need turning. I'll get Duncan and David.'

Jeb raised one weak hand, the pale veins prominent through the thin skin. 'No. You do it.'

Emmanuel's face paled at the thought of touching his brother's ailing body.

'But that's why we have servants,' he blustered.

Jeb's eyes slid sidelong, anticipating the look on his brother's face when he said, 'I'd prefer an act of brotherly love – if you can bare to touch me.'

Emmanuel steeled himself, his fingers opening and closing into the palms of his hands as he anticipated what it would be like. Was pleurisy contagious? He swallowed the dryness of his mouth and made an instant decision.

'Servants are best suited for physical work.' He sprang for the bell pull at the side of the fireplace.

The colour of their skin accentuated by white wigs and gloves and standing at over six feet, Duncan and David, the twin footmen, born in the West Indies of a slave mother and an unknown father, appeared immediately.

'Quickly,' said Emmanuel, as Jeb turned red in the face.

Once the task was complete, they left in unison, closing the door softly behind them.

'What's done is done,' Emmanuel repeated, choosing to revert to their earlier conversation rather than dwell on Jeb's illness. 'She'll fit in. She'll have to.' He went back to the window.

Jeb was not fooled. He smiled, his mouth lifting to one side of his face. 'Verity will insist she does.'

Emmanuel stiffened.

Jeb guessed that Emmanuel had not told his wife about the paternity of her children's new nanny.

'She'll be glad of help when the baby comes,' said Emmanuel. 'I've given orders for one of the attic rooms to be opened up for her.' He countered Jeb's accusing gaze. 'I know no one's been up there for years. But it will do.'

'Ah!' Jeb exclaimed.

'I told her she was from Barbados and my brother's household. Enough, I think.'

Jeb noticed Emmanuel's angry glare, but pretended he didn't. 'Pretty,' he fought for breath, 'is she?'

Emmanuel reached for another cigar and grumbled in the affirmative.

'Eighteen… years,' Jeb murmured thoughtfully.

'That evening…' said Emmanuel, his eyes glazing as his voice faded. 'It seems such a long time ago now. I can barely remember being so young and the evening being so balmy, so full of excitement.'

'I remember it well,' said Jeb, his voice stiff with resentment. 'You were married to your first wife. And I was young, and full of energy, able to move, to walk…' He took a deep breath, the sound it made resembling a handful of castanets all clicking at variance with each other. He squeezed his eyes tightly shut as he recalled the butler, Caradoc, and the sickening way the candlestick had come down on his head. 'We're *all* responsible for that girl, Manny.'

Emmanuel poured himself another brandy. 'So you say, Jeb, so you say. But I have other more important matters on my mind. The business with Conrad Heinkel. I'm convinced that sugar prices are going to plummet, what with the imports of beet sugar coming in from Europe now. I'm pursuing a partnership arrangement at present, but Heinkel is a widower and it would make life easier if Horatia considered him as a husband. I might try to persuade her.'

–

While the men smoked and talked in the dining room, Emmanuel's daughter from his first marriage, Horatia, and her stepmother, Lady Verity, sat drinking coffee from bone china cups in the drawing room.

'Prince Charles is gone,' Lady Verity wailed into her coffee, her face crumpled with despair.

'Post a reward,' Horatia suggested dispassionately.

'I have done.' Verity dabbed at her red-rimmed eyes. 'Two guineas in fact.' She got up from her chair, the back of her hand resting against her forehead. 'I've barely slept a wink since he's been gone. I fear dreadfully not seeing him again.'

Horatia grimaced. 'He's a dog. You make him sound like a lover.'

Lady Verity threw her a disparaging look. There was little love lost between them.

'Horatia, you are just like your father. You have no compassion.'

'I saw George today, your youngest son.'

'I know who he is,' snapped Verity.

Horatia flicked at the corners of her lips with a damask napkin. 'He's still wearing a dress. Do you think that's wise?' she asked, the apparent innocence of her manner masking a veiled accusation that Verity was not a good mother.

Choosing retreat rather than attempting to portray herself as anything but the selfish person she was, Verity said, 'I have a headache. Do forgive me. I must go.'

'Nothing I said, I trust?' said Horatia with a forced smile.

'My delicate condition.' Verity rested her square hands on her swollen belly. 'Children are a blessing, but they are also a great responsibility.'

Horatia raised her eyes to heaven. Children, pregnancy and complaining about her lot formed the centre of Verity's conversation and were a handy shield under attack. Horatia sometimes wondered what Verity had talked about when her father was courting her.

'Lucky that you have a nanny, nursemaids and a governess to help you out,' Horatia said.

'Good staff are not easy to get,' replied Verity. 'One has to make do.'

Horatia hid her smile behind her cup. Verity was not clever. Her father had married the woman for other attributes, she decided, but could not think what they might be.

The clock in the hall struck nine. 'Goodnight, Horatia,' said Verity.

'Goodnight,' said Horatia, her jaw aching with the effort of appearing gracious.

Immediately Verity had gone, Horatia slid her fingers into the small, lace-edged pocket that swung from a silken cord into the folds of her dress. Slowly she slid the cheroot out of the pocket, bent over a candle until the end was glowing and a sliver of smoke curled upwards.

Closing her eyes, she drew in the sweet humours, expelled rings of powdery grey smoke and thought how good it would be to accompany it with a brandy, which was in the dining room along with her father.

I want some, she said to herself, and made her way across the marble-floored hallway, a plume of smoke from the burning cheroot wafting out behind her. She thought of the big leather armchair in the library where she could stretch out, her feet on the desk, with a brandy and her cheroot.

The dining-room door was ajar. She paused, her fingers touching the cut glass of the door handle, just as the last part of Jeb and Emmanuel's conversation drifted out.

So far she had resisted the advances of Josiah Benson, a man who, unlike most, appreciated her business brain. Rather than marry a man of her father's choosing, whoever Conrad Heinkel was, she'd stall him by allowing Josiah to call on her.

—

By mid-afternoon, the west wing in the vicinity of the Reverend Strong's room was silent and bereft of servants. The sun slanted in through the high windows along the corridor outside, dust motes floating like crystals in the strong light.

Nelson strode along the corridor. He paused outside his uncle's suite and listened. Not a sound. Softly, trusting his uncle was in a drugged and dreamless sleep, he opened the door and stepped into the room.

The curtains were drawn. They usually were of an afternoon. And Jeb was indeed asleep, his mouth open and his chest rattling.

Nelson made for the tray of medicines, salves and ointments sitting on a tray at the side of the bed. Carefully, he brought a small bottle out of his pocket and took out the stopper.

After careful scrutiny of the collection of bottles and boxes, he found the one he was looking for, took out the stopper, and poured its contents into his own bottle, which was of a different colour and type. Once that was done and the bottle was back in his pocket, he filled the empty one up from the jug of water conveniently left on the tray.

Just as silently as he'd entered, he let himself out of the room.

–

Home, thought Tom Strong, gazing at the forest of chimneys that sprang from the roof of Marstone Court and could be seen for miles around.

The house itself was surrounded by over two hundred acres of parkland and occupied the Avon Valley below Leigh Woods, looking towards the new colonnades and crescents that were springing up all over Clifton.

'Glad to be back?' asked John the coachman, a jovial man with a round, red face, and an equally round wife.

Tom thought carefully before answering. He always did. If things weren't said right, they could easily be misconstrued, like giving orders on a ship.

'It's good to see Bristol again.'

'I s'pose you'll be seeing the Reverend Strong first?'

This question needed less consideration. 'Unless anything more pressing occurs, I shall indeed see the Reverend. There's little time to spare.'

'Back to your ship that quick, are ye?'

Tom thought of the last time he'd seen Jeb. He smiled sadly. 'Has there been some miracle in my absence?'

The coachman looked uncomfortable that a question was now being asked of him. 'No,' he said, frowning.

'Then I think we can agree that it's the Reverend who has little time to spare.'

The coachman sighed. 'He's a good man. He don't deserve to be suffering.'

'No,' said Tom. 'He doesn't.'

The comment affected Tom enormously. He would not be captain of a Bridgetown packet if it hadn't been for the Reverend Strong. He would not be well fed, well clothed and the adopted member of a wealthy and powerful family of sugar barons if it hadn't been for Jeb, and yet, somehow, he'd never been able to show his gratefulness like other people did. He'd always felt like second best, an afterthought following the disappearance of Jeb's real son. Because of that, his discourse with Jeb was always terse, even rebellious, and yet Tom loved Jeb. He just couldn't put his feelings into words.

Sheep scattered as they got closer to the house. For a brief moment, Tom thought he saw a thin figure bound through the trees with them like some latter-day Pan. He assumed a shepherd was herding the sheep with a view to leaving the parkland for a nearby meadow. The parkland grass was now quite short, so the sheep would not be needed for a while. He thought he heard a dog bark, presumed it was a sheepdog, though it seemed a little high-pitched for such a large dog.

'Is the shepherd local?' he asked the coachman.

'What shepherd?'

Tom explained. The coachman pulled up the horse, and the stiff springs of the wooden-bodied chaise bounced to a halt. Both men peered across the parkland towards the trees where most of the sheep seemed to be congregating.

There was nothing.

'Just a shadow,' said Tom. 'I've been at sea too long.'

The coachman urged the horse forward. Tom leaned back into his seat, his eyes closed and his hands clasped behind his head. There had been a figure and a dog, and if it wasn't a shepherd, it might be a poacher. There were plenty of rabbits on this estate to feed an army and he'd no objection to them taking a few.

The coachman cleared his throat as if about to say something. 'I'm a simple man with few vices, but I wonder if...' He cleared his throat again.

Tom thought about helping him out, but decided to stay silent.

'I was wondering if... you was off into Bristol sometime...'

'And you want to come?'

'Well...'

'I know a nice little tavern, a bawdy house where the women have milk-white bosoms and the softest hands you've ever—'

'Oh no! No!'

The coachman's big, round eyes seemed to grow to the size of saucers at Tom's teasing.

'A fight,' he said, his face as flustered as his words. 'I like a bit of fisticuffs, you know, and don't mind putting on a shilling on you, Captain Tom, if I've got one to spare. I just wondered...'

'I'll let you know,' said Tom, and thought he heard a dog yelp before the park returned to silence, broken only by the rustling of the trees.

–

A fire blazed in the nursery grate and steam rose from a row of collars, cuffs and handkerchiefs draped over a high brass fender.

The four children born to Sir Emmanuel Strong and his second wife, Verity, were sitting stiff-backed around the table in the middle of the room. They sat silently, hands folded in their laps, willing themselves to be still, but gradually losing the concentration to do so.

'I'm cold,' whispered Rupert, afraid that Mrs Grainger might hear him.

'So am I,' exclaimed his sister Caroline, who was eleven years old and the eldest. 'I'm going to warm myself.'

Rupert and Arthur gasped in astonishment. Their younger brother George, springy curls falling around his face, began to cry.

'Shush, Georgie,' said Rupert, keeping his voice low. 'Mrs Grainger will hear you.'

At the mention of Mrs Grainger, the governess, George's despair deepened. He sank off his chair to the floor, his legs splayed out from beneath the green calico dress he was wearing.

Mrs Grainger was responsible for teaching them everything from their basic ABC to a smattering of French and a little drawing. She had a round face, small eyes and a mean mouth and wore dresses of stiff fabrics like serge and bombazine.

'I wish Peters was still here,' said Arthur, who was only three years older than George and had only discarded wearing the same dress George was presently wearing, some two years before.

'Well, she isn't,' snapped Caroline as she leaned over the fender, rubbing her hands before the glowing coals.

'Poor Peters,' Rupert muttered.

Their last nurse had lasted at Marstone Court for only six months and they'd loved her. They'd also loved the nurse before that, and the one before that again who had lasted a shorter time than the other two had done. All the nurses were called Peters, firstly because it was easiest for the children to remember one name and thus have a sense of continuity and security, and secondly, busy, wealthy people like the Strongs had neither the time nor the inclination to learn new names. The original Peters had been nurse to Horatia and Nelson when they were children.

None of the more recent Peters, those employed as nurses to the children Lady Verity had produced, were any good at all, according to Mrs Grainger, who hadn't even been at Marstone Court when the original Peters had been nurse.

'Slack and lazy,' she'd exclaimed when Caroline had asked her why the last Peters had left. 'We can't have slack and lazy people looking after the children of quality folk.'

Caroline had wanted to point out that Mrs Grainger had said the same thing about the last two. It occurred to her that she'd said the same thing about the ones before that, though she couldn't quite remember. She'd been younger then and, besides, being too outspoken might mean being locked in the attic, Mrs Grainger's favourite punishment, where old furniture, carpets and paintings were stored. The room was thick with dust, had shuttered windows and rough wooden floors. Only Georgie had escaped the attic so far, but the day would come, Caroline told herself. Georgie would do something wrong and Mrs Grainger's beady little eyes would twinkle wickedly and a cruel smile would warp her fat face. Caroline wasn't sure how she would protect Georgie from Mrs Grainger. Sometimes she considered telling her parents, but Mrs Grainger was clever. Caroline could almost hear her now.

'And who are your long-suffering parents likely to believe? An upright adult adored by her younger charges, or a spoilt girl in need of having the birch across her backside.'

Much as she'd like to believe her brothers would back her up, Caroline knew that Mrs Grainger would make sure they didn't. When trouble threatened she would be overly kind to them, buying their silence with bull's-eyes she kept in a bag in her pocket. Then she'd school them in a little ditty that they were to sing at the top of their voices as they marched down the stairs to see their parents in that magic hour between five and six o'clock in the afternoon:

*Mrs Grainger makes us work,*
*At my sums I do not shirk.*
*Just to please her gives me joy,*

83

*She says I'm a clever boy.*

What else could her parents believe of a woman who inspired such songs of praise? During the periods when a nurse was in residence, the cruelty ceased. Only in the schoolroom had Mrs Grainger continued to hold sway and she'd been clever. Her favourite punishment had become the attic rather than the cane because it showed no trace, but sometimes her temper got the better of her. George's sobbing was getting louder.

'Come on, Georgie. Stop crying.' Rupert got behind his brother, tucked his hands under the boy's armpits and heaved him back on to the chair.

'Don't let us down, Georgie Porgie,' he said, mopping the wet eyes with his handkerchief. 'You know what Mrs Grainger is like.' George did indeed know what Mrs Grainger was like and immediately burst into more copious tears.

'Come on,' said Rupert once he'd settled Georgie into his chair and had climbed back on to his. 'She'll be back soon and she told us not to move. We'll get one hell of a whacking if she knows we have.'

'You shouldn't say that word,' said Caroline. 'It's not nice.'

Rupert pushed his dark curls back from his shiny forehead and said proudly, 'Tom says it all the time.'

'I know he does, but that doesn't make it nice.'

Rupert wasn't giving in. 'Would it be better if we said heaven of a whacking instead?' He stressed 'we'. Tom was the person he admired most in the whole wide world. He told him tales of the sea, spoke eloquently of the places he'd been to, the people he'd seen. Rupert longed to escape into the big wide world, the one that existed beyond the close confines of the nursery and Marstone Court. Unusually for boys of his age, he was actually looking forward to being sent away to school, possibly to Queen Elizabeth's in Bristol, though he'd like to go a lot further. Although only eight years old, he had already made his mind up to be a sea captain when he grew up. With sails unfurled and beating before a trade wind, he would sail the world and see all the wonderful places Tom Strong had told him about.

Unwilling to surrender to Mrs Grainger's will, Caroline sauntered to the window and looked out. They were on the fourth floor of the house, just beneath the attics. The best thing about the room was the view. Acres of rolling grassland, trees in the park and, beyond the wall, the fertile ground that was Ashton, where plump cattle grazed and wild ducks and geese waded on the marshy land towards the river.

The nursery was self-contained. Everything the children might need was up here – except their parents. It would be bearable if it weren't for Mrs Grainger. Despair settled on each child and they might have remained silent and still if a scrabbling, scratching sound hadn't come from the chimney.

'The sweep!' exclaimed Caroline who spent a lot of time gazing from the window. 'I saw him arrive before breakfast. He's come to sweep the chimney up in the attic for our new nurse.'

'Why doesn't she have Peters's old room?' asked Arthur, the second oldest son.

'I don't know,' Rupert shrugged, then ran to the fireplace and tried to peer up the chimney.

The other children gathered round as the noise continued, louder now as if someone were trying to kick their way through the wall.

'Will his brush come out?' Arthur asked. He was normally the quietest child, but his curiosity was aroused.

'He doesn't use the big brush in this part of the chimney,' Caroline explained. 'It's too narrow and has bends in it so he sends his boy up with a hand brush. I expect he's stuck.'

Rupert turned pale. 'Do you think they will get him out?'

Caroline didn't answer. Like him she was gazing wide-eyed at the fireplace, feeling fear for the boy and relief that it wasn't her stuck up the chimney with just a small brush and dead starlings for company.

## Chapter Seven

Down in the drawing room, Lady Verity Strong tugged at the bell pull beside the glass doors that opened out on to a promenade bounded by a curving balustrade and Grecian style statuary.

'That noise,' she shouted, holding her head with both hands. 'I can't stand it!'

The sound filtering down the chimney seemed to clang in her brain. Eyes closed and hands covering her ears, she strode up and down the room, side to side, to the door that opened on to the main hallway, and back to the double glass doors that led out to the balcony with a view of the gardens beyond.

She was almost at screaming point. Why didn't someone come?

'Hurry, girl! Hurry!'

It was Edith who entered, a plump, common type who mostly attended to the Reverend Strong's needs, cleared up the mess from his bed or the sodden sheets of her youngest son, George. She appeared to be carrying something that smelled of horse dung and mouse droppings.

Verity wrinkled her nose. First the din from the fireplace, and now this. 'Where's Soames?' she demanded.

Soames was her personal maid, an upright person with high cheekbones and deep-set eyes either side of a thin nose with pinched nostrils.

'Beg yer pardon, ma'am...' Edith began, 'but Charlie's – sorry – Prince Charles 'as been brought back again. There's a man at the back door...'

The bundle Edith was carrying leaped from her arms and scampered across the floor towards Verity.

'Prince Charles! My darling.' Displaying greater affection for the dog than she did for her own children, Lady Verity swooped as low as she could in her condition, and lifted the little brown and white spaniel up from the floor.

'My darling,' she wailed, as the dog wagged its tail and licked her face. 'My best, most beautiful darling!'

Edith dropped a swift curtsy. 'Begging your pardon, ma'am, but there's a man outside. 'Twas him that found it and he noticed there's a reward—'

'Give it him,' Verity snapped, her attention wrapped up in the dog. 'Tell Cook to take it out of the nursery budget. Two sovereigns, wasn't it? Give him three.' She hugged the little dog close. 'My darling Prince is worth it, aren't you, my sweet? Now, you really must stop running away, you naughty little dog.' She kissed the creature's nose and cuddled it like a baby.

Hiding a smile, Edith turned to go, meaning to head for the kitchen and demand of Cook the reward for the return of the little dog.

But Lady Verity hadn't finished with her.

'I want it stopped immediately.'

Edith was flustered. 'Er... what exactly do you mean, Madam?' she asked, afraid the mistress of Marstone Court might be referring to the frequency of her dog's vanishing, and the fact that it was always Edith who brought him back.

'The noise! That dreadful, thudding, scratching noise.'

'Yes, ma'am,' said a relieved Edith and went on to explain. 'If you remember rightly, the new nurse is to have the old room up in the attic and the chimney needed sweeping.'

'He must do it quietly.'

'Sorry, ma'am, but it's the sweep's boy you see. He's gone and got 'imself stuck.'

Clutching the dog to her bosom, Lady Verity slumped into a chair. She was bloated, ungainly and unreasonable. Her confinement was near and she was paler than normal.

'I think that's very careless of him. He should consider his customers' sensibilities and get himself a smaller sweep. Obviously this one's got far too big for the job. Now go downstairs and see that the matter is taken care of.'

Edith dropped another curtsy. 'Yes, ma'am.'

What was Lady Verity actually asking her to do? She could hardly tell the sweep that he wasn't to come back until he'd found himself a smaller boy. What would they do with the one stuck up the chimney? Never you mind, Edith, she thought, you'll think of something when you get there.

87

But first she made her way to the kitchen. Cook counted the coins into Edith's outstretched hand.

'Is it the same man who found him?' she asked Edith.

Edith saw the suspicion in her eyes. 'He might be. Dirty sort he is, but then, dirty people all look the same to me.'

After pocketing the coins, she made her way to the dining room. This was the oldest part of the house and its fireplace was a monstrous construction of white marble, a monument to wealth and the sugar trade. Figures with African features, their bodies bent almost double with the weight of the mantelpiece, gazed into the room.

A vast sheet had been spread over the floor. Dust covers protected the furniture, which had been moved away from the fireplace and closer to the windows.

The sweep, his moleskin trousers tied with string 'Yorks' just below the knees, was bending into the fireplace, his head up the chimney.

'I said it was best to stick to cleaning the main chimneys. That one up top ain't been used for years. And bit of a narrow opening. That's why I sent him in this way. It's a long climb, but there's a bit more room in this grate. My boy's a bit chubby, you see. Gets it from his mother's side of the family, I'm told.' He added, 'He's an orphan and been with me a long time now.'

Mouth pursed and brow furrowed, Duncan the footman stood with his hands clasped behind his back, eyeing the sweep with the utmost disdain. Dealing with tradesmen was not usually one of his duties.

The sweep's head reappeared. 'He's up there somewheres,' he said apologetically. 'There's bits of old flue branching off from the main 'un.' He shook his head dolefully. 'I said it 'ud be blocked. I said them old flues were dangerous. But,' he sighed heavily and bent for his long brush, 'we're going to have to get him down.'

Duncan's nostrils dilated. '*You* are going to have to get him down.'

The sweep pushed his hat back on his head and ducked beneath the mantelpiece. Half his body disappeared up the chimney.

'Willy! Willy! Where are you, Willy?' His voice echoed inside the tall chimney.

Duncan turned his attention to Edith. 'Well?'

Edith cursed herself for feeling so awkward in Duncan's presence. What was he anyway? Nothing but a jumped-up slave in a smart suit and a white wig, but the fact that he spoke in such a superior manner, plus his height, unnerved her. She felt herself reddening before she managed to say, 'Lady Verity sent me to find out what all the noise was about.'

He gazed at her as if she were an absolute idiot. It made her want to hide her rough, square hands and check her appearance in the nearest mirror. 'Well, you've found out. The matter will be dealt with as quickly as possible.'

'And how will that be?' she asked nervously.

Duncan's expression was unchanged. 'Either the boy comes down or he doesn't.'

The sweep re-emerged from the chimney looking concerned. 'I can't hear anythink any more. I think p'raps Willy's passed out.' Although Duncan was unmoved, Edith gasped with fear and clasped her hands in front of her. 'The poor child! What's to be done?'

The sweep took off his hat and wiped the sweat from his brow leaving a white line through the black soot.

Duncan fixed his eyes on the fireplace as he came to a decision. 'It's unfortunate, but I can't really see what we can do. You'll just have to pack up your things and go home. We can't have this mess in the dining room all day, and certainly not tonight. Sir Emmanuel has a dinner party tonight. Guests are expected.'

Edith's jaw almost fell to her chest. She couldn't believe her ears. 'You mean leave him up there?'

Duncan shrugged. 'We have no choice.'

The sweep glared at the footman. 'He's got to come down.'

Duncan's eyebrows shot skywards. 'Really? And how do we get him down? Are you going to go up there?'

The sweep shook his head! His eyes were like stars in the sootiness of his face. 'I'm too big. I'd get stuck too. So would you.'

Duncan's height seemed to double as he pulled himself straight in order to emphasize his complete unsuitability for such a venture. His voice rang with authority. 'My good man, I have no intention of going up the chimney.'

Edith felt helpless but couldn't bear the thought of leaving the boy up there. 'Well, someone has to do something!'

The sweep lifted his hat and scratched his head, half turned towards the door, saw someone standing there, and took a second look.

The man's hair was dark and fell unfashionably to his shoulders. He had blue eyes and broad shoulders, and was an imposing figure. He wore a leather jerkin over a linen shirt, and suede trousers tucked into calf-length sea boots.

Tom Strong dropped his sea chest on the floor. 'What's all this noise about?'

–

Edith sighed with a mix of relief and adoration. It was as though the power of the tides had swept into the room. The salt smell of the Atlantic permeated his clothes and clung stiffly to his hair.

'There's a boy stuck up the chimney,' Edith exclaimed, her legs weakening. This was only the second time she'd met Tom Strong. Her legs had wobbled then at the sight of him, and they did the same now.

'He's a chimney sweep,' Duncan added unhurriedly, as if it wasn't really quite as important as Edith's emotional outburst indicated. 'I don't think we can do very much at all.'

The sweep took off his hat, recognizing that Tom Strong was more than a servant in this house, and touched his forelock with obvious reverence.

'If you could help, sir,' he pleaded. 'Though he's getting too big and too old for the job, I'd miss Willy. Intended learning him the whole trade, as you might say. I was told to sweep the attic chimney this time round, but the opening up there's too small, so I sent my boy up this way.'

The sweep had an odd way of speaking, but Tom understood. 'Then we have to get him down.'

The footman sniffed, his disdain far from diminished and his pride dented. Duncan did not like tradesmen or staff going over his head. He needed to feel in control of everything to do with the running of Marstone Court. 'There's nothing we can do,' he repeated. He sounded petulant, almost childish.

Tom ignored him. He'd met men of every race, creed, colour and social class, and got on with them all. Duncan was a man he didn't like.

'We'd better be quick,' he said suddenly, and headed for the stairs. Edith followed. 'What are you going to do, Master Tom?'

Tom bounded up two stairs at a time and Edith followed, her skirts bunched up almost to her knees. She'd be almost indecent if she weren't wearing Lady Verity's cast-off pantaloons.

'You're too big. We're all too big,' Duncan called after them.

'Well, if I'm too big to get up there and get the boy down, then someone small has to do it,' Tom called over his shoulder.

Edith was left puffing down on the second landing by the time Tom had reached the nursery. He flung open the door and all four children gasped with joy and tumbled off their chairs to greet him.

He barely gave them a chance to hug him, before he said, 'Rupert! We have an emergency. I need you to do some climbing.'

Rupert didn't need telling twice. 'Super,' he shouted and was out of the door and bounding along the passage with Tom. Unwilling to be left to explain the situation to Mrs Grainger, the other three followed, Caroline holding young Georgie's hand.

Rather than going all the way back down to the dining room, Tom led Rupert, the other three children and a flushed and puffing Edith into the room where the new nurse was going to be housed. The fireplace was much smaller than those on the lower floors, the mantelpiece and surround made of wood and painted green.

Tom dismantled as much of the grate as he could, removing a few loose firebricks and the stones above with his bare hands. Stooping low in the gap left by the absence of ironwork, he looked up the chimney. From this height he should have been able to see a patch of sky high above him. To his great dismay, he saw only darkness. Something or someone was blocking the main flue.

'Damn it,' he muttered and forced his shoulders up into the narrow gap. It was hopeless. His shirt tore on rough edges that grazed his arms. He had no alternative but to retreat and do what he'd intended in the first place. He stripped off his jerkin and shirt, and beckoned Rupert over. 'Take off your clothes.'

'Everything?' Rupert asked as he began unbuttoning his breeches, jacket and linen shirt that scratched his skin and left a red rash around his neck.

'Down to your drawers.'

'Aye, aye, sir,' said Rupert, his face pink with excitement.

'I think we need this,' said Tom, detaching a rope from around the mantelpiece, obviously the place where a past occupant had hung a little laundry to dry. Rupert was now stripped down to his drawers and his feet were bare. Tom tied the rope around his waist.

'Now listen,' he said, glad to see that Rupert's expression was as intense as his own. 'I want you to climb up that chimney just like you would a mast on a ship in exactly the way I told you.'

'Aye, aye, Cap'n,' said Rupert, and saluted smartly.

'Take this.' He slid a knife from the silver scabbard hanging from his belt. Originating from North Africa, it had a cruel curve but was light enough for a boy to use. 'Stab it gently into whatever's blocking the flue, then use it like a spade, digging a little at a time, but only a little, mark you. Understand?'

Rupert would have saluted again, but Tom didn't give him time. He pushed him towards the grate and interlocked his hands to form a stirrup.

'Try to push the blockage back towards me, but keep to the side. It'll come down in a rush and you might come down too. I'll hold this end of the rope so if you do get buried in soot, I can pull you out quickly. Will you be all right?'

Edith gasped. 'Oh my God!'

Neither Tom nor Rupert acknowledged her.

Again Tom asked, 'Understand?'

Rupert, his face shining with excitement, nodded and put his bare foot into Tom's hand.

'Then up you go.'

Tom was aware that Edith and the other children were close, but he couldn't possibly spare the time to look at them. He knew by their silence that they were waiting with baited breath, wondering who would come back down, if anyone. It was a risk to send Rupert up at all, but the lad was brave and if there was the slightest chance of saving the chimney sweep's boy, they had to take it. He gritted his teeth as soot trickled down, hopeful that Rupert would come down unharmed. He was not so sure about the sweep's boy, who might be buried beneath a fall above the blockage. God help him, he prayed, and hoped for the best.

Small amounts of soot and stones fell as Rupert climbed higher. Tom watched, his head craned backwards as he encouraged him.

'Steady there... Keep looking up... Remember what I taught you.'

On occasion the boys had accompanied him to the *Miriam Strong*, the training ship set up by Jeb, where, after an initial wariness, they had mixed in with the apprentices and learned seamanship, including how to climb the rigging. Rupert had shown an aptitude for climbing. But you couldn't get suffocated on open rigging, and that was Tom's greatest fear. If the soot and other debris came down, he had to pull the rope quickly in order to get Rupert out. Hopefully they'd get the sweep's boy out too. At worst he'd be given a Christian burial.

Rupert braced his bare legs across the flue, his toes gripping the rough brickwork like the claws of a bird gripping a branch.

The sweep was close by, his brow knotted with concern and his hands resting on bent knees. The others, including Duncan, watched from a distance, Edith with her arms around the children who would be in the fireplace with their brother if they could.

Rupert stopped climbing. One foot slid; his legs trembled as he sought to gain a more secure foothold.

Tom felt his heart hurtle into his mouth, but refrained from asking if he was all right. The boy needed to concentrate. Shouting wouldn't help.

At last Rupert shouted, 'I'm there.'

Tom let out a sigh of relief. 'Good lad. Now then, carefully, very carefully, poke the knife into the left side of the blockage and lean to the right.'

It suddenly occurred to Tom that the boy was swapping the knife from his right hand to his left and he cursed himself. What was he thinking of? The boy was right-handed. He should have instructed him to lean to the left and stab at the right. Tom folded his lips inward and wished his throat didn't feel so dry. What if Rupert got killed? How could he live with it?

He wanted to tell Rupert to be careful, but he dare not panic the boy. Best leave him to get on with it.

The first trickle came down like black water, hitting the bare grate and forming dark clouds to rise mistily around Tom's legs. The second trickle was grittier and faster, granules of unburned coal dust glistening and scattering as they hit the ground, rebounded and flew into the air.

Tom tensed and tightened his grip on the rope. At the slightest sign of things going wrong, he would pull Rupert back down.

Suddenly the trickle became a torrent, smacking him in the face. Instantly recognizing the danger, he pulled on the rope. Too easily, it fell towards him along with the debris, but there was no sign of Rupert. Tom couldn't breathe, he couldn't see, but he forced himself upwards, reaching out, trying to feel for the boy's legs.

Falling stones became larger, hitting him in the face. As an unmistakable stickiness seeped from his forehead, he knew he was injured. But still he scrabbled in the dark grittiness of it all, cursing himself for not checking that the rope wasn't tighter.

There was never any question of giving up. The debris was coming down and the boy would come down too – hopefully alive. Hopefully both boys.

In an instant, Tom was knocked backwards as the inside of the chimney collapsed in on itself. The main bulk of the deluge was Rupert, who came down black with soot, coughing and rubbing the dirt from his eyes. Tom grabbed hold of the boy and heaved him to his feet. Edith grabbed him, and although mindful not to dirty her clothes too much, she checked him over, fussing with his hair and brushing the soot from his cheeks with the corner of her apron.

Tom rubbed the dirt from his own eyes and bent almost double as he coughed the dust from his throat. The discomfort was bearable because, although the rope had broken, Rupert was all right. But what about the sweep's boy?

Edith was clucking like a mother hen. 'Thank God you're all right. Thank God! Let's get you washed up.'

Tom found it irritating but also sad that Rupert was receiving comfort from a servant and not from his parents.

More soot began to fall, and Tom cocked his ears.

Edith continued to fuss.

Tom shouted at her. 'Shut up!'

Edith looked hurt before turning indignant. 'The boy needs some soft words after what he's been through!'

'Shut up, woman! Listen!'

They obeyed; Duncan with his pristine crispness, the children full of excitement, almost as if the whole thing were a specially laid on dramatic performance, and Edith, her snow-white apron now streaked with soot.

Something was moving in the chimney and it was coming closer. A sudden fall of soot and old birds' nests were followed by a pair of feet, which then became legs encased in a pair of ragged trousers. The sweep's boy.

They all sighed with relief and their tense faces broke into smiles. But things were not quite over.

'Get back!' shouted the boy as he swung out from beneath the mantel-piece and into the room. 'The bloody lot's coming down!'

The sound of falling grit became a rumble. Clouds of thick, black dust billowed from the grate. Twigs, soot, feathers and dead birds lay on the floor – and something else. The children gaped and Edith screamed, then covered her face with her hands.

Up until now Duncan had shown nothing but disdain for the proceedings. Now he stood round-eyed, his jaw dropped and his mouth wide open.

'Oh Lord!' said the sweep.

'Bloody 'ell,' said his apprentice.

Tom blinked the dust from his eyes. He'd come home smelling of the sea and full of tales for the boys about the sights and sounds he'd seen and heard. Now he smelled of dead soot, and nothing he'd seen could compare to what lay at his feet.

Amid the rubble, lay the mummified, semi-smoked remains of a long-dead child, fragile locks of dark gold hair clinging to his scalp.

Tom closed his eyes.

The sweep took off his hat.

'Get the children cleaned up and back in the nursery,' Tom ordered Edith. His voice was resonant; the sort of tone he used on ship to get things done quickly and with the least fuss.

'Come along, come along,' trilled Edith, impatient to get them out of the room, and away from the small body that had fallen from the chimney.

Duncan followed them, and Tom, the sweep and the sweep's boy were the only ones left.

The sweep had his hat in his hand and was scratching his head. 'He's not one of my boys,' he said, 'but then I only bin doing these chims for about fifteen years. Didn't come up from Taunton to take over from me uncle till then. Mind you, he never told me nothing about no boy getting stuck up there, well, at least, not at Marstone Court. By the looks of him, he's been up thur for years, seeing as that's part of the old chim.'

Tom didn't contradict him. 'We can at least make sure the boy has a decent burial.'

The sweep nodded. 'I'll bring me cart round to the stable yard.'

All three stared at the body. The boy's skin was the colour of well-smoked bacon left too long in the smoke house. Tufts of corn-coloured hair clung to the dried-out skull. Birds must have taken some, thought Tom, but did not venture the information. Few stomachs could cope with it.

Tom plucked a piece of cloth that still bore some resemblance to its original colour. He fingered its softness and it was then that his worst fear took form. He made an immediate decision. 'Bring that chest over,' he said, nodding to an old oak coffer beneath the window.

As the sweep and his boy heaved the chest away from the wall, Tom ripped down a curtain and carefully wrapped it around the body.

'Tis a fine coffin,' said the sweep as he lifted the heavy lid.

Tom placed the fragile little bundle inside the chest. 'He deserves it.' He dipped into the money pouch that hung from his belt, withdrew two sovereigns and passed it to the sweep. 'Please see the boy is properly buried.'

'That's more than enough,' the sweep said, eyeing the gleaming coins.

'And for your trouble,' Tom added.

The sweep touched his forelock. 'Thank ye, sir.'

Tom patted the carved lid of the chest. 'Rest in Peace,' he said softly. Inside, his heart ached with a terrible knowledge.

It took all three of them to carry the chest down the back stairs, past the kitchen and sculleries, and out into the handcart alongside the sweep's brushes, his bags and his pails.

'Sad business,' said the sweep.

'Sadder than you could imagine,' murmured Tom.

Tom made for his room. Horatia was waiting for him at the top of the stairs, her face beaming with delight.

'I heard you were home,' she said. 'Are you joining us for dinner?'

'I'd like to see Jeb before then.'

She shook her head. 'He doesn't join us for dinner at all now. He's a lot worse.'

Tom sighed.

'Why do you never call him Father? He'd like you to.'

Tom didn't meet Horatia's gaze. 'He doesn't mind me calling him Jeb.'

He wouldn't admit to not feeling worthy of calling him Father. He was grateful to Jeb of course, but even after all these years, he couldn't help regarding himself as no more than a substitute for Jeb's real son, Jasper.

'He sleeps a lot nowadays.' She looked concerned. 'It won't be long, Tom. It might be best that you stay on here for a while. Another sea voyage and he may not be here when you get back. And no exciting stories of your exploits, please. A surge of excitement or shock could kill him.'

Tom thought of the portrait of Jasper hanging on the wall in Jeb's house, the piece of velvet he'd plucked from the body in the chimney.

Horatia did not allow him to dwell on matters. 'You're filthy,' she said, her gaze raking him from head to toe. 'And smellier than usual,' she added. She had never been able to hide her weakness for Tom. It was the only true weakness she possessed, which was perhaps why she countered her warm expression with a sarcastic comment.

'The sweep needed a hand with something.'

'So I heard,' said Horatia, looping her arm through his and walking with Tom to his room. 'You know servants can't resist gossip. Neither can I, come to that.'

'Of course not,' said Tom wryly. 'You're a woman.'

Horatia's face fell. 'Oh, Tom! Don't say that. You know I'm not like other women. I sometimes think I should have been born a man. What do you think? Would you have preferred it if I had?'

Tom did not feel inclined to respond to her obvious insult to his masculinity. He said, 'I think it very wise of you not to be like other women. It sets you apart.'

Her face brightened and her voice oozed honey. 'Does it really?'

'Yes,' said Tom. 'It will suit you to be a life-long spinster.'

He left her outside his bedroom door looking unsure whether he was extolling or vilifying her independent spirit.

Once inside his room, he splashed cold water on to his face, wetted his hair and welcomed the coldness as it trickled from the nape of his neck, around his shoulders and over his chest.

Closing his eyes, he wondered how he was going to face Jeb. He'd probably know by now. Gossip spread quickly. He'd have been told it was a sweep's boy, from years back, perhaps from before the Strong family had bought the estate and extended the house.

Thank God, thought Tom.

With a mix of fear and amazement, he fingered the piece of brown velvet he'd taken from the body. He had to keep Jeb from knowing his son's true fate, but for his own peace of mind, he had to find out how on earth Jasper had got there.

Edith left Rupert outside the laundry-room door. 'Wait here,' she ordered, and dashed back towards the icehouse, thanking Michael and all his angels that Captain Strong had not discovered the skinny figure lurking there.

Hair as stiff as a brush, and legs not much thicker than a broom handle, the figure Tom had earlier espied among the sheep, stepped from behind the water butt. 'Where's me money?'

Edith wrinkled her nose at her brother Spike. 'You stink!'

'Never mind that. Where's me money?' He held out his grimy hand.

Edith sighed resignedly as she dropped a coin into the dirt-encrusted palm. 'One guinea. There you are. Now shove off before I dunk you in the tub along with the boy in there.'

Pale blue eyes opened wide in a face that was as dirty as his palms. 'Hot water? What you trying to do, kill me? Look,' he said, sliding his hand over a greasy coat shoulder, 'bit of dirt keeps the weather off. See?' Water picked up from the edge of the butt, trickled over his shoulder without seeping into the cloth.

Edith was unimpressed. 'Go,' she hissed, and pushed him hard enough to set his legs running whether he'd wanted them to or not.

By the time she got back to where she'd left Rupert, his brothers and sister had arrived, possibly to give him moral support, or more likely, to escape the dictates of the tyrannical Mrs Grainger.

Entering the laundry room was like being immersed in warm soup. Clouds of steam hung in the air, and puddles of water splashed underfoot.

Mrs McTavish, the laundress, was heaving a sheet out from a large wooden tub with a boiler stick that was soft and white from years of immersion in thick, soapy water.

'Have you finished with that water, Mrs McTavish?' Edith asked the big, red-armed woman.

Mrs McTavish looked up sharply, her small blue eyes softening as she saw Rupert. 'Have ya bin down the coalhole, bairn?'

'Up one, more like,' said Edith. 'I thought it best to scrub him down here.'

'I know, I know,' said Mrs McTavish shaking her head. 'Taking water up them flights of stairs is hard work.' She reached out and pinched Rupert's cheek. 'The water needs more hot in it, but I see no wrong in you getting in there first, so long as you don't mind a few soaked linens floating 'round you.'

Rupert was already peeling off his underwear. His limbs, face and neck were pot black. The rest of his body was white as marble.

'You look like a gypsy horse, one that pulls caravans,' said Caroline and laughed nervously. She was putting a brave face on going upstairs late for lessons.

Edith was worried herself. Mrs Grainger terrified her. Excuses could be made for Rupert, but not for all of them. 'You really should be at your lessons,' she said.

'It's cold up there,' said Arthur.

'And Mrs Grainger is a bitch,' said Caroline.

'Miss Caroline! Now where in the world did you pick up language like that?' Edith sounded suitably shocked, though in all honesty, she heartily agreed.

'I heard Tom use that word in the stables when Sadie, the coachman's dog, was having her puppies. He said that Sadie wasn't the only bitch at Marstone Court. I think he meant my half-sister Horatia, though it could just as easily have been my mother.'

Edith and Kath McTavish exchanged looks. It wasn't their place to comment, and they didn't need to. Both knew what the other was thinking.

'Now that's enough of that,' said Edith, as a naked Rupert climbed into the tub of hot, soapy water just as one last item of laundry bubbled to the surface.

Rupert pulled the item from the water. 'Drawers!' he said, and pushed them towards Mrs McTavish who got them out, wrung them and fed them through the mangle.

'Now the rest of you had better be going,' she said, rolling her sleeves further up her fat, red arms and reaching for the soap and scrubbing brush.

'We'd better wait for Rupert,' said the defiant Caroline. 'Mrs Grainger might worry if we're not all together.'

Edith wasn't fooled. As Mrs McTavish worked the water pump so she could swill bits of lint off the scrubbing brush, she muttered, 'More likely to be waiting there with a birch cane.'

Mrs McTavish nudged her and nodded at George who was clinging to her apron string, his lip quivering. As he burst into tears, a trickle of urine ran from under his dress and down into his shoes. Poor mite, thought Edith, and felt like crying herself. Every time Mrs Grainger's name was mentioned, George wet himself.

'I hear the Captain's home,' said Mrs McTavish.

Edith's cheeks dimpled as she recalled the hot flush that had swept over her face when she'd seen him strip off his jerkin and shirt, ready to climb the chimney if need be.

'I saw him earlier. He asked for my help with something.'

Mrs McTavish was instantly attentive. 'What?'

'Nothing really,' Edith flustered.

Mrs McTavish kept her gaze fixed on Edith's plump face. 'Nothing don't turn a lass pink as a poached salmon, does it now?' Edith flushed pinker.

'The sweep's boy got stuck in the chimney,' she said, the words tumbling out more quickly than she was thinking.

'Captain Tom sent me up after him,' shouted a boastful Rupert as he bobbed and dipped among the extra washing Mrs McTavish had added to the tub.

A small voice came from behind Edith's skirt. 'He was dead, wasn't he, Edith? He was dead.'

Edith patted George's head and turned him swiftly towards the door. 'Come along, Caroline, Arthur. Take your brother and go back to the nursery. Rupert and I will be along shortly.'

After Rupert had been scrubbed and dried, he scurried with Edith back to the nursery, both slightly scared of meeting Mrs Grainger before they got there.

'Why doesn't Captain Tom want anyone to know about the dead boy?' Rupert asked Edith.

'No doubt he has his reasons.'

–

There was no response when Tom knocked at Jeb's door, so he let himself in. The curtains were drawn and the room smelt of lavender, which appeared to be scattered all over the floor.

He expected Jeb to look ill, but hadn't expected him to have shrunk into a skeletal parody of the figure he'd once been. The sound of his breathing seemed similar to the whirring of a clock between the falling of the weights, only louder and more worn.

Tom called to mind Horatia's comment about not returning to sea. She was right. He couldn't possibly go back now.

His gaze went automatically to the portrait of Jasper Strong, his fresh face smiling out into the room, his cheeks rosy. He was wearing a brown velvet suit and his hair was the colour of corn.

Overcome by his feelings, and knowing that he had to compose himself before seeing Jeb, Tom let himself out of the room. Filled with a mix of anger and despair, he clenched his fists, wanting to take a swipe at life for being so unfair to those he loved.

Nelson caught him on his way to the stables. 'Off to Bristol already?'

'I need to.'

'To vent your frustration,' stated Nelson matter-of-factly.

It was odd; Nelson seemed to latch on to human emotions without any need for explanation.

'Give my apologies, will you?'

Nelson nodded, a half smile on his face. 'Might have come with you, but Father wouldn't be pleased. Cousin Adelaide is coming. Father's hoping for a family alliance.'

'A marriage?'

Tom couldn't help his tone. It was just that Nelson didn't seem the marrying sort. In his own way, he was as independent as his sister and a considered thinker, although more inclined towards art than business.

'A dire arrangement,' said Nelson with obvious disdain.

He walked with Tom to the stables and watched as Tom tightened his horse's girth.

'Will you fight tonight?'

Tom grimaced. 'If I can.'

It had always been the same. He had to relieve his anger somehow. Unlike Emmanuel, Nelson's father, he seldom lost his temper, and, unlike Nelson, he was a good boxer. Bare-knuckle fighting helped him cope.

Nelson held the horse's head as Tom mounted. 'Nice to see you home, Tom. I'll see you when you get back and tell you about everything you've missed.'

'Like how pretty your little bride is?' Tom asked with a hint of sarcasm.

Nelson shook a finger at him and laughed. 'Beauty is in the eye of the beholder, Tom. And I'm an artist, remember? I seek perfection, a hint of the exotic.' He shook his head forlornly. 'And Cousin Adelaide is neither perfect nor exotic.'

'Does such a woman exist?' asked Tom.

'Oh yes,' said Nelson, a faraway look in his eyes.

But Tom had already kicked his heels into his horse's side and didn't hear.

## Chapter Eight

The tall stacks of Conrad Heinkel's sugar refinery snorted sweet-smelling smoke into the atmosphere above the pan-tiled roof of the Fourteen Stars. The seventeenth-century tavern had arched windows and upper storeys that jutted over the road. It also sagged at one corner, so leaned for support on the building next door, which housed the stables and vehicles of Bennetts Carriers.

Carters, ostlers, stable lads and clerks were thirsty at the end of their days' labour at Bennetts, so appreciated having an inn next door. The inn provided refreshment, and after working hours, Bennetts became a venue for cockfights, dogfights, and bareknuckle boxing.

Inside, where the horses and closed vans were kept, the air was thick with smoke, noise, the sweet scent of hay and the tang of horse droppings and liberally sprayed urine.

Bales of hay and straw formed an adequate ring, though hardly enough to keep either the gathered men or their enthusiasm at bay. Some men pressed close, their faces red with excitement, eyes bulging, and spittle flying from their mouths as they shouted odds, oaths and encouragement at the two half-naked men who fought bare-knuckled over the sawdust and scattered straw.

'Half a crown on the captain!'

The bet was taken and passed on around the ring among the press of sweating men. Storm lanterns hung from heavy beams, their flickering light throwing giant shadows on to the plastered walls and making ugly the features of men aroused by greed and violence.

Both men fought of their own volition. Both were middle-weights, though Tom Strong's opponent was thicker-set, his muscles less defined than Tom's, obviously a man who'd never pulled on ropes in heavy seas or shinned up ragged rigging as the ship rolled from side to side in a gale.

By virtue of his calling, Tom's body was hard and lithe, and he moved quickly. He was regarded as a sporting type, a man's man, though he never attended cockfights, bull baiting or other so-called gentlemanly sports. He only fought men, whom, he argued, fought out of choice; animals were goaded to do so.

He was stripped to his drawers, his body glistening with sweat. Long strands of dark hair had escaped the strip of leather tying it at the nape of his neck, and strayed damply around his neck and shoulders.

Quick on his feet, his eyes never leaving his opponent's face, he lashed out with a left, skipped quickly back, then in with a right. There was a cracking of bones as his bare fist met his opponent's chin. Victory was close at hand and even though the crowd had not heard the blow, they saw it and could smell that the fight was almost over. Their excited shouts turned into bellows of approval as his opponent's knees buckled, his eyes rolled in his head and he slid to the ground.

A wild cheering went up as a small man with greedy eyes and a goatee beard grabbed Tom's wrist and raised his arm triumphantly above his head.

'Bristol's very own Wild Rover, Tom Strong!'

In that moment of triumph with his arm held high, Tom smelled himself and remembered that he hadn't been home for two days. Getting drunk and fighting was hardly going to help matters, but the prospect of going back to Marstone Court, facing Jeb and not disclosing the truth about the boy in the chimney, was a grave responsibility. He'd had to get things straight in his mind. He must lie, of course. There was no alternative. He knew beyond a shadow of doubt that the boy in the chimney was Jasper Strong, but why had he climbed the chimney in the first place? On no account could Jeb be told the truth. He was too weak, too close to dying.

'My money,' he said impatiently, dragging his arm from the referee's grasp.

The beady-eyed little man, oddly dapper in waistcoat and breeches, though his back was humped and his legs were too short for his body, was good at organizing these events and supplemented his income with a share of the take. He eyed Tom with the same appraising look he'd give to a horse. 'Want me to fix you a few more fights? There's a travelling champion coming to Bristol at Whitsuntide. There'll be a booth up on the

Downs along with the coconut shies, the bearded lady and all them other strange things people like to look at.'

'I'll think about it.' Tom clicked the fingers of his open hand in front of the little man's face. 'The money, Stoke.'

Stoke shook his head solemnly and counted ten sovereigns into Tom's hand. 'Might be a different kettle of fish if you needed the money, eh? I mean, really needed it. Luck of the devil you had, Strong, getting yerself adopted by that family.'

His response was curt. 'I prefer to earn my own money.'

Over the years, Jeb Strong had made sure Tom had been accepted fully into the Strong family and he'd never felt awkward with any of them, though he preferred being away at sea. But after setting eyes on the sad remains of Jeb and Miriam's real son, he now felt like a cuckoo in the nest, a usurper of the rightful heir. He had no intention of sharing his emotions with anyone, however, so turned away and looked for his clothes, finally seeing Sally Ward waving them at him. He smiled at her and shook his head.

'Give me my clothes, Sal. I'm turning cold.'

'And I'm turning thirty,' she said with a high-pitched laugh. That's a lie, thought Tom, but didn't say so. Sally Ward was well past thirty but still trying to look eighteen with the help of rouge and smudges of soot around her eyes. There was a hopeful look in her eyes and a kind of urgency in the way she fussed around him.

'Fancy spending some of that money on me?' She winked at him saucily and stood as provocatively as she knew how, her bosoms bubbling over the top of a bodice that was far too tight for her.

Tom took his trousers, shirt and leather jerkin from her outstretched hand, and smelled the gin on her breath. 'I need it for other things.'

'What, you? Tom Strong? The Strongs got bags of cash!'

Tom clenched his jaw as he fastened his trousers. 'I like the freedom,' he said.

Tom had a wild reputation. No one could really understand why he mingled with prostitutes, street fighters and people in poor man's boots, the sort made to fit either foot rather than favouring left or right. If asked, he couldn't really explain. In the past he might have said he was trying to maintain a link with the life he'd been born into, just in case Jasper had returned. Now, perhaps, he was merely enjoying their company, and recognizing in them something his mother had once been.

Sally was fawning all over him. He would have pushed her aside then and there, but noticed the dark bruise beneath her right eye. One man pushing her around was enough without him doing it too. Sally took his lack of action as encouragement. Before he'd had a chance to fasten his shirt, she was up against him, her hands running down his bare chest and carrying on downwards to squeeze and rub against his private parts. Although reluctant to linger, he felt himself hardening; only natural, of course. Sally was a professional.

'No,' he said firmly and took her hand off his groin.

She pursed her lips and looked petulant. 'Are you sure you won't change your mind, sweetheart? I'll do anything you want for a good price, and I'll make all your bruises feel better.'

He smiled, gripped her shoulders firmly but gently and pushed her away. 'Winning makes my bruises feel better.'

She pouted like a young girl though still tried to look happy. Tom wasn't deceived. He saw the worry in her eyes and guessed she was concerned that she might not make enough to live on by morning and Stoke would give her another beating.

'How's Clarence?' he asked, averting his eyes as he finished buttoning his shirt and pulling on his jerkin.

All pretence at being a young coquette disappeared and lines of worry showed up more prominently around her eyes and in the sudden downcast mould of her mouth. 'He's got a bit of a cough at present. Somebody told me that I should give him plenty of oranges. There's lots of them coming in on the packets from Spain now, so he said.'

Tom guessed that the advice had come from one of her clients, possibly a doctor. He wondered if he was the same man who had hit her, but doubted it. Stoke was her pimp and the likeliest culprit. 'Have you bought some oranges?' he asked her.

'I did, when I had the money. It don't go far, and some of it goes astray, you might say.' She shrugged and jerked her head over to where Stoke was watching her with keen and greedy eyes. Besides horses and fights, Stoke also looked after the dollies who plied their trade around the ancient lanes and by-ways between Steep Street, Christmas Steps and Trenchard Street.

Trade could be brisk depending on the forest of masts that sprouted like spruce trees along St Augustine's Quay in the heart of the city.

Cuthbert Stoke was almost a bona fide businessman, though not quite. He had fingers in many different pies. Not only did he act as procurer and take a cut of the doxies' earnings, but he also rented them rooms in buildings he owned. Most dated from the seventeenth century, damp yards at their rear, plaster flaking from walls on the upper floors, and evil-smelling growths blackening them at ground and basement level.

Tom stared Stoke out until the man turned away and the crowd finally obscured the view.

He looked into Sally's face and she smiled hopefully, perhaps thinking he had changed his mind. Not only was she past her first bloom, but he could hear a wheezing in her chest that hadn't been there on the last occasion he'd seen her. He might be wrong, but there was a fair chance she had consumption.

Guilt and compassion got the better of him. 'I'll walk you home,' he said, took her arm and led her to the door. I'm being a coward, he thought. In his mind he was in Jeb's bedroom, the sick man propped up on a multitude of pillows. After the first greetings – how the trip went, if the weather was good, had they run before the trade winds – Jeb would relate all the happenings at Marstone Court. Tom would tell him about his voyage, the things he'd seen and the places he'd visited.

Looking like the cat that got the cream, Sally threw the end of her shawl over her shoulder and linked arms with Tom. 'Get out the bleedin' way and let a lady through,' she shouted with a sly look and a voice like a foghorn.

Sally talked and played the tart all the way from the Counterslip, over St Augustine's bridge and along the quay. She lived in a shabby room at the top of the Christmas Steps, a steep warren shaded by overhanging gables and dating from a time when men had worn doublet and hose and there'd been an abbey close by, stretching along the banks of the Frome. Nothing much had changed in hundreds of years, except that the buildings had got shabbier. But it was easy to imagine medieval apprentices shouting the wares of their masters from the dark doorways of the ground-floor shops, or a careless servant tipping night slops from the first floor into the alley below.

Unfortunately for Sally, she lived in a room on the ground floor. Once the door to the street had closed behind them, Tom's nostrils were assailed with the sickly smell of rotting plaster and middens that emptied into cess pools, which in turn seeped into the Frome where it sank or floated backwards and forwards on the ever-changing tide. The river itself was only a tributary of the larger Avon and the Floating Harbour and wound into the city from the east. The Floating Harbour was a godsend to shipping. In previous times ships had lain on mud at low tide. Wooden stanchions, fixed across from the stone quays, had stopped them sticking fast between tides. Since the construction of the Floating Harbour they sat in deep water. The water was welcome; the sewage that came with the Frome was not.

A small glow came from the fireplace where burnt pieces of Radstock coal tried unsuccessfully to warm and lighten the room.

Sally flung her shawl on to an unmade wooden bed of rough timbers and straw-filled mattress. 'I'll light a candle.'

The glow from the fire lit her face as she bent, lit a taper then a candle, snuffing the former and laying it carefully aside for future use.

A cast-iron pot hung on a trivet above the fire. Not smelling anything appetizing, he assumed it was empty, unless its contents were congealed on account of the fire being so low.

'There!' said Sally spinning round and clasping her arms about him. 'Now you can have your money's worth.'

He reached round his back and unclasped her hands. 'I told you. No.'

She looked hurt. 'Ain't I good enough for you any more?'

He avoided her eyes. 'Where's your son?'

She shrugged. 'Out somewhere.'

Tom was appalled. What was he? Nine years old? It was close to midnight and his mother didn't know where he was, though Tom guessed from experience that it suited her for Clarence to be out of the way. There was only one bed in the room. She could hardly service her clients with him lying beside her.

Tom looked at the dying embers in the grate. 'Do you have any coal?'

'Cold, are you? I can make you warm.'

As he picked up a poker and did his best to revive the dying glow, he heard the rustling of petticoats. Even before he turned around, he knew what sight would greet him.

'Like it,' she asked coquettishly. Her thighs were bare and her woollen stockings were held up with garters made of string.

'Cover yourself.'

'Don't you want—?'

To Tom's relief, footsteps sounded in the passage outside. Clarence Ward crept in from the street. The latch on the door rattled obstinately as he opened it. Still suffering the aftermath of drinking too much gin, Sally was slow to drop her dress.

A pale face appeared from around the door. Clarence was thin and had the streetwise look of a child used to desperation. Whatever he thought about his mother's lewd display, it flashed only momentarily into his eyes, then disappeared as if he accepted what must be done to survive. But it angers him, thought Tom, and he probably wants to kill me, just like I wanted to kill the men my mother went with.

Sally dropped her skirts and was immediately on the defensive. 'Where've you bin, you little toe rag?'

Coins rattled in ragged pockets as she shook him, jerking him closer to her side. She held out her hand and clicked her fingers.

'Give it here!'

The boy's gaze stayed fixed on Tom's face. 'Only if you promise to send him away.'

'I ain't doing no such thing! He's a friend!'

The boy poked out his tongue. Sally shook him and something sprinkled from his pockets and on to the floor. Tom heard the gritty sound of sugar being ground beneath the boy's bare feet.

'Sugar!' Sally exclaimed. 'You bin down that Hole in the Wall again?'

Tom smiled to himself. An old pastime and still going strong; boys with nothing to lose would bust a barrel of sugar when no one was looking, scoop as much of it as possible into a sack, then sell it down at the Hole in the Wall, the centre of smuggling and thieving in the city. The hole referred to in the name of the place really existed and through it a lookout was posted to sound the warning should the excise men appear.

'I got money,' the boy exclaimed and brought what looked like silver coins from his pocket – four shillings, Tom guessed; the going rate for stolen sugar hadn't risen in years.

Sally was livid. 'This ain't a good way to earn a living, Clarence!'

The boy turned cocky. 'It's better than opening yer legs for any raggledy man that comes calling.'

She clipped his ear. 'Cheeky little bastard.'

The boy dodged away, rubbing his ear as he looked from her to Tom and back again. 'Got to earn some money, ain't I?'

So far Tom had been disinclined to interfere, but this last comment goaded him into action. He stepped closer, his presence seeming to dominate the room. 'There are other ways to earn a living, lad.'

The boy eyed him warily. Sally's shouting and shaking of the boy had caused her to cough. She turned away and grabbed a piece of unidentifiable cloth – probably some item of undergarment – and coughed up a mixture of blood and phlegm.

Both man and boy looked at her, their eyes filled with concern. Tom's fears were realized. Sally had consumption. Her days on earth were numbered.

Tom's fingers went to the money in his pocket. His voice was firm. 'Your mother needs medicine, and you need to make an honest living.'

'What like?' said Clarence, his eyes still fixed on his coughing mother.

Tom knew he had hit the right spot. He recognized the aggression in the boy's voice for what it was; a mix of anger and outright despair, though he'd known worse. At least for now the boy had a room to live in, though it wouldn't last, Tom thought sourly. From boarding house, to room, to a dark doorway; he'd known them all. He pushed the memory of his own childhood to the back of his mind. He had to if he was to help Sally and her lad, and he felt obliged to do so. It wasn't that the lad was his; he couldn't be. It was just that he had an affinity with Clarence. Their mothers had come out of the same mould. Jeb had been there to help him, and he was here to help Clarence.

He adopted a cheery voice but found he couldn't smile. 'Do you fancy getting away from Bristol? How about going to sea and seeing the world? It's a big place, you know.'

Something sparkled in the boy's eyes then was swiftly gone. Tom sensed his defensiveness. It was so familiar; so much part of his own childhood when he'd hated every man who had handled his own mother and the gin palaces for degrading her mind, which in turn degraded her body.

The boy shrugged. 'I might do. There again I might not.'

Tom knew better than to approach the boy, lay his hands on him and preach in a fatherly manner about mending his ways. A seed had be planted and allowed to grow in the boy's mind, but he also had to be aware of the consequences of his actions should he carry on the way he was.

'If you get caught you won't be around to look after your mother.'

'I'll send her money from prison.'

'Not if you're in Australia. They deport hundreds of thieves there, so I hear.'

The boy looked thoughtful. Getting deported as a result of his crimes had obviously never occurred to him.

Sally stopped coughing and her face began to assume something of the radiance he remembered from her youth.

'Could you really get him a place on a ship?' she asked.

'I can do better than that. How's about you give up this place and go to live with your sister at Portishead?'

The sister ran a pub there and, following the death of her husband, had asked Sally to help out.

'But Clarence—'

'What if I get him a place at the Merchant Seaman's Apprenticeship School? He'll be fed and warm while he's being taught a trade along with a lot of boys like him. What do you say?'

She looked at him as if he were a plaster saint just lately come to life and the boy looked at his mother as if he were suddenly little more than a toddler, as if whatever she said was the God's truth.

'Well! Just imagine! My boy at a proper school and learning 'ow to be a sea captain. Ain't that lovely?'

Tom didn't point out that most of the boys ended up as able seamen rather than captains, though some did a lot better than others. He could see the sudden hope in her eyes and also the love she bore for her son. She wanted something better for him than she'd had for herself and it touched his heart.

The cynical look dropped from the boy's eyes as he looked intensely at his mother. 'As long as you go and live with Auntie Annie, then I'll do it.'

Sally nodded. 'I couldn't think of anything better. Can't you just imagine me serving great flagons of porter? It'll suit me all right it will.'

Tom felt pleased for them both and chanced rubbing the boy's head. 'Meet me at ten-thirty tomorrow morning outside St Nicholas's church.'

'Is that where the school is?' the boy asked.

Tom shook his head. 'No. Come with your bundle. I'll take you there. You can ride pillion behind me.'

Although being surly was a hard habit to break, the boy's eyes brightened. It wasn't every day he got to ride pillion on a horse and attend a proper school.

Sally accompanied Tom out on to the steps when he left. The fine night had turned to rain. Water dripped from the overhanging buildings and made the cobbles treacherously slippery.

Tom reached for the prize money in his pocket. He had ten guineas in all. 'Here's three guineas,' he said and pressed the coins into her hand. 'Now get out of here and to your sister's.'

She glowed with gratitude. 'You're a good man, Tom.'

He brushed her gratefulness aside. 'You're sick, Sal, and Clarence deserves a chance. Don't worry. I'll take care of him.'

Tears glistened in her eyes as she clasped his hand between hers. 'If you want to tumble with me, I'll do it for free—'

He shook his head. 'No offence, I hope?'

Her dark eyebrows knitted above her pert nose. 'Then why are you being so kind to me?'

He smiled weakly. 'I used to know a mother and son just like you and Clarence.'

He didn't explain any more than that but thinking about the past made him want to immerse himself in it. Besides, it would help put off the dreaded moment at Marstone Court when he'd have to face Jeb. He chose to walk up the Christmas Steps and then along to Steep Street. By the time he got there his shoulders were soaked and his heart ached.

The past always had the same effect on him. He thought of how good Jeb and his wife had been to him, their daughters becoming like sisters. He thought of how Jeb talked about his son and what he might be doing in heaven.

He thought about having a few drinks, the heat of rum burning into his throat and sending his mind into oblivion. But away from the docks, he asked himself if he really was thirsty or merely a coward, putting off the moment of returning to Marstone Court and Jeb.

He found himself walking up Steep Street, a curse of a climb that twisted upwards and led to the ferry at Aust and the main road to Gloucester. Shabby signs advertising chimney sweeps swung and creaked from buildings on both sides of the road. During the day hooves and iron-rimmed wheels hammered over the cobbles and street urchins ran and dived for apples fallen from a passing cart or scrabbled for cast-off peelings thrown into heaps for the scavengers with their thin ponies and smelly carts, to sweep up and take away.

Many of the streets around the docks were narrow. Like Christmas Steps, the upper floors of old buildings almost touched over the steep winding alleyways that were laughingly referred to as roads. He had a quick drink in the Ship Inn, a low place where the smoke from a thousand pipes of Navy shag had blackened the ceiling and permeated the walls with its gut-churning smell.

One nip of Jamaica Rum was enough. Tom swigged it back quickly, hoping it would dispel the vision of Sally with her skirts up and Clarence with that desperate look in his eyes. Suddenly he felt sick and in need of seeing the one person who could make him feel better. Jeb Strong was the most important person in his life and he was probably wondering why he hadn't come in to see him before going off to enjoy himself.

'Are you off, Tom?' said the landlord.

Silently Tom waved his hand over his shoulder and was gone. He collected his horse from Bennetts stables, mounted, then crossed the river and travelled southwards out of the city, glad to leave the smog behind him, though the smell of his own unwashed body and thoughts of Jasper Strong travelled with him.

## Chapter Nine

Marstone Court rose in fairytale splendour among the meadows. Sandstone turrets, quoins and mullions sparkled in the misty sunshine of an autumn day. Swathes of red, gold and brown trees bounded the acres of parkland, and fields of corn and fat cattle tumbled like giant patchwork beyond the high walls to the River Avon.

The original house had been built in the latter years of the sixteenth century and purchased by Isaiah Strong in 1770. He had spent a fortune modernizing it, ripping out oak panelling, enlarging rooms and adding painted, gilt-edged ceilings that would not have disgraced Versailles. He could well afford it, thanks to the triangular trade; outward-bound ships taking cheap trade goods to Africa that were exchanged for slaves, packed tight into stinking holds, who in turn were taken to the West Indies to provide labour on the plantations. On the last leg of the trip, sugar, molasses and rum were loaded and brought to Bristol. Isaiah Strong had done very well and on his death his estate had gone to his son Samson, who in turn had passed it on in equal measures to his three sons, Emmanuel, Otis and Jeb.

Tom reined in his horse and looked at the mansion as if seeing it for the very first time. He'd never quite been able to call it home. Too large, too gaudy and too intimidating for his taste; always Jeb's house.

After stabling his horse, he headed for the opulent staircase that swept up from the chequered floor of the reception hall where alabaster pillars formed a colonnade around the room and gilt cherubs clung to French mirrors and the legs of marble-topped tables. The Strongs had never succumbed to the Regency fashion for understatement. Wealth and power were reflected in their love of the ostentatious.

The Reverend Jebediah Strong was asleep though upright, propped up against a mountain of pillows. His eyes were closed, but his mouth was open. A rattling sound came from his chest and his hands shook as if attempting a never-ending task for which he had too many fingers.

Tom paused. Was it only two days ago he'd stood in this same spot watching him sleep? Jeb looked far older than his fifty-eight years. When had he started to look old? Not in two days surely?

Grateful for a moment to compose himself, Tom rubbed a thumb and finger into the corners of his eyes and breathed a deep sigh. At the sound of it, the man in the bed stirred, his eyelids fluttered before he opened them.

'You're awake!' Tom smiled as if his confidence was an infection he could pass on to the sick man. 'I didn't mean to wake you.'

A weak smile twitched at the old man's mouth. 'I smelled the sea. I knew immediately that the prodigal son had returned.'

He didn't mention knowing that Tom had been home for two days. Tom breathed a sigh of relief. Hopefully, no one had told him. He pulled up a chair. 'Anything interesting happen while I was gone?'

Jeb smiled ruefully. 'As in life, nothing ever happens at Marstone Court unless you make it happen. Tell me about the places you've been to, the sights you've seen.'

Tom smiled. 'I'll tell you everything.' He made his tales as vivid as possible so Jeb could see, smell, hear and feel the things he'd done and seen. Porpoises, dolphins, flying fish, and great whales spouting water from their heads; Tom described them all. He spoke of the smell of the sea, the warm aroma of land just over the horizon, ocean-side villages rising on stilts above the waters, brown-skinned women wearing little more than tablecloths and necklaces of flowers. It was the most he could do for a man unable to escape his ailing body.

When he'd finished, Jeb sighed, his breath rattling dryly in his chest.

'I can't wait to get back,' Tom added.

Jeb nodded weakly.

Just then, the soulful note of a lone church bell sounded from the village. Tom shivered inside but made a big show of walking to the window and looking at the clouds, the grass, the trees, anything but let Jeb see his expression and perhaps guess...

'God bless,' Jeb said softly. 'A poor village boy going into an early grave, so Edith tells me.'

Tom closed his eyes in thanks. He would have kissed Edith if she'd been there. She hadn't mentioned to Jeb that the boy had been found in an upstairs chimney. The dear soul had understood that sudden shocks were dangerous to a man as sick as Jeb. Hopefully she'd keep the gossip at bay.

'I'm going down to the *Miriam Strong* later,' said Tom, changing the subject as he turned back from the window. 'I've got a new recruit, a deserving case I think would benefit greatly from a bit of education.'

'Good work, Tom. Good work indeed.' Jeb beamed. 'I recall the boat was about to be broken up when I bought her,' he said. 'But with a little bribery… if you've got money and someone else hasn't, you can buy anything.'

A fit of coughing racked Jeb's body and his eyes rolled in his head. 'Turn me on to my other side,' he said.

Gently, Tom eased him so that his right side was favoured over his left, his weight hardly seeming to dent the pillows.

'Indulge an old man,' Jeb said, his breath whistling through his teeth as he fought to keep talking. 'Let's talk about how it used to be; Miriam and the girls; and Jasper.'

'Tell me,' Tom said, his smile feeling tight on his lips.

And so Jeb told him – as he had many times before. Tom sat quietly, remarking only where it was necessary, and all the time he listened to the bell tolling in the church tower. Then it stopped and he knew that Jasper had at last been put to rest.

Tom waited until Jeb was snoring before leaving the room and its close-kept smells of camphor, liquorice and the unmistakable presence of terminal sickness. As he closed the door behind him, he saw the hem of a grey silk dress disappear behind a lacquered Chinese cabinet along the corridor. At the sound of his first footfall, Horatia stepped out, a vision of glorious womanhood, her blonde hair and blue eyes adding immediate lift to the grey creation she wore.

She rushed up to him, grabbed his shoulders and kissed him on both cheeks.

'What was that for?'

'For being kind to Uncle Jeb.'

'Thank you.' It seemed to Tom as if she were waiting for him to kiss her back, but he wouldn't. So far as he was concerned, to take advantage of her affection would be easy, but ungrateful. He dare not.

She linked her arm with his as they made their way along the thickly carpeted landing and said breathlessly, 'It seems so long since we last saw you.'

'A year. That's all. Supplies for the plantation, rum for Savannah, sugar and tobacco for Bristol. A nice round trip.'

'Lucrative, no doubt, though not so lucrative as in my grandfather's day, of course.'

Tom shook his head. 'No slaves, thank God!'

'Poor savages. Now they have to stay in Africa and eat each other.'

'I don't think they do that.'

Horatia's idea of artful conversation had always vexed him. As a child she'd baited him and as an adult she sometimes bored him.

'Never mind whether they do or don't. It was a good trade. This house was built on it. And are those people really that much better off? I don't think so. But there, that's in the past. The future is there for those with ambition. Do you have ambition, Tom?'

She was studying his face, but he feared looking at her. Horatia always had plans, and he was never sure where he might fit into them.

'My only ambition is to see more of the world.'

'Back to sea? Again? Don't you want to settle down, Tom? Don't you want to see what can be achieved on land without risking life and limb?'

He sensed the questions were leading somewhere. 'I like the sea.' They stopped at the bottom of the stairs, Horatia still smiling and Tom being polite. She hugged his arm close to her side.

'Surely we should see more of you, things being the way they are with Uncle Jeb?'

Tom frowned and felt suddenly cold, anticipating he was going to hear the news he most dreaded. 'How long?' he asked.

She shook her head and gripped his arm tighter as if to give him comfort. 'I've already told you, if you go away for another year, he won't be here when you get back.'

He closed his eyes as if that would shut out the thought of Jeb's passing.

Horatia took his hands between hers and looked at him intently. 'I understand how you feel, Tom, and I know you'd want to be here when he goes.'

Tom nodded. It was true, but he couldn't say it. The words stuck in his throat.

'And there is more than one reason for you being here...' Tom frowned. What was she up to?

'Father wants to see you,' she said. 'I believe he's in the library. Will you go there now?'

It wasn't usual to be summoned to see Sir Emmanuel on returning home, but perhaps in the circumstances it was only to be expected. 'If it's about,' he began, but stopped what he was going to say and looked up at the first-floor balcony. 'What's that noise?'

What initially seemed to be a humming came along the landing towards the stairs. Mrs Grainger came into view, three of Emmanuel's children trotting along behind her. The children were singing and looking straight ahead as they came down the stairs. Tom and a smiling Horatia stood back and watched. Tom strained his ears to catch the words.

*Oh, I am just a child,*
*So lowly, meek and mild.*
*And Mrs Grainger's taught me grace,*
*To hold my tongue, and know my place.*

Once she was down the stairs, her charges following, Mrs Grainger, a woman with frizzy red curls escaping from a bun plastered back with goose grease, nodded a tight greeting and bobbed a curtsy. The three children continued to chant and smile.

If Tom hadn't been so concerned about Jeb, he would have noticed their eyes were not smiling and that Caroline, the eldest daughter by Emmanuel's second wife, threw him a withering look.

Horatia had already lost interest. 'Never mind Verity's children, Tom. Listen to me,' she said.

As if they were nothing to do with her father, and therefore of no consequence to her, he thought. Horatia resented Verity – that much was obvious.

'There's something I want to talk to you about—'

Frowning, Tom looked after the small file of teacher and pupils disappearing down another well-used passageway. 'I thought Verity had four children,' he said.

'She has,' Horatia answered, annoyed that he was paying more attention to the children than he was to her.

'So where's the fourth?'

Horatia sighed. 'Lying down in the nursery, I expect. Does it matter?' She clasped his hands more tightly and held them against her cleavage. He could feel her heart and the inside curves of each breast, and knew she had done it deliberately.

Jeb and Jasper were still large in Tom's thoughts. He was only vaguely aware of Horatia telling him of a future Bristol where the ships wouldn't have to wind their way upriver, and steam power rather than sail power would change their world for ever.

'I'll think about it,' he said, without knowing what she had asked and disentangling her hands from his. Although she still smiled, he could see she was disappointed, but he had no intention of giving her hope. Having Edith smirking at him like a puppy dog was bad enough, though he couldn't in all honesty envisage Horatia sinking quite that low.

'Tom Strong, you have not heard a word I said!'

He was about to lie, then thought better of it and shook his head. 'I'm sorry. Do excuse me. I have so much on my mind at present.' More than you could ever know, he thought.

'Tom, we've been friends since childhood and—'

'Yes,' he said trying to sound more uplifted. 'We had a happy childhood, didn't we?' It wasn't exactly the truth. 'But I was part of it because Jeb's son went missing.'

'True,' said Horatia. 'The silly boy. He was always climbing.' 'How old were you when he disappeared?'

'Disappeared? He drowned. He fell off the tree and drowned. You should know that.'

She shrugged her beautiful shoulders and stretched her neck so he could see the whiteness of it, the way it curved from her collar to her chin. She was flirting with him.

'I think I was about ten, perhaps eleven.'

'Do you remember what he was like?'

She frowned and looked at him searchingly. 'Why are you asking me these questions?'

'Jeb's about to die. He talks about his family a lot.'

She nodded. 'Yes. Of course.'

'Was Jasper especially close to anyone? Like you or Nelson?' 'Naturally. We were cousins.'

'Did you play games with him – like you did with me?' Horatia's taunts had sometimes made his life a misery.

Her smile vanished. 'I don't remember.' Her wide skirt knocked against him as she suddenly turned to leave. 'I have to go now.' Why had she suddenly become agitated? he wondered. Was it regret? And for whom?

'Did he drown?'

Horatia shrugged. 'There'd been a lot of rain. The river had broken its banks and flooded the meadows.'

'What do you think?'

'I was only a child at the time. The gardeners searched the grounds. They've all moved on now apart from one. He helps in the churchyard in the village now.'

The silk gown rustled seductively as she walked away. He watched her go, though his thoughts were elsewhere. Before she disappeared, he headed for the main staircase and the library. He didn't see her stop and turn to watch him, or the desire in her eyes. The sound of children singing floated from the dining room. It crossed his mind that the fourth child must be ill and he would have asked Horatia if that was so. Although she hated Verity, she seemed to care for her stepbrothers and sister. No doubt he would hear if it were serious.

–

There was a faint chink of light shining beneath the locked door of the attic, where little George was crying bitterly, his skirts bundled around his legs. A splinter of dry wood had pierced his bare bottom, but he dare not move. Mrs Grainger had foretold dire consequences with the birch should he move an inch. She'd already laced it across Caroline's backside because she'd protested at her treatment of him. So he sat in the darkness and dust, accompanied by the smell of his wet drawers, which Mrs Grainger had tied around his neck. Gradually his crying became sobs and he wished he were elsewhere with Peters, or someone like her who would give him cuddles. Comforted by the thought of all those kind-hearted girls who had shared the same name, he fell asleep, his chin falling on to the wetness of his drawers.

—

The library walls were dark with books, the gilt of their spines glinting in the sparse light piercing the draped windows.

Emmanuel was sitting at his desk, both hands folded over a thick book he'd been reading prior to Tom entering the room.

'Tom! I've seen little of you since you moored up.' His voice was strident though not deep. His face was flushed and his clothes were newly fashioned and finely cut, no doubt purchased to better hide the increasing corpulence of his figure. Emmanuel Strong had a big appetite for everything.

'I've only been back two days, sir.'

Emmanuel waved his hand at the winged armchair directly opposite his own. Tom sat down.

'You've seen my brother, Tom?'

'Yes.'

'My brother has led a blameless life. No doubt he has a place in heaven.' He arched his eyebrows in subtle amusement. 'Hopefully he'll put a good word in for me when he gets there.'

Most people would have considered the comment utterly tasteless, but Tom knew the brothers well. If Emmanuel had said it to his face, Jeb would have laughed and promised he'd do what he could to assist his errant brother enter the Kingdom of Heaven.

Emmanuel poured claret from a cut-glass decanter into two short glasses. He handed one to Tom, his eyes flicking between Tom and the drink as he began to speak.

'Jeb has little time left and I know you would wish to be here when he dies. I also know that you are a man who bores easily. Oh, my daughter would probably find time to entertain you, but women's company can get tiresome after a while, don't you agree?'

Tom wasn't inclined to give a direct answer. Instead he said, 'I believe you have something in mind to keep me occupied.'

'Ah!' exclaimed Emmanuel with a sly wink. 'One of the hens in the coup has already clucked in your ear.'

Tom smiled politely. 'Horatia is very kind.'

Emmanuel's face darkened at the mention of his daughter's kindness, interpreting it as an intimacy he didn't feel Tom deserved.

'A warning, Tom; treat her as your sister, nothing else, mark you, if you catch my meaning. Hmm?'

He raised his eyebrows questioningly. Tom had no qualms about putting Emmanuel's mind at rest.

'I have never regarded her as anything more.'

Emmanuel's jowls trembled as he nodded and said, 'Good man. Good man. Not that I consider you unworthy of joining this family. Although I was never entirely in agreement with my brother and his charity work, I will abide by his wishes that you be given the same opportunities to succeed as my own son. But I'd rather you didn't pursue my daughter. It wouldn't be right.'

'And no doubt she is destined for better things,' said Tom with an even smile, though he would bet that Horatia's plans for marriage were at variance with that of her father.

Emmanuel showed no embarrassment at his obvious prejudice. He leaned forward, and Tom found his gaze fixing on the dents in Emmanuel's puce nose.

'We're talking business here, Tom. To that end, and bearing in mind Jeb's imminent demise, I have a proposition for you.' Emmanuel struggled his portly form out of the chair and strolled to the window where he held back a tasselled drape.

'The Strongs have owned plantations in the West Indies, principally in Barbados, for many years. My grandfather started it, and my father extended the business. Rather than pay shipping companies to transport his goods, he set up his own. Thanks to him, the Strongs now own plantations and shipping.' He sighed, his breath misting the cold glass of the windowpane. 'They were powerful men, Tom, giants of their time. And I want to be one too. I wish to make a mark on this family, create an increase in its wealth with an eye on future expansion.'

He turned from the window. 'The sugar refining process is the only part of the business we do not control. I want that too, Tom. In fact, I'm determined to have it.'

It was like sitting in the path of a storm. And I've done that enough times, thought Tom, but at least with a ship you can veer away. There was little chance of that with Emmanuel. The man possessed the same passion for business that some men had for women or fine horses. Some of that passion was reflected in the eyes of his daughter, though not Nelson, who treated business more casually, as though what would be was luck more than judgement.

'To that end, I have agreed with Conrad Heinkel, who owns the largest refinery in Bristol, that I will purchase shares in his establishment. But,' he said, raising his finger, 'I wish to buy at the right price. At present I have agreed a very good price, which I do not want to pay.'

Tom shrugged. He wasn't at all sure where all this was going. 'Can't you afford it?'

Emmanuel looked astounded at first, then rocked with laughter. 'Of course I can. But that's not the point.'

Hand resting on the back of the chair, he leaned over Tom's shoulder. 'It's the fun of playing the game, getting the refinery for as little as possible.'

'Hardly a game,' said Tom, suddenly seeing that business was only a sport if you were already successful and had everything you wanted.

'Prior to my purchase of these shares, I asked Conrad if he would employ a member of my family in order to put my mind at rest that things are run as they should be.'

Tom frowned. The Heinkel Sugar Refinery was a well-known, part of the city skyline, the biggest refinery in the city. 'But surely this refinery is already successful. Why does he contemplate taking on a partner?'

Emmanuel smiled broadly and tapped the side of his nose. 'The British do not trust foreigners. It has been noticed that the Germans have too much control in the trade. They are both the instigators and main membership of the Sugar Bakers Association. Nothing gets refined without their involvement. Serves our own right, of course. In the past we made so much money from slaves and sugar, we weren't interested in refining. The Germans were already doing it, were good at it, and were offered good money to come over and boil up the cane we brought over. In they came from Hanover and suchlike to do what we didn't want to do. Now they are being accused of keeping their skills to themselves, of controlling output. There are rumblings in Parliament—'

'Prompted by the Merchant Venturers Association?' said Tom without a hint of surprise and earned a slap on the back.

'You're a clever young fellow, Tom, and obviously see my point. Rather than risk confrontation and possible legislation against what is already regarded as a foreign monopoly, Conrad Heinkel agreed that I should become a partner.'

'So what is my part to be in all this?' asked Tom, wary that Emmanuel might be asking him to use his brawn rather than his brain to bring about some particular event.

Emmanuel poured more drinks. Holding the glass up to the light as if to study its contents better, he said, 'Nothing for the present. Just be a part of the refinery and ingratiate yourself. When the time comes, I will tell you what I want you to do.'

Deep inside, Tom wanted to say no, but what harm would it do? It would indeed prevent him becoming bored and he couldn't go back to sea, not until Jeb was gone. Staying in England would also allow him time to investigate Jasper's disappearance...

This was becoming increasingly important to him. If Jasper had not disappeared, Tom would never have known the privilege of living as a member of the Strong family. He owed him everything.

Tom had always been aware of Emmanuel's ruthless ambition, so taking advantage of hostile legislation was characteristic. But he couldn't help thinking that Emmanuel had an ulterior motive and wondered what it was – until Horatia swept into the room and saved the biggest smile for him. On seeing the expression on her father's face, Tom guessed that Emmanuel wanted to keep them as far apart as possible.

## Chapter Ten

Charcoal scratched across the paper, its fine dust flicking upwards on to Nelson's cuffs and staining his fingers black.

He was drawing a likeness of Adelaide Tillingham, his cousin – and bride, if his father had anything to do with it.

Adelaide was posed on a chair over which was draped a large piece of red velvet that might once have been a curtain. She had an upturned nose, which Nelson gave a slightly pig-like quality on paper. Her eyes were small and looked smaller by dint of her thick, black eyebrows, which Nelson drew meeting in the middle.

The most beautiful part about her was the silk embroidered shawl that Nelson had placed over her shoulders. It was red, a colour she'd protested was too garish. It was decorated with a Chinese dragon embroidered in gold silk thread. Madame Sybil had given it him years ago, 'As a memento, *mon cher.*'

Adelaide's mother was sitting close by, her bulging eyes flicking between the young couple, ready to detect and act swiftly at any hint of impropriety. Every so often, she glanced down at her crochet hook before shoving it through the first stitch of a seven-sectioned shell. But her eyes did not linger.

Nelson smiled to himself. Just in case I poke her daughter in the time it takes her to complete her stitch.

He'd been sketching for an hour and Adelaide was beginning to fidget.

'Mother, can I see it now?' she asked.

Nelson shook his head. Why didn't she ask *him*?

Right on cue, her mother asked, 'Is it ready?'

Piqued by their impolite treatment, Nelson threw the stub of charcoal into the fireplace, and placed the drawing into his red leather folder. 'That's enough for today,' he said and got to his feet.

'Mamma!' Adelaide exclaimed, looking almost ready to cry.

'I want to see it,' her mother demanded, her lace-covered fist stabbing Nelson with the crochet hook as she grabbed the folder with her other hand.

Nelson sighed and looked up at the ceiling as he waited for the inevitable cries of anguish.

Both women peered avidly at the drawing he'd placed on top of another in the folder.

Adelaide wailed, 'Mamma! I don't look like that. I don't look like that at all!'

'My daughter looks like a pig!' shouted her mother. 'And what's this?'

Nelson turned quickly. 'Put it back!'

'She's naked!' Mrs Tillingham exclaimed.

'No, she's not!' Nelson grabbed the latest sketch he'd done of Blanche. She was exactly as he remembered her, dark, exotic and alluring.

Mrs Tillingham was red in the face. 'She looks like a savage! I will not allow my daughter to marry a man who paints half-naked savages.'

Nelson's spirits rose to astronomic heights. He'd been unable to convince his father that Adelaide was not the bride for him. Now it looked as though Adelaide and her mother had made up their own minds.

He scratched his head but hid his grin before he said, 'I was looking forward to painting my new wife without her clothes on. Are you quite sure?'

He congratulated himself on his expression, a mix of pathos and outright amusement.

Mrs Tillingham bustled Adelaide towards the door. 'Come along, my dear child. This man is not for you. Scoundrel!' she shouted before slamming the door.

Nelson waited until it was safe before breaking into laughter. Saved by a sketch! He almost fell on to the draped dragon counterpane that Madame Sybil had given him. As fingers touched the roughness of the gold thread, his laughing broke out anew. If only Adelaide and her mother had known the origins of the red coverlet and the couplings he'd enjoyed upon it.

—

Conrad Heinkel wore dark, conservative clothes and muttered little prayers to the Almighty, mostly in German, when things weren't going quite right. He was a widower, and although the refinery was a dangerous place of great heat and dark labours, Heinkel seemed loath to let his two children out of his sight. They followed him everywhere.

'They have to learn how men toil for their daily bread. They must understand that nothing in life comes easily,' he told Tom.

Tom agreed with that, although his own life had been much harder. Conrad took him around the refinery and outlined the production method. Tom caught on quickly, and although he didn't need to, opted to spend most of his time with the workforce rather than in the offices. Management, he suggested to Conrad, needs to lead from the front not push from behind. Most men would have chosen the easier option.

The heat was oppressive and a thunderous roar sounded from the furnaces that heated the bulbous stills in which cane sugar was being refined. Men, stripped to their breeches, shovelled coal continuously into the row of arched furnaces, sweat and coal dust running in streaks down their backs.

A few days after Tom's arrival at the refinery, Emmanuel Strong came visiting with Horatia in tow. Emmanuel's expression was like thunder. Horatia was tight-lipped and stiff-backed, her eyes fixed straight ahead. Tom guessed she'd been told by her father to wait outside. Obviously, Horatia had refused.

Still seething, Emmanuel needed to vent his anger on someone else. He spotted Tom scooping impurities off a bubbling sugar vat with a long-handled ladle. The bowl of the ladle was the size of a large saucepan and its handle was over ten feet long. Though it afforded distance between the scooper and the vat, Tom's shirt was wringing wet and clung to his body.

Emmanuel brought his head close to Tom's ear and shouted, 'Where's the man that should be doing this?'

Without turning from his task, Tom shouted back, 'Got overcome by the heat. Gone outside.'

Emmanuel was in no mood for sensible explanations. 'He shouldn't leave his post and you shouldn't be doing that.'

Tom eyed him sidelong, but avoided looking at Horatia. 'And have the man faint? Bull's blood in the sugar's one thing. It takes out the impurities. A man of fifty with a hairy body and sweating like a horse only adds them.'

The noise increased as a tub of lime was tipped on to the charcoal filter beds through which the sugar seeped before being pulsed through a vacuum and spun round until it was pure.

Emmanuel moved away, and Tom bent back to his task. Assuming that Horatia had gone with her father, he stripped off his sweat-soaked shirt and tossed it at one of the small square windows, which had wide, clean ledges.

Most of the men in the refinery stripped to the waist when the heat became unbearable. Semi-nakedness had never worried Tom. Like most seamen, he'd seen varying degrees of nakedness all over the world.

He thought he heard one of the chargehands calling to him. When he looked, he saw Horatia. She had not gone with her father but was standing just a few yards away, her mouth open, looking at his body.

He heard Emmanuel shouting for her to come. When she did, he pushed her through the door after which he came marching back to Tom, his face red with anger as much as heat.

'Remember what I said,' he growled into Tom's ear. 'She's not for you. Be warned, Tom. So long as my brother is alive, you'll not be on the streets. But once he's gone, if you touch my daughter...'

Tom stretched himself to his full height, his fists clenched. The day had finally come when one of the Strong family had made it plain that he wasn't really one of them, that he never could be. The knowledge hurt far more than he had expected, though deep down he'd always known it.

For Jeb's sake, he wouldn't hit Emmanuel. For Jeb's sake, he wouldn't shout what was in his heart. He had to be at Marstone Court when Jeb died. He owed the old man that. He reached for his shirt.

The stink and feel of sugar covered his hair and body. He was sickened by the smell of it, the heat of the boiling pans and the sight of men with scald marks that disfigured their bodies.

Tom shouted to Conrad that he was going out and felt Conrad's eyes following him. Although he hated to let Conrad down, he'd had enough and needed fresh air.

Once outside, he felt like a convict, released early and intent on supping the full cup of freedom. His steps quickened and, try as he might, he couldn't stop himself walking along Rosemary Street and towards the quay where he'd berthed his ship. It wasn't due to sail for three days under her new captain.

The tide was in, that much was apparent just by the wheeling and shrieking of the gulls. A ship was already making her way out, men climbing about her rigging, loosening sails ready for the moment they were out in the channel and setting a course. For now a pilot cutter was rowing her out of the harbour and down the Avon. Even without seeing her name or having a closer view, Tom knew the ship was his. Captain Rogers had cast off early. Tom turned away, thought about going back to the refinery, but couldn't. He needed to feel a deck beneath his feet. He needed a ship, any ship, and headed to the spot just below St Mary Redcliffe church where the *Miriam Strong* was moored.

When he got there, a group of boys were practising knots under the watchful eyes – or rather one eye – of Jimmy Palmer, mate on one of Tom's many voyages and now confined to land without an eye and the fingers of his right hand. His eye had gone in a fight with a mad ship's cook off the coast of Tierra del Fuego and his fingers had been shorn off by ropes racing through his hands in the heart of a gale.

'Captain Strong aboard!'

At Jimmy's cry, the group of boys let fall pieces of rope with which they were practising half-hitches and bow lines, and saluted Tom as if he were a grand admiral of the Royal Navy, not merely a captain on a fleet of vessels taking manufactured goods across the Atlantic and bringing back sugar, rum and molasses.

Tom shook Jimmy's hand, which felt more like a fist. The boys stood to attention until Tom told them to go back to their knots.

None of them was exactly neat as a new pin. All had been deloused, most washed their face and hands every day, but the more subtle niceties such as not letting wind in company, were not rigidly adhered to. Clarence, he was told, had made a good friend, a boy called Joe, who had a harelip and continuously running snot.

Tom perceived that Jimmy was worried about something and asked what was wrong, despite his own problems.

Jimmy sucked on his pipe. 'Will you take a drink with me?'

Tom nodded and followed him down below. Jimmy brought out a flat-bottomed decanter from one of the neat and narrow cupboards a master carpenter had spent time and trouble fitting into the sloping side of the ship.

Jimmy poured a measure of rum into two glasses. 'Someone wants this berth or this boat,' he said after downing his rum in one swift swallow. 'Must do. I'm told by the Venturers or Port Authority, or whatever they are nowadays, that there's a party waitin' to pay two hundred pounds a year berthing fee.'

'Two hundred!' Tom was so surprised, he could barely get the words out. 'Someone wants to pay two hundred pounds for this berth?'

'So it seems.'

Jimmy poured each of them another shot and they drank those too. Both studied the inner walls of the ship as other men study the neck and shoulders of a beautiful woman.

Ships got you like that, thought Tom. Even when they were lying like a dead whale on the mud, their great weight supported by the huge wooden stanchions beneath, they were still a thing of beauty.

'What's to do?' asked Jimmy eventually.

Tom looked towards the curve of the wharf and a host of decrepit warehouses. At one time they had held sugar, tobacco and tea. Too old and damp, they hadn't been used for years. But someone wanted their berth, so it stood to reason, thought Tom, that someone had plans for them too. Emmanuel would know. He'd be bound to.

'I'll ask some questions, Jim,' he said and drained his glass.

He followed his old mate back up on deck, and laughed as the boys raced to be first to climb the rigging. As he shaded his eyes against the weak sunlight and watched them, he could almost believe he was at sea again, the deck heaving beneath his feet, the sails unfurling and cracking like whips in the wind. He knew the *Miriam Strong* would have sailed well and asked himself the same questions he'd asked Jeb Strong a hundred times before; what was her real name and how had he come by her?

As he watched the boys carry out more drills and disciplines of seaman-ship, his earlier unease was completely forgotten. Helping these boys towards a better future was more important to him.

If his attention hadn't been taken up with the ship and the boys, plus Jimmy's pronouncement about the rise in berthing fees, he might have noticed that he was being watched.

Hidden in a corner where the chimney from a glass works cast lengthy shadows, Reuben Trout stuffed a clay pipe with black shag, struck a flint and lit it. He was being paid well to keep watch on the comings and goings around the training ship, and also to keep an eye on Tom Strong. Watching had become his livelihood. What was more, he liked the job, far easier than keeping drunken seamen in order. Besides he was older than when he'd first come across Tom on that chilly winter's night, but he was still fit enough to keep watch.

He didn't care much for Tom. Never had. Blood and breeding will out, that was Reuben Trout's creed. Tom Strong was not a born gentleman. He had come from the gutter, and, in Reuben's opinion, he'd never quite left it behind.

—

After leaving the *Miriam Strong*, Tom made his way back to the refinery in the hope of finding Emmanuel. He was lucky. Emmanuel was helping Horatia up into the carriage. Tom got there in time to grab the door before it was closed.

Emmanuel was surprised. 'What the devil—?'

'I want to talk to you.'

Tom gripped the coach door with one hand, and Emmanuel's sleeve with the other. He could barely control his anger.

'What do you want with the *Miriam Strong's* berth?'

Emmanuel looked puzzled at first, but his tone turned surly. 'What would I want with a run-down berth presently occupied by a run-down ship?'

'Why would anyone want to offer two hundred pounds for a run-down berth?'

'I can't imagine.'

'I don't believe you.'

Emmanuel expelled air down his nose like an impatient horse. 'You obviously think me a very hard man, Tom, if you think I'd steal my brother's little project from under his nose. Believe it or not, but I wouldn't do that.'

Tom glared at him, unsure now. 'I need to know,' he said at last.

'Why? No one else in Bristol has enough money to outbid us over that berth. While my brother lives, no one gets that berth. No one at all!'

After they'd gone, it occurred to Tom that Horatia had been extraordinarily silent. Her father had probably laid down the law about men and marriage yet again.

Thoughtfully he stroked back a stray lock of hair that had tangled with his lips. Emmanuel could be telling the truth. A powerful bond existed between the three brothers. Although Emmanuel was more ambitious than either Jeb, whom he knew, or Otis, about whom he'd heard many good things, they looked after each other.

'I need to think and I need a drink,' he said and promptly took himself into the Fourteen Stars, which was just a short walk away.

By the time Sally appeared, Tom had done little thinking and far too much drinking.

'What's yer problem?' Sally said, stroking his cheek.

'I've become a landlubber,' he replied, looking sorry for himself.

'Oh, never mind,' she cooed against his ear. 'Let me make things better for you.'

He turned bleary eyes on her. 'You're supposed to be in Portishead with your sister.'

He was vaguely aware of someone leaning over his shoulder, asking Sally if Tom had a few spare sovereigns in his pocket.

'I don't know,' she blurted, then almost screeched as Stoke gripped her hair so tight, she thought she could feel it ripping out of her head.

'Find out,' he hissed.

Her head burned, but when she felt her hair it was still there. With Stoke's eyes upon her, she delved into Tom's pockets and felt money. Before lifting any, she glanced back to Stoke, who had now turned his attention to a rough-looking man with a boil on his face. They looked over, then laughed and looked away again.

Damn the man! Well, if Stoke was trying to set her up with that ugly bloke, he was very much mistaken. She was off.

She half rose, fully meaning to scarper before Stoke could get any of Tom's money off her, and before he told her to earn it by being 'nice' to his ugly companion.

A crowd of seamen pushed into the bar, blocking the view of Stoke and his friend. They looked rough too. She couldn't leave Tom with this sort of company in the state he was in, not after he'd been so kind.

She bent close to Tom's ear. 'Won't be long, Tom. I'm going to get your German friend that you told me about.'

She kept low as she made her way across the room and out of the door. The Heinkel Sugar Refinery was only just along the road, and she knew that Herr Heinkel had a house in Rosemary Lane. She raced there as fast as her legs could go, her boots slapping on the uneven cobbles.

The door was dark blue and had a brass knocker set two-thirds of the way up. There was a boot scraper to one side of the door, an oil light fixed into a cast-iron bracket on the other.

Grasping the knocker, she gave it a heavy rap, then repeated it again and again and again.

There was no time to spare. If she were unlucky, Stoke or any of those men would have gone through Tom's pockets and worse by the time they got back.

A maid in nightcap and gown, a shawl thrown over her shoulders, appeared. She looked shocked by Sally's smudged eyes and thin face.

'I need to speak to Mr Heinkel,' she blurted.

The woman frowned. 'At this time of night?'

'It's important.'

'Well, come back in the morning.'

The woman started to close the door.

'No!' screeched Sally. 'I have to see him. It's about Captain Strong, Tom Strong!'

A voice suddenly boomed from the top of the stairs inside the house. 'Who is it, Mary?'

Sally didn't give her chance to answer. 'Sally Ward! It's Captain Tom. He needs your help.'

A man in a bed-gown and wearing a nightcap came halfway down the stairs. Conrad Heinkel was frowning. 'What is wrong?'

Sally breathlessly explained, though elaborated, and did not mention that she'd been ordered to go through Tom's pockets. It made people nervous to invite thieves into the house.

'He was upset about his father and not being able to go back to sea, and the training ship and everything... and now he's drunk. He needs to get home and I couldn't think of anywhere else to come.'

Conrad's response was immediate.

'Harness a horse and get out the carriage, he said to two male servants that had appeared. 'Collect the Captain from whatever gutter he's fallen into, and take him home. But be discreet.' The servants looked at him blankly. 'Quietly! Without disturbing the family,' he said and wished he were back in Hanover, where servants jumped to it without lengthy instructions and blank looks.

Outside and beyond Conrad's hearing, they unleashed a barrage of reasons why they shouldn't be doing this.

'Putting us out of our way for a tart? Look at it. Long past her best, that one. Wouldn't give you tuppence for a ride!'

Sally ignored their jibes and took them to the tavern table over which Tom was sprawled. Thankfully Stoke was nowhere in sight.

'I can go with you,' Sally said brightly, excited by the thought of taking a coach ride out to Marstone Court.

'No need. We know the way.'

Sally tried again. 'Just for the fun of it,' she added.

Staggering beneath the weight of Tom's body made the men even grumpier. At last they had him in the chaise. Then they turned to her and said, 'You can go now. We'll take over from here.'

They laughed as they drove off. Sally watched them go, left alone in the darkness, the only light falling from the narrow windows of the Fourteen Stars.

Unwilling to go back to the tavern, she headed off towards St Augustine's Bridge and her cold, damp room at the bottom of the Christmas Steps. At least Tom would be safe and warm in his own bed tonight.

–

Fearful of footpads, Heinkel's servants kept a fast pace out through the village of Bedminster and along the road to Ashton. By the time they got there, Marstone Court was in darkness, but they did manage to rouse the gateman, saying that they'd brought Mr Tom Strong home from the city.

The gateman rubbed his eyes.

'He's been working hard at the refinery,' the coach driver said. 'Mr Heinkel ordered us to bring him home.'

'Working at this time of night? Strayed into an inn no doubt,' the gateman grumbled as he cranked open the gates. 'Now, don't you be long,' he added as they drove through. 'My bed's still warm and I want to get back in it. And don't go waking the whole bloody house or the master will be fetching a flintlock to you!'

The coachman and his colleague took his warning to heart and stopped some distance from the house. Discretion being the better part of valour, they left Tom lying beneath a tree to the side of the house.

'Will he be all right?' said the coachman to his colleague.

'The night dew will do him good,' said the other man as he heaved himself up inside the coach and made himself comfortable in the warm spot lately occupied by Tom Strong.

Peeved that he'd been left sitting up on top all alone, the coachman continued, 'Are you sure no one's seen us?'

'Only the moon,' said the man, and slammed the door shut.

Nervously but as quietly as possible, the coachman turned the horses' heads back down the drive towards the gate, unaware that other eyes watched from high on the fourth floor. Caroline, a light sleeper, had heard the carriage and was looking out of the window on to the moonlit scene below.

'It's Captain Tom,' she whispered.

Rupert pushed her to one side so he could get a better view.

Arthur knelt on the window seat, peered out and asked, 'Is he dead?'

Georgie was still sound asleep, chewing at the woollen mittens he was forced to wear to stop him sucking his thumbs. Mrs Grainger had given him a concoction to make him sleep. 'Tincture of poppy seed and dandelion,' she'd said when Edith had asked what it was.

'He can't stay out there all night. We have to rescue him,' Caroline pronounced.

They spoke in whispers and were extremely quiet finding their slippers and sneaking out of their room.

'The back stairs,' whispered Caroline.

Rupert was thinking about how big Tom was. 'How are we going to get him in?'

Everyone bumped into Caroline as she stopped to think. 'We'll get Edith up. She'll help us.' And off they trotted along the landing and down the back stairs.

Edith's hair was in rag curls and she was dreaming of suet pudding with treacle, her lips smacking together as though it were real. Caroline tugged one of the ragged bumps of hair. Edith frowned and smacked at her hand. Caroline persisted until a disgruntled Edith woke up.

'It's Captain Tom. We've got to help him.' She explained about the coach and how the two men had left Tom beneath a tree.

Edith reached for her shawl and pulled on her boots.

The door at the bottom of the stairs squeaked as they tugged it open. The three children, Edith and the meagre flame of half a wax candle filed out into the night.

They trod lightly, the wetness of the grass seeping into the children's slippers. Edith shivered beneath her shawl and asked herself why she was doing this. If Grainger found them out here, the children would get the birch across their backsides and she'd get the sack. She wasn't sure which was worse.

Moonlight filtering through the tree dappled Tom's body.

'He's too big to carry all the way to the house,' whispered Rupert.

Edith knelt down at his side, Caroline opposite her. 'We have to wake him.' She patted his cheeks in the attempt. He groaned but didn't open his eyes.

'Let me,' said Rupert and proceeded to slap Tom's cheeks in quick, sharp slaps that sounded almost like gunshots in the silence.

'Not so loud,' said Edith. 'We need to wake him, but quietly.'

'My knees are wet,' moaned Arthur.

'Grass! Wet grass,' said Edith grabbing handfuls of it and rubbing it over Tom's flushed cheeks. His eyes flickered and his groans were almost words.

'Again,' said Caroline, and immediately repeated what Edith had done.

This time he was almost coherent, though his sentences were unfinished. 'Someone must have… he couldn't have climbed… Jasper… why?'

'Soon 'ave you inside, sir,' Edith whispered. 'All together now…'

With great difficulty, they got him to his feet, Edith on one side, Caroline to the other and the two boys following behind, Arthur holding the flickering candle.

'He's heavy,' said Caroline.

Edith agreed. 'We'll never get him up all them stairs to his own bed.' She panted while she thought about it. 'I know. The laundry room.'

'Won't it be locked?' asked Arthur.

'Goodness,' Rupert muttered, 'who'd want to steal our dirty laundry?'

Edith giggled at the thought of a masked burglar running off with armfuls of pantalets or Lady Verity's whalebone corsets.

They staggered as far as the laundry door, which was open, just as Edith had said.

Baskets piled high with white twill, cotton and linen shone silver in the moonlight that filtered through two small windows.

'Oh, me goodness! Me legs are going,' said Edith, her knees bending beneath the weight.

Rupert had the presence of mind to tip the laundry from the baskets and spread it on the floor.

'Careful,' whispered Edith, as they slowly lowered Tom on to his makeshift bed.

Caroline shoved a folded sheet beneath his head and Edith covered him with a pair of chintz curtains.

For a few minutes they knelt silently at his side, panting after the exertion, their white breath drifting like smoke through patches of moonlight.

'Will he be better in the morning?' asked Arthur.

'Mostly, though his head will be aching – but that's his fault. Just you remember that, Arthur – You shouldn't oughter, drink too much porter.'

Arthur frowned. 'I don't understand.'

Edith grabbed his elbow and jerked him to his feet. 'I'm glad to 'ear it, young master. Let it be a lesson to you.'

That the statement made little sense to any one didn't really matter. Edith had done her bit for Captain Tom. She felt proud. If there was anyone in this house she'd help at the drop of a hat, it was him.

Rupert would have lingered, but Edith ushered him out and made sure everyone was back in their beds before she went to hers. Despite the discomfort of having her hair in rags, Edith fell asleep minutes after her head hit the pillow.

Safe in the knowledge that everyone was sleeping soundly, Rupert slid from his bed, dressed quickly and made his way along the dark corridors, down the servants' stairs and back to the laundry.

Tom was fast asleep, not a pretty sight at all with his mouth open and snoring loudly. But Rupert was determined to make sure that Tom woke up in the morning. In the meantime, he bundled himself in more laundry and fell asleep, his body curled up and his hand resting on Tom's shoulder.

A cockerel crowing at a nearby farm woke Tom before six o'clock. He started then blinked, surprised to see where he was and who was laid sound asleep close by.

He tried to move without disturbing the boy, but Rupert opened his eyes, saw Tom looking at him and smiled. 'I'm glad you're better,' he said, his face shining with innocence.

Tom's throat felt dry as a sun-drenched beach, but he managed to ask how he'd got from Bristol to the laundry room.

'A coach brought you and left you on the grass. We brought you here.'

'We?'

Rupert got to his feet and as he stretched, explained everything.

'So where are you going now?' Tom asked, as Rupert made his way swiftly to the door.

Rupert's young eyes were suddenly fearful, not at all as brightly alert as when he'd first awoken and smiled at him. 'Mrs Grainger mustn't catch me here. I have to go.'

Tom pushed himself up on to his elbows. It felt as though a Zulu warrior was beating a war drum inside his head. He winced, closed his eyes then counted to five before reopening them. The way the children went around singing the praises of their governess had never quite rung true in his book, but Verity and Emmanuel seemed to think it quite wonderful – probably because it suited them. They preferred to provide the more material needs of their children, without the emotional involvement.

Tom said, 'You don't like her very much, do you?'

Rupert averted his eyes. A tuft of grass pushing up through the flagstone floor seemed suddenly to be more interesting. He kicked idly at it with his slippered foot. Finally, he shook his head.

Tom felt for him. The Strong children were well dressed, well fed and lived in a fine house, but they were little more than orphans. 'Do you want me to tell your parents you don't like her?'

Rupert's eyes grew round with fear. 'No. Please. You don't know her. Besides, there's a new Peters coming today. Things will be better when she gets here.'

Tom frowned. He knew the name, but the amount of drink he'd consumed had muddled his brain. 'Peters?'

Rupert's face brightened. 'A new nurse. You see, if we have a nurse, things aren't so bad with Mrs Grainger – until she gets rid of her, that is.' His face turned crestfallen. 'She always gets rid of them in the end.'

Perhaps a witness to Mrs Grainger's persecution was the best option for now. 'When did you say this new nurse is coming?'

Rupert opened the door. Tom could see he was agitated, wanting to stay but too afraid. 'She arrives on the ship from Barbados today. Mrs Grainger says she's black and we'll only see her in daylight. She frightened George and made him cry.'

Tom wondered at Mrs Grainger's narrow-mindedness. He'd met people of all colours all over the world and only found differences in cultures, not in human nature. Poor children, having a woman like that governing their lives.

'There you are then,' Tom exclaimed in a show of cheerfulness, and shook Rupert's shoulder. 'She'll be here by teatime.'

Rupert shook his head. 'No, she won't. Mrs Grainger said she'd have to stay on the ship until tomorrow. The coachman's ill, you see, so there's no one to collect her.'

Tom rubbed at his aching head and closed his eyes tightly shut. He had been thinking of taking a bath, walking in the wind, then visiting Jeb following a light luncheon. Twenty blacksmiths were hammering nails into his head. He supposed a trip into Bristol would clear his head just as well. He sighed resignedly. 'I'll find out what ship she arrives on.'

'*Ianthe*, at midday.' Rupert grinned. 'I told Nelson that Mrs Grainger had locked George in the attic, and Nelson told me not to worry because our new nurse was arriving at midday on the *Ianthe*."

'Did he now?'

Tom couldn't help being surprised that Nelson should know the comings and goings of servants unless they were involved in looking after him personally. Tom struggled to his feet, swore and winced as he hit the top of his head on a low-hanging beam.

He rubbed at yet another hammering ache. 'At midday, you say?'

'Yes, Captain.'

He squeezed the ache from his eyes with his thumbs and winced as the first light of daybreak pierced the windows. Damn it, he wouldn't leave the children without a nurse for one more day.

Rupert lingered by the door. 'She won't eat us, will she, Captain?'

'The nurse? Good grief, no. I've heard of many fine men brought up by Negro nurses out in the colonies.' He grinned. 'Not one inch of them was chewed. You've nothing to fear.'

Hesitantly, because he still wasn't sure, Rupert's expression brightened as he said, 'I'll tell George that we'll have a new nurse by tomorrow and that she won't eat him.'

'Today!' Tom exclaimed, tucking his shirt into his trousers. 'By mid-afternoon, *Ianthe* will be tied up and cargo and passengers will be unloaded. I'll collect her then.'

'You will?' Rupert exclaimed.

'I will,' said Tom. 'Now, what's this nurse's name?'

Rupert frowned. 'Peters. It's always Peters, although I think Mamma wanted to call this one Brown or Black. Father told her that would be cruel, and besides, we're used to the name Peters, but Nelson said that her real name is Blanche Bianca.'

'Of course,' said Tom, remembering now that the Strongs' combined memories were such that they couldn't be bothered to call a person by their correct name. But how did Nelson know her real name?

'I'll find her,' he said, and followed Rupert out of the door.

After breakfasting on dry bread and water, Tom washed himself and strode down to the gatehouse. The smell of fat frying drifted out of the open door along with the gateman. After the usual formalities, he asked whose carriage had brought him home.

'Mr Heinkel's, so I understand.'

'Oh, Lord!' Tom was mortified. Not only had he run out on Conrad, but the man had also rescued him from himself and got him home safely.

He thanked the gateman and strode around the grounds before judging it time to leave for the city. He would collect the new nurse from the *Ianthe* and would also see Conrad to apologize for his behaviour.

One of the stable lads was on hand to help him harness a horse. 'The governess cart will do,' he said, when the lad asked him which carriage he was taking. 'I need the fresh air.'

It didn't matter that the day was grey and cold and threatening to rain. The stiff breeze that froze his ears and pulled at his hair, also helped to clear his head. When he got to the quay, he left the horse in the hands of a lad who looked in need of sixpence. 'Take a shilling,' he said, and flipped the lad a coin.

The masts of the *Ianthe* were not yet in view. Tom checked his timepiece. The tide was only just coming in and the ship would come in with it, the rowers of the pilot, or one of the new paddle steamer tugs, helped by six knots of incoming water.

He strolled along the quay, eyeing the fast sailing barques that came up from Seville, their holds filled with dewy-skinned oranges.

Further along the quay another ship, *The Pride of Cork,* was unloading a cargo of pigs, fattened on the rich pastureland of south-east Ireland. The pigs were squealing and honking, weaving this way and that beneath the canes of their keepers.

Tom watched the scene idly. It soothed his soul and helped him cope with life ashore and the refinery, where men baked red in the heat from the sugar pans. He was doing it for Jeb. A familiar voice called out and disrupted his thoughts.

'Feeling better now?' It was Sally.

Tom rubbed at his head and smiled. 'A bit. Did I get very drunk?'

Sally rested her hands on her hips and smiled saucily. 'Too drunk to be of use to a girl like me.' She beckoned him close. 'I called you a carriage.'

Tom frowned.

'The German's house is right next to the refinery. He got his coachman out to take you home.'

'Yes, I'll have to apologize to Mr Heinkel for my intrusion. But thank you anyway.'

Sally was nervously biting her blackened fingernails. A flea swung from a strand of hair trailing out from beneath her bonnet. 'Can I talk to you, Tom?'

Sally smelled bad; not just dirty because she was poor, but because she was ill, the pungent, slightly acidic smell of sickness clinging to her skin and her clothes. A straw hat with a blue silk bow on the side threw shadows over her face and made the grey circles under her eyes seem greyer.

Remembering their last meeting, Tom sighed. 'I thought you were going to your sister's?'

She shrugged. 'Well, you know what Portis'ead's like. Then there's me sister... me life wouldn't be me own.'

It was second nature for Tom to help others, mostly as a result of the kindness Jeb Strong had shown to him, but also because he couldn't help it. Normally he would have washed his hands of Sally long ago. But like his mother, she walked the streets for a living.

'So where's the money I gave you?' he asked her.

She shrugged again and began twisting the corners of her shawl. 'I spent some on gin... and a hat.'

'So I see,' he said, taking in the floppy blue bow. 'Isn't it a little grand for St Augustine's Quay?'

She smiled and touched the brim lovingly. 'Paid two bob for it. Don't you think it's nice?'

'I suppose so.' He didn't mention that it looked more suited to summer than this time of year. Besides, it wasn't terribly important. What did irk him was that he'd given her money in order for her to leave her squalid life and Stoke behind.

'So what else did you spend it on?'

She looked coy suddenly, acting as if she were a courtesan dressed in silks and satins, not a streetwalker in a stained dress and a dirty hat. 'Come and buy me a drink, and I'll tell you all about it.'

He didn't want to go with her. *Ianthe* would be coming upriver now, past Shirehampton village and around the Horseshoe Bend, and between the steep, high cliffs of the Avon Gorge. But he had an inkling as to where a proportion of his money might have gone, and it made him angry. 'Come on.' Grasping her elbow none too gently, he guided her towards a dockside tavern.

Horatia closed the heavy door softly behind her. The library was dark and smelled of the books that lined the walls from floor to ceiling. A high-backed couch sat between a large desk and a leather chair, half of its length hidden behind a four-panelled screen depicting hunting scenes from Greek myths; a semi-naked Diana chasing a white stag through an ever darkening glade.

Neither the scene nor the furniture was easily seen because the wooden shutters that covered the windows had not been unfastened as they should have been. Horatia's skirts rustled like a host of dry leaves as she bustled to the window, making a mental note to speak to the housekeeper about it. The servants were up at five, so there was no excuse for them to be closed.

In other circumstances, she would have called for a servant to open them rather than wrestle with the iron stave that slotted behind the shutters and hinged into the wall on the right-hand side. But time and secrecy were of the utmost.

Carefully, she opened the shutters. Just as she congratulated herself for carrying out the task so quietly, the iron bar slid from her hand and thudded against the wall.

'Damn it,' she said, as it swung out and chipped a particularly fine Ming vase that matched another on the other side of the window.

'Horatia?' It was said in a long, lazy way, as if the speaker was having a problem with his tongue.

She spun round just as a limp hand flopped over the back of the couch. Nelson was sprawled full-length, a stupid smile on his face and faraway look in his eyes.

A Bristol Blue port glass fell from his hand to the floor and rolled out of sight.

'What are you doing here?' Horatia asked.

'I don't want to be here,' he said with a languid smile. 'I want to be in Barbados. I want to feel warm again... so I can write... so I can paint... so I can bide my while with...' His voice fell away.

Horatia eyed her brother's languid expression, the way his eyes seemed to whirl around in his head.

She judged it safe enough to carry out her task. After checking her brother was paying her no attention, she fetched a note out of her pocket, unfolded the thick, creamy paper and read it again:

My dear Miss Strong,

May I first say how I much appreciate the pleasure of being received by you as a friend, and in this regard I am only too pleased to continue advising you in your business matters, but perhaps with the desire of winning your favourable regard?

Horatia skipped Josiah Benson's protestations of love and affection, and went on to the paragraphs that most interested her.

...I have therefore done as you requested and bought stocks in Mr Brunel's Great Western Railway, which, we both agree, is the transport system of the future – imagine, London in a matter of hours!

Of course, the income envisaged from this enterprise is nothing when compared to 'our secret' plan. I am making enquiries in this regard, though with obvious discretion. As we know, there are a number of parties who could unsettle our project should it be discovered before the right and proper time.

May I ask for your forbearance and your permission to use whatever and whoever possible to fulfil our glorious objectives?

Yours affectionately,

Josiah Benson

Horatia's eyes glittered with excitement and her heart palpitated like a young maid faced with her first marriage proposal. Josiah Benson was now her most trusted friend and business adviser. Of course, he'd like to be much more, but so long as she played her games with him, promised him everything, but gave little in return, she would keep him where she wanted him. He was the conduit through which she could participate in the world of business and men.

Before Nelson had chance to rise, she sat swiftly at the desk and wrote a note giving Josiah her full permission to use all means at his disposal to achieve their objectives. She then rang for a servant.

David, Duncan's twin brother appeared. He was as tall as his brother, just as dark, but didn't have the same seductive way of looking at her. She told him to go away and send Duncan.

The corner of David's mouth twitched as if he were longing to smile. Horatia glared at him.

He left quickly and sent his brother.

Duncan's eyes seemed to mock her as she handed him the note, though his expression remained unchanged.

'Take it to Mr Benson,' she said, her voice necessarily soft as she placed a finger on her mouth, then pointed towards the chaise.

They were not alone. Duncan knew when it was wise to be politic and take his leave.

'Who was that?' Nelson mumbled. He tried to raise himself from the chaise, but rolled off and on to the floor.

'A servant,' she said, standing over him.

'I've lost my virgin bride,' he said blearily.

'How careless of you.'

'I upset her mother,' he said once he was on his hands and knees.

Horatia smiled. 'How jolly!'

At last on his feet, Nelson said, 'Father didn't think so.'

'I'm not surprised,' said Horatia as she tucked Josiah's note into her pocket. 'He was very hopeful of marrying at least one of us off.'

'I'm going to stand my ground,' he said grandly, hitching his thumbs into his waistcoat.

'I don't doubt it. You can be quite stubborn when you wish.'

'I told him I wanted to become more involved with the family business before settling down. Anyway, there are lots of girls like Adelaide of good family and with fortunes that would bond easily with ours. He seemed to like that.'

'Was it the truth?'

Nelson slammed open the library window and took deep breaths in front if it. 'Of course. Father isn't going to live for ever. Someone has to take over.'

Horatia's smile vanished. It hurt her immeasurably to think that her younger brother was regarded as more capable of running the family business than she.

She suddenly remembered a conversation she'd overheard between her father and her uncle regarding the girl Nelson had been involved with in Barbados.

'Wouldn't you prefer to go back to Barbados and take over from Uncle Otis? You could trust me to run things here.'

Nelson's stupor seemed to dissipate. 'That would depend on what was waiting for me there.'

## Chapter Eleven

Blanche wrapped her arms around herself as the cold wind whipped her hair across her face and stung her eyes. The sky was grey and heavy, and the river was the colour of mud as it curled its way through the high cliffs of the Avon Gorge towards the centre of Bristol.

*Ianthe,* the ship that had brought her from Bridgetown, had furled her sails and was being rowed up the river by a bevy of brutish men all heaving in time, their oars dipping, rising and dipping again into the murky water.

They were sweating, their faces burned red raw by the ice-cold wind. Sweating, Blanche decided, was something she would never do in this wet, cold country. 'They must be freezing,' she muttered.

'Won't stop 'em rowing,' said the first mate who was close by. 'They'll row their hearts out. 'Tis their last day, you see. Steam's taking over from men.' He pointed to a boat chugging in the opposite direction to them, regardless of wind and tide. Smoke plumed like a giant feather from its coal-black stack. 'The master – Sir Emmanuel, that is – gave them this last day of rowing one of his ships up the river. He's employed them the longest, I'll give 'im 'is due. But there. That's progress for you. Keeps them warm though,' he added.

'I'm glad for them,' said Blanche, almost envious of their plight – at least of being warm. I don't think I'll ever be warm again, she thought, and squeezed her eyes tightly shut.

A fall of water escaped from a furled sail, as the ship lurched in the wind. Some of the sailors grinned. Soaked through, Blanche gritted her teeth, opened her eyes and caught a glimpse of terraced houses rising in tiers above the steep-sided gorge. The houses looked opulent and made her feel better. Things were bound to improve. England and Bristol couldn't be grey and miserable all the time.

By the time *Ianthe* had moored at St Augustine's Quay, a steady drizzle was falling. A colonnade of buildings with over-hanging upper floors, some with the curved scrolls and ormolu of Dutch brickwork, towered towards the water. The cobbled quay, slick with mud and oily tar, divided the houses from the ships. A bridge crossed the water some way distant, packed with people hurrying, carrying bundles, pushing handcarts and dodging every conceivable piece of horse traffic ever invented. It was as busy as Bridgetown, but very different; the houses looked hard and cold, and the air left a sooty taste in the mouth and smelled of iron, coal and a sickly mix of sugar and horse dung.

'I'm to be met,' she said to the first mate as he carried her chest down the gangplank, Blanche treading carefully behind him.

'Aye,' he said with an exhausted sigh and put it down beside her. 'If you're sure. Captain Briggs did say it were best for you to stay aboard. You'll get plenty cold waitin' here.'

'I couldn't get any colder,' she said brusquely as she wrapped her cloak around her. 'I won't be waiting long. They'll send a servant to collect me. I'm family, you know.'

He touched his forelock as if he recognized that fact. It pleased her, made her feel warmer inside even though she was soaked to the skin.

She held on to the hope that someone would be waiting for her and, just as steadfastly, she also gripped the thick shawl and woollen cloak that covered her shivering shoulders.

The quay was alive with men and movement. Eyes bright with curiosity watched her as she paced beside the leather-bound chest, which held all her worldly goods; her shoes, her mother's jewels, a little money, and the high-waisted dresses made in Barbados.

A lank young man of barely sixteen rested his hands on his knees, stared at her and asked, 'You a darkie?' He leered and added, 'Didn't know they looked like you.'

'She's a Spaniard!' shouted another man. 'Came up from Seville with the oranges.'

'Creole!' shouted another. 'Ship's come from the Sugar Islands, not Spain.'

Ignoring the shouts and lewd appraisal of labourers offloading hogsheads of sugar, rum and molasses, she scrutinized the length of quay, turning her nose up at the smell of muddy water and questionable effluent that floated around the ship. As if the smell wasn't bad enough, the noise hammered at her head. Sledges sliding over cobbles, some pulled by men, some by horses or donkeys, rattled and grated.

Nothing she heard or saw could dent her confidence, until she saw the dresses the women were wearing. Panic set in as she realized that fashions in Barbados were far behind those of Bristol. She'd seen a few women in Barbados wearing wide dresses with tight bodices and layers of frills from waist to hem. She'd considered them the exception to fashion rather than the norm. What a fool she'd look in her empire-line dresses with their high waists, low necklines and flimsy materials. Her spirits sank.

Much as she searched, she couldn't see the grand carriage she'd expected to meet her. Wagons, sleds, dogcarts and handcarts crowded the quay. Only one other form of conveyance stood waiting.

Her gaze settled on a governess cart, pulled by a white-socked bay with a docked tail and an arched neck. That must be it, I suppose, she thought with a plummeting heart. An enclosed carriage would have been far preferable in this weather and she'd so hoped that Nelson would be here to greet her. Why wasn't he?

She looked around her. Men heaved ropes and rolled barrels or leaned on walls and capstans, smoking clay pipes, but none looked likely to be the driver. A skinny boy with jug ears, which helped support an oversize cap, held the docked bay's head.

The wind whipped the light wool of her skirt around her legs as she approached him. It was the thickest she owned, though not thick enough for this climate. She swept towards the cart, her hand flat on her stomach as if to keep the butterflies within under control. 'Is this the carriage from Marstone Court?' she asked, unwilling to call it a cart, governess or otherwise.

The boy squinted up at her. 'Yeah.'

'So where is the driver?'

He pointed to a dark doorway from which came an abundance of noise each time it swung open before slamming shut again.

'Oh, is he now?' she muttered through chattering teeth.

The sight of a carved statue above the door stopped her in her tracks. It depicted a half-naked woman with long plaits and a skirt of what looked like leaves, and she was standing on a stone shelf that jutted out from the main building. It looked rough and primitive, not at all the sort of thing she'd expected to see in a Christian country. But nothing was quite as she'd expected it to be. If only her mother was here. Sighing, she closed her eyes, imagined her mother's voice and what she would say.

'I'm with you,' she whispered. She talked to herself quite often nowadays, almost as if she were mother as well as daughter. A little mad perhaps, but she must keep her spirits up. What was past was past. Purposefully, she stood and read the words beneath the carved idol. In stout letters it said, *'La Sauvage Noblesse'*.

'The Noble Savage,' she murmured.

Beneath that, was a scrawled handmade sign:

*Beer tuppence,*
*Gin penny a gill.*
*Drunk for a shilling, dead drunk for two.*

A tavern! A common dockside tavern! Damn the man, leaving her waiting here while he was inside drinking his fill and all in the Strong family's time.

'Well, we'll see about that,' she said.

Feeling warmer than she had since leaving Barbados, due to her anger rather than a rise in temperature, she swept through the door.

Heads turned, eyes narrowed through clouds of thick smoke, and flaccid lips sucked thoughtfully on chewed pipe stems as she entered.

'I'm looking for the driver of the bay horse outside,' she said, her voice seeming to bounce off the low ceiling and daubed walls.

A man with greasy hair and smoking a clay pipe pointed a blackened fingernail towards an alcove close to where huge barrels of beer were ranged on racks. Above them, a row of pewter mugs dripped from a blackened beam. 'He's over there.' He grinned as he added, 'He's got company,' then spat a goblet of phlegm into a brass spittoon close to his feet.

Ugly habits were of no consequence to Blanche. She was almost certain by now that the driver could not possibly be Nelson. He would not frequent such a place as this. It was obviously some servant taking advantage of the situation. The nerve! Well, she'd deal with him.

Stiffly determined, she walked towards where the man had indicated. Low mutterings and conversations of the dark interior resumed as she espied the man she presumed to be the rig's driver. A woman sat opposite him over a rough trestle, shielded from the other customers by a stout wooden pillar.

The man was tanned, with dark hair and blue eyes. On seeing her, his mouth fell open.

The woman looked up and started to rise. 'Nosey parker! Who d'you think yer looking at?'

'My name is Blanche Bianca. I've come from Barbados and expected to be met. I did not expect to have to enter such a place,' she waved her hands at her surroundings, 'as this!'

'She wants me,' said Tom when he'd at last found his voice. He was taken aback at her appearance. The West Indies bred plump nurses with big breasts and motherly dispositions; at least, that was what he'd heard. He'd taken little notice in the homegrown nurses previously appointed at Marstone Court. None of them had been particularly engrossing. But Blanche Bianca! He'd never seen anything quite like her.

'What's she want you for!' The woman sounded surprised.

Blanche was cold, tired and not in the mood to be charitable. 'Well, I wouldn't be wanting the likes of you,' she said. She would have said more, but the flame from a tallow candle flared and threw light over the woman's haggard face. Dull eyes looked out from under shadowed brows. Her cheeks were heavily rouged and her hat might have been quite grand at one time, but was now edged with grease, its ribbon dirty.

The man got to his feet. 'I have to go, Sal.' His gaze stayed fixed on Blanche.

Sal looked at Blanche then back at him. 'Oh, yeah! Too good for the likes of me, but her...'

'It's not what you think,' he said. 'Now, here's a few coins for you. Buy yourself a meat pie or a bit of fish down at the market.'

He was tall, his hair tied at the nape of his neck like the sailors on board the ship from Barbados. Blanche took in that much, but didn't want to linger. She shivered. Most of all, she wanted to be warm.

'Can we go now?' she said, turning towards the door. 'The family will be expecting me.'

'More than you can imagine,' he said, and got to the door before she did. 'Do excuse me, but I have an errand to run before getting back to Marstone Court. I've promised you'll be there by teatime.'

As he held the door for her to pass through, his eyes seemed to smile as much as his mouth, perhaps more so. He was genuinely glad to see her. His smile and welcome was the warmest thing she'd seen since leaving Barbados.

It wasn't easy, but she had to remind herself that he was only a servant. 'The sooner the better,' she said, holding her head high as she made for the cart. 'Though we might have got there sooner if I hadn't had to search for you in a common dockside tavern in the company of a trollop!'

Tom studied the grey eyes, the dark hair that tumbled out from beneath her bonnet. Her skin was dusky brown, her eyelashes long and black. She was one of the most beautiful women he had ever seen, if not *the* most beautiful, and she moved like a ship gliding over water, regal, soundlessly and as though her course of action was already decided.

No red-blooded male could resist her, he thought, and yet her sharp rebuke at finding him in a tavern and her haughty manner with Sally had offended him. Lovely as she was, Blanche Bianca was acting like a lady of means, not like a servant at all. It wouldn't hurt to bring her down a peg.

The cart sagged slightly as he loaded her brass-bound chest, then got up beside her. 'You've a sharp tongue, Mrs Peters,' he said.

'My name's Bianca. Miss Bianca. And I expected to see better sights on arrival in this city than the inside of a tavern.'

'Yes, Mrs Peters.'

Hadn't the man heard right? 'Bianca! My name is Blanche Bianca,' she said as loudly and as stridently as she could.

'Not for long,' he muttered, but she didn't bother to ask what he meant by it.

'Who was that woman?' she asked. 'Why did you give her money?'

'Because she needs it.'

He knew she wanted to ask him what Sal had done in return. He wouldn't enlighten her that as a member of the Strong family, albeit by adoption, he had responsibilities. Giving a little to the poor and needy was expected. Wealth was easily shared with those who had nothing. He felt

Although puzzled, not to mention strangely attracted to her driver, Blanche sighed and sunk into her seat. She was tired and had not eaten properly for days. The food served on ship had been difficult to keep down, possibly because boiled mutton that was salted before being cooked, didn't agree with her, and possibly because the heaving of the sea made any food difficult to digest. But they couldn't leave, not if they were on Strong family business. It wouldn't do to be petulant in front of the servants.

Goodness knew how many stairs there were between the small window and the ground, but whoever had shouted was obviously on their way down. Blanche eyed the door to their left, willing whoever it was to come out of there before she froze to death.

Eventually a big, red-faced man came tumbling out, closely followed by two golden-haired children. He glanced at her, took a second look and bowed his head slightly. 'Good day, madam,' he said reverentially.

She returned the greeting. He looked important, even wealthy in a solid, conservative kind of way. He wore good clothes, and men standing around doffed their hats respectfully. The children smiled at her, and she smiled back. Intrigued by her presence, they approached the cart.

'Tom, you have recovered?' asked the big man.

His eyes kept sliding to her; his accent was not Bristolian or Barbadian, but similar to that of the Dutch planters and shippers that had called into Bridgetown on occasion.

Tom looked contrite. 'Conrad, I have to apologize.'

His voice dropped almost to a whisper, but Blanche could still hear him.

'My behaviour was unforgivable, but Emmanuel Strong makes me lose my temper...'

The man called Conrad shook his head and held up his hand. 'No need to do that. I understand.' He leaned closer. 'You must realize why I went into business with him, Tom, but that does not mean I have to like him.'

Tom nodded and ran both hands over his head, a spontaneous gesture of relief. 'I don't like him much either. Whatever I can do to help you, I will. I think you know that.'

Conrad smiled. 'You are so like Jebediah. I know,' he added, putting up his hand in order to halt Tom's instant protest, 'you are not of his blood.' He poked a thick, strong finger at Tom's chest. 'But you are of his heart.'

If Tom had been a woman, he would have blushed. As it was, he managed to contain the surge of emotion he felt in his heart. 'I value your friendship,' he said to Conrad. He grinned and raised his eyes. 'And I value you getting me home safely. My behaviour was inexcusable.'

Conrad shrugged. 'We all behave badly sometimes. Did anyone see you arrive in my coach?'

Tom shook his head.

Conrad looked relieved. 'Then you will be coming back to work?'

'Yes,' said Tom.

Blanche found herself listening intently to every word, her gaze flicking from one man to another. They were big men, one golden, one dark, and both seemingly of the same mind.

She let her hand dangle over the side of the gig, tapping her fingers impatiently against the shiny black paintwork, and felt a pair of tiny hands slide into hers. She looked down into two expectant faces.

'I have broken my kite,' said the boy, lifting a limp, torn thing that looked as though it had crashed. He had a bright, open expression and his hair was as blond as that of his father, who was clearly Conrad.

'Can you mend kites?' asked the girl, a shadow of her brother, not so big but just as bright in countenance and with hair as golden.

'What happened to it?' Blanche asked, bending down so she could talk to them better.

Sighing as if the weight of the world were on his shoulders, he said, 'The wind blew it into a tree.'

The children watched with intense interest as Blanche examined the torn muslin. 'I'm sure that if you asked your mother, she's bound to have some scrap of material in her work basket to patch it with.'

'Our mother's dead,' said the girl in a matter-of-fact manner.

'Oh!' It sounded pathetic, but there was no point saying she was sorry because Blanche had never known the woman. Instead she said, 'My mother's dead too.'

The girl jerked her chin in affirmation. The boy said nothing. Acceptance had set in ages ago, thought Blanche.

She suggested they take off the muslin and mend it with newspaper. 'It'll work just as well. I made one when I was a child. It had a tail as long as an alligator.'

'What's an alligator?' the boy asked, as she stepped down from the vehicle.

As she explained what that was, she sensed she was being watched. When she glanced up, her eyes met those of the children's father, who was watching her with great interest over Tom's shoulder. Tom turned to see where Conrad was looking. His expression, which had been relatively serious, now seemed surprised.

Feeling herself reddening, Blanche looked away. 'Now, let me show you what to do,' she said and began to show how it could be mended. 'Remove the muslin and glue the paper to the frame. Make lots and lots of bows for the tail by twisting pieces of paper around the string.'

The children giggled with delight, as much for her attention to them as for her description of how to mend their kite. She sensed their mother had spent a great deal of time with them before she'd died and that they were missing her very much.

Tom said, 'When you've finished playing, we'll get going.' He sounded amused.

Conrad and his children watched them leave. She waved and first the children then their father waved back. She smiled. These people, as well as Tom, had made her day feel considerably warmer.

'They were very nice.'

'Yes,' said Tom.

'He was foreign?'

'German. Most sugar refiners are German.'

'Why is that?'

Tom congratulated himself. He had told her things about the city and had whetted her appetite for knowledge. Now she was asking him questions that he was pleased to answer. It made him feel good, that she needed him, even though they'd only just met.

'The Germans have a refining tradition. They are master sugar bakers. We British preferred growing sugar. Larger fortunes were made growing sugar rather than refining it.'

'Because sugar was expensive?' asked Blanche not wanting to appear ignorant, coming as she did from Barbados.

'Because labour was cheap,' Tom replied and could have bitten off his tongue.

It had been a few years since the slaves were freed. Mentioning that time and that trade made him feel guilty. The whole period, so far as he was concerned, should never have happened. But many men of means still bemoaned its passing.

'Slaves,' said Blanche in little more than a whisper.

Tom felt a need to explain, to lay the ghosts that haunted a whole country. 'It was to do with white labour being so short, and the slave trade in Africa already being in existence. It was just a step away to load them on to ships...'

Blanche cut him dead. 'My mother was a slave.'

Tom stared.

Blanche stiffened. She hadn't meant to admit that. 'You mustn't tell anyone.'

Tom's eyes swept from her to the road ahead and back again. 'Of course I won't.'

'The family knows, of course.'

'Ah yes, but you wouldn't want the servants to find out,' said Tom with a sharp nod. He could easily imagine how it would be. Gossip and intimidation, especially about a newcomer, sprang easily into existence in the small world of a country house.

'I'm a ward of the family,' she blurted, instantly hating herself because she sounded pompous and ashamed of her mother. She tried again. 'My mother died so they have to take care of me.'

'Is that so?' said Tom, as warning bells sounded in his head. No one had told him she was to be a ward of the family. Rupert had assured him she was to be their nurse, and so had the coachman who'd risen from his sickbed in order to thank him for making the trip. If he hadn't had such an aching head, he would have gone looking for Nelson and asked him for the details, but he'd taken Rupert's word and that of the coachman as proof enough.

The horse eased into a trot as they left the narrow streets and dark buildings of the city behind. The road and the river ran between flat farmland, lush water meadows and marshy bogs where pigs jostled and grunted among the couch grass.

Despite the sombre weather, everything was new and exciting and aroused her interest. The sky was grey, the grass was limp with rain, even the river was brown not blue like the sea she was used to or the gurgling stream over which she had leapt the first time she'd met Nelson.

There must have been a faraway look in her eyes, judging by Tom's expression when she caught him glancing at her. It was as though he were trying to weigh up what she was thinking.

Holding her head to one side, her chin high, she asked if she'd grown horns.

At first he seemed taken aback, then collected himself and pointed just below her eye. 'You've got dirt on your face.'

She touched where he indicated. 'It's not dirt. It's a beauty spot. A real one.'

He nodded at the explanation, as if satisfied, but every so often she felt his eyes on her.

'You're not what I expected,' he said.

'What were you told to expect?'

She couldn't help the quaver of apprehension. Some inbuilt instinct was telling her that things would not go that smoothly in this country. Trying to expel her unease was useless. It sat there, like a sleeping moth.

Just when she thought she had it under control, she heard him sigh and say, 'I don't think you've been told the truth, young woman.'

Although he'd spread a blanket over their legs, Blanche shivered, as much from the wetness of her clothes as from the nervous chill that coursed down her spine. A series of loud sneezes proved impossible to stop.

'What do you mean?'

She tried to hold her head high, though it was almost impossible against the continually driving rain that spattered her face and ran down her nose.

'Your nose is running,' he said and despite himself, dotted her nose with his finger.

She rubbed it off on the corner of her sleeve; like a child, he thought. And she'd come here in all innocence, supposing she'd be a ward of the family not a servant. He had to tell her the truth and give her time to arrive at Marstone Court with her dignity intact.

They stopped in a narrow lane.

'Look, Blanche Bianca, we need to talk about why you're here.'

'I'm to be a ward...' she said, her voice faltering as she studied the look in Tom's eyes and remembered what the solicitor had really said, something about being bonded.

Tom took hold of her hand in both of his. They felt strong and warm. Her first inclination was to pull back, but she changed her mind.

'I'm given to understand that you're here to be nurse to the younger members of the Strong family, four of them in fact, and one more on the way.'

Blanche shook her head. 'No, no, no! I am not a servant! I have been brought over here because my mother died and my father...'

She stopped herself. She'd made a promise and signed a paper at the solicitor's in Barbados.

Tom shook his head and smiled sadly. 'Miss Bianca, I offered to pick you up because the coachman is sick at the moment. All I was told was that a new nurse was coming over from Barbados to help in the confinement of Lady Verity Strong.'

Blanche could hardly believe her ears. 'A nurse!'

He immediately regretted being so blunt. 'Perhaps I've got it wrong.'

'You certainly have,' she said, her chest heaving with a sickening apprehension that she may indeed have read things wrongly. She also remembered the look in Betsy's eyes when she'd mentioned being bonded, and her comment about the Strongs only caring about sugar. Whatever the truth of the matter, she couldn't help but retaliate.

'What would you know? Men who frequent low places with cheap doxies aren't likely to be party to the business of respectable people!'

'I've already told you. Sally is an old friend and I've been trying to help her and her son.'

'And why would you want to help the child of a woman like that, as if I didn't know?' She stared at him accusingly.

'I have my reasons,' he said, dropped her hand and gripped the reins tightly. The rain clamped his hair to his head and dripped off his chin. He clucked and the horse moved forward.

They would have continued for some time in silence if the wind hadn't chosen that moment to lift her bonnet and send it bouncing on to her shoulders. Only the fact that the ribbons secured it around her neck kept it from flying away. Wisps of hair floated around her face and the rain and the spray from the road flew into her face.

'Damn this weather,' she said as she attempted to get her bonnet back on her head.

The driver burst into laughter. 'Now, now! That's hardly the right kind of language for the nursery. Think of the effect on your young charges!'

At first she wanted to laugh, but her wounded pride was not easily healed. 'I am not a nurse!'

But deep down she knew he was speaking the truth. She had merely blinded herself to it, refusing to acknowledge what bonded really meant and caught up in the excitement of seeing Nelson again.

At last he said, 'I know how it is to be close to a family, yet not regarded as one of them.'

'I beg your pardon?' Blanche protested. 'What would a coachman know about it?'

Tom was persistent. 'I know how it is to be part of the Strong family, yet not part of it. Jeb Strong adopted me when I was just a child. His own son had died in an accident.'

He swallowed hard as he remembered the body in the chimney.

'Even before his son died, he'd been engaged in good works since some incident back in his youth. I was one of those good works. All the same, I'm not a Strong. Sometimes I can see resentment in the faces of servants, even tradesmen. But I accept that. I was not born a Strong. I never can be a Strong – except in name.'

Blanche was speechless. Being told she had been brought to England as a servant was not the future she'd foreseen, but Tom had spoken with an emotional intensity that affected her deeply. It seemed at odds with his rugged appearance.

'I'm sorry,' he said at last.

Once her throat and lips were less dry, she said, 'I too have secrets. Some of them hurt.'

She noticed that little creases appeared around his eyes when he smiled, and their blueness intensified. 'If ever you need to share your hurts, bring them to me. It might help.'

'Thank you,' she said and immediately fell into a thoughtful silence. She'd expected so much from living in England. Tom had punctured her imagined world and yet, at the same time, he'd offered her his friendship. Deep inside a small voice told her to value that. In time she would need it.

The size and splendour of Marstone Court finally came into view.

The house was larger and grander than anything she'd ever seen, built of honey-coloured stone extensions filtering off from either side of the original building. Steps led up to a pillared portico built to resemble the entrance to a Greek temple, each pillar joined to its neighbour by ornate railings of wrought ironwork. There were so many chimneys, and so many windows, like a deck of playing cards laid out over a table. In the centre of the roof was a glass dome that would glint like crystal in sunlight.

Blanche caught her breath. 'I can't go in. I can't possibly go in.'

'Don't be afraid,' he said.

Her eyes flashed. 'I'm not,' she snapped, and wished she wasn't.

Tom helped her down before pulling a brass handle to one side of the door. Somewhere deep within the house, a bell rang.

A black servant wearing a white wig and the most splendid livery she'd ever seen in her life opened the door.

Tom laid her trunk before the footman's buckled shoes. 'Here you are, Duncan. It's all yours now.' With that, he turned to go.

Acknowledging Blanche with the most disdainful of looks, Duncan's nostrils flared like a fiery horse. 'Begging your pardon, Captain Strong, but servants are supposed to go round to the rear entrance.'

Tom turned back. He'd never liked Duncan and was in no doubt that it showed in his face. 'Inconvenient,' he said.

Blanche caught the note of warning in his voice.

The footman bristled, hairs on his upper lip seeming to stand proud as he said, 'May I also point out that it is not my job to handle luggage? I will instruct a porter.'

Tom re-entered, walking slowly, purposefully, as if he were measuring his paces, until there were only inches between them. His voice was little above a rumble. 'Don't tempt me, Duncan. I dislike you as much as you dislike me.'

Blanche almost wanted to cheer with delight when she saw the fierceness in Tom's eyes and saw the footman's eyes flicker with fear. 'I'll get it done, Captain Strong.' His voice was laced with defiance.

'I'll do it myself, Duncan,' Tom said. Pushing the footman aside, he lifted the chest that had once belonged to her grandfather.

'Follow me, Miss Bianca,' he called over his shoulder.

Blanche followed him up a grand staircase that swept up in marble splendour to the first floor. Above her the staircase spiralled out of view up into the glass dome, the sky lending its natural light.

The footman lingered in the hall below them looking perplexed. 'The back staircase is for servants,' he shouted up at them.

'I'm not a servant,' Tom shouted back.

Wider stairs became ever more narrow as they climbed higher. At last they were in a brown painted corridor, doors on either side.

Tom stopped occasionally, seemingly trying to work out which door was the right one. At last he came to a standstill.

'This is it,' he said at last.

Blanche sensed hesitation. It seemed strange in such a confident man. 'You don't seem very sure.'

Yes, he was hesitant, but had no intention of telling her the reason why. Soot, debris, and the body had all been removed from the room – but not from his mind.

'This is where the chimney divides.' He took a firm grip of the brass knob and flung the door open in one sweeping gesture. 'The chimney was swept just for you. I believe you have this floor of the house to yourself.'

He set her sea chest beside the bed and stood, feeling sorry for her and wondering if there was any way he could make things better.

Blanche ran her fingers over the patchwork bedspread and glanced down on to the unlit coals of the reinstalled fire grate.

Tom cleared his throat. 'Did you have better than this is Barbados?'

'It was painted white, and had polished floorboards and blue shutters opening out on to a veranda.' Her voice was melodic, her accent a mix of West Indian and West Country, picked up from the English overseers on the Rivermead Plantation.

She looked out over the slop yard and the stables beyond. 'I had a view of the Caribbean,' she said wistfully.

She didn't need to tell him how disappointed she was. He could see it in her eyes.

'I'll pick you flowers from the garden,' he said cheerfully. 'That should brighten it up.'

A bemused smile twitched her lips. 'At this time of year?'

He smiled too. 'Perhaps not. But at least you have food,' he said, indicating the bread, cheese, two apples and a pitcher of water on top of the chest of drawers.

'Yes.' She didn't sound very impressed.

'I think it best you get out of those wet things.' he said, indicating the soggy dress that dragged on her frame. 'Perhaps if you made yourself comfortable...'

Blanche didn't reply. She was numb with cold, tired and disappointed, though she blamed herself for the latter. How foolish she'd been to think that the family was going to adopt her, to think that Nelson would be waiting for her, to think that she was ever likely to rise much above her mother's station in life.

She sensed rather than heard Tom taking his leave of her.

'Remember what I told you,' he said, pausing by the door, his face full of concern and his tone sincere. 'If you ever need anyone to share your concerns...'

'She nodded, her mouth tightly shut and her eyes big and moist.

Tom closed the door behind him, but lingered, assuming she'd burst into tears. He heard nothing but a big sigh. Blanche Bianca, he reasoned, was made of sterner stuff. Too proud to display her despair, she would keep it all inside, but at some time it was bound to burst out.

–

In his house next to the refinery, passed to him by his father, Conrad Heinkel oversaw his children's bedtime prayers, a habit he'd inherited from his wife Lottie who'd died in childbirth some years earlier.

After the usual prayers, Lisel, his daughter, added, 'And bless our move to the new house with the garden on Redcliffe Parade, and if you can find us a new mother, God, make her just like the pretty lady who helped us with our kites. Amen.'

'Amen,' echoed her brother.

'Amen,' whispered Conrad from his place by the door.

## Chapter Twelve

Too tired even to eat the bread and cheese, Blanche collapsed on the bed, still fully dressed and wet through. Where was Nelson? She wondered. Why wasn't he here to greet her?

When she slept she dreamed Nelson was showing her St Mary Redcliffe church, the Old Vic theatre, the wide lawns of Queen Square and the grandeur of the Avon Gorge; the places he'd talked to her about. She woke up shivering.

'Just dreams,' she murmured, tears of anger stinging her eyes. 'Dreams don't count.'

In a parody of her mother's voice, she added, 'Let's get you out of these wet clothes, Blanche, my girl.'

Bonnet, cape and shawl, all heavy with wetness, were removed and slumped to the floor. Damp at the sleeves and sodden around the hem, her dress clung to her body. Shivering, she dragged a blanket off the bed and wrapped it around herself, its woollen roughness scratching her skin.

A church clock struck twelve. It was already noon! She'd slept for more than two hours and now she was hungry.

As she ate the bread and cheese and sipped some water, she studied her surroundings – and wished she were back at home in Barbados.

The room nestled under the eaves and had a small window with bars across it. Walls of duck-egg blue reflected the cold north light that eased through the window, making the plain room seem even colder. Pegs for hanging her clothes lined the walls at chin height. There was a bed, one chair plus a large chest of drawers on which sat a mirror that swung in its frame. A smaller chest stood beside it on twig-thin legs. When she tried to open the top drawer, a lid sprang open to reveal a porcelain basin complete with stopper and soap. Opening the cupboard lower down revealed a matching jug. A simple washstand, beautifully hidden. She dipped her hand into the jug. The water was cool and the Turkish towel that hung from a hook on the cabinet's side was thin and had taken on the coldness of the room.

'Dear God,' she exclaimed, took a deep breath and closed her eyes. Oh, to be back in Barbados where the sun was warm and washing with cold water was a delight rather than an ordeal.

She shivered again. It was the warmest dress she owned and the soft wool clung stubbornly to her limbs as she tried to peel it off. When her bodice was hanging around her waist and her breasts were bare, someone knocked at the door.

'Who's there?'

'My name's Edith. My room's along the end of the landing next to the attic stairs.' The voice was loud, like that of a market woman selling live chickens or fresh fish. 'I thought you might need some help in unpacking.'

The door flew open and Edith swept in, her bright smile freezing and her face reddening at the sight of Blanche bare-breasted, her cotton chemise barely reaching to her knees.

'Oh! Sorry!'

Cold air concerned Blanche more so than modesty. 'Well, don't just stand there! Come in and close the door. It's cold enough in here as it is and if I don't get out of these damp things, I'll be stone dead cold!'

Edith pushed the door behind her and stood looking awkward. She had a round face, pink cheeks that looked like splashed paint and big breasts that strained against the bib of her apron. Blanche guessed Edith liked her food. Her eyes strayed to the contents of the open chest.

'Looks like you got lovely things.' She peered closer and trailed her fingers over the soft silks, the muslins, the pretty bonnets and soft kid gloves, the shell-studded jewellery box and finally the silver stopper of the blue scent bottle, which she pulled out and held up to the light.

'I've seen one like this before,' she said dreamily.

Blanche stopped straightening her dress. 'Where?'

Edith shrugged. 'Don't know for sure... but... oh, yes. I was sent to collect it from a shop near John Street. I was given a letter to go with it and was then told to take it to one of the ships going to the Sugar Islands.'

'A letter?'

'Yes.'

Suddenly Blanche felt as though she were melting. 'Who was the letter from?'

'The master writing to his brother, I expect. Mr Otis runs the plantation. Did you know him?'

For a moment it was difficult to answer. 'Everyone on the island knows him. He's a very important man.'

Edith nodded as though she did and didn't understand.

'It's very precious,' she said, took it from Edith and placed it back in the chest beneath the jewellery box, her hand shaking slightly.

Edith watched with interest as Blanche chose a pale blue linen dress to wear. Heavier than muslin, she'd always thought it ugly, but it might keep her warm. 'Well,' she said as she shrugged her arms into her sleeves and turned her back towards Edith, 'are you going to help me?'

Edith blinked herself into sudden alertness. 'Sorry. I was just thinkin' I ain't ever seen anyone as dark-skinned as you – only they blokes that comes over from America looking for work and begging on the streets. Runaway slaves, they is, oh and some of the seamen.' She giggled before returning to her constant stream of words. 'But then not naked! I ain't seen any of them naked, or even almost naked, no matter what colour their skins. My, my! Just look! You're covered in goose pimples. You must be freezing. Why ain't you lit the fire? Ain't you got no tinder box?'

Blanche made a big thing of closing her sea chest. 'I don't think so.' The truth was, she'd never used one and wasn't too sure what it looked like.

Edith failed to notice her unease. 'Haven't you looked? If you ain't, I can go and get one, but there must be one 'ere somewhere. Here it is,' she said, retrieving a tin box from the narrow mantelpiece.

'Of course.'

'I'll get this lit in no time,' Edith said, her large rump hiding the spluttering spark from Blanche's view.

Feeling a little stupid, Blanche thought some sort of explanation was in order. The truth was the only one she had to offer. 'I'm no good at lighting fires. I've never had to do it.'

'Lucky you! What sort of 'ouse did you come from then?'

'We had servants,' said Blanche.

Still on her knees, Edith twisted round. 'Now we ain't gonna 'ave tall stories, are we? We gets enough of them from Captain Tom.' Faced with

Edith's scepticism, Blanche counselled herself to be careful in what she said. 'My uncle and my aunt acted as servants. They did lots of things. And then there was the heat and my mother was ill...'

'Oh, the poor woman!' Edith assumed that Viola had been an invalid and the relatives had rallied round. The bright smile returned and she slapped her hips.

'Fancy not being able to light a fire,' she said.

Fingers of flame began licking over the coal. 'There!' Edith pronounced and got to her feet, just as Blanche was examining herself in the mirror, trying to see whether she looked out of place in the dress she'd chosen to wear. Once her hair was brushed, she'd look quite respectable. Suddenly she felt Edith's eyes on her.

'Is something wrong?'

Edith hesitated and bit her lower lip. 'Well. A few things...'

'Go on.'

'I don't want you to think I'm being rude, but... it's your clothes.'

'What's the matter with my clothes?'

Edith blushed and slammed her eyes. 'You forgot your pantalets. You're not wearing any.'

Blanche stared at her uncomprehending. 'Pantalets?'

Edith grinned, turned pink, lifted her gathered skirt, overcome by embarrassment, dropped it, and then lifted it again. 'Like these. I'd catch me death without 'em. Just imagine, one gust of wind blowing up off the river, me skirt up over me head, and me ass... ets on full view!'

Blanche *could* imagine and, for what seemed the first time since her arrival she smiled, then burst out laughing.

Edith cleared her throat and nodded to where the dress lay flat across Blanche's stomach and clung to her limbs. 'There's paintings in the house with women dressed like that, but they don't wear such dresses now. Can see why too. It's showing all you got. Enough to give the Missus apoplexy! As for the men... well! I mean, look at that neckline, lean forward and one of your boobies is likely to escape.'

Blanche looked at Edith's dress, then at her own. 'I'll have to do something. I can't possibly be seen looking like this.'

Using both hands to lift the heavy lid, she re-opened her sea chest, and looked at the pinks, mauves, pale lemons and greens. 'I left Barbados feeling like a queen, arid I come here feeling like…' She couldn't think of the right word, opposite to queen.

'They don't look very warm,' observed Edith, her rough fingers running over the soft fabrics. 'And you do know them that's way above stairs – nurses, governesses and suchlike – have got to provide their own frocks. Has to be modest, mind you. Course,' she said, smoothing her hands down over the bulging bodice of her grey, full-skirted dress, 'different for us ordinary servants. Not likely to 'ave a decent frock hanging in a cupboard.' She burst out laughing. 'Not likely to 'ave a cupboard either, come to that.'

Blanche eyed the mass of lightweight muslins, silks and lace. She sighed resignedly. 'The green wool and the grey-and-black striped are passable if I wear a lace dress or a muslin underneath and an apron on top. It's not ideal, but will do for now, at least until I can get them altered. But for now, I'll have to wear two dresses at a time.'

'Aprons are provided. I've already made them up for you. Three of white linen and one of rubber.' On seeing Blanche's perplexed expression, she went on, 'For those little wet moments when the new baby arrives.'

'I just need dresses,' moaned Blanche.

Edith bubbled. 'I'm quite a turn with a needle. Sewed all me own aprons, and darned these knickers meself,' she added, exposing her pantalets for further admiration, just in case Blanche hadn't seen enough of them the first time. 'I'll make you some underwear too. Don't know how women in this country ever managed without them.'

Blanche stripped off the blue dress, put on the fine muslin she used to wear to her mother's soirées, then put the linen dress on top of that.

'You need an apron to nip in yer waistline and hide all that naked bosom.' She spun on her heel, dragged open a drawer and got out a broad-bibbed apron. Once Blanche had tied the four-inch wide apron strings, Edith stood back to observe her handiwork. She looked pleased, until her eyes rested on Blanche's bosom. 'Too much of yer boobies showing.' Edith poked at the bare bits of Blanche's breasts. 'Now what are we going to do about them?'

'Well, I ain't sending them back,' said Blanche, her hands on her hips. 'Find me a kerchief like the one you're wearing.'

'Better than that, 'ave this one,' Edith returned, and tucked it into the bib of the apron. 'Can't be offended at that!' she exclaimed, slapping her hands together as if dusting them with flour.

'I'm almost respectable,' said Blanche. 'Almost!' She fussed with her hair, trying to get the mass of dark curls back into some sort of order. During the Atlantic crossing, the style had become less and less elaborate as time went on, the cluster of side curls becoming a tangle due to the salty air and the brisk winds. Fastening her hair into a bulky bun with pins was about all she had been able to do and she had promised herself she'd do better once she was on dry land again. But for now the bun would have to suffice.

At last it was tidy, and she examined the result.

Edith said, 'Servants are expected to keep things plain and simple.'

'I am,' Blanche said.

'Plain?' exclaimed Edith. 'Your skin's the colour of caramel. Can see your eyes now. Funny colour, ain't they? Strange 'aving grey eyes with your skin colour. That's funny too,' she added, deftly touching the dark mole that sat below Blanche's right eye. 'Is it real?'

'Try picking it off and I'll scream,' said Blanche, brushing Edith's hand away just in case she was tempted to try it.

Although tired, Blanche found the energy to get to her feet and started to put her things away. Edith offered to help, buzzing around, chattering like a parrot as she plucked mittens from among the dresses, popped them into a drawer along with lace-edged handkerchiefs, white silk stockings, ribbons, silk shawls and bags of scented lavender. She placed the jewellery box and the scent bottle on top of the chest of drawers.

Edith was just about to hang her parasol on to a hook, when Blanche pounced on it. 'I'll take that.' She cuddled it to her breast.

Edith looked at it fondly. 'Pretty, that. I had a parasol once. Me brother got it for me. Don't know where he got it, but it was black with pictures woven in silk. Ever so pretty it was. In Bristol one day, and it was gone. Somebody pinched it from off me arm, they did. Can't trust anyone these days, can ya?'

Edith spoke loudly, so it was hard to ignore what she was saying. Thoughts of Barbados and her mother drifted into Blanche's mind. She said, 'The last time I used this parasol was just before my mother died.'

'Do you miss her a lot?' asked Edith.

'Very much.'

'I miss my mum too,' said Edith wistfully.

Edith went on to tell Blanche of the mining village she used to live in. 'Deep Pit, Oldland Common,' she said. 'It was a deep mine all right, but not when the men got down there. Three foot 'igh it was. Rotten place. No wonder me dad and the men out there were so rotten. If you treat men like animals, they're going to act like 'em, ain't they?'

Blanche agreed.

'But never mind,' Edith went on. 'Me dad got killed. Best thing that ever happened. Still down that mine so far as I know. Coal collapsed and fell in on top of 'im. Saved on the funeral expenses it did.'

It seemed odd to Blanche that Edith showed no sign of grief for either parent. 'When did your mother go?' she asked.

Edith's lips slapped together as she folded a black, silver-edged shawl and stroked it before placing it in a drawer. 'She went from Oldland Common just after me father died. Got a place in the Pithay, in the centre of the city, along with me brothers and a cousin. Ain't nothing special, but it's home. I'll take you to see them some time,' said Edith. 'But let's visit Cook first fer some grub while you get yerself acquainted with the household, the servants that is, you won't be meeting the family, of course. The housekeeper will look you over, see if you suit, whether you wash behind yer ears, go to church on Sunday and know how to speak to yer betters like what I do. They're all looking forward to meeting you. Funny, but we all thought you'd be the same colour as Duncan and David, the footmen.'

Blanche recalled the footman who'd opened the front door. He'd towered above her, intimidating, disdainful, and as different to her as it was likely to be.

—

Duncan was in a foul mood. He'd come back from his journey into Bristol, soaking wet and still seething from Josiah Benson's treatment of him. The man owned an estate sandwiched between the village of Horfield and Almondsbury, yet did most of his business from Clifton Gentleman's Club, which was where Duncan had gone with the message. In Duncan's opinion, Josiah Benson was as far from being a gentleman as it was possible to be.

At the club, he'd been made to wait in the vestibule while a manservant had taken Horatia's message in on a silver tray. Waiting outside was expected. After Duncan had waited a few minutes, he heard men laughing. They'd been drinking. Laughter following heavy drinking was different and more frequent than when men were sober.

Elegantly dressed in tight-fitting trousers and a silk-lined frock coat, Benson came out accompanied by two companions. All were smiling, smoking cigars and their faces were red as the port they'd likely been drinking.

Duncan had cringed and gritted his teeth as Benson looked him up and down. He'd guessed what was coming. Benson had said it all before, mostly after too much port.

Just as he'd expected, Benson turned to his companions. 'So, what do you think? How much do you reckon he'd have fetched in the old days?'

The other men laughed. One of them, a white-whiskered man in a grey suit, had walked around him as if he were a prize steer. 'That tall? That handsome? Two hundred of any man's money.' Then he'd sneered, 'Three hundred of a woman's.'

They'd laughed. Benson had added, 'There are two of these in the Strong household.'

The white-whiskered man raised his eyebrows. 'Both serving Miss Horatia?'

Duncan had wanted to grab hold of the whiskers, drag the man forward and slam his forehead against his, hear it crack, see him slide unconscious, even dead, to the ground.

Benson threw the man a warning look. 'Have a care, Claude Smythe. I intend making that lady my wife.'

The man apologized.

Benson headed for a desk close to the door, dipped a nib in the inkwell and scribbled on a piece of paper.

He lowered his voice as he said, 'I want you to tell Trout to keep a closer eye on Captain Strong. I want to know who he meets and where he goes. Then take this note to your mistress.'

He pressed the note into Duncan's hand. Duncan slipped it into the small leather pouch that hung from his belt.

Josiah Benson looked smug. Emmanuel had impressed on him it would be a good idea to have Tom followed. Logically, he thought it a waste of time, but Emmanuel had offered to split the costs so long as he didn't tell Horatia he had a hand in things.

'Let her think it's all to do with this railway and steamship business,' he'd said to Josiah, who'd almost dropped to his knees when Emmanuel slapped him heartily around the shoulders. 'In no time at all, my dear boy, she'll be yours. Mark my words.'

He'd half suspected that Emmanuel had ulterior motives, but dismissed them. All the man cared about was seeing his daughter well wed. It was understandable.

Duncan hated having to see Trout, who frequented one of the most stinking, quayside taverns in the city. He also hated being treated as if he were still a slave but, most of all, he hated hearing his mistress insulted. Duncan was extremely loyal to Miss Horatia, in fact, he loved her and fancied she felt the same, though nothing could ever be mentioned, of course. Both colour and class were against them, so he was content to desire from afar.

Horatia had snatched the note swiftly from the tray.

'Go,' she ordered as she ripped open the note.

Wounded by her sharpness, he headed below stairs. He couldn't take his anger out on his mistress, so someone had to suffer.

There was no one in the servant's hall when he entered. As usual, everyone was gathered in the warm kitchen around the cook's big pine table, sipping their afternoon tea. All eyes turned expectantly in his direction, and their conversation ceased.

'Have you seen the new nurse?' Cook asked Duncan, a trickle of tea seeping from the corner of her mouth.

'She's very pretty,' said one of the parlour maids, a dark-haired girl with hazel eyes called Kitty Ray.

'Is that right?' Cook eyed Duncan for confirmation.

'Yes,' he said in a clipped manner. 'I suppose she is.'

Cook poured him tea and he dragged out a chair.

'She's going to look more than pretty beside Edith,' laughed Kitty. 'Under nurses don't come much plainer than her.'

Everyone laughed, except Duncan. Tom's treatment of him still smarted, and all on account of the new nurse.

Cups danced in saucers as he brought his fist down hard on the table. 'This new nurse has airs and graces far above her station. I'll not have it in this house.'

'All nurses are like that,' said Cook with an injured expression.

'This one is more so,' Duncan said, his eyes travelling slowly over everyone gathered around the table, his voice sliding like velvet over his vowels. 'Her name is Blanche Bianca, but the name Mrs Brown would be more convenient for the master and mistress to remember, and for us too. Is that clear?'

Parlour maids, kitchen maids, valet, butler and footmen, all exchanged glances. Duncan's presence was as big as his body. He eyed each of them in an imperious way that left them in no doubt that the new nurse would indeed be called Mrs Brown.

'And don't make her too welcome,' he added. 'She's not likely to be staying any longer than her predecessors.'

## Chapter Thirteen

The warm air and delicious smells of baked bread, caramel pudding and a juicy haunch of venison on a Dutch spit, met Blanche and Edith as they entered the kitchen.

Conversation ceased as hostile eyes turned in her direction.

'This is Blanche,' trilled Edith. 'She's from Barbados.'

No one said a word. Then Cook sniffed and wiped her nose on her sleeve. 'Well, that ain't what I 'eard. I 'eard 'er name's Mrs Brown.'

'Her name is Mrs Brown,' said Duncan and sipped his tea. Without his wig, his hair was cropped, like the backside of a sheep just after shearing.

'That's what I thought,' said Cook, fetching Blanche a sidelong look of outright contempt. 'She looks brown so the name suits.'

Although still tired, their animosity revived her spirits.

'My name is Blanche Bianca, not Brown.'

She said it loudly, aiming it like a burst of cannon at the cook's turned back.

A few faces turned in her direction. The more placid stared down at the table, doing their best to appear dumb, blind and deaf.

Blanche glared at Duncan. 'And if I am brown enough to be called Brown, why aren't you called Black instead of Duncan?'

No one said a thing, though Edith tried. 'Come on, you lot! You told me earlier that you wanted to meet her. What's the matter with you all?'

Blanche felt like cheering. Edith was gutsy, quite capable of standing up to anyone.

The triumphal moment was short-lived. Duncan turned accusing eyes on Edith. 'How is the dog trade going, Edith? Lucrative still, no doubt. It would be very bad for Lady Verity to find out about it.'

Edith suddenly seemed smaller.

'To save you waiting to eat with the children, you can eat here,' said Cook to Edith, setting a white dish on to the table.

Blanche heard her stomach rumble. She'd had nothing to eat save the bread and cheese since the ship had docked around eight-thirty that morning.

Hungry too, Edith started to make her way to her place on the bench. 'What about—?'

Cook pressed a large meaty hand on to Edith's shoulder. 'Never mind Brown. I'll deal with her.'

'Bianca!' Blanche snapped. 'Blanche Bianca. I'm not Brown.'

Cook's eyes were pale as frogspawn. 'Well, you ain't none too white, are you?' A controlled snigger ran around the table, as she ladled the good-smelling broth into a white china bowl. 'You can have yours 'ere,' she said, dumping the bowl down hard on to the end of a long pine side table. Some of the broth slopped on to the surface, which was stained with the blood of six pheasants, whose innards and dissected heads were no more than two feet from her food. 'Here's yer spoon.'

Cook wiped the spoon with her apron before setting it down next to the bowl. 'And here's some bread,' she added, cutting a thick slice from the loaf that sat on the main table then throwing it at the side table, its edge catching some of the black blood that lay in puddles beside the dead birds.

Blanche picked up the piece of bread and threw it back, hard. 'I've not come here to eat with servants!' It hit Cook in the eye with a resounding thwack.

'Wahhh!' wailed the cook, wiping at the flecked blood with her fingers. 'How dare you do this to me! I'm the cook, and you're just the daughter of a darkie b—'

Blanche was across the room, one fine, long finger pointing like the muzzle of a pistol between the cook's eyes. 'Don't you dare,' Blanche snarled.

'You're going back on that boat, girl,' Duncan shouted, reached to grab her, but almost jumped out of his skin as a heavy hand crushed his shoulder.

'I didn't know the circus had come to town,' said Tom. Duncan was flung aside.

Cook, maids and footmen subsided into chairs and subdued smiles as the captain entered, an ebony pipe clenched in the corner of his mouth. Even the cook patted her hair and pinched some colour into her cheeks. He ignored them all and looked straight at Blanche and smiled.

'My dear Miss Bianca, are the staff neglecting you?' He swiftly took in the separate bowl setting and the blood-soaked table. 'You must be starving,' he said.

'Famished.'

A little ash from his pipe freckled the velvet lapels of his jacket and the curling pattern of his brocade waistcoat as he looked around the room.

Blanche was now as smitten with him as everyone else, her mouth hanging slightly open and her eyes wide with surprise.

He looked smarter, more of a gentleman than that morning, but still vital, confident in his own strength and power.

'And where is Monsieur le Chef? Where is Monsieur Leon and Monsieur Pierre?' he asked, bending slightly to sniff the roasting venison.

'It's their day off, Captain,' ventured the cook as she struggled to her feet, her progress hampered by the full folds of her gathered skirt.

'Then it's down to you to provide us with our repast, Cook. Now fetch fresh bread and soup for both of us. We'll dine in the servants' hall, seeing as none of you are using it. Oh, and slice up some ham, pickles and tomatoes. And if you've got some cinnamon cake, well, you know it's my favourite.' He beamed at her broadly, as though, thought Blanche, he were the bridegroom and the cook his blushing bride.

Cook's animosity disappeared. She was all smiles and curtsying as she bobbed between the soup kettle and the breadboard.

Tom glanced swiftly, yet purposefully at Duncan. 'And bring wine.'

The footman winced under Tom's gaze, but struggled swiftly to his feet.

'And perhaps tea for Miss Bianca,' Tom added. 'Come with me,' he said to her, taking hold of her hand.

Dumbstruck, Blanche allowed herself to be led. Before Tom had entered the kitchen, it had seemed full of backbiting, intimidation and spitefulness. Now the sun's rays hit the copper pans and the dull yellow of the walls and high ceiling where tea towels and aprons hung from wooden stretchers. His palm was warm, his fingers gentle though callused with the scars of a dozen voyages.

'Keep your head high,' he murmured as he led her out of the kitchen and along the stone passageway to the servant's hall.

'I intend to,' she replied, her heart fluttering with mixed feelings, a surge of emotion that for once did not include Nelson. Tom was like a breath of fresh air, hurricane even, and she wasn't sure whether she should stand firm against his onslaught or bend with the breeze.

There were comfortable chairs around the walls of the servants' hall, and a dining table and chairs in the middle. Light from arched windows set high in the wall threw patches of sunlight on to the red-brick floor.

'It's stopped raining,' said Blanche.

Tom laughed. 'It does sometimes.'

He pulled out a chair for her. Blanche, her legs aching and her stomach empty, sat down. He sat across from her, his hands spread flat on the table and looked at her from below dark eyebrows. 'They appear to be giving you a hard time already.'

'I understand it's something that comes with the position of nurse; not quite belonging to below stairs or above, but somewhere in the middle, trusted by no one.'

He studied his hands, as if he were searching for something in his scratched knuckles. He decided, as he had on many occasions, that truth was the best course of action.

'It's not your only problem, is it? The whole household knows about your mother being of certain parentage and kept by Uncle Otis. It was bound to come out.'

'It's a man's world. A woman has to survive as best she can,' said Blanche, aching to add that Otis was her father, but not daring to do so.

'I understand your grandfather was a sea captain.'

She nodded and looked into his eyes. 'I'm not sure who my father was.'

Tom grinned. 'Neither am I.'

Kitty Ray the parlour maid came along with a silver tray of food and tea. Duncan followed, two claret glasses in one hand, a dust-covered wine bottle in the other.

Tom and Blanche waited until both servants had withdrawn before continuing their conversation. Tom poured wine. Blanche began on the soup after tearing the bread into four equal pieces. After a few spoonfuls, her stomach ceased rumbling.

'Why are you being kind to me?' she asked him suddenly.

He stared at her then smiled as if a funny thought had occurred to him. 'I don't know. I just feel perhaps...' He paused as he thought it through, swallowed a spoonful of soup and said finally, 'I should be kind to you because you deserve it.'

Blanche thought of the scent bottle that had arrived in Barbados every year.

'Did you love your mother?'

He seemed taken by surprise at first, but collected himself. 'My mother was a whore, and I lived my life in the dark alleys around the docks. I was starving when the Reverend Strong found me.'

'You were very lucky.'

He put down his soup spoon and took a big gulp of the claret, then wiped his mouth on the sleeve of his coat.

'And Jasper, his real son, was very unlucky,' he said. 'I used to think what would happen if Jeb's true son reappeared, that he was never drowned, but had been picked up by a fishing boat and taken on as a cabin boy? What would Jeb do then? And yes, I did love my mother. No matter what she was, I still loved her.'

He said it so endearingly, so sincerely, that she paused in moving the spoon closer to her mouth and looked into his face. His eyes were very blue, his gaze very intense. She could well understand why the housemaids, and even the cook, smartened themselves up when he appeared.

'And your mother? Did you love her?'

Blanche nodded. 'It didn't matter that she wasn't married, or that I didn't know my father. She was my mother.'

Tom put down his spoon and covered her hand with his. 'We have a lot in common.'

'We're both eating soup,' she said with a smile.

'No,' he said, shaking his head and smiling in a way that was both sad and ironic. 'We were both born outside the Strong family to – let's say – women of independent spirit, but have been drawn in like herring caught in a net. Who knows whether either of us will ever escape?'

–

'I'll take that, Rosa,' said Cook to one of the kitchen maids as she took a tea tray out of her hand. 'Mr Nelson wants to see me.'

Rosa looked surprised, but Cook ignored her.

Mr Nelson, the master's son, was waiting when she entered his room.

She said, 'Your tea, sir,' and dropped a little curtsy. 'If there's anything else I can do for you, sir...?'

'Yes, there is,' said Nelson, and gave her a brown paper package tied up with string. 'This is the secret ingredient for my biscuits, Cook. The substance is medicinal and is to be included when you bake me some biscuits. Almond ones, I think. But please note that these biscuits are for me and me alone. Is that clear?'

He said it in the way his father said things, as if a disobeyed order could lead to a spell in prison.

'Oh yes, sir!' exclaimed Cook as though he'd spoken with the utmost courtesy, her rosy cheeks swelling with the strength of her smile.

It always amazed Nelson what the servants put up with. He'd yet to see one stand their ground; certainly not Cook, he decided. She lived for the Strong family and Marstone Court, and would die in service here.

'They'll be baked this afternoon and cool by this evening. If that's to your liking?'

He nodded as imperiously as he knew how. 'Very good. And remember. No one is to know about these biscuits, and no one is to touch a crumb except me. Do I have your promise, Cook?'

'You do, sir,' she said and dropped another grateful curtsy.

After she'd left, Nelson breathed a sigh of relief. He was sweating and had called in on the family doctor earlier that day, explained his symptoms and been given a good look over by the old man.

'It could be drink,' said the doctor into Nelson's open mouth.

'I drink less than my father,' Nelson snapped. He tensed as the doctor pulled down the rim of each eye in turn.

'You are taking something to cause this,' said the doctor as he peered up Nelson's nostrils.

Nelson shrugged. 'I take nothing except...' He paused, unwilling to think that the dragon powder he'd been introduced to by the little Chinese girl, and the odd trickle of Uncle Jeb's medicine, was worse than rum or brandy. 'A little laudanum and suchlike.'

The doctor nodded sagely. 'Up until a few months ago, I would have said this was of no consequence. But some of my profession are now saying that it is worse to take opiates than it is to drink brandy. I suggest you desist and see how you get on.'

Nelson felt his heart palpitate at the dire words. 'What do I do when I feel tired, when I lack energy for... certain tasks?' He was thinking of women, but found he could not mention such intimacies.

The doctor eyed him from over the top of his wire-framed spectacles. 'Take a spoonful of sugar, in fact, take two.' He chuckled at the thought of it. 'Less expensive than opiates, especially for you, my dear fellow.'

'And if I deign not to follow your advice?'

The doctor scratched his head, his fine eyebrows meeting the many wrinkles of his freckled forehead.

'Personality can change, health can be damaged – this is what is being said.' He waved his hands. 'Of course, it may not be so, but perhaps you should try some alternatives. I have something that may help.'

He opened a double-fronted cabinet to reveal bottles, jars, boxes and potions of all description and colour. He handed over what looked like a plug of tobacco.

Nelson eyed it suspiciously. 'Do I smoke it?'

'Certainly not,' said the doctor. 'Mix it with sugar – plenty of sugar. Bake it in a cake, if you like. I'm sure you'll find it enjoyable.'

Later that night, Nelson stole along to Jeb's room, regretting that he'd taken the old man's laudanum.

'Please forgive me,' he said looking down on his uncle's sleeping form.

Quietly, so as not to be disturbed, he replaced what he'd taken. As silently as he came, he left. He felt pleased with himself that he'd so easily given up the practice introduced to him by the exotic Lucy Lee. He also felt excited. Blanche Bianca had arrived from Barbados. He hadn't come across her yet, but he'd seek her out as soon as he could, though he had to be careful. This was England, not Barbados, and she was only a servant.

—

The next day she was to meet the mistress of Marstone Court, Lady Verity Strong, and afterwards the children who frequented the floor next down from hers.

It was David, Duncan's twin, who collected her from her room and took her to the opulent surroundings where the family lived. There were carpets, curtains, portraits and pastoral scenes the size of houses, plasterwork ceilings, the scrolls and sweeps of flowers and fruit gilded with real gold, as if they were really growing in exceptionally strong sunlight. Statues of Greek gods and heroes looked blindly across wide passageways at lacquered Chinese cabinets inlaid with mother-of-pearl and smelling of sandalwood. Crystal chandeliers holding hundreds of candles hung overhead. At night they must look like a firmament of stars, thought Blanche.

Tables were fashioned in the Baroque style, heavy and oozing with gilt leaves and voluptuous legs, the tops fashioned from the best Italian marble. Sconces holding six candles or more were set in the wall between each window and in front of vast mirrors fashioned in the Venetian style with etched edges of coloured glass.

'There are more mirrors than paintings,' Blanche whispered in amazement.

'Lady Verity likes mirrors,' David whispered back. 'She thinks family portraits are old-fashioned.'

Hands resting softly on her very round stomach, Lady Verity Strong was sitting alone in front of a lace-curtained window. Encased in Turkish slippers with turned-up toes, her feet rested on a footstool. Prince Charles, her adored brown and white spaniel, was curled up in what remained of her lap.

Round-faced and plump, she had once been pretty, though the shape and pinkness of her mean little mouth gave her a petulant look; attractive on a young woman, but less so on a matronly mother of four with a fifth on the way.

She wore a white lace cap that sat like a handkerchief on her head, fronds of lace trailing down with her curls at either side of her face. Slowly she turned to face Blanche, her eyebrows raising slightly as though surprised at what she saw.

'You're taller than I expected,' she said, running her eyes over the unfashionable dress, improved by Edith's helpful additions of calico petticoats and stiffly starched apron. 'I expected someone darker.'

At the sound of his mistress's voice, the little dog awoke and jumped down from her lap and snuffled around the hem of Blanche's dress. Blanche gritted her teeth.

'Come here, Prince Charles! Come here!'

The dog ignored her and continued its sniffing.

Lady Verity snorted with indignation, but chose to snap at Blanche rather than at the dog.

'You will look after the children. You will assist the monthly nurse, who will deal with the baby during its first few weeks. You will officiate at their meals, take them for walks, have some part in their education, mend their clothes and make clothes when necessary. Edith, the under nurse will help you. She will take you to meet them after they've finished their posture hour.'

Blanche didn't know what a monthly nurse was and neither did she understand what posture hour meant, but she wasn't going to betray her ignorance. She'd rely on Edith to tell her. Besides, she had the distinct impression that Lady Verity didn't want her here. Best not to antagonize lest she get sent back to Barbados, she decided.

Lady Verity took a deep breath and tried to hold her head high, a difficult task on a woman with three chins. 'Your mother was Negro. Is that right?'

The statement was meant to sting, and it did.

*You might be called Blanche, but you ain't properly white*, Betsy had said.

If Verity had turned round, she would have seen Blanche's blazing eyes. As it was, Blanche spoke as though each word was ground from her teeth. 'Her father, my grandfather, was from Bristol. He was a sea captain.'

'And your mother had no husband?'

Blanche detected a slight tremble in her voice, a sudden wavering when people are suppressing a sob of despair or wish to anger someone.

It was almost on her tongue to proclaim that Otis Strong was suspected, but she kept her promise to say nothing. 'That's right.'

'Ah! No matter. You are only a servant. I take it you can read and write?'

'Yes. I also speak some French and I've been taught to paint and draw.'

Lady Verity's eyebrows shot up. 'Really? Well, I don't know that I approve of servants of your ancestry and situation being educated at all. But never mind. Mrs Grainger, the children's governess, might find you of some use. I see no need to introduce you to the rest of the family. You're not important enough for that.

'Prince Charles,' she called as she waved her away.

The dog ignored her, sat in front of Blanche and held up his front paws, obviously begging for a titbit judging by his enthusiasm and the roundness of his belly.

Blanche knelt down and tickled the delicate little chin. The dog panted, its tongue long and pink, and its eyes big as saucers. 'Hello, beautiful,' she said, and the dog rolled over.

'Prince Charles!' Verity shouted, her face red with anger.

The dog looked from Blanche to his mistress and back to Blanche again.

Lady Verity half rose from her chair, almost as if she were about to give chase, which of course was impossible. 'Are you still here?' she shouted.

Blanche headed for the door. The dog followed.

'*Prince Charles!*' Verity shouted again.

Influenced by the anger in her voice, the dog threw Blanche one last soulful look before pattering towards his mistress and the window. Just before he got there, he lifted his leg and peed on the leg of a chair.

Without curtsying, without expressing the slightest word of subservience, Blanche retreated and closed the door behind her.

Edith was waiting for her outside. 'I'm to take you to meet the children.'

'So I understand.'

How d'you get on?' she asked, her face pink with enthusiasm.

'The dog was friendly. Can't say the same for the bitch though,' said Blanche.

Edith clapped her hands over her mouth and shook with laughter. She was still laughing as they climbed the stairs to the nursery floor.

During a gap in Edith's giggles, Blanche asked her what a monthly nurse was.

'She comes in the month after the baby's born. Does everything that's needed while the mother rests in bed. My gawd, not a bit like my mother. She 'ad thirteen babies altogether. They didn't all last, mind you, but she did make 'em and birth 'em. Sometimes I wonders whether rich folks ever really do either of it. I swears to God, they'd get someone else to do that for 'em if they could.'

Just before they entered the nursery, Blanche remembered something else she'd wanted to ask. 'What did Lady Strong mean by a posture hour?'

Edith looked at her meaningfully, her hand on the door handle. 'You're about to find out,' she said with a grimace, and swung the door open.

Little effort had been made to make the room a cheery place for children. Sunlight glared through an un-shaded window and into her eyes. For a few seconds the rest of the room seemed in darkness. A step further and out of the sunlight, she finally focused on a scene she would take to her grave. Four children were sitting still and upright on straight-backed chairs. The youngest one, no more than three or four years old, was crying piteously. The next one up in years was sitting stony-faced and still, the only sign of movement his quivering bottom lip. All four heads bobbed in her direction as she entered. The older children looked more stoical though the girl she judged to be the eldest had a defiant look about her. She looked directly into Blanche's face and asked, 'Are you the new nurse?'

Unable to find her voice, Blanche nodded.

'You're not very black,' one of the boys exclaimed.

'Not very black at all,' said the eldest boy with obvious disappointment.

The girl looked to Edith. 'I think our posture hour is up, Clements.' She jerked her chin at the youngest child whose tears had combined with a runny nose and made a mess of his face. 'You'd better un-strap George first before he starts screaming.'

'You do Arthur,' said Edith to Blanche, jerking her head at the second smallest child as she went behind the chair of the youngest. 'I'll do George.'

Blanche went behind the second chair and saw why the children were sitting so still and so upright. As she undid the straps, she couldn't help her anger spilling over into words. 'What kind of family is this that tortures children? And I'm the colonial, the savage from the Sugar Islands. Would I do this? No! No, I would not.'

'Do you eat people?' asked the eldest boy with a hopeful expression.

'Not lately,' Blanche answered.

His face dropped. 'That's a shame.'

'But I might develop a taste for the human flesh of whoever strapped you into these things.'

'They're backboards,' said Edith, and proceeded to show and explain how they worked. 'The board is put like this so the biggest part of the board is resting against the back, then the arms are crooked behind these long pieces…' She proceeded to demonstrate how the arms were hooked over the thinner pieces. The latter were not unlike racket handles in some odd ball game although there were two, one on each side. The whole thing was strapped to the child and the wrists were attached at the front. 'It's to improve posture,' Edith said awkwardly. The expression in her eyes said it all.

'Mrs Grainger persuaded our mother it would be good for us,' said the girl, her chin jutting defiantly and a look in her eyes that Blanche had never thought to see in a child of her age.

'You can eat Miss Grainger if you like,' said the eldest boy, smiling brightly as he rubbed the feeling back into his arms. 'Though I think she'd be all gristle.'

Edith poured water from a large jug into a china bowl, dipped in a cloth and handed it to Blanche, muttering so the children wouldn't hear, 'Your first job. Get rid of that boy's snotty nose before I throw up.'

Blanche put an arm around the little boy and wiped his grubby face. 'Come on, now,' she said softly. Once she'd done that, she rubbed at the little boy's arms to get the blood flowing again. 'There! Better?' She gave him a big hug.

His smile was worth it, but she couldn't help noticing what a pale little boy he was and wondered how often he got to play in the sunshine.

'You're nice,' he said. 'Are you our new Peters?'

'She's a darkie,' said the girl. 'If you remember rightly, Mother said she thought it best to call her Mrs Black or Mrs Brown rather than Peters.'

Blanche grimaced. Duncan's suggestion no doubt.

The oldest girl eyed Blanche thoughtfully. 'Mrs Grainger told us you were black and probably a cannibal. She said you should stay in your own country. I wish *she'd* stayed in Nuneaton. It's a village, I think.' She cocked her head and frowned. 'You don't look very black.'

Blanche exchanged a glance with Edith who was suppressing an impish grin. She had to remind herself that these were only children. Perhaps she was prejudging Mrs Grainger, but so far, she didn't like the sound of her.

'My father was white. So was my grandfather on my mother's side,' she said through gritted teeth, her jaw aching with the effort of keeping her temper. 'And his mother was an actress and a friend of Mrs Siddons.'

There followed a quick intake of breath from everyone in the room. Edith nudged her arm and whispered, 'Heard all about them actresses. Lead a right life, they do. Seen gentlemen out with them round and about the Pithay were me ma lives now.'

Blanche realized immediately that actresses were not quite so respectable as her mother had led her to believe.

The boy interested in cannibals marched up to her and introduced himself in a manner she was quite unprepared for. 'My name is Rupert, and this is Arthur,' he said, indicating the second smallest boy. 'My sister's name is Caroline. Don't mind her, she's terribly bossy. George, of course, you've already met. He's still in dresses for the moment, but he'll be breeched once he stops peeing his drawers.'

Edith explained that it was quite usual for boys to wear dresses at least up until about three years old. George was taking a little longer than his brothers had done.

A floor clock, the top of which almost scratched the ceiling, chimed four times. The eldest children exchanged glances. George burst into tears, ran to Blanche's side and promptly buried his face in her dress. Blanche dropped to her knees.

'Come on, George,' Edith moaned, reaching for the hairbrush. She looked at Blanche and said softly, 'They go down to the dining room to see their parents at four o'clock every day for tea. Sometimes you're required to go down with them, but not today apparently. That task falls to Mrs Grainger. I've been told to help you set up supper in the nursery.'

Blanche prised George's head from the folds of her apron. Tearful blue eyes looked up at her and his bottom lip quivered again. 'Don't you want to see your mother and father, George?'

Caroline came over and took hold of his hand. 'He doesn't like Mrs Grainger.'

Edith clapped her hands. 'Come on, children. It's teatime. Let's get you ready before Mrs Grainger collects you.'

Blanche straightened collars and sleeves while Edith brushed the children's hair.

Mrs Grainger wore a mauve dress with a tight collar and had tight lips to match. A pince-nez swung from her neck on a silver chain and although her dress and the fullness of her skirt were reasonably restrained, she swept into the room like a flag ship heading for battle. The moment she saw Blanche, she stopped and sniffed.

'Good day to you, young woman. I am Mrs Grainger. I trust you have been informed of your duties by the housekeeper and by Lady Verity?'

Blanche had met the housekeeper that morning, a less tense meeting than that with Lady Verity.

'I have.'

'Good. Today I will take the children down to see their parents. In future it will be your duty. Come along, children.'

Blanche felt George grip her apron again and made an instant decision. 'You don't need to do that. I can take them down.'

The jaw tightened, a broad brow stiffened above hard, black eyes. 'It is not for you to decide,' she said, her mouth moving as though she were taking bites from a hard apple.

Blanche felt the children's eyes on her, recognizing her as a possible protector. She heard Edith's quick intake of breath and didn't hear her breathe out. All of them were terrified of this woman. But not me, she thought. Not me!

'As the children's nurse and their governess we have equal duty to the children.'

A slow smile crossed the wide-jawed face. 'I was here before you, young woman. I will be here when you are gone.'

Cowed and silent, the children watched round-eyed. Hidden until now by the folds of her skirt, Mrs Grainger brought up her right hand in which she held a short, thin cane. She flicked it towards the open door. 'Come along, children.'

The children trooped out of the door like a flock of young chicks, some half grown and already thinking of fleeing the nest. Caroline held tightly to her little brother's hand and threw Blanche a helpless look before she left and the door closed behind them.

'So that's Mrs Grainger,' said Blanche.

'Right ole witch, ain't she?' Edith said. She began to tidy the room.

'She enjoys being cruel,' Blanche said thoughtfully as she unfolded a tablecloth and laid it on the table. Knives and teaspoons were brought out from an ancient oak dresser that had definitely seen better days.

Edith sighed. 'Cold with it. But then the only warm woman in this house is Cook, and that's only because she toasts her backside against the fire. Mind you, Lady Verity's the mistress in name only. It's Miss Horatia who really rules the roost. Even Mrs Grainger is all smirks and smiles when that one's around. Miss Horatia is Sir Emmanuel's daughter—'

'I know,' said Blanche and paused in what she was doing as she remembered the things Nelson had said, the things they'd done together.

Edith looked surprised that she knew, but took it some other servant had told her and went on. 'The gaggle of geese you've just met are the product of the second marriage. Horatia and her brother Nelson are the children by his first wife. She died after her third child was born.'

'And Nelson,' said Blanche, her heart already beating hard at the mention of his name, 'do you see much of him?'

'Nah!' said Edith as though mention of him left a nasty taste on her tongue. 'Bit of a pansy that one. I prefer Captain Strong. He might not be a blood relation, but he's the bloke I'd most like to curl up to in a storm at sea, I can tell you!'

Tom had been kind, but it was Nelson who had written poetry for her, had captured her in oils and appeared to be the key to her happiness. She had to let Nelson know she was here. He couldn't know or he'd have come to see her already.

The sound of footsteps coming up the stairs and along the bare boards outside the room prevented anything else being said.

'Now who's that up here snooping? Not that old bag Grainger again,' said Edith.

'I hope not,' said Blanche.

'Stop grinding yer teeth,' said Edith.

'I can't help it. I feel I want to bite her.'

'It might be the ghost that lives up in the attic,' whispered Edith.

Blanche laughed. 'I don't believe you.'

'It's true, I tell you.'

The door swung open to reveal a pair of dusty, leather boots, masculine legs and a smiling Tom Strong.

'Not with feet like that,' said Blanche.

Tom filled the doorway, his hands behind his back. 'Ladies! I've come to make you an offer you can't refuse.'

Edith reddened and giggled as she attempted to hide her blushes with her hands. 'You can make me any offer you like, Captain Tom!'

Blanche hid a smile. It was obvious that Edith adored the man. She could understand why, but told herself that she was less enamoured of him. He lacked Nelson's grace and soft manner, but conceded that he was attractive. He has depth, said the small voice deep inside. Her mother's voice, she decided.

Since that morning Tom had thought long and hard about how he might get Blanche on her own again. It wasn't in his nature to bring flowers, to court her with sweet words and fine manners, like Nelson, for instance. His feelings were sincere and he was convinced she would see through his friendliness and recognize his esteem for what it really was. He'd concocted a plan.

'Hopefully,' he said, 'tomorrow will be fine. How about taking your young charges for a drive in the city? I know it's Saturday, but I need to call in at the refinery and then to the *Miriam Strong*. What do you think?'

Edith answered for both of them. 'I think the youngsters would love it. So would I, come to that. What about you, Blanche?'

Tom's intention had been that Blanche would be in sole charge of the children, but he couldn't possibly leave Edith out if she wanted to come too. He'd seen the way she looked at him. He looked at Blanche, his teeth aching as he held his smile, waiting apprehensively for her to answer.

'Yes,' she said.

His eyes sparkled mischievously. Tomorrow wasn't soon enough.

'And tonight, after the children have eaten supper...' With a flourish, he brought out a brightly coloured kite from behind his back. 'We go flying,' he said.

Blanche laughed.

'Well, fancy you thinking of that then,' Edith said.

'Fancy,' echoed Blanche, a swift understanding passing between them. He'd overheard her conversation with Conrad Heinkel's children and was trying to please her. She was deeply touched.

–

Once the children were ushered from their presence, Lady Verity slammed a knife against a plate so hard that it broke. 'You should have told me!'

Emmanuel Strong turned from the anger of his wife's face. When they'd first married, he'd thought himself a lucky man to be marrying a woman half his age. Although of a wealthy family, their fortune was as pennies compared to that of the Strong family. But even so, he hadn't married her for that. She was younger than him and the appetites of his youth had not diminished that much.

'Look at me, damn you!'

Astounded at her outburst, he turned from the window where he'd been watching the object of her anger running across the grass with the nursemaid, Edith. Tom ran out in front of them flying a kite. Determined rather than nervous, he straightened his waistcoat and cleared his throat. 'It was Jeb's idea – and Otis's too come to that. How could I refuse?'

She pursed her lips and her pink cheeks flared brighter. 'You insult me!'

He shook his head and walked the length of the table to her side. She shrugged aside the heavy hand he placed on her shoulder.

Sir Emmanuel Strong had spent all his life in the sugar trade and other schemes connected with shipping, building and lining a nest already comfortably cushioned by previous generations. Business had been his lifeblood over that period, but now, middle-aged, he had a need for a family and a woman with whom to share his wealth. What he did not need were petty jealousies.

He sighed. 'Her mother's dead. It's only right that she should come and live here. Isn't it enough that she's a servant?'

'Pah!' Verity pushed herself to her feet and faced her husband so that her nose was level with his chin. 'And a servant she shall be! She's the one who'll take care of all these brats you landed me with.'

Emmanuel was shocked. He adored his children – all of them. They too were part of his wealth, pawns in an increasingly material world.

'Verity! You're talking about your own children!'

She pointed a finger at him. 'You wanted them. That's why you married me. I'm a brood mare on whom you sire stock to carry on your name and your business. That's all I am!'

To some extent she was telling the truth. He'd convinced himself that she wanted a family too. It shook him to the core to find this was not the case.

She sat back down then and helped herself to the last of the blancmange and jelly, added fruit cake and poured cream over the lot.

Affection dead in his chest, Emmanuel watched as she used a tablespoon to ladle food into her mouth. Such a small mouth, yet such a big appetite.

Suddenly all the passion he'd felt for his wife when she'd been little more than a girl, was snuffed out. She made him feel sick.

As his heart hardened, he waved his arm over the table, indicating the food still sitting there from teatime. 'The leftovers go into the swill bucket for the pigs – should you chance to leave them anything!'

A blob of blancmange hung from her mouth and her eyes froze to malice then burned into anger.

'Stay away from me!'

A plate of bread and butter flew through the air, followed by what was left of an apple tart and a bowl of strawberry jam. Streaks of food ran over silk wall hangings of palest green, pink and white almond blossom, hand-painted by an artist who had never been to China but thought he knew what it was like.

Emmanuel ducked it all and as he reached the door, he said with undisguised malice, 'I'm glad that girl's here. Hopefully my children might know a woman with a warm heart. That will be good for them.'

Verity reached for the sugar bowl, her eyes still blazing. 'So long as she stays upstairs with them, and out of my sight!'

## Chapter Fourteen

Blanche Bianca. Her name was like a song, thought Tom. He watched her run through the wet grass until the kite took flight, the children skipping and laughing around her. Her hair had come loose, pins, ribbons and bonnet flying off into the grass.

Puffing and panting some way behind, Edith tried to keep pace, but gave up and bent almost double, her hands resting on her knees as she fought to catch her breath.

'Blow me,' she said, her cheeks red with exertion. 'She runs like the wind. No one can catch her.'

'I can,' murmured Tom.

He ran after her, his strong legs hurling him through the grass, over the gravel drive and through the trees, circling around so she came upon him rather than him catching her up. Engrossed with the kite and the children, she didn't see his manoeuvring and ran full pelt into him, bounced off and blushed when he held her shoulders to prevent her from stumbling.

Her first inclination was to laugh and run away, just like a child playing a game. Perhaps it was the warmth of his palms on her arms, or the fact that they were both panting, their breath mingling as they faced each other, but they lingered, laughing into each other's faces, then pausing as if the very same thought had come to both of them at the very same time.

Loose and flowing, her hair rose on the wind and flicked over his eyes and lips, breaking the spell.

'I didn't want you to fall and hurt yourself,' said Tom gruffly, as though he needed to make an excuse.

'You cheated. You cut through the trees.'

'I'd never catch you without cheating.' He feigned great disappointment, but took the opportunity to drink in her warm complexion and the tumbling wildness of her hair that no hairpin or ribbon seemed capable of holding in place. 'You run too fast.'

'I know.' She smiled at him almost wickedly, before running away, laughing wildly, and the children running behind her, leaping to catch the tail of the kite.

Mesmerized, he watched her. He'd never seen a woman move like she did. And yet she seemed unaware of her allure, either that or she didn't care what effect she was having on him.

'I'll catch you again,' he called after her.

'You'll have to run fast,' she called back.

'I will,' he shouted.

Before she disappeared among the trees, he saw her smile and was almost certain she was daring him, perhaps even inviting him to try again.

Suddenly he became vaguely aware of a breathless panting at his side. Without bothering to look, he guessed it was Edith.

'My,' said Edith, struggling to catch her breath, 'all this running around is too much for me. I'll keep you company instead, shall I?'

He gave a mumbled response, his gaze still fixed on Blanche. He didn't see the disappointment on Edith's face.

Edith repeated what she'd already said more loudly.

He glanced down at her. 'No need. I have to go.'

Judging by the look on her face, she didn't believe him, but he felt no obligation to enlighten her.

'Perhaps you would tender my apologies to Miss Bianca.'

Edith did not say whether she would or wouldn't. It was then he noticed her sullen expression and regretted being so abrupt.

'Miss Clements,' he said, taking her hand, 'reluctantly, I have to take my leave of you *all*. I trust you will forgive me.'

Edith giggled as he kissed her hand.

'You promise you'll render my most profound apologies?'

'Oh yes!' said Edith, her face as bright as a beetroot.

It wasn't a lie, in fact. After Horatia had told him that one of the gardeners from the time of Jasper's disappearance still lived in the village, he'd made arrangements to meet him there.

Without looking back, he made his way through the twilight to the village and St Mary's churchyard.

Josh Carter had been one of twenty-eight gardeners employed in those days. He was old, but still fit enough to keep the churchyard in reasonable order.

A few blades of grass had already sprouted on the unmarked grave of the boy found in the chimney. It had been a lucky coincidence that this particular spot was not too distant from the mausoleum of the Strong family, a marble edifice, flanked by Corinthian columns and roofed in green copper tiles.

Something scurried off into the stunted foliage beneath the hedge surrounding the graveyard. A rabbit, thought Tom, or a fox.

He stood there, hands in the pockets of his leather jerkin, staring at the gold lettering on the front of the building above the pillared portico: 'Comes the blind Fury with th' abhorred shears, And slits the thin-spun life, but not the praise.'

Milton, if he remembered rightly.

The building shouted wealth and status, the words regret, if not outright indignation, that death dared curtail members of such a powerful and wealthy family. Their names were emblazoned beneath the frieze and between the pillars. Miriam Strong and three of her daughters – Patience, Piety and Charity – had died of cholera and all in the same year. He'd been away at sea for the first time, serving as a cabin boy on a wool packet. He remembered Jeb's desolation on his return, the emptiness of Littledean. Ruth and Rachel had married. Only Leah had remained and had been worried then about her father's health. As it deteriorated, Emmanuel had insisted they move into Marstone Court, as Leah had married a missionary whose work was taking them to China.

So long ago, he thought, and promised himself that Jasper would eventually lie with his sisters.

He walked slowly around the stone structure, eyeing as he did more names on other panels around the outside walls. The name of Samson Strong stood out bold and shiny. His wife's name, Amelia, was etched quite a bit further down. Their bodies weren't there, of course, because they'd died at sea. The name dividing husband and wife was obliterated by mud, almost as if someone had applied it with a stonemason's trowel or an artist's palette knife. He was just about to bend down, pluck a bunch of grass and wipe the mud away, when the smell of black tobacco drifted to him on the air. A stooped figure walked slowly towards him, his long coat seeming to weight him closer to the ground and his wide-brimmed hat shielding his features.

'Cap'n,' said the man.

'Josh.'

Neither man met the other's eyes.

The old man sucked on his pipe in one corner of his mouth and blew the resulting smoke out of the other. 'Chill night.'

'Frost before dawn, I reckon,' Tom responded and they both sniffed the air; the countryman and the mariner, both dependent on the weather for their livelihood.

The old man nodded. It was sixty years since first he turned the earth at Marstone Court, following in his father's footsteps as head gardener. There was nothing much Josh didn't know about the family.

They both stood silently, regarding the mausoleum.

'Nice woman,' said Josh with a jerk of his chin at Miriam Strong's name.

'And married to a good man.'

'Yep!'

'And lovely children.'

'Lovely girls.' Josh's smile exposed teeth yellowed by time and tobacco. His two front ones seemed obscenely long and at variance to the others in his mouth. Tom was fascinated by them and had to force himself to concentrate on the question he wanted to ask. 'Do you remember the time Jeb's son went missing?'

Josh chewed on his pipe, but with his molars rather than the thin, long incisors. 'Nearly twenty years ago. Long time. Lot of things growed since then... tomatoes, cabbages, potatoes, turnips...'

The list seemed to go on and on. Obviously, the garden had been the mainstay of the old man's life.

Tom waited patiently and tried to keep his gaze fixed on the mausoleum. It was no use. Try as he might, his gaze kept drifting back to Josh's face, especially his teeth.

'It was someone's birthday party,' Josh was saying. 'Everyone was there. It was a dry day, first for weeks. Ground was too wet for peas that year. River was in full flood.' He shook his head sagely. 'The boy should never have gone near that river.'

He didn't, thought Tom. 'Was everyone invited to the party?' Josh nodded. 'Even the house servants.'

Tom frowned. It wasn't usual for servants to attend a family party. 'Why was everyone summoned to be there?'

'Because of the ship.'

Tom was even more confused. 'You mean the *Miriam Strong*?'

Josh shrugged. 'It was a painting of a boat. The master had had it done in London. Beautiful painting, it was. And we all had to look at it, and he spouted on about it for a while...'

Josh chuckled and shook his head as if being proud of a painting was as nothing to being proud of an onion bed or a cabbage patch. 'It was on display. S'pose it's in the 'ouse now.'

Tom went on a mental tour of Marstone Court. There were a number of paintings of ships on the walls of Marstone Court. One above all others came to mind. It was a painting of a Strong vessel, splashes of colour and light giving the ship a ghostly appearance as though both it and the landscape were melting into the sunset.

Josh chewed on his pipe and his eyelids creased into wrinkled lines. 'Red sky mornin' after the boy drowned. I knew it would be as bad a day as the one before when I saw that.'

Tom frowned. 'Something else happened the following day?'

Josh jerked his chin in affirmation. 'Master caught a poacher. Cheeky blighter he was too. Kept his stash down in the cellar so we found out later. Him and one of the farmer's lads were in it together. Poacher killed the deer, farmer's lad brought sides of pork and beef up from the farm, and took back a deer.'

Tom's mind worked quickly. Was there a connection?

'Can I speak to him?' Tom asked.

'Oh, no, no, no,' laughed Josh. 'Poacher made the mistake of runnin' and the master filled 'im with holes.'

'He shot him?'

'Stone dead.' Josh spat into the grass.

Tom thanked Josh for his help, and would have left immediately, but a bat flew down from the church belfry, swooping low over their heads. Both men ducked and something fell from Josh's mouth and into the grass. Josh went down on to his knees to search for it, his pipe jiggling at the side of his mouth.

'Lost me teeth,' he said.

'I'll help you,' said Tom.

'No need to.' There was a cracking sound as Josh straightened and triumphantly brandished the offending items.

Tom could say nothing, but watched as Josh wiped his two front teeth on his coat then pushed them back into the gap in his gums.

Josh saw him looking and grinned. 'Had a pig slaughtered a while back. He didn't need them and I did.'

Keeping a straight face, Tom thanked him again, and was just about to go when Josh suddenly said, 'Farmer's lad that was in on it is still alive though. Got sent to Australia, though I heard he'd come back.'

'What was his name?'

The old man's brow wrinkled with the effort of thinking. 'Funny name. Had relatives down in the city somewheres.' Josh tapped his pipe against his protruding teeth. 'Farmer... Fenner... Fenton... something like... I know!' he exclaimed suddenly, his upper teeth dropping on to his lower lip. 'Fenwick! A chap called Fenwick.'

–

Despite protests from Mrs Grainger, kite-flying after tea and before supper became a frequent event. Tom had intervened, a fact that was obvious seeing as he appeared as if by magic the moment they were out in the park.

He ran with the children, laughed with them and, when it was wet or too cold to go out, they would settle around the nursery fire and he would tell them stories of the sea, of the places he'd been, the things he'd seen.

Blanche and Edith were as enthralled as the children, their faces warmed as much by the vividly told tales as by the flickering flames.

'... And then the giant sea monster slid slowly beneath the waves, its giant tail lashing the air as though it were waving goodbye.'

As the story ended, Tom dotted the noses of each listener, including Edith, and finally Blanche.

'And there you have it,' he said, gazing boldly into her eyes. 'The tale ends with a tail.'

It didn't occur to her that she was gazing back at him with the same intensity, until she became aware of the silence and four upturned faces with bemused expressions, plus another that looked a little put out.

He made excuses to leave after that.

Later, after the children were in bed and everything cleared away, Edith made herself and Blanche weak tea and they pulled up chairs to the nursery fire. The nursery was warmer than their own rooms as the children were allowed more coal and candles.

Blanche hardly noticed Edith's constant prattling as she sipped her tea and stared into the flames. What was it about Tom that unnerved her?

'I make a good fire,' Edith was saying proudly. 'That's what comes of being the eldest of eight and with a sick mother, though after having eight babes and a few miscarriages, what can you expect? We used to wrap them up in straw and throw them on the fire; that's why it needed to be good, you see.' She laughed suddenly as she realized what she'd said. 'I mean that we threw the miscarriages on the fire, not the born alive babes! Have you got any brothers and sisters?'

She told her she hadn't any and grinned to herself. Edith had boasted earlier of having thirteen brothers and sisters, now it was eight.

Edith's next question took her by surprise. 'You ain't got no plans on Captain Strong, have you?'

'Plans?'

'You wouldn't be sweet on him, would you?'

Blanche looked down into her tea. She'd had no intention of telling anyone about Nelson, but confiding in someone might help her. Hopefully it would also take her mind off Tom.

'I didn't come here to see Captain Strong. I came to see Nelson.'

Edith gasped and covered her mouth with her hand.

Blanche bit her bottom lip as she thought things through. Should she tell Edith more? Besides Tom, she was the only true friend she'd found since arriving in England. She decided to take the risk.

As she told the tale, Edith's eyes got wider and wider and her chin fell.

'I haven't seen him yet,' Blanche said finally.

Edith's expression remained shocked. It was a minute or so before she blinked it away and tried to say something positive. 'I suppose you have to see him… I mean… he'd want to know, even if he is going to… marry his first cousin.' Blanche was amazed.

The meagre light from the candle they'd lit flickered as the floor clock chimed the half past. It would be half an hour before the family sat down for dinner.

Blanche got to her feet. 'I'm going to go down to the dining room and see him.'

Edith looked aghast. 'You can't do that!'

Blanche tidied her hair. It didn't look as shiny as it normally did, but once the kettle on the fire had boiled, Edith would fetch more water and they'd both wash their hair as Edith had already proposed. It would be clean tomorrow. It would have to bide for today.

The prospect of trying to see Nelson was exciting, although, as Edith had pointed out, it could mean her being sent back to Barbados immediately. But she had to try.

'I see no reason why I can't.'

'You'll get the sack.'

'Have you ever been into the dining room?'

'Well, yes, but only first thing to lay the fires before anyone else is around. Servants have to be invisible, you see.'

Blanche gritted her teeth. Well, I am not invisible. I am a woman of flesh and blood.' As Nelson knows well, she thought, and could almost feel his body lying against hers, just as they had on the beach in Barbados.

What will you do if anyone sees you?' Edith sounded appalled.

Blanche shrugged. 'I'll tell them it's such a big house, I lost my way. Have you ever got caught when you shouldn't have been there?'

'Oh yes.' Edith took the teacups and put them on the tray with the other bits of crockery and cutlery from teatime. 'I got up late, then the fire wouldn't light properly. The sticks were damp, you see. The butler caught me.'

'And what did he say.'

Edith grinned. 'The family were coming into breakfast so I couldn't shoot out past them. He got me to hide beneath the table. That's when I learned about Mr Nelson refusing to marry his cousin.'

'Are you sure?' Blanche gasped with delight. The news was music to her ears, loud trumpets and beating drums rather than wistful violins.

Blanche sprang to her feet. 'I have to see him.' She swept to the door.

Edith wrung her plump, pink hands. 'Blanche, you can't!'

'I can and I will.' Suddenly she felt that what she'd really come here for was within her reach. Nelson had refused to marry his cousin, and although he may not have voiced his reason, she truly believed that she was it. Edith squealed with fright as Blanche grabbed her shoulders. 'You have to show me where the dining room is.'

Edith shook her head, and her pink cheeks got pinker. 'I can't. I might get dismissed. I couldn't afford that, Blanche, much as I'd like to help you, but there's me poor old mother and me starving little brothers to think about!'

'I don't believe you've got a mother.'

'Yes, I have!'

'And a lover too?'

Edith's face went bright pink. 'Well, no... I didn't say I did.'

'I have! And I want to see him. Tell me how to get there.' Edith sighed. 'I'm not going with you, mind.'

'Do you really think I'd want you with us? Two's company, Edith.'

Directed by Edith, Blanche made her way downstairs, the plain walls and thin matting giving way to plusher furnishings.

From the main landing that circled the marble pillared hall, she watched as a footman, possibly Duncan, raised a long taper to the myriad candles of a chandelier. According to Edith, there were two other footmen besides Duncan and David, but they weren't paid so much because they weren't as tall. It seemed odd to Blanche that people could be paid by the inch, but apparently it was so.

The smell of succulent food, possibly seven courses or more as was usual in this house, wafted up to her. A second footman, resplendent in blue livery edged with gold braid, glided soundlessly across the marble floor carrying a large soup tureen. Blanche flattened herself against the wall, peered round when she judged it safe, and saw him disappear down a passage.

Once he'd gone, she began the final descent to the marble hall and the passage the footman had taken which was sure to lead to the dining room. When the coast seemed clear, she gathered her skirts and went down into the hall. Just as she was about to turn to her left, a door to her right opened and a woman with high cheekbones and piercing blue eyes strode confidently towards her.

Blanche froze in amazement. Nelson! Good God, she looked just like Nelson, except she was wearing a dress. Her jaw was stronger, the way she moved filled with intent.

Horatia swept towards her, frowning. 'Do you want something?'

Blanche had learned enough since arriving to know that as a servant in England she should appear humble. She gave a polite little nod, just as one lady might give another in greeting, but there was nothing servile about it. Damn it, she would *not* be servile! She couldn't do it.

'My name's Blanche Bianca and I'm from Barbados,' she blurted. 'Perhaps Nelson's told you about me.'

Blanche noticed the tightening of Horatia Strong's jaw, the way her nostrils dilated as if she were reining in her emotions. Her voice was as cold as her eyes. 'I know who you are and where you are from. I asked you what you were doing here. You belong upstairs in the nursery.'

'I was hoping to see Nelson,' she said truthfully. 'We met in Barbados.' It was brazen, but Blanche didn't care.

'Ah!' The disdainful look stayed fixed on her face.

'I want to let him know I'm here.'

There was no subservience in the way Blanche spoke or held her head, her grey eyes defiant.

'See him?' Horatia asked incredulously. 'My brother is in London, not that it's anything to do with you!' Blue brocade swished like a passing bird as Horatia circled her.

*As if I'm a damn horse.*

'How dare you!' Horatia's face was close to her own. Blanche turned her head to face her. It was as if they were rivals for the same man, though how could that be? Horatia was Nelson's sister.

'I dare,' Blanche said in a low voice. 'I dare!'

Horatia's pale complexion began turning red. 'Get back to the nursery where you belong.'

Blanche held her ground and shook her head. 'I do not belong in the nursery. I was not told that I was destined for the nursery. If I had known I would never have left Barbados.'

This was too much for Horatia Strong.

The slap from the lace-covered hand caught Blanche across the mouth. She tasted blood on her lips and felt it trickle down her chin.

She did not look away, or cry or do any of the things an upset inferior would do. She was her mother's daughter. She smiled triumphantly. 'You, madam, are supposed to be a lady.'

As Horatia raised her hand again, the doors to the library opened. Both women looked towards Emmanuel Strong. Blanche blinked. If Horatia was a feminine, though stronger version of Nelson, then Emmanuel was an older version of his son, the same height, but more corpulent, ruddy faced and powerfully intimidating.

Blanche slid her eyes sidelong to Horatia. *More like his daughter.*

His stomach pressed against his waistcoat like sausage filling tightly packed in its skin. A gold watch chain gleamed against the dark pattern and a white cravat and winged collar framed his face.

Lady Verity came to her husband's side, a dark grey pelisse sitting heavily over her dress. It was trimmed with velvet and must have been hot as well as heavy.

Horatia didn't give her father time to ask what was going on. 'This impertinent little trollop should be sent back to Barbados immediately. I don't want her in this house. I want her out.'

'I agree,' said Lady Verity.

Horatia glared at her in surprise. They hated each other and had, it seemed, both made vows never to agree with any suggestion the other made.

Blanche tried to look beyond them, to catch a glimpse of Nelson. She saw no one. She was aware that Emmanuel Strong did not once look in her direction, as if rich men like him had more important things to consider than uppity servants.

'Ladies,' he said in a loud voice, 'to the dining room, please.' He offered his wife and daughter his arms and they left, leaving Blanche feeling alien and inconsequential, but unbowed.

Duncan followed them and glared at her as he passed. 'Know your place, *woman*.' The word was laced with contempt.

Fire in her belly and in her eyes, Blanche swiped at the trickling blood with the back of her hand.

Suddenly the whole idea of coming here seemed like a bad joke. Otis Strong had misled her. But she refused to admit that she had allowed herself to believe the unbelievable, that the Strong family would accept her as a long-lost daughter.

Bristol was cold. Barbados was still a warm place in her mind, and if Nelson didn't want her, then she would go home. Some of her jewellery – enough to sell and pay her passage – was in the sea chest. Someone, somewhere in this city would buy it, although she didn't know who and she couldn't remember her way around the city. She remembered the dock, the mix of dark doorways, the frowning upper storeys of timber-framed inns, and the mix of sailors speaking in a range of dialects and languages. The city terrified her. She needed someone who knew the city well. Tom.

Back in her room, she got her mother's shell-covered jewellery box out from her sea chest. Just as she'd retrieved it, she heard footsteps outside the door – hesitant footsteps – as though someone was trying to be very quiet and failing miserably.

'What happened?' Edith murmured on opening the door. Then, seeing the blood at the corner of Blanche's mouth, 'Who did that?'

'I want to go home,' Blanche blurted. Her eyes stung with tears, but damn it, she wouldn't break down and cry. She would not!

'Oh dear,' said Edith.

It seemed odd to Blanche that Edith didn't try to dissuade her. After all, hadn't they become good friends? But Edith's attitude became clearer after Blanche asked where Tom went on his frequent errands.

'Why?' Edith snapped and eyed Blanche with a mix of suspicion and downright jealousy.

Blanche explained about raising money for the trip home by selling her mother's jewels. They weren't exactly diamonds – at least, she didn't think they were – but she was convinced they did have some value.

'Oh well, if that's all… ' said Edith, brightening. 'Some people reckon he's got a sweetheart in the village and that's the errand he refers to, but I know different.'

Edith beamed at the thought of knowing a secret no one else was party to.

'He goes to the churchyard. Did you hear about the sweep's boy who got stuck up the chimney?'

Blanche nodded. 'Where would Marstone Court be without gossip?' she said lamely.

'Well, I think it upset Captain Strong. It was 'im that found the little lad, you see – all tanned he was, like a piece of cured leather or a side of salted bacon. So he goes to St Mary's churchyard and says a little prayer. In fact, I saw him head that way not so long ago. Then he goes off to Bristol.'

Blanche felt her trust in Tom was confirmed and decided to ask him for his help right away. She couldn't wait a minute longer.

Edith reminded her that it was dark out. 'Take my cloak,' she offered. 'It's warmer than yours.'

Although the wool smelled musty, Blanche thanked Edith and pulled the hood over her head, clutching the jewellery box beneath her arm.

'I won't be long,' she added as she ran out of the door.

Moonlight blinked between the branches of dormant trees. April was still a month off and only a few brave leaves had so far sprouted.

She ran as fast as she could, cutting through the grass and beneath the trees. After letting herself out of the small pedestrian gate that formed part of the main gate of Marstone Court, she set off for the village that Edith reckoned was about two miles distant.

–

Tom had said his usual prayer over Jasper's body. Usually he walked to the churchyard, but tonight had gone by horse, meaning to continue into Bristol. He had an early start the following morning assisting Conrad fire up the new centrifugal system that would separate the sugar from the impurities far faster than ever before. Conrad had suggested he stay the night there and Tom had agreed. No matter his uncle's ambitions, he liked the big German, a man not afraid to get physically involved with the machines and methods of refining.

He turned his horse's head towards Bristol, lightening the sadness of Jasper's death by thinking of Blanche and the way she had run through the long grass.

Thinking of the rhythm of her bounding grace, he heard sounds that seemed to echo his thoughts.

'Tom!'

Reining in his horse, he turned in the saddle.

'Blanche?'

A dream! It must be a dream. He blinked, narrowed his eyes and blinked again, felt the night air on his skin, heard the call of an owl from a barn across the fields. He could smell, hear and see, which meant Blanche was real. There she was, racing towards him, her hood falling from her head, both her hair and her cloak billowing out behind her. For a moment, Tom could barely breathe. Touched by moonlight, it was the loveliest sight he'd ever seen in his life.

'I needed to see you,' she said, looking up at him, her breath silver on the frosty air, her mouth slightly open.

The first thought that entered his head was that he wanted to close that slightly open mouth with a kiss. His horse spun round as he dismounted and he caught her in his arms to prevent her being knocked to the ground.

'I need to go into Bristol,' she exclaimed, her breath warm against her cheek.

It hadn't been her original plan to go into the city. She'd been going to ask him to sell her mother's jewellery, but she'd had second thoughts. It was silly, but she wanted to be with them until the very minute they were sold. They'd been part of her life for so long. It seemed only right.

She explained about wanting to raise money to go back to Barbados and that she couldn't possibly let the box and its contents out of her sight. 'There's nothing for me here,' she said finally.

A pang of anguish gripped Tom's heart. He had no intention of offering her the money to go home. He wanted her here. Hopefully, her mother's jewels were of no value and she'd have to stay. But he could not refuse to help her.

'Perhaps in a few days' time…?' he began.

'No!' Blanche shook her head decidedly. 'I want to leave as soon as possible.'

He frowned and pulled her cloak more closely beneath her chin as he thought things through. 'You're a determined woman, Blanche Bianca. Are you sure that's what you want?'

'I want to sell them and get away as quickly as possible.'

Tom thought of people he knew in the more unsavoury parts of the city, who would indeed pay instant cash and no questions asked, and balked at the idea of taking her there. She'd turn heads and invite comment and he'd have to protect her. He could tell by her expression that she wouldn't take no for an answer.

'Come on,' he said and helped her up on to the horse. Although Blanche was no heavyweight, the horse would be pretty much all in by the time they got to the city. He'd already arranged to stay overnight with Conrad. Hopefully one more bed would be available and someone could take Blanche back to Marstone Court in the morning before anyone would notice she'd gone.

After folding her cloak around herself, she wrapped her arms around him. 'You feel cold,' she said shivering.

'You feel warm,' he said softly, and was almost convinced that she squeezed him more tightly in response.

For a while the only sound was the even tempo of the horse's hooves on the frozen road. The night sparkled with frost.

'Look at those stars,' she said suddenly.

'Like diamonds,' he said.

'You can wish upon a star. I'm going to make a wish.'

'What will you wish for?'

'I can't tell you,' she said laughing. 'If I do, it won't come true. Make your own wish.'

'All right.'

The front of her body was warm against his and she'd wrapped her cloak over her arms, which were entwined around him. Tonight, he thought, looking up at the stars, there was only one thing he wanted.

'What was your wish?' she asked suddenly, and made him fear that she could hear his thoughts.

He laughed and shook his head. 'I couldn't possibly tell you. You might slap my face.'

She laughed too, even though she half expected he was telling the truth and it might possibly refer to her.

They fell to silence. Tom wondered if she'd guessed what he'd wished for. He wondered if his next question might be misinterpreted as a consequence.

'When's your day off?' he asked over his shoulder.

'Tomorrow,' she answered.

'Just as well. You won't be going back to Marstone Court until the morning. Is that all right with you?'

'I don't care if I never go back there again, though I have to collect my belongings,' she added. 'Where are we going?'

Tom had racked his brains for a suitable person who would deal with Blanche's jewellery quickly and with cash.

'A place I know, somewhere you can buy and sell anything.'

The Druids Arms had small windows, which let in little light during the day and let out just as little at night. Tallow candles smouldered in metal holders fixed to the walls and half a tree trunk smouldered like a burning beast beneath an eight-foot bessemer.

In one corner of the broad inglenook a bread oven door hung from one hinge. At the other end a brace of mackerel dripped moisture on to the ashes as they slowly smoked and turned brown. Their smell permeated the thick clouds of black shag smoked in handmade pipes, and the sweat of men home from the sea and not keen on fresh water for either drinking or washing.

Inside the tavern, it was light enough for Tom to see the slight nick at the side of her mouth. He asked her about it. Blanche chose to lie.

'I was sewing a button on to one of George's dresses and was stupid enough to break the thread with my teeth. I should have used scissors.' She didn't meet his eyes.

He seemed to believe her, and looked across the room, nodding towards the person he was obviously seeking.

'Aggie Pike,' he said over his shoulder.

Blanche followed him, searching for a woman among the brute-faced men.

Aggie Pike was not at all what Blanche had expected. Neither was the method of greeting between Aggie and Tom.

'Tom!' shouted Aggie. She rolled up her sleeve and plonked her elbow on the table.

Blanche could hardly believe her eyes. Even in Barbados she'd seen nothing quite like this. Tom was arm-wrestling with a woman. As he did so, he explained to her that Aggie was a barge owner who hauled goods along the Avon and up the Severn to the Forest of Dean and Gloucester. She had arms like legs of ham.

'Strong as an ox,' Tom muttered as he strained to keep his arm upright.

Blanche sat on a three-legged stool, trying not to notice the looks she was getting from the pipe-smoking men, the lank-haired youths, and the odd doxy thinking she had competition.

Elbows on table, and hands tightly clenched, Aggie and Tom faced each other across the table. Tom gritted his teeth. Aggie chatted as she chewed a clay pipe that jiggled at the side of her mouth.

She finished telling him about her last voyage and how she'd dumped her latest husband off at Sharpness. Tom wondered whether it was the truth that she'd ever had a husband in the first place. She was far from pretty. In fact, the rear end of her barge looked better than she did.

'Are you sucking that thing, or have you really got enough teeth left to hold on to it?' he asked.

She took the pipe from her mouth. 'Look,' she said and opened her mouth wide. 'Six here,' she said, pointing to teeth the colour of rotten meat. Her breath smelled rotten too. 'And seven here,' she added, pulling down her bottom lip so he could see them more clearly.

Blanche winced. She'd seen better teeth on a dead barracuda.

Tom's idea had been to break her concentration while she showed him her gummy mouth, but the rotten teeth, thick with tar, protruding like nails from blood red gums, only distracted him. Her grip and the strength in her muscles were as good as ever.

'Fancy a kiss then,' she sniggered, leaning forward so that he got the full visual impact of her gummy mouth and fetid breath.

Tough though he was, Tom couldn't cope with that. His arm slammed to the table and laughter exploded around him at the sight of his disgusted expression.

Aggie laughed uproariously with them. 'I'm too much of a woman for you, Tom Strong,' she shouted. She glanced at Blanche and winked. 'Mind you, if you don't want the captain, I can find a berth for him on me boat fast as you like.'

There was more laughter. Aggie lapped it all up, smiling round at everyone like a prima donna at the end of a performance.

Blanche didn't correct Aggie that there was nothing between her and Tom, and then wondered why.

'Now, let's get down to business,' Aggie said once all the attention had died down.

She leaned more closely across the table. Tom got closer too, holding his hands over his mouth.

'Now, what you got for me then, Tom?' Aggie asked in a low voice.

Tom nodded at Blanche. 'My friend has some jewellery to sell. She needs money quickly so she can get a fast boat home.'

'Home?' asked Aggie with raised eyebrows. 'And where might that be?'

'Barbados,' said Blanche.

Aggie's smile bestowed a sweetness to her face that hadn't been there before. Her voice became dreamy.

'I remember a man I met there once, long ago, mind you.'

Tom explained that Aggie had disguised herself as a boy and stowed away to sea when she was younger.

Aggie went on, 'He looked a bit like you, though darker mind, quite a bit darker. Now,' she said abruptly once the vision had cleared from her mind, 'let's see what you got to sell, and I'll tell you whether I'm interested.'

Blanche fetched out the small box, wondering why the lid felt so wet, then realizing it was because her hands were sweaty and she'd been gripping it tightly. She opened it and turned it to face Aggie, who looked, blinked, then smiled. 'There's a few things here, enough to get you a passage home.'

She poked at the contents. Her fingernails were black and her hands grubby. 'This is nice,' she said, fetching out a silver locket that held a small miniature of Blanche's mother painted by a local artist.

Blanche grabbed it back. 'Not that,' she snapped. The moment she did it, she had second thoughts. She needed the money. She had to get away. Sighing, she dangled it reluctantly and said, 'I suppose it has to.'

'I think I'd like that for myself,' Tom said in a gruff voice she hadn't heard before. 'Here. Four sovereigns.' He took it and placed it round his neck. 'P'raps Aggie will give you enough so that you can buy it back off me.'

She saw him put something in it before clamping it shut, but gave her attention to Aggie, who was choosing what she'd buy.

'This, this and this,' she said having chosen two brooches; one of coral and the other green stone set in silver. The last was a single pearl pendant on a thin gold chain. 'I'll give you ten sovereigns, more than enough for your trip home.'

Blanche couldn't answer. Her eyes were fixed on the jewellery box. All it now contained was a pair of earrings with red stones. They were a little duller compared to the other items. Perhaps that was why Aggie didn't want them, thought Blanche.

As if reading her thoughts, Aggie suddenly said, 'The earrings look to be glass, though I can manage another sovereign for them if you want me to take 'em off yer hands.'

All I have left of my mother, thought Blanche, her heart almost breaking at the thought of it. 'No,' she said, and snapped the lid shut. 'I'll keep them.'

'Not stolen, are they?' asked Aggie.

'No. They were my mother's,' Blanche said quietly. 'I want something to remember her by.'

Aggie scooped up the jewellery and shoved it down beneath her grubby neckline.

Blanche watched guiltily as Aggie counted out the money. What would her mother think of her? What would she have done in the circumstances?

*If one man don't want you, there's sure to be another that will.*

She could feel Tom looking at her and turned to face him. 'I had to do it,' she said, her voice trembling a little.

He smiled at her and looked deeply into her eyes. 'I know,' he said softly, as though he really did. 'I know.' He nodded at the money. 'Do you want me to look after it for you?'

'It's all right,' she said, putting the money into the shell-covered box with the earrings.

Aggie straightened on her stool and offered Blanche her hand. 'Glad to 'ave bin of some help.'

Blanche shook it.

Aggie offered it to Tom, who hesitated as Aggie's loose lips tilted in a lop-sided smile. Grotesque as Aggie was, Blanche thought it only polite that Tom should shake her hand. When he did slide his hand into Aggie's, she understood the reason for his hesitance. Aggie promptly pulled him forward at the speed of lightening and planted a sloppy wet kiss on his mouth.

Drinkers of every age burst into ribald laughter. 'Put 'im down, Agg. Ain't you had anything to eat today?'

Blanche laughed too. Aggie was disgusting. No man in his right mind would want to kiss her. And she doubted whether Aggie made a habit of kissing men in dockside taverns. Tom, she decided, was the obvious exception. Men seemed in awe of his physical presence and treated him with respect, as though he were a storm waiting to break. Women adored him, not that she'd seen him in the company of many. She could only judge by the way she herself was responding to him. In the absence of Nelson seeking her out, it was easy to do.

–

Conrad Heinkel sat smoking his pipe, his feet resting on a footstool, a brandy in his hand, and a tureen of beef stew sitting on the table whetting his appetite and making his stomach rumble.

The clock in the hall struck eleven o'clock just as Tom Strong arrived. As he'd already sent the servants to bed, Conrad got up and answered the door himself.

'Tom!' he cried, throwing his arms around him.

It was like being hugged by a bear. 'You're breaking my arms,' laughed Tom. He was glad when Conrad let him go, but less so when he saw the way he looked at Blanche.

'The kite lady!' Conrad exclaimed delightedly.

Blanche found herself blushing as Conrad bowed and kissed her hand. She hoped he didn't notice the musty smell of Edith's cloak and wished she'd given it more attention before accepting it. She also hoped it wasn't riddled with fleas. Not content with nipping her, they'd probably colonize her companions too.

'Let me take your coats,' Conrad said.

'Someone lent it to me,' Blanche said as she passed the cloak over, just in case their host had an acute sense of smell.

Tom felt a need to explain Blanche's presence. 'Blanche had an errand, which needed my assistance. I hope you don't think it an imposition…?' Tom stopped as he saw the beaming smile spreading across Conrad's face and realized that Blanche's presence was far from being an imposition. He instantly felt jealous, an emotion he'd seldom felt before.

'I have supper for you,' Conrad said. 'Eat.' He pointed his pipe at the tureen.

It was late when they'd finished and Conrad had given them two or three brandies.

Blanche much appreciated the warmth it gave her and felt happier than she had for a long time. Tom seemed less so.

With her permission, Tom had told Conrad about selling the jewellery so Blanche could go home. Conrad's jovial smile seemed to falter.

'But why?' he asked in a sad, strained voice that reminded her of a child told to go to bed.

Perhaps it was the brandy, but more likely a combination of that and her kindly companions, but Blanche told everything that had happened, even her conviction that her father was Otis Strong.

Conrad shook his head. 'That is wrong. Bringing you over here as a servant.' He turned his eyes on Tom, whom he knew was a member of the Strong family in name only. 'What do you think, Tom?'

Tom had drowned the last of his brandy and was sitting forward in his chair, elbows resting on knees, hands clenched tightly together. He was staring at the floor, though not seeing it. In his mind he saw Jasper half buried among fallen debris.

'At least you don't have anything to prove,' he said.

Blanche stiffened. 'Of course I do! I have to prove who my father is, that I'm a Strong.'

Tom jerked his head up and glared at her. 'And I don't,' he said resolutely. 'Well, that's true at least.' He reached for the brandy and filled his glass to the brim. 'I replaced a dead boy. I'm second best. Always will be.' He swigged the brandy down in one gulp.

Blanche exchanged a concerned look with Conrad. She sensed he was thinking the same; that there was more to these maudlin comments than met the eye. This was a different Tom to the confident, charismatic man they'd both come to know.

Conrad sighed and put his empty glass on the table. 'You are a good man, Tom. Jeb made a wise decision.'

Tom smiled sardonically, his mouth tilting up at one side. 'Did he? I wonder what he'd say if he knew that Jasper did not drown. What would he say if he'd known that his dear son had been in the house all this time, close but silent and dead?'

Astounded by the implication of what he was saying, Blanche started to rise from her chair. 'Tom—'

Conrad's voice was as warm as the firm hand he placed on her shoulder. 'What do you mean, Tom?'

As Tom buried his head in his hands, the whole story came out. Blanche sat mesmerized, barely aware that Conrad's hand was still on her shoulder. She'd heard of the boy in the chimney, but like everyone else, had presumed it was the sweep's boy. Now it seemed otherwise.

Tom took the locket he had bought from Blanche out from his shirt and clicked it open. He showed them the lock of hair, the piece of material. He smiled at Blanche. 'A little bit of your past, and a little bit of mine – both together.'

Both Conrad and Blanche stared at it, lost for words. At last Blanche asked, 'How did he get there?'

Tom shrugged. 'I don't know. None of the servants presently in the house were there then. Servants don't stay at Marstone Court for too long, besides, they were all gathered in the same place as members of the family when Jasper went missing. An old gardener who lives in the village told me the name of someone who might shed some light on it, though I did hear he'd gone abroad. But I'll do what I can,' he said, adding grimly, 'I'll damn well find him.'

## Chapter Fifteen

From early the next day, Tom and Conrad were kept busy at the refinery, so Blanche was taken back to Marstone Court in Conrad's carriage and in time for tea.

After taking the stairs two at a time, she went straight to her room and began to hurl clothes into the musty sea chest that had once belonged to her grandfather.

Busying herself helped keep myriad misgivings at bay. She had the money to go home, but still had a nagging doubt about doing so. If only Nelson had sought her out, things might have been different.

Edith was supposed to be overseeing the children's tea in the nursery, but couldn't resist clumping up the stairs to ask Blanche whose coach she'd come home in, and where she had been.

'Servants aren't supposed to stay out all night. It's not good for their moral health,' said Edith as she bundled her cloak over her arm and checked its condition in case Blanche had made it worse than it already was.

'That won't matter for much longer,' said Blanche, smoothing out her own clothes so they would lie flat on the transatlantic voyage home.

'You got the money?' asked Edith, her eyes wide with admiration.

Blanche beamed with satisfaction. 'I did.' Her smile disappeared as she thought about Nelson and her disappointment at coming all this way and not seeing him. And she wouldn't even be saying goodbye to him. But she'd say goodbye to Tom, Conrad and the Strong children.

'Who's with the children at present?' she asked.

Edith blushed. 'They're all right. They're eating.'

A burst of sunlight suddenly lit the budding trees and green parklands, which made the room they were in look even colder in its northern light.

'Have they been for a walk today?' Blanche asked. The children loved playing beneath the trees and running through the grass.

'Well,' Edith began, 'Mrs Grainger said—'

Blanche grabbed her one and only warm cloak and a pale green bonnet with pink roses at the side. 'Mrs Grainger saw no need to go for a walk? She hates exercise of any description, which is why she has such a wide derrière!'

Edith burst into laughter.

The children should have been sitting around the table in the nursery, but when they got there, they were in a huddle in the middle of the floor. A lot of laughter and chuckling was going on. They sprung apart the minute the door opened, their frightened expressions melting away when they saw it was only Edith returning and that Blanche was with her.

'Goodness,' said Rupert. 'We thought it was the Gorgon.'

Blanche clasped her hands before her as she announced, 'I hear you have not taken your exercise today. Therefore, if you can find our kite...'

She had fully expected them to go rushing off for the kite and their outdoor clothes. Instead they all stood there, silently grinning.

Blanche looked from Caroline to Rupert to Arthur and then to George, whose smile was too wide to control.

'George!' Blanche exclaimed. 'You're wearing breeches!'

The little boy seemed to swell with pride. 'I'm nearly four,' he said happily.

Edith, never too keen on exercise, decided to stay in the nursery and polish off the jam roly poly and custard that the children had left.

Running and laughing, Blanche led the children around the side of the orangery towards a hillock that shielded the main house from a broad meadow, which led towards a style and a footpath to the village.

The hillock proved a wonderful place for launching the kite. The children took it in turns to run down, but there was little wind so the kite did not fly as high as it could.

'Let me,' said Blanche. Laughingly, she ran down the hillock, the kite soaring high above her as she raced through the long grass, the hem of her skirt sodden, her shoes soaking, and the evening air turning her cheeks crimson.

She handed the kite over to the children and turned her gaze to the setting sun that glowed a burning orange in the western sky.

West to Barbados, she thought to herself, and remembered how warm the sun had felt on her skin, how the breeze had blown her hair as she'd ran along the beach.

Suddenly, she began to run towards the setting sun, foolishly thinking that if she ran fast enough, she would get home without a ship. It was pure fantasy, but the joy of running was very real. She didn't care about her wet shoes, her damp dress; she was running like she used to.

Exhilarated by the evening air, she ran on, skirted the hillock, raced towards the stile. Bypassing where the children played with their kite, she ran towards the orangery, her hair flowing over her face, pretending it was a warm wind when the truth was very different. Scooping her hair back from her face, she noticed a figure standing in the orangery door, watching her, his hands resting on the hips of his beige trousers, his hair turned to gold by the setting sun.

It was Nelson.

She slowed and came to a standstill.

He was smiling, his eyes bright with longing. 'You still run like the wind, Blanche.'

Heart palpitating and too breathless to speak, Blanche stared at him with undisguised delight. 'You're here!' she said at last.

'Of course I am.'

He held out his arms as if it were only right that she should fall into them.

'Where have you been?'

His arms dropped slowly to his side and his smile stiffened.

'I've been ill. I had to see a doctor.'

'Why did you leave Barbados? Why did you send me no word?'

She couldn't help being angry with him. He should have been more considerate, otherwise how could she believe that he loved her?

'I was engaged to be married. The family insisted I go home and fulfil my obligations. When I got here, I called the marriage off.'

Blanche was overwhelmed with relief, but she wasn't going to let it show, and besides, just because that particular engagement was terminated, didn't automatically mean that the family would approve of him marrying her.

He stood to the side of the orangery door and spread one arm in invitation. Blanche glanced over her shoulder. The children were playing. She followed him and he closed the door.

'I'm not going to run away,' she said hotly.

'I'm not going to chance it,' he replied.

He looked so handsome, so well groomed, and so... smug. Well, thought Blanche, I'll show him!

'I've arranged to go back to Barbados,' she said. She brushed the dust off the leaf of a large tropical plant.

He spread his arms, amazed. 'Why would you do that?'

Blanche grimaced. Didn't he know? Couldn't he see?

'I have been brought here as a servant, Nelson, to be a nurse to your stepbrothers and sister.'

'Ah yes,' he said, thoughtfully tapping his chin as he considered the implications. 'And this is England.'

She wasn't quite sure what he meant by that. Despite herself, a thrill ran through her as she looked again on his fine face and fair hair. Even the way he stood brimmed with confidence and invited attention.

Sighing, Nelson laid his hands on her shoulders and smiled down into her face. 'England is so...' He seemed to search for the right word, and finally said, 'different. Social niceties and moral rules are more lax in the colonies than they are here. I'm sure you've noticed that.'

'I've noticed a lot of things,' she replied hotly, but didn't voice them. Children strapped to chairs and seeing little of their parents was cruel. Being wealthy was all very well, but there were other, more important things in life.

It was impossible to dwell on them. Nelson attracted her still. Just his touching her, made her legs feel as though they'd turned to water.

He ran his fingers down her cheek then took her chin in his hand, raised her lips to his and kissed her as lightly as a butterfly landing on a flower.

'We'll both go to Barbados,' he pronounced. 'It's the only way.'

–

Edith insisted on helping her, scuttling around her like a bantam hen searching for her eggs. Her pale blue eyes were almost popping out of their sockets with a mixture of fear and excitement as she ventured a host of excuses as to why Blanche couldn't leave. On the one hand, Blanche was her dearest friend. On the other, she'd prefer to have Tom to herself, no matter how frail her chance of capturing his affection.

'You can't leave without properly giving in your notice,' she said, folding clothes and handing them to Blanche for packing.

Stays, shoes and underwear went into the chest, followed by a handful of muslin sachets one of which broke, leaving the scent of dried lavender heavy on the air.

'Yes, I can.'

'How will I cope with that old cow Grainger and the baby when it comes?'

Blanche ignored her and went on packing.

Edith continued. 'And how are you going to get into Bristol? The coachman won't take you. He'll be afraid of losing his position here, which comes complete with his home above the coach house.'

Blanche tutted disdainfully. 'Two rooms to house a wife and four children; is that too much to lose?'

She smiled as she thought of Nelson's plan. He was going to bribe the coachman and the captain of the next ship to Barbados. And when they got there, they would throw themselves on the mercy of his Uncle Otis, and categorically accuse him of being Blanche's father. How could he possibly refuse a marriage between cousins now that Nelson was free? Even Otis's shrewish wife would be loath to object. Slowly she folded a shawl, put it in the chest on top of the other clothes – a rainbow of blues, mauves, yellows and greens – then remembered the English weather and took it out again.

Edith slumped on to the bed and nibbled her fingernails, which were already short. She'd always kept them so, a habit she'd started in the days when she used to blacklead the grates. No matter how careful she was, it always got stuck beneath her nails. 'My ma says that it ain't no use running away from providence. You got to stand and face it and do yer best.'

Blanche raised an eyebrow and placed her parasol into the chest. 'What's that got to do with anything? Anyway, last week you told me you were an orphan.' Blanche threw her big white aprons to one side. She certainly wouldn't want them in Barbados. 'I think you make up family histories to suit the moment.'

'I don't!' Edith had the cheek to sound hurt.

'You also told me you have eight brothers and sisters the week before last, then last week it was twelve. You also told me your father died down a mine, and then you told me he got drowned at sea.'

Edith flushed and buried her bitten nails beneath her armpits. 'I wasn't lying, it's just that I get a bit carried away sometimes. I gets it from me father, so me mother says. And me cousin. Fen 'as got lots of sayings too. He's cleverer than me, an' he says you got to take advantage of things if they're put in yer path – otherwise you'll trip over yer own feet.'

Blanche laughed and shook her head, rested her hands on the lid of the sea chest and took stock of the situation.

'I'll ask Tom to take us instead of the coachman,' she said, and wondered if she should ask Nelson first before taking the decision, or whether she should show her commitment to their plan by arranging it herself.

Edith bit her bottom lip, her nose wrinkling. The less Blanche had to do with Tom, the better as far as she was concerned, even though she was running away with Nelson. It was just that Blanche and Tom looked so good together, and they talked a lot, their conversation moving easily from one subject to another.

She shook her head and tutted like a judge. 'Oh, I don't know that he can do that. He's with the Reverend Strong as much as he can be, on account of the poor gentleman is dying by the day,' said Edith. 'He tries to feed him sometimes, which isn't as hard as it sounds. The poor gentleman's not taking solids, of course, just milky sop that I wouldn't feed to a pig, but then gentry got weaker stomachs than the likes of us, and my ma reckons that plenty of fat greases yer insides and makes yer bowels work properly so as you don't have to—'

'I'd like to see him,' Blanche said, disinclined to hear the more intimate details of the Clements's lavatory habits. 'Tom, that is. And right away. I'm sure Nelson would trust him to take us and that Tom can keep our trip a secret.'

Edith's face was as bright as sunrise. 'Oh, yes!' she exclaimed, her freckles diminishing in the pinkness of her complexion. 'The captain's an honourable man. He'd never let a secret slip out.'

'I'm sure he wouldn't.' Blanche hid her smile and pretended to smooth out a non-existent crease in a pale blue dress.

A dreamy look came to Edith's face. 'Me ma always says that you should never snitch on family and friends. You should keep the faith, she always says.'

'A very wise woman, your mother. Shame I won't get to meet her.'

Edith looked crestfallen. She'd never considered the idea of Blanche meeting her family, but now it was mentioned, she found the idea attractive. 'That is a shame! Tell you what, if you decide not to go, or if Nelson marries that washed-out cousin of his, you can come with me on yer next day off and meet her – and the rest of the family too. How does that sound?'

Blanche stiffened at Edith's careless statement. She would die if Nelson married his cousin, and there was *no* chance that she would change her mind about running away with him. After all, Nelson was the reason she'd come here in the first place.

She managed to smile appreciatively. 'It sounds wonderful.'

'Do you promise?'

Edith was the one and only friend she'd made since coming to England, apart from Tom. There was no point in upsetting her now. 'Of course.'

Blanche slammed the lid down on her trunk. 'I'd better find Tom, in any case. I've never been to the Reverend Strong's rooms. Will you take me there?'

The Reverend Strong had a suite of rooms at the end of a corridor on the first floor of the west wing. The view through the floor-to-ceiling windows was spectacular, and Jeb's bed had been turned round so he could see it better. Presently, an orange sun hung low in the west between the cliffs of the Avon Gorge.

As they traversed the landing between the stairs and corridors, Blanche glanced down into the hall. One of the footmen, possibly Duncan – though it might have been David – looked up at her. His expression was a mix of surprise and indignation as he jerked his head round, causing his white powdered wig to slip. She fancied his inclination was to run up the stairs and ask what they were doing there, but he was carrying a silver meat dish with a domed cover and obviously did not want to present the dish cold.

Tom was sitting on the edge of Jeb Strong's bed, spooning what looked like a milk pudding into the Reverend's mouth. He swallowed it painfully, Tom gently scooping the excess from his chin.

Jeb's face froze, his gaze fixed beyond Tom and on to Blanche as she entered the room behind Edith.

The smell of sickness and crushed lavender was overwhelming. Blanche felt her nose beginning to wrinkle, but managed to control it. Although it was Tom she was looking for, her eyes met the astonished stare of Jeb Strong.

She knew from her mother that Jeb Strong was the youngest son, yet surely he looked the oldest? Apart from a few sparse hairs, his head was like a snowball stuck on a series of sticks that barely disturbed the smoothness of a cut velvet counterpane. His eyes rolled in his head. Saliva dribbled from the corner of his mouth.

Lifting a trembling finger, he pointed and after struggling to find his voice, murmured, 'Viola...'

His voice was barely above a whisper, yet to Blanche it was like a thunderclap. A member of the Strong family had admitted knowing her mother.

Tom frowned at his foster father and wiped the spittle away from the crusted corners of the old man's mouth. 'Calm down, now. Calm down. It's just Edith and the new nurse.'

Blanche almost ran to the side of the bed behind Tom.

'Blanche!' she exclaimed excitedly. 'My name's Blanche Bianca and Viola was my mother. Did you know her? Did you know her very well?'

She was aware that Tom was glaring at her, his expression a mix of surprise and warning. Blanche ignored him. Jeb had her undivided attention.

Jeb Strong nodded weakly. 'Ye... s.' His reply was long and drawn out, like a regretful sigh.

Edith took the opportunity to apologize to Tom for interrupting, wringing her hands, her gaze fixed adoringly on him.

Tom stood up, his broad back blocking Blanche's view.

'I think you should go,' he said over his shoulder.

'I can't go,' she said, her eyes bright with excitement. 'I have to ask about my mother. I have to ask the Reverend how well he knew her.'

Tom looked angry, far removed from the man who'd offered her friendship from the moment she'd arrived. 'You're over-exciting him,' he said grimly.

Blanche was adamant. She could see from Jeb's face that he wanted to talk to her. 'It's important.'

Tom remained resolute, still barricading her from getting too close. 'I think you should go.'

She threw him an angry look, retreated, then rushed round to the other side of the bed

'Tell me,' she said, leaning close to the old man, smelling his ailing breath, seeing more closely the pallor of his face and the liver spots that had prematurely aged his paper-thin skin.

Turning mournful eyes up into her face, he struggled to speak. 'Yo... ung.' The word strung out on his breath.

Blanche nodded that she understood. He was telling her he'd been so young at the time.

'Beau... ti... ful.' His voice was barely above a whisper.

She wasn't sure whether he meant her mother had been beautiful or that she was. She presumed the former. He'd known her mother. He could surely confirm once and for all that Otis was her father.

His eyes turned sadly wistful as he studied her dark complexion, and the startling contrast of her steel grey eyes. He sighed regretfully. 'Vio... la... Hea... ven.'

Blanche sensed that Tom was still glaring at her, his anger mounting, but she did not move.

She leaned closer to Jeb. 'Will you tell me who my father is?' she whispered. 'Will you?' He seemed to nod, though she couldn't be sure.

'Pat... ience,' he said haltingly, then pointed, the tip of his finger touching the mole beneath her eye. 'Pat... ience.'

Hooded lids of loose skin closed halfway over his eyes, as if he were remembering, as if he were afraid to look at her. His voice was as watery as his eyes, which then rolled upwards as he opened them again seemingly uncomprehending who she was.

'You have to go now,' said Tom, pulling her away from the bed.

He looked and seemed agitated, his eyes darting between her and the dozing form of Jeb Strong.

'I want to ask—' Blanche began, but Tom was already manoeuvring her towards the door while Edith wiped Jeb's mouth.

Suddenly, the old man's eyes blinked open, his mouth seemed to slip to one side and he began to drool. 'Tom...' he slurred.

Tom had been going to bundle her out of the door. A few fast-paced strides and he was back at the bed, bending over Jeb and admonishing him. 'See. Now you've tired yourself out.'

Jeb's throat gurgled as his body filled with fluid.

'We'll turn you now, Reverend Strong! We'll turn you now,' cried Edith, panic making her cheeks turn pink and her lower lip hang with worry.

Tom took charge. 'Use the pillows!'

Edith understood him, and Blanche assisted. Using the pillows to cushion their grip on his thin limbs, Tom and Edith turned Jeb on to his left side.

Still hovering over him, Tom threw Blanche a glance. Obviously he was blaming her for Jeb's condition. 'I think you should leave.'

He gripped both her shoulders and turned her from the bedside. His shirt must have been clean a few days ago. Now it hung loose, unbuttoned from the neck and halfway towards his navel. She smelled the fresh sweat and saw where tanned skin melted into white and for a split second she wondered how it would feel to the touch, if his thigh muscles would feel harder than Nelson's... She felt her cheeks burning.

'Can't you see the man needs his rest?'

'He can confirm that my father was – is Otis Strong.'

'Not now.'

'Yes! Now!'

Tom's expression hardened and she could see his chest rising and falling rapidly against the looseness of his shirt. His face, his eyes and his lips were close enough to caress as he said, '*I'd* like to know who my father was, but I never will. Now go!'

Edith, who was trying to manage alone, called out, 'Captain Strong!'

Eyes closed, Jeb's head lay back against the pillows, his mouth wide open like the starving young of some scrawny-necked bird. Tom glared at Blanche, his hair tumbled over his tired eyes. 'Get out! Now!'

'Tom!' Edith was struggling. Saliva shone in a runny line over Jeb's bluish chin. Tom helped Edith carefully push him further on to his left side.

'He's not going to die, is he?' asked Blanche. 'He mustn't,' she said more quietly. 'Not yet, God, please not yet.'

Tom just turned away to lean on the bed, his face creased with concern as he looked down into Jeb Strong's pale face.

Edith applied a cold compress to Jeb's forehead. Spittle ran from the corner of the old man's mouth, his lips moving weakly. 'Patience,' he said again, the word drawn out like a breathless sigh.

Another angry look from Tom, and Blanche left the room, but lingered outside, straining to hear what was going on. Things had not turned out as she'd planned. She'd been going to ask Tom to take her and Nelson to Bristol where they would get a ship to Barbados. Suddenly, the island of her birth seemed a lifetime away. And gnawing within her was the same question she'd been asking herself all her life. Who was she? Who was her father? She had half hoped that by going back to Barbados with Nelson by her side, that Otis might have enlightened her. But now the answer seemed much closer. It was here in Bristol on the lips of a dying man.

As time went on, she sat down on a hall chair, wrapped her feet round its barley twist legs, and prepared to wait until Tom came out. She felt bad about upsetting him. He'd been kind to her. Her thoughts were confused. Running away with Nelson didn't seem so urgent now. She hoped he'd understand why she had to stay longer and briefly wondered what she would do if he didn't. Those evenings at the beach were beginning to seem wonderful memories. In England her relationship with Nelson seemed to have turned a corner, or a page. Something was different.

Tom looked tired when he came out. He was rubbing his eyes with finger and thumb as if he would push them from their sockets. 'I'm sorry,' he said, as she got to her feet.

Blanche said nothing, but gave a curt nod of her head as if she understood his reasons for turning her out, but did not approve. Her resolve to be cold towards him melted when she saw fear, regret and apprehension dance through his eyes.

Cupping her elbow in the palm of his hand, he said, 'I want to speak to you.'

He took her to a window seat from where they could see an inky black sky scattered with stars. The sun had long since gone to bed.

He smelled of maleness, well-worn cotton and the warm cosiness of soft leather. For a while he said nothing, as if expecting her to say something first. Blanche couldn't think of anything appropriate. Prior to this evening, her thoughts were of Nelson and her in Barbados. Now the Reverend Strong had taken centre stage, telling her to have patience. Perhaps he would tell her more when he felt better.

'How is he?' she asked.

Tom shook his head. 'He'll survive tonight, but...'

He spread his hands helplessly. Sympathetic to his despair, Blanche took hold of one of them. Tom looked surprised.

'I'll pray for him,' she said.

Tom nodded, his eyes dark with worry.

She sensed he wanted to say much more and that he felt ashamed that he'd ordered her from the room. It was easy to forgive him.

'He's sleeping now,' he said. 'Edith's staying with him and has opened a fresh bottle of laudanum. She reckoned the last one didn't work, no matter how much she gave him.'

'Ah,' she said, and her thoughts went back to Miss Pinkerty and the many potions and powders made from plants, roots and animal's blood, some administered hand in hand with superstitious ritual, passed down over the centuries. But there were some similarities between the old ways and the new, the Sugar Islands and England. The potion she'd given her mother to ease her pain had undeniably been laudanum – poppy juice mixed with rum. It surprised her to remember Miss Pinkerty's respect, even fear for the concoction.

*A little is a medicine, too much is a poison.*

'Will you tell him about his son?' she asked, the story he'd told her at Conrad Heinkel's still fresh in her mind.

He shook his head. 'I can't. The truth will kill him. Do you think I'm right not to?'

It flattered her that he'd asked her opinion. She could say it was only right that he should be told about his son. But she didn't want him to die, not until he'd told her about Otis.

'I think you're right,' she lied.

'So when do you go back to Barbados?'

She tucked a stray wisp of hair behind her ear. 'I think I've changed my mind.'

His face cracked into a grin. 'After me having to wrestle Aggie Pike before bargaining?'

Blanche nodded almost imperceptibly. 'I thought about it. But I've decided not to. I have to stay. Destiny brought me here, and only destiny can send me on my way.'

Tom sighed. 'I know how you feel.'

She looked away. She didn't want to snap at him, but the hot retort was waiting to be said. How could he know how she felt? She'd been brought here, presuming she'd be welcomed as a member of the family, or at least live something like the life she was used to. Instead, she was a servant.

She stood and looked out of the window towards the picture-book trees that edged the gravel drive. 'I'm different. It takes more time to fit in.'

'I'm different too.'

'It's not the same as being from somewhere else.'

'Doesn't the gutter count? My mother was a whore. She died at the hands of a client who then threw her in the river. They found her among the sewage and rubbish. That's what a man thought of my mother. He had no reason to do that, none at all. She was just trying to survive.'

Blanche bit her lip. 'My father is a very rich man and a member of this family. That's why they brought me here. My mother kept their secret and they kept us in style. She expected them to keep their part of the bargain and look after me even when she was no longer around. Then – this.' She shrugged.

'We have a lot in common,' he said.

He was right. Their mothers were sisters in survival. Both she and Tom were outsiders at Marstone Court, but in different ways.

Perhaps they might have confided more, but Mrs Grainger was marching from the other end of the passageway, the stiff bombazine of her full skirt reminding Tom, as always, of a battleship in full sail, though twice as frightening.

Blanche got up. 'I have to go.'

'So do I.'

Despite wanting to get to the children before Mrs Grainger, she watched him go, his head bowed forward as if he were crying.

After Mrs Grainger had come and gone from the nursery and the children were put to bed, she left the wider, brighter rooms and corridors behind, and went back to the draughty room beneath the rafters and unpacked her sea chest. The Reverend Strong had told her to have patience. She had to stay. She had to know. She hoped Nelson would understand.

## Chapter Sixteen

A warm breeze was blowing in from the tropics and the last flight of sugar birds had flown inland to their night roosts in the trees or beneath the eaves of houses and mills.

Someone was singing and the tinkling of wine glasses came from inside a well-lit house with a long veranda. In her dream Blanche floated towards it, her heart full of joy because she was about to see her mother again. Why, she would say, have you been so long, child?

And there she was, walking along the veranda, the frail muslin of her empire-line dress no more than a cobweb around her body. Just as Blanche started to move towards her, a roll of thunder sounded. Slowly the orange glow of the setting sun faded away along with the dream, but the thunder continued.

'Wake up, Blanche! Wake up!'

Strong hands gripped and shook her shoulder.

Blanche blinked. Edith was bending over her, a candle in one hand and a rough woollen shawl clutched haphazardly around her shoulders.

'The baby's coming. You're wanted.'

Bleary-eyed, Blanche got out of bed and reached for a shawl to throw over her nightgown.

Edith grabbed her arm just before she got to the door.

'You've got to dress, Blanche. You can't go down like that.'

Blanche shook her off. 'Is the baby going to care how I'm dressed?'

'No, but Lady Verity—'

'Pah!'

Blanche took off along the draughty corridor and down the three flights of stairs to the first floor. Housemaids were standing outside the bedroom door of Sir Emmanuel and Lady Strong. Two held pails of steaming water, others had clean linen and towels. The housekeeper, a Mrs Hedron, was standing over them like an army sergeant major, just in case they should make a move before she gave them leave.

Her chin seemed almost to disappear into her collar and her eyes almost popped out of her head when she saw Blanche.

'Brown!' she said, her face a picture of bruised respectability. 'You are not properly dressed.'

'The baby won't be wearing any clothes at all, and Lady Verity won't be at her most dignified either. And please take note that my name is not Brown.'

Mrs Hedron looked as though she'd been slapped with a wet fish. Even the maids sucked in their breath. She managed to collect herself.

'One does not talk of one's betters in such a vulgar manner.'

Blanche was in no mood to justify her comments. 'Is the doctor here?' she asked jauntily.

Mrs Hedron's black eyebrows rocketed skywards. 'Yes, but he's not ready for us yet.'

Blanche was about to say that if that was the case, why had she been called from her bed, but the voice of Emmanuel Strong intervened.

'Mrs Brown. Would you come down here, please.'

He was standing in the hall down below, paintings of his ancestors at his back beneath the galleried landing that ran around three walls of the marble reception hall. He did not appear to have heard what she had said.

From the top of the stairs she saw him pass into the broad doorway of the library.

Mrs Hedron looked as though she were about to burst a blood vessel. 'Surely you're not going down like that?'

Blanche said nothing but smiled in a wickedly coquettish way, the voluminous folds of her cotton nightgown swinging around her bare, brown legs as she headed for the top of the stairs.

He was drinking something darkly golden from a squat cut glass. Not rum, she decided, but perhaps whisky. Judging by the redness of his face, he'd had more than one. Such is childbirth, she thought.

He looked at her awkwardly. 'Close the door.'

At first she hesitated. Suddenly she felt vulnerable, dressed as she was in her nightclothes. But he's drunk, she decided, and I'm strong and can move quickly if I have to. Confident that she could handle anything he attempted or said, she closed the door and turned boldly to face him.

He was standing in front of the fireplace, wearing a quilted smoking jacket and a round hat with a long silk tassel, which hung over his right ear. He had an awkward look in his eyes as though he couldn't quite focus. She'd seen gentlemen and working men take on that look after they'd had a few slurps of rum. Truth, or the truth as they saw it, bubbled to the surface, inhibitions unlocked by alcohol.

'I'm sure you'll do your best by my latest child. I know it isn't really what you're used to but you must understand, it's the best I could do in the circumstances.'

Blanche frowned and renewed hope surged in her chest. 'My father—' she began.

'Could have been anybody.' He laughed into his glass. 'Pretty thing. Kept a good table and entertained well, so I understand.'

'Otis—' she began.

'Don't be ridiculous,' he snapped. 'My brother was fond of her, but he didn't own her. And he was fond of *you*.' He pointed a finger at her. 'Just be grateful for that. Your mother was less than respectable. She didn't want you going down that particular path, which is why you are here, young lady. As I have said, be grateful!'

She had it in mind to say more, but the thought of the agreement she'd signed made her hesitate. In time Reverend Strong would tell her the truth. Sir Emmanuel would never do that.

She started for the door, and glanced back in time to see Emmanuel tilting his head backwards as he upended his glass and tipped the contents down his throat. His balance tottered along with his legs. They gave way and he fell forward on to the couch the drink slopping on to her nightgown. She immediately imagined Mrs Hedron's face; a nurse in charge of a newborn baby smelling of drink and dressed in a nightgown.

Just as she reached the door, it swung open, almost sending her flying back into the room.

'Nelson!'

They stood staring at each other, both looking startled and stuck for words. Suddenly he burst into poetry, just as he had in Barbados:

*Oh nymphet of my wildest dreams,*
*The sea in your hair, at your feet,*
*Your heart and mine in glorious meet,*
*And erre the sun god's glorious path...*


He was looking at her as though already seeing her naked, her hair streaming over her shoulders and her body aching with desire. It was hard to find the words.

'I'm not going to Barbados with you,' she blurted.

'What?'

Blanche felt cold in her cotton nightgown.

'I have to stay here — at least, for now.'

She didn't want to tell him about the Reverend Strong having known her mother and about to confirm Otis as her father. Back in Barbados when she'd voiced the subject, he'd considered it of little consequence.

'I wish I didn't know my father,' he'd said with a grimace. 'But unfortunately I do, and he is not a man you'd like to get to know well, I can tell you.'

'Give me a little time,' she said, wondering at her own lack of emotion. After all, weren't they made for each other? Hadn't they said as much in Barbados?

'Do I have any choice?'

'I'm sorry,' she said apologetically. 'Do you forgive me?'

Nelson sighed heavily, his eyes still raking her body with great interest. 'How can I not forgive you?'

Smiling, he held out his arms. In an instant they were wrapped in a tight embrace, her head on his shoulder.

'Blanche,' he said, stroking her hair back from her face.

She closed her eyes tightly, relishing the feel of his body through the flimsiness of her nightgown. His hardness pressed against her pelvis, almost painful, but pleasurable too.

Completely forgetting that Nelson's father was lying out of sight and comatose on the sofa, she allowed Nelson to take liberties. He breathed heavily, his hands fondling her neck, her shoulders and her breasts, untying the garment at the neck so he could more easily slip his fingers inside and run his thumb over her nipple.

Things might have gone further if Nelson's father hadn't woken up and poked his head up over the back of the sofa.

'Stop that! Stop that at once!'

Clothes dishevelled, his face still red and his eyes blazing with anger, he struggled to his feet. Blanche stepped back. Earlier Emmanuel had looked at her with something resembling affection. Now he looked as though he could kill her, as though she were just a servant again – or something much worse.

He staggered between them, pushing them apart with clenched fists, then looked from one to the other.

'I forbid you to see each other. Do you hear me? I forbid it!'

Nelson gaped and seemed uncertain what he should do. Blanche seized the initiative. Feeling small and insignificant, but not daring to let it show, she stood with head held high and said, 'You have to understand. We fell in love in Barbados. We met on the beach.'

Emmanuel Strong could not have looked any angrier. He glared first at his son. 'So that was why your Uncle Otis sent you home before time. And he said nothing, though that's typical of the man. He always was soft.'

Nelson shook his head so hard that his slicked-back hair fell forward around his face in silky blond strands. 'I don't understand.' He glanced at Blanche. 'She's everything I desire in a woman.'

'You will not think of each other like that,' growled Emmanuel, his face like thunder.

'Because I'm a servant?' said Blanche.

'As good enough a reason as any,' he snapped. 'You are a servant.'

'I wasn't a servant back in Barbados,' she said with a look that left her master in no doubt as to what, or rather whom she was referring.

His hesitance passed, Sir Emmanuel Strong's eyes glittered. 'Well, you are *here.*' His face, already swollen with the effects of good brandy, turned redder and redder. 'Out!' he shouted at Nelson, and pointed to the door. 'Within the week I want you working in my stead in London, and while you're there you can attend on Adelaide Tillingham again. That's the woman for you, my boy.'

'She's the one you've picked for me,' Nelson snapped defiantly, 'not the one I want.'

'While you are under my roof, you obey my wishes. You will marry Adelaide Tillingham—'

'Along with her fortune,' Nelson interrupted. He turned to Blanche. 'My father wishes to breed a dynasty, a family as well as a company, to control the sugar industry.' He turned back to his father. 'It's a bit like being put out to stud. You even made sure I knew what to do in order to achieve your ambition, didn't you, Father?'

Emmanuel bristled with rage. 'Get out of here!'

Nelson bowed in mock respect. 'I will, Father, but only because your presence and your ambition make me sick.' He bowed to Blanche, his eyes locking with hers.

Emmanuel turned his attention to Blanche. 'And as for you—'

She was burning inside, trying to understand this sudden venting of such a terrible anger. There could be only one explanation.

'Just because my mother was once a slave doesn't mean you can treat me as one.'

The colour seemed to drain from his face. Hot anger had turned cold and the sound of his voice sliced into her heart. 'If that is what you wish to believe, then so be it. Nelson is not for you. It is only for the sake of the regard this family had for your mother that I will allow you to stay. But tread carefully, my dear, or back to Barbados you will go.'

Blanche opened her mouth to protest, but this time there was a knock on the door that turned out to be Mrs Hedron. She curtsied and said, 'The nurse is needed.'

Blanche attempted to catch his eye before she left to follow Mrs Hedron back up the stairs, but he refused to look at her.

I'll speak to him again, she thought, and convinced herself that somehow she would win Sir Emmanuel round. The whole scenario lay heavy on her mind until the sight of the baby softened her resolution. She was sure that Nelson would seek her out again. In the meantime, the children would occupy her time and with Edith's help she would visit the Reverend Strong again, the one man likely to tell her the thing she most wanted to know.

Nelson had breakfast brought to the privacy of his room. He'd slept badly the night before on account of the racket going on around his stepmother's door.

Duncan brought breakfast on a silver tray, complete with chunks of sugar cut straight from the loaf, cream in a small silver jug, and a wooden box inlaid with jade and ivory figures. There were also kippers, bacon, kidneys, lamb chops and eggs – plenty of variety to satisfy his appetite.

'Your tea, sir. Shall I pour?' asked Duncan.

'Please,' said Nelson.

'And your biscuits, sir. Shall I place them on the plate for you?'

'No,' said Nelson. 'I can deal with those myself.'

Heaven. He could sit here in his favourite chair, drink China tea and indulge in two or three of the delicious biscuits Cook made for him. She'd asked him if the ground-up leaves he gave her as a special ingredient were sage or basil. 'I was just wondering, sir,' she had said, embarrassed by her own boldness.

'Just medicinal,' he'd told her. 'Something, my dear lady, with which I could not possibly do without.'

## Chapter Seventeen

The smell of linseed and oil paints overwhelmed the sweeter smell of the dark green leaves that shaded the orangery from strong sunlight.

Tom paused. If he'd known Nelson was here, he would have gone elsewhere to think about the problems facing him at the refinery.

Softly, he retraced his steps, but as if by instinct alone, Nelson sensed his presence and stopped painting, his brush poised over his shoulder. 'A beautiful subject, don't you think?'

Intrigued, Tom moved closer, looked at the portrait, and felt his breath catching in his throat. Nelson was an excellent artist. He'd not only captured Blanche's likeness in oils, but also her very essence, the spark in her eyes. Not only that but the sleeves of Blanche's dress were halfway down her arms and her breasts were bare above her bodice. Tom clenched his jaw.

'This is how I remember her in Barbados,' Nelson said, his eyes searching Tom's face for a reaction. 'I've always liked exotic women. They're so sensual, don't you think?'

Tom said nothing to Nelson's inference that he knew Blanche intimately and merely nodded.

Nelson turned back to the painting, his blue eyes hooded. 'I saw you coming out of her room. I would appreciate it if you did not visit her again.'

Tom flinched. It wasn't like Nelson to give him ultimatums. Their relationship had always been cordial, perhaps because they'd both lost their mothers when children. Perhaps also because both, in their own way, were relatively easy-going.

'You didn't see me coming out of her room. You saw me leaving the nursery. I go kite-flying with her and the children.'

'All the same, old boy,' said Nelson in a slow, low drawl. 'You shouldn't be quite so attentive. She might get the wrong idea.'

'And your intentions,' Tom said, flicking his fingers in a brisk tap of the painting, 'are strictly dishonourable. After all, she is only a servant. Your father would disapprove!'

Nelson shrugged. 'I wouldn't be the first in this family to set up a little love nest. In fact, such arrangements run in the best of families.'

'And what makes you think Blanche would agree to be a mistress?'

Nelson dipped his brush in yellow ochre. 'We care for each other, so should not let that stand in our way. As a servant she's almost penniless. As a mistress she'd be kept in style. I think she'd agree to that.'

Tom barely controlled his anger. The Strongs thought everything had a price, including a young girl's honour. It didn't matter that Blanche had been brought up in a free and easy manner and might have given herself back in Barbados. As far as he was concerned, she still deserved some respect. He stood, head bowed and fists clenched.

Nelson carried on painting, but watched Tom warily, just in case he had to defend himself, though God knows he was no match for Tom's brawn. Of course he couldn't offer Blanche marriage, but that didn't stop him feeling possessive about her. She was still his and he wanted to continue the relationship they'd begun in Barbados in whatever form it might take.

Then the door between the orangery and the main house opened. Tom looked up, hoping to see Blanche, but was disappointed. As usual, Edith blushed the moment she set eyes on him.

'Beggin' yer pardon, Captain Tom, but me and Blanche got today off and I was goin' into Bristol to see me mother and Blanche promised she'd go with me. But there's no carter going that way, and I wondered...'

'I should have known it was your day off,' said Tom, determined to hold her attention so she wouldn't look at the revealing portrait of Blanche. 'Is that your Sunday best you're wearing? You look very...' He searched for the right word to describe the blue striped dress that did nothing to enhance Edith's plump features, '...nice.'

Edith simpered and smoothed the coarse wool of her full-skirted dress and straightened her bonnet. 'Yes, it is. Do you like it?'

'I do,' he said, taking hold of her elbow. 'Now you just tell me where you and Blanche want to go and I'll take you there. I don't mind putting myself out to take two pretty girls into the city.'

'Oooh, you are kind, Captain Tom. Me mother'll feed you when we get there. I'm sure she will! And we'll be back for the evening service at St Mary's in the village. I promise.'

Tom had intended going into Bristol to see Conrad Heinkel anyway, so it was hardly out of his way, but he wasn't going to tell Nelson that.

'A pleasure. Best to set off as soon as possible, that way you'll have plenty of time with your mother,' said Tom as he guided her towards the door. 'She lives in the Pithay, I believe?'

He didn't look back to see Nelson's reaction. If he had he would have seen a mix of malice and outright jealousy on his face.

—

Blanche could hardly believe she was keeping her promise to visit Edith's mother. And all because she wasn't going to Barbados.

Edith did most of the talking all the way into the city, her chatter directed at Tom.

'My father used to climb up the masts, swing from the crow's nest and do things with the rigging...' She went on and on.

So Edith's father was now a seaman. Blanche smiled down into her lap.

In a rare gap where he could get a word in, Tom leaned towards Blanche and said, 'I have to see Mr Heinkel on a matter of some urgency. If you want me, you know where I am.'

The wind was rattling the rigging of the baroques and brigantines moored at the quay when Tom dropped Blanche and Edith at St Augustine's Bridge.

'He seemed quieter than usual,' Blanche remarked, as they ran up through St James Barton, where a fair had been held since medieval times around the parish church. Today it was empty and shepherd's purse flickered among the grass like lightly fallen snow.

'He was *very* quiet,' said Edith.

'Perhaps he's worrying about the Reverend Strong,' said Blanche.

'P'raps he's in love,' said Edith, whispering the remark against her ear, though there was no one around to hear it.

'I wonder who with,' said Blanche, and smiled when she saw the hopeful blush seeping over Edith's face.

They laughed more as the breeze caught their clothes, Edith's skirt expanding like a balloon and exposing her knee-length pantalets, and Blanche's old-fashioned muslin clinging to her limbs beneath a second dress of lightweight wool. Shivering, she tugged her cloak around her. Wearing two dresses was not enough to be fashionable or to keep out the cold. She'd have to make some dresses.

Edith giggled. 'Can't imagine not wearing pantalets, not nowadays. Course, when I was younger I didn't wear 'em, but it ain't so important when you're just a nipper, is it?'

Blanche envied Edith her pantalets. 'I'm going to make some from my dresses,' she said decidedly. 'Then I'm going to buy some new material to make new dresses, or I would if I had the money. I've got a little aside from my voyage money, perhaps enough for one dress.'

Edith gripped her arm and nudged her warmly. 'Don't you worry. I can help out. You can pay me back when you've made up your mind about Barbados.'

Blanche smiled her thanks and wondered how Edith could possibly have money to lend when she earned less than Blanche.

The streets leading into the Pithay were narrow and the ancient cobbles were uneven causing Blanche and Edith to stumble and hold on to each other for safety. Black shadows, thrown by the jutting storeys of timber-framed houses, made the streets even darker. Blanche felt sorry for the people living there. She saw some of them, pale-faced and staring out from lop-sided doorways, the interiors behind them blacker than night. She smiled at them. 'Good day.'

She almost yelped when Edith nudged her in the ribs.

'Don't do that.' Edith spoke through the side of her mouth. 'They'll wonder what you're after – or what you're selling.'

They passed a pub called the Blue Bowl where three men leaned against a window beneath its crumbling façade. Blanche felt their eyes burning into her back and couldn't resist turning round.

Edith pinched her arm. 'Don't look!'

One of the men stepped forward, lifted his bowler and smiled. 'Ladies! Can I offer you a drink?'

Edith put her arm through Blanche's and gripped it tightly against her side. 'Say nothing! That's Stoke. If you dare smile, he'll think you're a dolly mop, or worse still a doxy, and he'll have you passed around like a parcel in no time.'

A shadow fell over them as they entered a place called Leonard Lane. It was far narrower than the centuries-old alleys they had left behind, where rats ran openly across the road pursued by throngs of stone-throwing children.

Following a swift glance over her shoulder, Edith sucked in her breath. 'Stoke's following us. Quick,' she said, tugging Blanche into yet another dark alley where the houses were even smaller, older and more tightly pressed together. Damp, musty smells rose from crumbling cellars where pale faces looked up through barred windows. A rotting door swung open from a stinking midden. Nearby a natural spring ran out of a wall and into a trough that overflowed into a muddy puddle and from there into a culvert. No wonder the river smelled as it did. Blanche was just about to wrinkle her nose and remark what a terrible place it was, when Edith said, 'This is where I live.'

It was not what Blanche had expected. She had had a vision of a small, poor but happy house, not this darkness, this smell.

The upper floor jutted out over the ground floor. Blanche looked up at the windows, small casements set in a crumbling gable beneath sloping clay tiles. Anyone with long arms could almost shake hands with someone leaning out of the window in the house opposite.

They passed an uphill alley called Cock and Bottle Lane, no more than the width of a man's shoulders. Wooden handrails were set into the patchwork of old mortar. Water had worn gullies between the slimy mix of cobblestones and moss. The door of the house just beyond the alley was open. Blanche flinched. The smell of it was bad enough, but it sounded as if the circus had come to town.

Dogs were barking. At first Blanche thought there must be dogs in the adjoining houses. Surely they couldn't all be in the same building?

She felt Edith's hand circle her wrist, and her worried face looked up into hers. 'We're not all that posh, mind you.'

Blanche didn't get chance to say that it didn't matter. At that moment a spotted dog came dashing out, wearing a very fine leather collar with brass studs and dragging a young man with corn-coloured hair that stood up from his head like the quills of a hedgehog.

'Edie!'

'Spike!'

'Can't stop,' said Spike. 'I'll be seeing you, Edie. Reckon you diddled me.'

'My brother,' said Edith, blushing. 'Take no notice.'

Dog and man bounded off down the street, though in all honesty, it was the dog doing the bounding and Spike, Edith's brother, being dragged along on the end of the lead as fast as his legs could carry him.

The sound of barking still resounded from within, bouncing off the walls of the small, squat houses that formed the lane.

Edith grabbed her arm. 'Come on. We ain't got all day.' She pulled Blanche through the door, the top of which barely skimmed her head.

The interior smelled of mildew and damp dogs. Once Blanche's eyes were accustomed to the gloom, she noticed the yellowing walls, the flaking plaster and the grass growing in untrodden corners. A broad-shouldered woman, her hair the same colour as that of Spike, but longer, laced with grey and tied back with string, was bending over three dogs, who were tied to stout nails in the wall. The dogs looked well bred but were filthy and straining at their collars. One was a type of hunting spaniel, and the other two the sort that ladies held in their laps or carried under their arms.

'Hello then, Mother,' said Edith. 'Busy, are ya?'

Without stopping what she was doing, Edith's mother said, 'Busy making a living. Not like you, our Edith, fed and watered in a grand house with gentlefolk. Some of us have to work.'

Blanche saw she was feeding meat to the dogs – it looked raw. 'Poor soul,' she said to one, 'only the tail end left for you, Muttie. Never mind. I'll catch you another one. A real big juicy one, I promise you.'

The dog yelped with pleasure as Edith's mother held the last piece of meat in front of its nose. If Blanche had not been made of sterner stuff, she would have fainted when she realized what it was. Dull yellow fat clung to the rear quarters of a rat, complete with tail.

Once just the tip of the tail was hanging from the little dog's mouth, Edith's mother looked up and wiped her hands on the sack that skirted her waist and served as an apron.

'Well, who's yer fine friend then, Edie?'

Blanche resisted the urge to suck in her breath at the sight of her face. At some time in her life, Mrs Clements had contracted smallpox. Her blue eyes narrowed above cheeks swollen red with blemished skin.

Edith leaned close to her and shouted against her left ear, 'This is my friend Blanche. She's from Barbados. Ain't she pretty?'

Edith's mother tutted through blackened teeth. 'Pretty is as pretty does.' Turning to her daughter, she asked in a quieter voice, 'Does she speak English?'

'Of course I do!'

Edith gave Blanche a nudge. 'Say it louder,' she whispered. 'She's a bit deaf.'

'I speak perfect English,' she shouted.

Edith's mother winced. 'No need to shout. I ain't deaf. Do you want something to eat?'

Blanche answered first. 'No, thank you. I ate before I came out.'

Edith's jaw dropped, and Blanche felt guilty. They'd had a bowl of salted porridge each, which Cook had delighted in telling them was made solely from water. 'Milk's all gone,' she'd said and pushed two slices of bread in their direction. Edith had eaten hers before realizing that Blanche had been served with stale bread, mould growing around the thick crust.

'You need to eat something,' said Edith.

Blanche shook her head. 'No.' Thankfully Edith's mother couldn't hear her rumbling stomach. She couldn't face eating something prepared by a woman who had just handled dead rats.

'We're having some grub now, Blanche. It won't be long,' shouted Mrs Clements, as if Blanche had not quite understood.

'Well, I...'

Her apology was drowned in a swell of barking as a figure ducked in through the doorway, then straightened and took off his silk topper that had a split from crown to band and part of its brim missing.

He slung something wrapped up in newspaper on to the table. The barking turned to whimpers and licking of lips. Whatever was in the parcel smelled good, and made Blanche's stomach rumble.

'Well, this is nice. Our Edie's brought company,' exclaimed the new arrival.

'My cousin, Fen,' Edith explained. She smiled at him with admiration and affection. He was in his thirties, thin-faced, long-nosed and too tall for the low ceiling. He appeared to be wearing three frock coats, sensible under the circumstances. The right sleeve of the top one compensated for the lack of sleeve in the one beneath that, and the third coat compensated for the lack of tails on the other two.

He raised his hat and bowed to her as if he were a gentleman and not wearing rags, and she were a lady of fashion, not one wearing a style that went out over twenty years ago.

'Pleased to meet you, I'm sure. Fenwick Clements the name. Sorry I weren't 'ere to extend the common courtesies of our family, but I 'ad to go out and about on an errand.'

Blanche guessed the 'errand' was finding food in someone else's pantry and bringing it home.

Mrs Clements placed her hands on her hips, leaned over the table and breathed in the appetizing smell coming from the parcel. 'What you got then?'

Fen trumpeted a fanfare. 'Tra, la, la, la!' With great aplomb, he unwrapped his prize and revealed a cooked ham, its skin brown and smoked and succulent juices trickling from the pink meat.

'Plates, our Edie!' shouted her mother, wiping her grimy hands over her apron.

Plates were found. Edith dusted each one off against her hip and her mother brandished a carving knife and a toasting fork, its prongs black with soot.

'Lovely,' said Edith to Blanche, the fatty juices running down her chin as she pushed a sliver of ham into her mouth.

Her hunger got the better of her and Blanche helped herself to a couple of lean slices.

Once all the meat was sliced off, Fen eyed Blanche as he chewed on the bone. 'You're pretty,' he said. 'Reckon you could marry a rich man given the chance.'

The food had been welcome, but the smell of the place, the stink of the dogs, dirt and drainage, was too intense to ignore. So was the look in Fen's pale, wandering eyes.

Blanche looked out to the alley through the open door. A thin shaft of sunlight, brave enough to pierce the gloom, had got thinner. 'We should be going,' she said to Edith.

Edith nodded and wiped her mouth on the back of her hand. Her mother was chopping up the bits of leftover fat and skin. The whole lot was being consigned to a copper pot in which sat a brown broth of dubious content. Blanche was glad not to be staying.

'You walking back?' asked Fen, about to offer his bone to one of the dogs, which licked it appreciatively.

'Don't waste that on a bloody dog!' Mrs Clements snatched the bone from Fen's hand. 'Give me that. It'll help flavour this broth for the nippers.' The bone slid into the thick broth.

Blanche forced herself to think of something else. Her eyes settled on the newspaper in which the ham had been wrapped. 'Do you read the news?' she said in an attempt at conversation.

Mrs Clements looked surprised. 'Got no time for reading.'

'I can read,' Fen said defensively, rubbing his greasy hands beneath his armpits. 'One of them Frys taught me when I was in clink. Quakers they are and believes that poor folk, in fact, *all* folk,' he added, lacing his thumbs through multi-matched lapels, 'should know 'ow to read.'

'Fen!' Edith threw her cousin a warning glance. Blanche was now party to the fact that he had been in prison.

'Oh. By the way, Edie, sorry I let the cat out of the bag with our Spike. I read out that the reward for that dog was two sovereigns.'

'How was I to know you was only giving 'im one and keeping the rest fer yerself?'

Ah, thought Blanche. So that's why Edith could afford to lend her money for dress material.

Fen offered to accompany them as far as Corn Street. 'Don't want that Stoke getting you embroiled in his nasty ways,' he said, winking at Blanche.

He cut a tall figure, striding beside them, doffing his hat to supposed gentry as if his clothes were still in good repair and his toes didn't peep through the end of his boots.

He left them in Penn Street. 'Goodbye, ladies,' he said, courteously lifting his battered hat like the gentleman he so wanted to be.

By the time they got to the sugar refinery on the Counterslip, the breeze had dropped and a light drizzle was falling.

'Big place, ain't it?' said an awestruck Edith, as they tilted their heads back and looked up at the towering building.

Six storeys high, it formed a large L shape, the main entrance being at the confluence of the straight lines. Three chimneys – two close to the road and one adjacent to the entrance – towered above Baroque pediments and arched windows. Barrels, sacks and square wooden chests were stacked high and ready for Monday morning, yet even though it was Sunday, the chimneys belched plumes of white smoke over the roofs of the city.

'Look at that,' said Edith. 'Seems we ain't the only ones to work on Sundays.'

'Just like us, they work for the Strongs. Besides, the fires can't be allowed to go cold. Someone has to tend them,' Blanche murmured.

Blanche remembered the sugar mills at home, the cane arriving in wagon loads straight from the fields to be fed incessantly into the mill before its liquid gold was drank by the sun.

In amongst the stacked sugar, charcoal and lime stood Tom's gig. The horse was standing on three legs, dozing into his oat bag, which was fastened to his harness. A cloud of flies buzzed around his head and his tail. Tom was not around.

Edith hung back. 'Shouldn't we wait out here for him?'

Without answering, Blanche pushed open one of the refinery's double doors, and was almost drowned by the sweet smell of raw muscavado.

Edith rushed in behind her. 'Wait for me!'

The heat hit them like a wave of dry sand. There were furnaces, bulb-shaped flasks the size of a house, and mountains of coal before each furnace. Channels ran almost at roof level. Blanche guessed they contained the raw muscavado on its way to becoming refined sugar. Although they were not burning at their fiercest, the sound of the furnaces rumbled through the air.

Edith grabbed Blanche's arm. 'I don't like it in here. Let's wait outside.'

Blanche pretended not to hear.

Edith clung to her arm so tightly it hurt. 'This is what hell must be like. Old Nick's going to appear at any minute,' she said, her voice trembling.

Blanche patted the hand that rested on her arm. 'It's just a sugar refinery,' she said reassuringly. Her gaze wandered over the dark interior, the chain hoists hanging from overhead beams, the metal-bound wooden ewers fixed to small trolleys; it was a world away from the green cane fields and the bright sky of Barbados. Men toiled in fields and factories just to add sweetness to life.

Suddenly a voice boomed, 'You women, what are you doing here?'

His shadow got to them before he did. He was huge, broad-shouldered and dressed in black. Blanche recognized him as Conrad Heinkel. He was carrying what looked like a Bible beneath his arm.

'Old Nick!' Edith exclaimed in a loud whisper.

'Don't be silly,' Blanche whispered back. To Conrad she said, 'We're waiting for Tom Strong.'

He looked them up and down. In the gloom, Blanche presumed he hadn't recognized her. She took a few steps closer into the light so that he could see her better. 'We met the other day, Mr Heinkel. I was with Tom then.'

He blinked and his expression brightened. 'Ah yes. The lady who mends kites.'

'That's right. And did your children manage to mend theirs?'

'Thanks to you, I have a house full of kites. You like children?'

She nodded. 'I do.'

'That is good,' he said. 'That is very good.'

Blanche wondered at his thoughtful expression and returned his smile.

'Conrad!' Tom appeared, a worried frown disappearing on seeing them there. 'Ladies. I hadn't expected you yet.'

'Refreshment before you leave,' Conrad said.

He showed them into a cosy office with checked curtains and a series of odd chairs arranged in a circle. As Conrad rummaged in a cupboard, Tom said, 'Make yourselves comfortable.'

They sat down. Conrad took great pride in making them coffee, which was why he'd been rummaging in the cupboard. Sweet and rich with cream, it tasted delicious. 'I insist you have one of these, he added. He undid a twist of paper. 'What is it?' Edith asked, but dipped her hand in first anyway and pulled out something resembling a stone.

Tom smiled. 'Eat it.'

Conrad said nothing, but kept his eyes fixed on Blanche as she bit into the hard, dark lump.

'Chocolate!' she exclaimed.

'Raw chocolate,' said Tom. 'Conrad and the other German sugar bakers are very fond of it, especially as a drink. They buy it raw from the Fry family. Go on. Eat it.'

'It's lovely!' Edith exclaimed as she gobbled greedily at a sizeable chunk.

Conrad laughed. He liked seeing people enjoy themselves. He also liked looking at Blanche and once or twice she looked back at him. After a few minutes he leaned towards Tom. 'I need to smoke. Shall we withdraw?'

A secretive look passed between the two men and Tom nodded.

They offered Edith and Blanche apologies and stepped outside. They had just finished a meeting with the Sugar Bakers Association which had taken place whilst Blanche and Edith had been in the Pithay. Certain other members of the association bought sugar at a cheaper price direct from the Strong plantation. After Emmanuel's strategy to take over Conrad's share of the company was explained, they all agreed that they would not bid for the three shiploads of raw sugar beet coming into port from the continent. These would all go to Conrad.

'I appreciate your warning, Tom,' said Conrad now. 'Tomorrow would have been too late to ward off your uncle's ambitions. The other members would have put in their bids for the sugar beet. With present stocks of raw cane and the beet, I can hold him off until the next shipments of sugar cane. This time he will not be able to persuade my colleagues to take more than they can cope with. In the meantime, I will try to raise funds to buy out his second payment on his portion of the company.'

'I trust I've given you enough time,' said Tom apologetically.

'It has to be enough.' Conrad nodded worriedly before he brightened again. 'Marstone Court has very pretty servants,' he said, nodding towards the closed door wherein Blanche and Edith still drank coffee and ate raw chocolate.

'Yes,' said Tom, taken slightly aback.

'She will make someone a very good wife. A good mother too, no doubt.'

Tom managed a curt nod and swallowed a sudden surge of jealousy. He'd noticed Conrad looking at Blanche but decided that his interest was merely paternal. Now he could see it was otherwise and it worried him. Unlike

Nelson, Conrad was a man of integrity, more likely to bestow honour than steal it away.

Due to the amount of ham she'd eaten at her mother's, plus the chocolate, Edith fell asleep on the way home, bundled on the floor at the back between the seats.

Tom kept glancing at Blanche, and made an effort to stop doing it, but failed. Her bonnet, which was pale mauve and had a wispy little feather floating at its side, lay in her lap. In the crisp night air and moonlight, her skin seemed almost silver, her hair like a black cloud around her head. She was exotically beautiful; no wonder Nelson wanted her. But Nelson would not marry her. Surely she knew that? She'd be a long-term mistress at best, at worst a dalliance until something new came along. Nelson had always liked exotic women, but in their place, mostly in Madame Sybil's, so he'd heard. Perhaps if Emmanuel had never taken his son to a brothel, he might never have become obsessed with foreign beauties – or developed a liking for opium.

He tried to convince himself that he would be telling Blanche the truth for her own good, but deep inside he knew otherwise. He didn't know when he'd first fallen in love with her, but it was there, tickling just beneath his heart and refusing to go away.

Staring steadfastly between the horse's ears, he took hold his courage, gave his jealousy full rein and said simply, 'Nelson will never marry you, neither here nor in Barbados.'

He sensed rather than saw the abrupt turn of her head, the look of surprise turning slowly to indignation.

He was right of course. Blanche was taken completely by surprise and was going to ask how he knew about Nelson, let alone that she'd considered going back to Barbados with him. Then she remembered Edith would do anything to ingratiate herself with Tom. She might keep her secret from the rest of the household, but she gushed openly in Tom's presence.

She stiffened, the only way she could control an angry outburst. 'I may not want him to marry me.'

'Hah!' Tom said scornfully. He didn't believe she'd settle for less than marriage.

He was right. Blanche had presumed Nelson would eventually marry her, though a little voice at the back of her mind nagged that it wouldn't be so.

'It's none of your business,' she muttered.

As the horse slowed to a tired amble, Tom sighed and shook his head. 'You're a fool. And it *is* my business. I'm the one who went touting your mother's bits and pieces to Aggie Pike for your return home.'

'I could have done it myself,' Blanche said hotly, though she knew it was far from the truth. She didn't know Bristol as well as Tom did, and she certainly didn't know the likes of Aggie Pike!

Tom barely tugged on the reins, but the tired horse sagged to a standstill, droopy between the shafts.

Tom wound the reins around the brake and took Blanche by her shoulders. 'I could marry you, Blanche. And I'm not tied up with the likes of Adelaide Tillingham.'

Shocked by his offer, her voice failed her. Her senses seemed heightened by his closeness, the seriousness of his expression and the warmth of his palms through her sleeves.

'He's not marrying her now,' she blurted once she'd found her voice.

'Of course he is,' said Tom, his hair waving around his face in the breeze. 'His father will insist. The Strongs aren't just a family, Blanche. They're a business. For them, marriage isn't about love. It's about business expansion and gathering more wealth, and more and more, and more. Don't you see that?'

Back in Barbados, she had been so sure about her feelings for Nelson, and almost as sure about his feelings for her. Deep inside she knew her passion wasn't quite what it had been back them. Think of those evenings, she thought, but when she did, they no longer seemed so golden. It was as if a sea mist had made the scene less colourful with the passing of time. Blanche stubbornly refused to relinquish the dream. She'd come to England for it.

Her face was flushed and her hair tumbled around her shoulders. Tom took advantage of Blanche's confusion. Still holding her shoulders, he kissed her – and Blanche did not resist.

In the stunned silence following his kiss, Tom gazed at her with more wonder than even Nelson with his palette of paint. He smiled nervously.

'Have you noticed how tired this old horse is? That's because he's having to pull us along by himself. It's a bit like us. If there were two horses pulling, it would make light work of things — just like in life.'

Blanche burst into an indignant laugh. 'Are you comparing me to a horse?'

Tom shrugged. 'I don't know fancy words, Blanche, but I know how I feel.'

He has integrity, thought Blanche. 'You're an honest man, Tom Strong, and your offer deserves consideration.'

He nodded thoughtfully. 'Good,' he said in a satisfied manner. 'Good.'

Her ears were getting cold, so Blanche put her bonnet back on as Tom reached for the reins.

'It's been an interesting day,' said Tom, as the horse ambled forward.

'Hmm,' said Blanche and smiled.

Between the back seats, Edith lay unblinking and very still. She had heard Tom proposing to Blanche, and knew that he'd kissed her. It just wasn't fair. Blanche already had Nelson. Wasn't that enough for her? Her bottom lip was trembling and a sob threatened. Bunching her hand into a tight fist, she pushed it into her mouth and wiped the tears from her eyes with the corner of her cloak. Well, she wouldn't be Blanche's friend any more, damn it, she wouldn't!

# Chapter Eighteen

Edith was being hostile towards Blanche, avoiding the nursery and spending more time below stairs with the rest of the servants.

Blanche considered asking her why, until the truth hit her. Edith must have heard Tom proposing to her. It occurred to her to explain, but what sort of explanation could she give? It had happened. There were no apologies to be made, so far as she was concerned. Tom had instigated everything.

Edith being less of a friend saddened her. When Blanche took the children kite-flying, Edith made excuses as to why she couldn't go. She only appeared when Tom did. Although Blanche saw him glancing at her and smiling as if he were thinking amusing and interesting thoughts, he never pressurized her for an answer to his proposal. They were rarely alone, and when it looked as though they might be, Blanche would run away, ostensibly to pull the kite up into the sky, but more so because she didn't know what to say should he ask her.

Besides looking after the older children, Blanche was now required to fill in for Mrs Frobisher, the monthly nurse, on her days off. One of those duties was taking the baby along to her mother to be fed.

'I know, I know,' Blanche said soothingly on one of those days, hugging the warm little body to her side as the baby turned red in the face and yelled for milk. 'Alicia May is hungry and needs her mother.'

Dr West was snapping his bag shut when she entered Lady Verity's room. Horatia was playing chaperone, sitting in a nursing chair and looking thoroughly disinterested. Prince Charles the spaniel was snoring on a purple silk cushion at the foot of the bed.

Dr West was a rotund man who advised brandy and water for minor ailments, and looked as if he took plenty of his own medicine. 'None of this getting out of bed after a fortnight,' he said. 'It may be unfashionable, but I advise all new mothers to stay in bed for one month following the birth.'

Blanche thought of her friend Lucy's mother and her strong brood. Two days following the births and she'd been up and about, hot steam rising from a cast-iron cauldron, as the sheets bloodied during the birth were boiled clean.

Horatia threw Blanche a withering glance then grimaced at the squalling bundle, and took advantage of Dr West's departure. 'I'll see you out, Doctor.' Swaying over its whalebone frame, her skirt swished like the sound of an ebbing tide over pebbles.

Verity's motherly façade left the room with the doctor and her stepdaughter.

'Bring it here,' she sighed, tugging at the tapes that fastened the bodice of her penoir.

Even as she handed her the baby, Blanche felt the full force of Lady Verity's pale blue eyes and knew she hated her.

'Stand over there,' Lady Verity ordered, jerking her chin at the window, her fingers poised over the flap of cotton that covered her swollen breast, already stained with milk flow.

Blanche obeyed. Englishwomen were prudish about exposing their bodies, even their breasts for baby-feeding. Back in Barbados, she'd seen women working in the fields, their babies tied around them, sucking at their nipples from beneath their arms. Their lives had been harsh, their children the greatest joy in their lives.

Turning her back to the room was almost like blotting out the present and all it represented. The view from the window, the spring leaves, the sprinkling of buttercups and daisies, were preferable to the dark blues, mauves and greens of the cluttered bedroom where the heavy furniture and velvet drapes of the new fashion stifled what light came through the windows.

A lone figure was walking down the gravelled drive, hair neatly tied for a change, and leather jacket straining across broad shoulders. Tom was going to the village, no more than a cluster of houses that straddled the road to Bristol. He's visiting Jasper, she thought. Her spirit followed him as well as her eyes until the road swerved right and he disappeared behind a stone folly, a watch-tower complete with castellated battlements and arrow slits carved to resemble a crusader's cross.

Tom was so unlike the rest of the family, so obviously of different blood – unlike Blanche, who *did* have Strong family blood, she was sure. But my mother wasn't a whore like his, she decided. Not in the strictest sense of the word.

*We women do what we have to do.*

She smiled. Her mother's voice had not quite left her, even though Barbados and that other life were many miles away.

The servants talked about Tom a lot, though they avoided including her in their conversations. Since the arrival of Alicia May, she'd spent little time below stairs. Nurses and governesses weren't expected to. They were the elite of the household, did not wear any uniform, and were not to be trusted, according to the maids, butlers and footmen. They were the only members of staff who were sometimes called upon to take tea with their employers, with the children in attendance of course.

Blanche didn't care that below stairs froze her out of their conversations. Unless she ate with the children in the nursery, she ate alone.

A sudden movement outside held her attention.

At first it seemed as though an animal, perhaps a deer, was running through the trees, following Tom but not wanting to be seen. A sudden flash of blue skirt exposed the truth, as Edith also disappeared behind the folly.

'Brown!' The sharp tone of Lady Verity's voice roused Blanche from her thoughts and the scene outside. 'Here, take this child. It's finished!'

A trickle of milk ran from the corner of the baby's mouth. Blanche wiped it away, placed the baby over her shoulder and made cooing noises as she patted the soft little back.

Lady Verity looked at her as though she were stupid, or at least disobedient. 'Don't do that here, Brown. Take her away and do it at your own convenience.'

Blanche clenched her jaw so hard she heard her teeth grind. For the sake of the child, Blanche let it go. Poor mite was getting precious little attention from its own mother and badly needed winding.

An amazing transformation suddenly took place in the heavy, airless room. The hairy bundle sleeping at the foot of the bed got up, wagged his tail and stretched, and his mistress's mood turned to delight.

'Come here, darling one,' she cooed. 'Come here to Mamma.'

Leaving the stifling warmth of Lady Verity's bedroom, Blanche turned back towards the nursery, and wondered at Edith running off after Tom. Would she get angry with him, accuse him of dallying with her? In all honesty he hadn't. His kindness towards Edith had moved her to make assumptions.

Due to her extra duties with regard to Alicia May, there had been little time to see the Reverend Strong. Tom or Edith had clearly told the household that her presence upset the Reverend and those times she had managed to visit the west wing, someone had appeared as if by magic and practically barricaded the door.

At first she thought about settling the sleeping baby into her lace-curtained crib, but thought better of it. No one had thought to show her to the Reverend Strong. He had few visitors. The only members of the family who visited regularly were Tom and Sir Emmanuel. Besides, she thought, smiling down at the pink-faced child, I'm sure he'd love to see Alicia May.

For once no one appeared as she approached the Reverend Strong's room. The door was well oiled and made no noise as she opened it. She stopped and listened, just in case he was not alone. The only sound she heard was the snuffling of Alicia May, now nestling contentedly in the crook of her right arm.

The room smelled of camphor and lavender. Sprigs of the latter had been sprinkled liberally over the floor. With each step, the dried flowers were crushed underfoot, and their perfume released.

Pale-faced, his skin glistening, the Reverend Strong lay immobile against a pile of pillows. His mouth was open and his eyes flickered as he hovered between sleep and full wakefulness. He looked very sick, much older than his fifty-odd years. So sad, she thought, that the man who seemed the best of the Strong brothers was the worst for health.

Clutching the baby gently to her chest, Blanche bent over him. 'Reverend Strong?'

The eyes flickered before opening. He blinked and seemed to brighten when he saw her face. A kind of restrained cackle came from his mouth as he tried to speak.

'Sshh,' she said, placing a finger against her lips. 'No need to tire yourself. See? I've brought Alicia May to see you.'

She held the sleeping baby up so he could see her better.

'Don't you think young life is beautiful?'

She smiled at the sleeping baby then looked into Jeb Strong's face. His expression was stomach-wrenching. He stared at the baby, closed his mouth and swallowed. A lone tear rolled from the corner of one eye.

If only he was well enough to tell me more, thought Blanche. It seemed that every time she saw him, his emotions overpowered his vocal cords. Poor man. She couldn't resist reaching out and, with her smallest finger, touching his tear.

An anguished, strangled sound came from his throat as his gaze shifted to her. He struggled for words, tried to lift his hand. She sensed he wanted to touch her. The baby was forgotten. He managed to lift one finger and pointed at the dark mole beneath her right eye.

'P... a... ti... ence,' he said, his breath drawing in like a captured sigh once the word was spoken.

'Patience,' Blanche echoed, and although she would be patient for Jeb Strong to get better and tell her more, time was running out for him.

His face suddenly creased as though in terrible pain, his eyes squeezed tightly shut as he broke into soundless sobs. 'S... i... nn... er,' he said weakly, poking one thin finger at his narrow chest. 'For... give... me.'

Unsure what she was supposed to forgive, and disappointed that she'd learned nothing more, she patted his hand. Seeing him agitated like this was upsetting. Finding out about her father was important, but not at the risk of upsetting Jeb Strong.

'Sshh,' she said, and began to sing softly, a lullaby her mother had sang to her.

*Echoes of the ocean, blowing through the trees,*
*Keep safe my sweet one, bring him home to me.*
*Sing to my child, sleeping in our bed.*
*Softly blow her tears away, for soon I'm sure we'll wed.*

His lips moved as his eyelids slowly closed. 'Patience,' he said one last time before his head fell to one side. He slept.

After closing the door behind her, a slow chill seemed to seep down her spine. First he'd told her to have patience, and now he was asking for her forgiveness.

The blood seemed to drain from her brain as a sudden and incredible thought came to her. Could it be that he was in some way responsible for her birth? Was it possible that *he* were her father?

She tried to sieve the facts. Otis was in Barbados, and her mother had lived in Barbados, but all three of the brothers had been there at various times. Jeb would not have been allowed to marry her mother, but he was a caring man. That much was obvious by his adoption of Tom and his past ministering to the poor. Was it possible that Otis and his brother had formed some sort of pact? Had it been agreed that Otis would look after Viola, her mother, whilst Jeb Strong had gone back to England to pursue his clerical career?

Blanche took Alicia May back to the room the child shared with the monthly nurse. Thoughts and suspicions about Tom, about Nelson and about her parentage whirled around in her mind. It seemed as though her head was filling with layer upon layer of questions for which no easy answers seemed forthcoming.

As she lay the baby down in her crib and covered her tiny form, the stress she'd suffered since arriving in this land, flooded over her and she cried long and bitterly. Her tears were not just for herself, but also for the unwanted children, the newborn babe, the boy with ringworm on the dockside, and the stinking squalor in which Edith's family lived.

Wrapped up in self-pity, she didn't hear the door open, the soft tread of fine leather shoes upon the woven richness of the Turkish carpet.

'Blanche?'

Recognizing the voice, she spun round. Nelson! Oh, it just wasn't fair! Why had he appeared now, when her cheeks were streaked with tears and her dress smelled of stale milk, regurgitated by the baby?

'I thought you'd been ordered to London,' she said, wiping her eyes.

He grinned boyishly. 'I disobeyed. Anyway, Father's gone into Bristol, no doubt still trying to get the better of Conrad Heinkel.'

Blanche remembered the kind man she'd met at the sugar refinery and hoped he had the courage to stand up to Nelson's father.

She grinned at his outfit of smock and floppy hat. 'Where are you going dressed like that?'

'Painting!' he exclaimed, spreading his arms wide.

'You didn't wear those clothes in Barbados.'

Gently, he kissed her cheek then whispered in her ear, 'At times I hardly wore anything in Barbados.'

Blanche felt her cheeks getting hot. 'Does the outfit help your artistic ability?'

He waved a finger at her in mock annoyance. 'One day I will be remembered as Turner will be remembered.'

She didn't know who Turner was, but presumed he was noteworthy. She studied Nelson's classic features.

'I'm sorry about Barbados,' she said, 'but I can't leave, not until Alicia May is a little older.' It seemed a weak excuse, but she couldn't help feeling sorry for the newborn, whose mother seemed uncaring about the child's welfare.

It was the best excuse she could think of. Tom had said that Nelson would have kept her as a mistress and would marry his cousin. She didn't want it confirmed so didn't mention it. Neither did she admit her real reason for staying.

He sighed and kissed her hair. 'We'll get there eventually, but in the meantime… when is your next day off?' He wrapped his arms around her.

'Tomorrow.'

He flushed with pleasure. 'Tomorrow I shall be painting a picture of the village church. Can you be there by noon?'

Blanche hesitated as she remembered what Tom had said. She could never be a wife, only a mistress, and even that might not be a permanent position. Nothing had really changed. She was being asked to meet him in secret. She was a fool to hope, but when she thought of Barbados, her mouth became dry and her heart beat against her ribs like a battering ram. She nodded. 'Yes.'

'I'll see you then,' he said, kissed each of her cheeks, then dashed away.

Blanche ran to the door and watched him go. Closing her eyes, she laid her head back against the door. Tomorrow she would prove to herself once and for all that she still felt the same about him, that their love would overcome all obstacles. But Tom's steady gaze haunted her. Surely she was a fool not to accept his proposal of marriage. But she couldn't help it. Memories of Barbados made her feel warm and happy, but could it be that the passion ignited on a sunlit island coloured her memories of Nelson? She shook her head and reached for her sewing box and one of George's shirts. Tonight she'd make herself busy, which would at least keep the doubts at bay and make time pass more quickly.

Mending the shirt was not enough to keep her occupied. It was her duty to iron and mend the children's clothes once they were returned from the laundry. A pile of hot coals glowed in the grate, warming the room and heating the core for the iron. Just as she was putting the glowing piece of iron into the casing with the help of a pair of tongs, someone knocked at the door and slowly pushed it open.

A mop of brown hair, then a pair of brown eyes appeared followed by a wide smile. 'Hello, Blanche. Can we visit you?'

Blanche smiled, up ended the iron and placed her hands on her hips. 'What better visitors could I have? Are the others with you?'

Rupert, Caroline, Arthur and George, the latter red-eyed as usual and sucking his thumb, filed into the room.

Blanche forced herself to forget about Nelson for the moment, and concentrate on them. 'Have you come to see Alicia May?'

'Yes,' said Caroline, always defensive about showing her feelings, like her mother, thought Blanche, and was instantly worried about the girl's future.

'And to see you,' added Rupert.

Blanche raised her finger before her lips. 'Speak softly. Your sister's sleeping and I've got lots to do.'

They dutifully filed round the crib and grinned down at their little sister. Rupert was fascinated by her tiny little fingers curling around his own.

'Aren't you supposed to be at your lessons?' Blanche asked.

'Mrs Grainger's got a cold and is confined to bed,' said Caroline. 'She left us some work to do, but we don't feel like doing it.'

Blanche shook her head. 'She won't like that.'

Rupert sighed in the worldly way of a young man far beyond his nine years. 'We know. She'll probably lay the birch across our backsides or a ruler across our hands. She might even lock us up in the attic with the spiders.'

At the mention of the attic, George promptly burst into tears.

'Rupert! You shouldn't frighten him like that.' Blanche knelt down, threw her arms around him and hugged him close. 'Oh, George! Spiders can't hurt you.' She shivered at the memory of sugar spiders. Thankfully, they wouldn't thrive in an English climate.

'It's not the spiders that frighten him,' said Rupert. 'It's those old paintings. Their eyes watch you. Even when it's dark, you know they're looking at you. Mamma felt like that about them, that's why she prefers mirrors.'

'You can't blame George,' said a know-it-all Caroline. 'It's usually him that ends up there. It wouldn't happen so often if he didn't wet the bed.'

Blanche hugged him even closer. She'd tried every way of getting him to stop wetting the bed, refusing drinks after six at night, rousing him from sleep every so often. Nothing had worked.

'We'll have to do something,' she said, though wasn't sure what. Lady Verity would bequeath the supervision of her children to anyone, so long as she wasn't bothered with them; Horatia was disinterested in her half-brothers and sisters; and Emmanuel counted his children in the same way he did his money – things to be accumulated, and perhaps used to gainful end. That left only Nelson and Tom. Tom knew something of what was going on. She thought of telling him to forget dead boys and do something to help those still living. But that would be unfair. It couldn't be easy stepping into a dead person's life and feeling somehow that you'd inherited his advantages by default.

That left Nelson. She purposely swept aside his inadequacies, resurrecting the man she thought she'd known in Barbados.

Between Nelson leaving and the children arriving, Duncan stayed hidden behind a dusty curtain in the nursery. Horatia called him her 'watcher', her eyes and ears below stairs. Oh, her father and stepmother didn't care much for what happened in the servant's kitchen, but she did. She knew the value of knowing what was going on. And she would certainly want to know what the children's latest nurse was up to.

## Chapter Nineteen

With each breath of wind, a shower of blossom blew like snowflakes among the mossy gravestones and marble mausoleums. Tom barely noticed. Walking through the long grass, he paused only to watch the fallen blossom form a fragrant drift around the tombstone of Jasper Strong. Old Josh was waiting for him there, his pipe sticking out like a twig from the side of his mouth, smoke curling around his head.

'Saw the old sweep who used to do the job before this one,' he said once the formalities were out of the way, 'the bugger that used to do the chimneys years ago, and asked 'im a few things on your behalf.'

Josh puffed on his pipe. He never rushed anything. As a boy, Tom remembered watching him toil in the garden. He'd seemed incredibly slow compared to the younger gardeners, dipping and rising with methodical frequency along the furrows and plants. At the end of a planting session, when beans and peas were being sown, or young cabbages transplanted to permanent spots, Josh had always planted more than anyone. Yet they'd appeared to be doing the job far faster than Josh. But that was his secret. He never rushed, but he never slowed either. He had one speed and it got the job done.

Tom waited.

'Drunken old bugger,' he said. 'Used to beat 'is missus and youngsters. Son showed me a broken finger. It was 'im that used to go up the chims for 'is father, so your boy going up the chim was nothing to do with 'im!'

Tom sighed. That much he'd already guessed. But why had Jasper climbed the chimney? Tom couldn't believe that the boy could have done it at his own volition. Someone must have suggested it. But who and, more to the point, why?

He was sombre when he left Josh and walked back through the cemetery. With head bowed, he walked past the rows of headstones capped with moss and bound with weeds, sad-eyed angels and ornate crosses. He kicked at the grass, sending clods of earth flying through the air. He finally came to the Strong mausoleum. He stopped, not because he wanted to admire it, more because he was disinclined to go back to the house until he had thought things through. So far, there was no one to blame for Jasper's death. He'd been just a boy who loved ships, who had wanted to climb masts but had climbed a chimney instead.

Mud clung to one of the names. It spoilt the look of the thing. Absent-mindedly, he plucked some wet grass and began rubbing the mud from the marble. Slowly the name was revealed. Tom straightened, surprised at what he saw, though not quite understanding its significance.

Grass rustled beneath the hem of a woman's dress. Tom turned, disappointed when he saw it was only Edith.

'Captain Tom. I was just out for a walk. I didn't expect to see you here.'

Tom instinctively knew that her presence was no accident. She was grinning broadly at him, her cheeks salmon pink and her eyes full of something more than excitement – hope perhaps.

Tom flung the grass to the ground, watching it scatter with the wind before rubbing his hand on his thigh. He was in no mood for Edith's mundane chatter. He spoke sharply. 'Where I go is my affair.'

The colour that adorned Edith's face seeped down into her neck. Even her ears turned pink. 'I didn't mean to be cheeky.'

She sounded genuinely regretful, and Tom felt sorry he'd snapped at her.

'Sometimes I like to be by myself,' he said, unable to stop his gaze straying to the name that had been hidden in mud. He sighed and shook his head. 'Though I really should find somewhere more interesting than a graveyard. Please don't mention I was here to anyone else. They'll think I'm mad.'

'Oh no, they won't,' Edith blurted. 'You ain't the only one who comes 'ere. Nelson comes here to paint, and even her ladyship came here, before she had the baby, of course.'

Tom frowned at the thought of Lady Verity visiting anywhere unless there was food on offer. 'Why would she?' he asked.

Edith shrugged. 'I don't know. She only came the once and brought me with her. And she walked! Can you believe that, her ladyship walking rather than getting the carriage out?' Frowning, she went on. 'Told me not to tell anyone too.' She beamed amiably, her broad face growing broader. 'But I can trust you, Captain Tom.'

'Where did she go?'

Edith shrugged again. 'I don't know. She told me to wait by the gate.'

Puzzled, Tom shook his head, his eyebrows knotted. 'Why would she want to come wandering around a churchyard?'

'There's the baby's christening.'

Tom looked at Edith. She was gazing at him adoringly, her eyes unusually round, as if she were trying to read his mind – or his heart. He couldn't believe that Verity would have come here to see the vicar about her baby's christening. More likely, she would have summoned him to the house. 'I don't really believe that, but then, I also do not believe that you were merely out for a walk. Was there something in particular you wanted to see me about?'

She could not possibly get any redder. He felt slightly smug. It confirmed his own masculinity, though in a hundred years, he could never feel any passion for her. That, unfortunately for both of them, lay in another direction.

'I was thinking how nice it was, that day we went into Bristol and that kind gentleman at the refinery gave us chocolate. I don't want to be forward, you understand, but I would just love to do that again. Wouldn't you?'

Tom smiled. Of course he would, if it meant having Blanche close to him again. He'd barely seen her since asking her to marry him.

'I would very much like to. Take my arm. I'll escort you back to the house.'

She took it gladly, slipping her plump, childlike arm through his. He felt her eyes feasting on him as she chattered like a magpie, mostly about her family; the things they'd done, the travelling, the achievements. Outrageous lies, perhaps, but entertaining.

'One more question,' said Tom. 'Were her ladyship's hands muddy?'

'Yes,' said Edith, 'I think they were.'

So Verity had rubbed mud onto the Strong mausoleum, but why?

He was successful in not meeting her gaze. Being kind to her was one thing. Encouraging her affection was quite another. He wondered how many admirers she'd had in her life. Not many, he thought, not many she'd want anyway.

'I thought you wouldn't have time for walking out, Edith, not with the arrival of our little Alicia May,' he said, and watched her face.

'I'm only a nursemaid. Brown is the nurse proper.' She said it contemptuously.

'You mean Blanche?'

'She's supposed to be called Brown, Lady Verity's orders.'

'I call people I like by their proper names, Edith. For instance, I never call you Clements, do I?'

Realizing she'd made a tactical error, she looked at him regretfully, opened her mouth then shut it again.

He could do without her adoration, and he wouldn't hurt her feelings, but he would not and could not tolerate her jealousy. He saw enough of that in Horatia.

'I'm taking the children down to the *Miriam Strong* tomorrow,' he said, returning to their earlier topic of conversation. 'A day out will do them good, besides which, it's time they learned more about ships and the sea. After all, they are members of the Strong family and will be expected to oversee its trade in years to come. And if they are to oversee its trade, they need to know about ships. The children will need female companions, of course.'

Edith was all attention.

'I shall require that both Blanche and you accompany us. The monthly nurse can look after the littlest Strong for the day. Perhaps you could approach Blanche with regard to this? I myself will clear the matter with Lady Verity.'

Adoration shone in her eyes and he felt the sweaty nervousness of her palms. He'd tried to sound formal but no matter how he spoke or looked at her, Edith remained in love with him.

Back at the house, they went their separate ways, Edith to see Blanche, apologize and blame the time of the month for her unfriendliness. She would do anything for the chance of a day out with Tom Strong.

Tom had no intention of asking Verity for her permission to take the children down to the ship. He would do it anyway, and the likes of Mrs Grainger wouldn't dare stand in his way.

In the meantime, he had a question to ask. He would have headed straight for Jeb's room, but was waylaid by Horatia, a vision in blue with velvet ribbons in her hair and a pearl-edged cameo at her throat.

'Father wants you,' she said, sliding her arm through his, and gripping him close as though they were conspirators in some treasonable plan.

She smelled of violets, which meant the dress was new. For his benefit? After a few weeks, the dress would smell of her body and be liberally sprinkled with rose water. Such heavy garments rarely got washed.

'Goodness,' she said, wrinkling her nose and suddenly pushing him away. 'You stink of smoke and grass. Where have you been?' He did think of telling her that after a day in the refinery, he'd visited one of the most iniquitous dens in the city before strolling around the graveyard, but decided against it. After all, Horatia was a lady. Although she had a cast-iron constitution, she feigned disgust if she so wished, but now he sensed the opposite was true. She rather liked his roughness, the dirt and sweat of hard walking, hard drinking – even of hard whoring. He sensed she viewed him as a challenge to be met and conquered. A lot of women had.

Tom let Horatia guide him to the study where Emmanuel Strong sat smoking behind his desk, an open accounts ledger spread out in front of him.

His eyes sparkled when he saw Tom. 'I've got something to ask you,' he said with something akin to excitement.

Tom grimaced. 'And I've got something to ask you.'

Emmanuel looked surprised, perhaps even a little wary. 'Ask.'

'It's a family matter. I know I'm not really family, but it's only the question of a name.'

Emmanuel had an open look, though some wariness remained in his eyes. 'Whose name?'

'A woman's.'

Puzzled, Emmanuel nodded for him to go on.

'Who was Patience Strong?'

Emmanuel stared at him. Then, to Tom's surprise, he burst out laughing.

Horatia smiled. 'Patience Strong was my grandmother.' Her smile wavered. She threw Emmanuel a look of contempt and said, 'My father has a lot in common with my grandfather. Both married twice.'

Tom shook his head and scratched at the base of his neck. He was puzzled.

Emmanuel said, 'Patience was my father's first wife.'

'I see.'

'Was there anything else you wanted to know about her?'

'Not really. Jeb was muttering something about patience. I thought he meant the virtue, then I saw the name at the cemetery.' He shrugged. 'He just got agitated. That's all.'

Emmanuel sighed as if relieved Tom hadn't asked him something more personal. 'Now, down to business,' he exclaimed and poured himself a large port from a flat-bottomed ship's decanter. Before Emmanuel had chance to replace the stopper, Tom had got himself an empty glass and glared at his adoptive uncle, as though daring him to send the stopper home. Begrudgingly, Emmanuel poured him a drink, though not as large a measure as he'd poured for himself.

Both men sipped before Emmanuel said, 'I hear the Germans are holding a lot of meetings lately. What are they up to?'

Tom almost choked on his drink. 'They're always holding meetings. Mostly it's to do with their church. They're Lutherans, aren't they?'

Emmanuel shook his head, his jowls flopping like those of an aged bulldog. 'They're foreigners and they all belong to the Master Sugar Bakers Association. I don't like guilds. I don't like anybody forming societies that can harm the trade of this country in general and this family in particular. There have been rumours and pamphlets—'

'Pamphlets written by people who think that anyone not born in this country has to be its enemy!'

Emmanuel's eyes were like jet beads and his face was red from too much drink. He was beginning to look older than he was, his jowls resting on his oversized cravat and his waistcoat straining around his girth. Wigs had been fashionable in previous years but not now. Emmanuel's hair was receding fast and his head was shiny with sweat.

'My only concern is for this family. Our plantations are not making as much as they were. It makes sense for us to control the refining process as well as growing the cane. It does not make sense for the process to be in the hands of these Germans.'

Tom wanted to hit him. It was true that the original guild members were all from the continent, mostly Hanseatic Germans, but some Dutch sugar bakers too. But the ruthless determination of Isaiah Strong, Emmanuel's grandfather, had founded a dynasty that was strong in both name and nature. No one was allowed to threaten the wealth and power they held so dear. Tom was in their power. Not until Jeb was dead would he feel free to leave and never return. Until then, he had to toe the line, or at least pretend to. But he *liked* Conrad Heinkel, and he would not betray him.

'What do you want me to do?'

Emmanuel drained his glass, poured himself another and took a large swig of that. 'I want you to find a way of gaining control of the refinery.'

Tom frowned. 'How do you want me to do this?'

Emmanuel downed his drink and poured himself another. Tom had barely touched his.

'Identify differences, such as religion, unpatriotic and unsociable behaviour, corruptive morals, et cetera. Sow the seeds of public outrage in the right part of the city and—'

'Eighteen thirty-one.'

Emmanuel pursed his lips at the mention of this date. In this year, the Bristol Riots had taken place and the most imposing buildings of the city had been burned down, including the Custom House on Queen Square. 'I want them run out of the city, preferably out of the country.'

'So you can buy the business for a song?'

'Of course.'

Tom slammed his glass down on the desk, causing some of the dark, red liquid to slop on to the leather top.

'God, but you're a bastard, Emmanuel Strong – *Sir* Emmanuel Strong! It's hard to believe that you're Jeb's brother, for a finer man never lived.'

'Fine?' Emmanuel cried. 'How little you know of the man. He committed the worst sin imaginable and thought by turning religious he might be spared the wrath of God!'

Emmanuel's eyes were bright with triumph. Tom was confused. Jeb was not capable of sin. He knew him well. It was impossible. He looked around him as if for moral support in his belief, and glanced at Horatia. She seemed distracted, smiling, as though she knew something far more interesting than either of them.

'There's nothing more to be said.' Tom headed for the door, Emmanuel calling out after him.

'How dare you walk out on me! Don't forget who you are! Nothing!'

Tom paused by the door, his face dark with anger. 'Well, I'd sooner be nothing than be Emmanuel Strong. A bastard! That's what you are. A low-down, stinking bastard!'

Emmanuel Strong staggered slightly. Trembling with rage, he laid his palms on the desk, then heaved a drawer open and brought out a pistol.

'Get out of my sight! Get out of my house! Get out! Get out!'

His face puce with anger, he aimed the pistol at Tom's chest, his hand shaking from the effect of his anger and too much drink.

'Father!'

Horatia grabbed the pistol from his waving arm, unclenched his fingers from around the stock, and took it from him.

'Go,' she shouted to Tom. 'I'll take care of him.'

Before Tom left the room, Emmanuel had sunk into his chair, his face still red and glistening with sweat, and his body trembling with anger.

Horatia grabbed Tom's sleeve before he'd got as far as the stairs. She looked worried. 'Don't leave, Tom. He doesn't mean it.'

Tom smiled and shook his head. 'Of course he does.'

'No. It's the drink—'

Tom raised a finger. 'Your father is never affected by drink, Horatia. He means it.'

'You can't leave. You can't. What about Uncle Jeb?'

Tom's own anger was making him grind his teeth and set his jaw. At the mention of Jeb, his tension slowly subsided. He nodded, surprised at the intensity of Horatia's expression, the concern, the fear and also the passion in her eyes.

'You're right. I can't leave.'

Horatia visibly relaxed. 'So you'll do as he asks?'

He didn't answer.

'You don't need to do it. It won't matter that much, Tom. Bristol's falling behind in the sugar stakes.' The secretiveness he'd seen earlier returned to her eyes. Her voice dropped to a whisper. 'As I told you before, there are other things besides sugar, Tom. With a little planning and a lot of courage, great achievements are possible.'

He said nothing. Horatia was surprising. She was beautiful, clever and more determined than her father could ever be. But she'd never been allowed to shine, simply because she was a woman.

Her eyes sparkled as she held his arm. 'We're going to build ships, Tom, big ships like the *Great Western*. I've invested my own money in the venture, but you mustn't tell Father.'

He frowned. 'You mean like Mr Brunel's ship rather than sailing ships?'

She nodded. 'Ships that can get to New York inside two weeks. Ships that can take the mail from London to New York in a fraction of the time it takes to sail there.'

He hadn't drunk enough for his head to reel, but it was certainly doing that now. First Sir Emmanuel Strong had laid this business of the sugar refinery at his door, damn him. And now it seemed Horatia had her own plans for the future of the Strong family.

'Don't breathe a word,' she added, her lips almost brushing his cheek.

Emmanuel Strong filled the doorway, his eyes bloodshot and anger still colouring his face. 'Aren't you bloody gone yet?'

Tom turned on his heel.

He went to his room where he broke out a bottle of rum. He would have preferred to have gone into Bristol, drink a little, fight a little, perhaps find Sally and have another try at getting her to go to Portishead to be with her sister. But he had to go into the sugar refinery tomorrow morning. He liked Conrad Heinkel. He liked the tough men who sweated over the sugar boilers, filled the furnaces, heaved the hogsheads and pulled on pulleys that opened shutters, valves and boiling pans. As he drank he considered finding Blanche and telling her all about it. One look at those deep grey eyes and he'd forget everything.

After finishing the bottle, he fell into a deep sleep, a world of dreams far from the problems that chased round and around in his mind. He never heard Horatia entering the room. He never saw the way she stared at him, her hand resting on her bosom as if she sought to stop her heart beating so hard.

Holding her breath, she leaned over him. 'Goodnight, Captain,' she said softly, and planted a kiss on his lips. She watched him for a while. No other man made her feel like he did. The look of him, the smell of him, invaded her dreams and occupied her mind in those moments when passion overrode her deep love of power. She was a woman in a man's world, but was striving to rise above the usual position of her sex. Men were easily used if handled correctly. She could wind them around her little finger – except Tom. He was her Achilles' heel, and she could neither admit to nor escape from it.

## Chapter Twenty

Following a warm bath and the administration of a little gripe water. Alicia May was put down to sleep. Normally Blanche would have eaten supper with the children, but since the baby's arrival a tray was brought up to her from the kitchen by one of the scullery maids and left without a word being said. Blanche had got used to the silent stare of whoever delivered it. She was sure that Duncan had given the order that she should be ostracized by the rest of the staff. In a close-knit household, it was only natural for jealousies and personal dislikes. Blanche did not let it worry her. The only servant whose silence hurt was Edith and she knew the reason for that. She would have tackled her about it on her day off when Edith would step in to take care of the baby, but Nelson's invitation took priority.

She was singing to the drowsy baby when the knock came at the door and Edith entered bearing her supper tray. 'It's roast mutton and apple pie. I got you a bit extra.' The words tumbled from Edith's mouth and she coloured up to her eyebrows as she said it. Blanche sensed the time of regret and forgiveness had arrived, but why now?

At the sound of Edith's resonant voice, Alicia May opened her mouth and yelled.

'You could be a little quieter,' said Blanche, and tried not to look surprised, but it was easy to see that Edith's attitude had changed. Blanche remembered seeing her running through the trees after Tom. What had been said to change Edith? She told herself she didn't feel jealous, only intrigued.

Edith stood with her hands behind her back, shifting her weight from one hip to the other and looking as if she were searching for something to say.

Blanche picked up the baby and swayed and hummed in a constant rhythm in an effort to stop Alicia May from yelling.

'Let me take her,' Edith offered.

Hungry for her own dinner, Blanche handed Edith the baby. 'I've got just the thing for you,' said Edith, looking down into the baby's face.

Alicia May continued to yell.

Blanche put down her spoon. 'Perhaps I should try—'

Edith spun away, one hand rummaging in the pocket of her apron. 'Now, don't you worry. Eat that food I got for you.' Blanche sat at the table and lifted the lid on the tray. Her mouth began to water. Cook certainly made a nice pastry. She thought of asking Edith why the change of heart, but decided it wasn't worth it. Tom meant nothing to her. She would tell Edith that, but not until after tomorrow when she'd met Nelson in the churchyard. She couldn't tell her until after then, and she wasn't exactly sure she knew why.

After a few mouthfuls, her attention went back to Edith who was tipping a spoonful of something into Alicia May's mouth. Blanche frowned. 'What's that?'

'Oh that's all right,' chirped Edith. 'It's only laudanum.' Blanche remembered Miss Pinkerty administering laudanum to her mother.

*Just wine and moondust. It will take you to paradise and back again, but take you to hell if you're not careful.*

'Give me that!' Blanche snatched the bottle from Edith.

Edith looked at her askance. 'There ain't no harm in it. My mother gave us a tot of Holland to shut us up. Didn't hurt us, did it? We're all hale and hearty.'

'Who gave you this?'

'Well, Mrs Grainger said—'

'Oh, did she?'

Blanche could barely control her anger. Already Mrs Grainger was infiltrating the life of the youngest member of the Strong family. 'You are not to give anything to that baby without my say-so. Is that clear?'

Edith pouted and her bottom lip quivered. Blanche took the baby from her and settled her in the crib. The child was already falling asleep, yet to Blanche's mind, it didn't seem a healthy sleep. Babies made comforting little noises before they fell asleep. Alicia May had gone out like a snuffed candle.

Blanche was angry. 'Whatever possessed you, Edith?'

Edith chewed at her lip before an avalanche of words fell out of her mouth. 'Well, I told Mrs Grainger that we were going out with Captain Tom tomorrow, and she said the duty nurse wouldn't be too pleased about that because she's got a lot of sewing to do and wouldn't want to be doing with a baby crying, and then she said she had just the thing to keep her quiet.'

Blanche opened a window, tipped the bottle, and let the contents drip on to the ground below.

'I didn't think it would do no harm,' simpered Edith. 'No different to the stuff she gives young George for his chest.'

Blanche spun round. 'Chest?'

Edith shrugged awkwardly. 'Something,' she said with a glum expression. 'Not laudanum though.'

Making a mental note to check what Mrs Grainger was giving George, Blanche resettled herself at the table and continued with her food. But it was hard to concentrate on eating. She was angry with Edith, angry with Mrs Grainger, and angry with a family that gave scant attention to its youngest and most vulnerable members. Tom's marriage proposal and Nelson's offer to run away with her were shuffled to the back of her mind. Then there was Edith. What was she up to? Rekindling their friendship, for certain. She could almost feel Edith's embarrassment, her aching to make friends and not being sure how to go about it.

At last she seemed to give in. 'I'm supposed to be going out tomorrow.'

Blanche continued eating.

At last all the pent-up tension seemed to break like a dam in full flood. Edith burst into tears and flung herself down on her knees next to the table and Blanche.

'Please be my friend again, Blanche. I think I should die if you weren't never me friend no more.'

Blanche pretended to think about it as she chewed her food. After all, it wasn't her fault that Tom had kissed her and asked her to marry him. She couldn't help it if it made Edith jealous. She said, 'I'll be your friend again, Edith, but on one condition.'

Edith's eyes were round with adoration. 'Anything, Blanche. Anything at all.'

'I want to be kept informed of any improvement in the Reverend Strong's health. I know some times are more lucid than others and that his mind returns and he speaks almost properly.'

Edith suddenly looked as if she were having second thoughts about her offer. 'Why?'

'I want to ask him some questions.'

'What sort of questions?'

'The sort that are important to me.'

Edith nodded thoughtfully and sprang to her feet. Sniffing first, she wiped her eyes and her nose on her apron.

'That's all right then!'

Her face brightened immediately, though Blanche sensed by the way she kept hopping from one leg to another that there was something else she wanted to say.

'Are your shoes on fire?' Blanche let her cutlery clatter on to her plate. 'Please tell me what else you want, Edith, then perhaps I can eat my supper in peace.'

Edith looked fit to explode with excitement. 'I just told you. We're going out with Captain Tom tomorrow. He's going to take the children down onto the *Miriam Strong*.'

'Yes, you did tell me. That's very good of him, but I can't go.'

Keeping her eyes downcast, she picked up her cutlery again.

'We have to. We're responsible for them children. We have to go.' Edith was almost begging.

Blanche sighed and laid the cutlery back down. 'We can't both go. Someone has to look after Alicia May and make sure no one gives her any more laudanum.' She wasn't going to admit to meeting Nelson. Edith would only ask her questions as to what she was expecting, were they going to go to Barbados and was he really going to marry his plain little cousin. She decided to make a joke of it.

'Perhaps you should ask your friend, Mrs Grainger.' She said it with an impish smile, knowing what to expect in response.

'I ain't going with that old Tartar! And I don't think Tom will be too keen either.'

Blanche hid her smile. No, Tom wouldn't be too keen.

Edith was too besotted with Tom to throw away the chance of spending most of the day with him. 'Seems a shame you can't come. I could have taken you and the children to see what dogs me brother's got,' she said, tracing her fingers around the edge of the washstand and not daring to look into Blanche's face.

Blanche had two reasons for hiding her expression. Firstly, it was hard to imagine the Strong children among those dark alleys or inside the dingy house where Edith's mother fed chopped-up rats to stolen dogs. Secondly, she didn't want Edith to see the sparkle in her eyes. She'd guess immediately that she was off to see Nelson.

'You'll have to go alone,' she said at last. 'I'm sure Tom won't mind.'

'Oh!' At first Edith looked quite put out, but soon she smiled with pleasure. 'Of course, I can manage the children by myself.'

Blanche smiled. 'And can you manage Captain Strong by yourself?'

Edith's face could not go any redder. 'I'll try,' she exclaimed, her voice trembling with excitement.

Blanche's tone became serious. 'And no more laudanum, not without mine or a doctor's consent.'

Edith nodded. 'But you had no need to waste it. Mr Nelson would have made use of it. Bottles, powders, and a bubbly thing with a long pipe...' She outlined the shape and size of the hookah with her hands.

Blanche froze. Muddled excerpts of past conversations flooded into her mind. Creative imagination. Artistic vision. She remembered him talking passionately of exploring his inner self, delving into the depths of his soul... the way his face had shone, the brilliance of his eyes.

'Shouldn't he take it either?' Edith asked.

'No,' she said softly, her appetite completely lost. 'He shouldn't.'

–

The children, Edith in the midst of them, came bounding down the steps to where Tom waited with the governess cart, the reins connected to the bridle of a high-stepping hackney. He'd opted for the governess cart because he'd used it to fetch Blanche when she'd first arrived in Bristol. He was certain she'd appreciate the thought, and because of its size, she'd have to sit up front with him in the driver's seat. He had it all worked out. But where was she?

He wound the reins and got down to help Edith get aboard, his eyes continually searching the arched doorway through which they'd come.

*Please come, Blanche. Don't keep me waiting.*

His impatience finally got the better of him. 'Where's Blanche?'

Looking a little miffed, Edith plumped herself down heavily in the front seat of the cart. 'Blanche isn't coming. It's just me.'

'It's her day off. Where is she?'

'Got other fish to fry,' snapped Edith.

To say that Tom was disappointed was putting it mildly. A whole day of children and Edith, he thought as he got up into the governess cart and took the reins. At present, Edith was silent, but before long she'd be chattering excitedly, her stories getting more bizarre the more excitable she got.

Tom stared straight ahead over the horse's back and urged it forward. His curiosity was hard to contain. 'Has Blanche got a sweetheart?' he asked Edith jokingly.

Edith shrugged and looked sour. 'P'raps she has. P'raps she ain't. But there you are, stands to reason 'e's more important to 'er than you and that boat of yours. But never mind. Don't you worry about that baggage,' she added, her voice sweetening along with her expression, 'we'll 'ave a wonderful day without 'er. Cook's packed a picnic and we can sit in Queen Square or on the boat and throw bread to the ducks. Won't that be wonderful?'

'Wonderful,' said Tom, and hoped for rain.

—

Lady Verity paced her room, the stiff bombazine of her mauve dress hissing each time she turned and re-trod the same expanse of floor between window and grand piano, the latter groaning beneath the weight of Hungarian glass ornaments bequeathed to her by an Austrian aunt.

'You're using my family,' she shouted at her husband.

Emmanuel was pouring himself a nip of rum. Women got more disagreeable as they got older, he thought, and eyed his wife's spreading body, bubbles of fat pressing against her bodice that corseting could no longer restrain.

Verity glared angrily at his brimming glass. 'For goodness' sake,' she screamed, 'it's early morning. Do you have to start drinking already?'

Calmly and slowly, Emmanuel downed his drink and promptly poured himself another. 'At least it's not Sunday, not that the vicar would notice.'

She stopped dead and stared at him, her fat face bursting with anger. 'To hell with the vicar! Did you hear what I said? What about my family?'

Emmanuel Strong was used to his wife's tirades and had put up with them in the past. But she'd been younger then, prettier and not nearly so fat. He thought of the women he'd known, the ones he still knew and those he had yet to meet. Verity had done her duty, but her matronly figure no longer interested him. Although in his late fifties, Emmanuel considered himself a handsome man, despite his increasing girth and his thinning hair. He chose to believe that the dark-haired beauty awaiting him in the city loved him as much for himself as his money.

Sensing his attention had strayed, Verity marched up to him and glared up into his face. 'Did you hear what I said, or are you going deaf? But there you are! What can I expect having married a man old enough to be my father!'

Emmanuel's features stiffened. He hated being reminded of his age, hated to think he was older than Otis and Jeb, and that the latter would soon be dead.

'You're making too much of this.' He shot her a warning look.

Verity chose to ignore it. 'No, I am not. My family were landed gentry when yours were still picking apples in Herefordshire. They married into some of the best families in Europe. But you wouldn't understand the significance of that.'

Emmanuel barely controlled his temper. 'Why should you care about Conrad Heinkel? He's only a distant cousin, and German, not Austrian.'

Verity took great pride in being related to Austrians, something to do with the long-running power of the Habsburgs. Germans, she'd always said, were blunt-headed militarists, ruthless in battle, and lacking the cultural refinement of their Austrian cousins. Emmanuel thought this a load of rubbish, though he'd never said so. Now she'd lost her looks, he no longer cared about her feelings.

Verity did not heed the warning signs; one more drink, the swiftness with which he drained the glass, slamming it down on the sideboard, refilling it and drinking again, the clenching of his jaw and fist. She kept on at him.

'You wouldn't have gained a share in the sugar refinery if it hadn't been for me,' she shouted, her shrill voice like nails scratching glass. 'He only trusted you to have a share because he trusted me.'

It was true that the refiners were a close-knit lot, foreigners and members of a secretive organization. He'd been lucky to get a share at all, but his whole purpose had been to seize control once he'd starved Heinkel of supplies. In the past, plantation owners had rarely got involving with refining. They'd made more than enough from planting in the days before slavery was abolished.

He poured yet another glass of rum. Like a long-suffering saint, Verity raised her eyes to the ceiling.

'Do you *have* to drink so much?'

Eyeing his wife over the rim of his glass, Emmanuel downed it in one gulp. 'It was a means to an end. I wanted more children to continue the family line, and you had the pedigree and the build to produce them. I chose you in the same way as a farmer might choose a cow.'

Verity's cheeks puffed up and reddened. 'Pity the bull was way past his prime,' she spat back at him, saw her husband's expression darken, and wished she'd kept quiet. She backed away, and Emmanuel followed.

He bore down on her, choosing his words carefully and speaking them precisely. 'You're the brood mare I chose to bear my children. You're the pan that warmed my bed, the receptacle for my seed. You opened your legs and I entered; without preamble, passion, or any erotic input from you whatsoever.'

Verity was every inch the flushed and affronted matron. 'You disgusting...' She raised her hand to slap his face. He caught her wrist.

'Let me go!'

'No.'

Struggling to free herself, she dared look into her eyes and saw reflected all that Emmanuel Strong had been, all that he'd become.

Still holding her wrist, he pressed down on her shoulder, down and down, until she was on her knees. She hit at him with her free hand, struggled against his grip, her protests stifled as he forced her head tight against his body.

'You promised to obey me, Verity, and obey me you shall. Whatever I want you to do, you will do.'

She continued to struggle, though not for long.

'That's right,' he said, as her struggles lessened. 'Stay as you are, and we will renew the more intimate side of our marriage to *my* satisfaction.'

Stiff-shouldered, Verity stayed still, her husband's hand holding her head against his crotch and leaving her in no doubt what he wanted her to do.

Later, she did not protest when he told her he was going out.

–

The next morning Emmanuel wrestled with his cravat into which he was trying to insert a silver pin. It was a job his valet usually carried out.

Susannah smiled up at him. 'Let me help you.' Her fingers burrowed under his.

He hadn't particularly wanted her near him. He might desire her again, and he'd had her twice already. Her body was too voluptuous and her smell too feminine. He just couldn't help himself. Twice. He prided himself on that; her so young and him so mature.

Susannah was as unlike Verity as it was possible to be. Verity used to smell of violets, but lately smelled of milk and stale sweat. As a lactating mother, the former was only to be expected. The latter was mostly due to the fact that she still squeezed herself into dresses that no longer fitted her.

As the smiling Susannah fastened the pin, he gazed down to her breasts, quivering gently between her raised arms. She was wearing a Chinese robe, the green silk of which was embroidered in gold thread with rampant dragons and pink-blossomed trees. The belt was unfastened. The robe gaped. His eyes roamed further, down over her belly, her thighs, all the way to her toes. No, not like Verity at all. Much darker. Much more exotic.

He smiled. 'Do you like your present?'

She smiled demurely and reached for a blue glass bottle. Her eyes locked on his, she lifted the stopper and dabbed perfume between her breasts.

'Do you?' she asked, her eyes full of promise.

Emmanuel groaned, tore resignedly at his cravat and sunk his face into her chest.

–

Blanche had refused to wear the corset and stiff petticoats that Edith had got her from Lady Verity's cast-offs. Instead she'd put on the old-style chemise, over which she wore a lemon dress. Spring was maturing towards summer and the thought of wearing stiff underwear and a bell-shaped skirt was too much to bear. It was also the dress she'd worn the last time she'd been with Nelson. Hopefully, it would seem as if the time apart had never happened.

Unfortunately, Bristol was not Barbados. The sun was bright, but the breeze was brisk and clutched at the filmy fabric of her skirt, fastening it around her body and limbs.

A man was scything the long grass among the older gravestones. He glanced at her passing, went back to his task, then stopped and looked at her again. It was almost as though he'd mistaken her for someone else.

Blanche nodded a greeting. He returned it, wiped his forehead with the back of his hand, then went back to his work.

Next to a copse of silver birch, Nelson was sitting on a stone, facing the church and his easel. Aware that this was a secret meeting and he wouldn't want anyone to see her, Blanche hid in the spangled shadows of the trees, carefully picking her way over the mossy ground. She stopped just behind him.

For a moment she stood silently, relishing the way his hair curled around the nape of his neck. He too was still, his hand steady as he sketched the details of the church and the leaning gravestones. She cast her mind back to their first meeting, how godlike he'd seemed with his hair tumbling over his eyes, his shirt undone and the faint smell of his sweat. If she concentrated very hard, she could imagine herself back there on the warm sand. Back then his presence had made her heart beat faster. Its beat was more hesitant now, lacked the frisson of excitement she remembered from Barbados.

No matter, she thought. The feelings will return once we do what we did back then. I know they will.

'Nelson.'

He looked around him before turning. His hand ceased sketching.

'You look like a wood nymph.'

She wanted to believe things could be as they were. Blinding herself with the memory of Barbadian evenings, she told herself that making love to Nelson now would somehow make everything right again. The idea was ridiculous, she thought afterwards – but she let it happen.

His body was warm against hers as he came closer. Her belly tightened at the smell of him, the feel of his hardening beneath the ridiculous smock he wore for his painting.

'I've been longing for this,' he said, his voice husky against her ear. 'I've lain in my bed and thought of you and Barbados and those wonderful nights staring at the sea.' He cupped her face with his hands. 'I can't believe we're alone at last.'

Blanche couldn't think of a single thing to say. More of her mother's words of advice flooded her mind.

*Mostly, you need a man to look after you.*

*Your looks won't last for ever.*

*Take advantage where and when you can.*

Back in Barbados she had been at the mercy of her feelings for Nelson. This was different.

Everything will be all right, she told herself. This is a new city, a new country and the first time Nelson and I have been alone together since Barbados.

They fell on to the mossy ground beneath the birch trees. He traced her breasts, her waist and her hips with his right hand, just as he might draw her if he'd had charcoal between his fingers. Her breasts strained against the low-necked bodice of her dress, her nipples slipping out above the thin fabric as she raised her arms and lost control in the onslaught of his kisses.

Afterwards she felt ashamed. Nelson lay on his back, smiling at the sky.

'You'll have to marry me now,' she said.

He drew a small phial from his pocket, pulled off the stopper and sipped at its contents.

'What's that?' she asked, her blood seeming to run cold.

'The doctor gave it me when I saw him in London. He said it would help wean me off my laudanum craving.' His lashes quivered on his cheeks as he closed his eyes.

Blanche felt uneasy. Suddenly she wished she hadn't come. 'Are you sure it will cure you?'

He began to laugh, and it felt as though it were at her. 'So he tells me.' He opened his eyes and looked up at her. 'It's very nice medicine. Do you want to try some?'

She shook her head and knew then, with certainty, that she'd made a terrible mistake.

–

The man scything the long grass looked up as Duncan passed and nodded a greeting but got none in return. The footman did not notice as Josh spat contemptuously into the grass. Duncan had seen the easel, the abandoned charcoal and paints. He'd been right to follow Blanche, correct in his assumption that she was meeting Nelson. On seeing the artist's materials, he had wondered why Nelson hadn't chosen a more interesting view. There were ornate glass windows along the nave of the church, for example, an obvious choice for an artist who cared for colour and form. Here there was a lack of contrast in the stonework, the unkept greenery and the ugly tombstones, most of which were covered in birds droppings. He shook his head. This particular spot was not suitable at all. All that could be seen were blank walls and gargoyles. But it was private.

He knew instinctively what he would find. They lay there in each other's arms, oblivious to him and the world in general. Like a spectator at the theatre, he watched them beneath the trees far longer than he needed to. Horatia would expect a full report, which suited him. He enjoyed watching other people doing such things, though he could never do them himself. Degrading and dirty, he thought.

When he got back to Marstone Court, the elms and oaks of the park were casting long shadows across the grass. Halfway up the drive, he heard the rumbling of carriage wheels and the sharp scuff of hooves against loose stones. The best carriage was coming down the drive pulled by four Cleveland bays. A newly created coat of arms decorated the dark green of the coach door. Gilt lines embellished the windows and doorframe. Through the polished glass, Duncan could see Sir Emmanuel Strong, his body stiff and his face red with either anger, port or both.

As prescribed by etiquette, Duncan became as a tree, unseeing, unfeeling and unnoticed. Yet another fight with Verity, no doubt. Stupid woman. Her ladyship was treading a thin line between toleration and open hostility; also between fidelity and adultery. Sir Emmanuel was a red-blooded man. He'd take his pleasure wherever he pleased, and might very well flaunt it if his wife wasn't careful. That's what wealth does for you, Duncan thought.

Upon seeing the coach leave, he knew where to find Horatia. She would be in her father's study, rummaging through his papers, which she often did when her father was out of the way.

In the house he straightened his cravat and pushed his white gloves more firmly on to his fingers before knocking on the study door.

'Well?' she said, looking up at him as she bent over what looked like endless lines on some kind of architect's drawing.

'Your brother met a woman today.'

He thought he saw contempt in her eyes as she sank into her father's brown leather chair. He chose not to believe it.

'Well, come along, Duncan. I don't employ you to be my eyes and ears in this place for you to be vague about your findings. Tell me the rest.'

Duncan licked his lips, not really because they were dry, but more because he wanted to relish the information. She would not be pleased. Not pleased at all. There were few times when a servant had power as he did now. He enjoyed the feeling.

'They did it beneath the trees at the back of the churchyard.'

Her tone was waspish. 'Don't play with me, Duncan. I can still have you whipped.'

He raised his eyebrows at the prospect, but lost none of his arrogance. 'Slavery is abolished, ma'am.'

A slow smile crossed her face. He went weak at the knees when she smiled like that.

'So, who was he with?'

Duncan told her.

## Chapter Twenty-One

Disappointed but feeling duty bound to keep his promise to the children, Tom took Edith and the children into Bristol, winding through the narrow streets around Redcliffe until they were on the quayside close to the Hole in the Wall tavern.

Since getting involved with the sugar refinery, he had not visited the ship as often as he'd liked. The sight of her took his breath away.

The *Miriam Strong* creaked like an old bed and her hawsers squealed against the drumheads of dockside capstans. A brisk breeze scuttled among the sails and sent clouds scudding across the sky. Sunshine followed shadow with regular frequency and if Tom glanced at her quickly, he could almost imagine her ploughing through a sea that was sometimes blue, sometimes green.

Jimmy Palmer held a finger to his mouth as Tom boarded. 'Mr Trinder's doing the schooling today. Before long, them boys will be writing better than me.'

From somewhere below decks came the sound of young voices reciting their tables.

'Can we join them?' asked Rupert with obvious longing.

'No.' Tom directed the children to the various decks and masts, giving them permission to climb, but insisting that Edith stay on deck with them.

All but one of the children scampered off. The youngest stayed close to Edith, clutching her hand tightly and sucking his thumb. There's something sad about that child, Tom thought but what would he know? He was a seaman, a bare-knuckle fighter who frequented all the places respectable men wouldn't or shouldn't visit.

Down in the cabin a bottle of rum and two glasses were placed against the rim of the table, a habit acquired on voyages so that the precious rum did not end up on the floor.

'They've been back,' said Jimmy, his brow creased with worry.

Tom sighed. 'So you've been approached again?'

Jimmy swigged back his drink, and promptly poured himself another. 'What does the Reverend say?'

Tom twirled his drink in his glass before answering. 'To tell you the truth, Jimmy, I haven't mentioned it to him. He's not far off dying and I don't want to hasten his journey without good cause. I'll see what I can scrape up of my own money. That should help.'

Jimmy jerked the decanter implying that Tom should take another drink. Although Tom wasn't in the mood for spirits, he swigged back what was left in the glass and held it out for a refill. It might not solve the problem, but it helped subdue his concern.

With a worried frown, Jimmy said, 'I don't think it's really the money they want, Tom. I think they're after this bit of the quayside, though God knows why! Look at it!' He nodded through the window at the huddled mess of old warehouses with broken windows and rotting doors. 'I think that lot was already old the day John Cabot left for Nova Scotia.'

Tom frowned as he thought about why someone would want this exact spot. It was close to the centre of the city, the last deep-water mooring before the Avon ambled off towards St Mary Redcliffe and Temple Meads Meadows. What was here or in either of those places – of interest to anyone?

Jimmy seemed to read his mind. 'So it can't be any big shipping company, can it?'

Tom had no reassurance to give him. 'The last mooring between here and Temple Meads Meadow...' he said and racked his brains for the answer.

The clumping of feet in strict timing signalled the fact that the boys' lesson was over, though Mr Trinder was still maintaining discipline.

By the time Tom and Jimmy got back up on deck, the boys were lined up in neat rows. Tom could have sworn that there were exactly ten inches between each boy and a ruler had been used to measure the gap to the last inch.

The Strong children watched from the upper deck, except young George, who had disengaged himself from Edith and had attached himself to one of the lines of boys, his back straight and his head held high.

Mr Trinder, who had once been a ship's surgeon and before that a teacher in tactics at Dartmouth Naval Academy, shouted, ''Ten… shun!' The boys clicked their bare heels and saluted smartly. A little late, but just as smartly, George did the same.

'Class dismissed!'

The words were hardly out of his mouth before the boys relaxed and began to horse around as boys are wont to do. George joined in. Tom smiled. It was the happiest he'd ever seen the boy.

Rupert was instantly in the fore of things. He loved the ship and had met the boys before. Arthur, a little more restrained than his brother, held back but not for long. Caroline did her best, but the boys seemed uncomfortable in her presence, turning their backs each time she tried to join in.

Tom smiled. Every so often, Caroline reminded him of Horatia, though she didn't frighten him half as much.

'Permission to approach captain, sir?'

Clarence, Sally's son, marched stiffly forward, his face fuller than when he'd last seen him. Amazing what good food and a warm bed could do.

This was a ship and, as such, traditional protocol was maintained. 'Permission granted,' said Tom.

He saw Clarence wince as he snapped to attention.

'Cane?' he asked, raising one eyebrow.

Clarence nodded.

'For what?'

'Daydreaming.'

'Boy, you'll learn nothing by daydreaming. Is there anything you have learned today?'

'Yes, sir!'

'And what was that?'

The boy's eyes, so similar to those of his mother, shone like a newly minted guinea. In a sing-song voice that crackled with the onslaught of early puberty, he recited: 'A mack'rel sky and mares' tails / Make lofty ships carry low sails.'

Tom recognized the ditty as something Jimmy would have taught him rather than Mr Trinder. Nothing changes, he thought. Practical men with practical ways still rule the seas. He said, 'You sound a keen seaman, young Clarence.'

The way Clarence swelled with pride touched Tom's heart.

'Very keen, sir.'

'Glad to hear it.' Tom saluted. 'Relieved of duty, Able Seaman Ward.'

He'd expected the boy to rush off then, to gang up with the other boys who were now standing in single file, waiting to go down below, collect their tin plates and spoons and devour their midday meal.

Clarence didn't move. He had a serious expression, the sort that most folk would not associate with a boy of his age, but Tom knew how it was to be a child and fend for oneself. Wisdom beyond his years, he thought, and remembered how he'd felt when he'd first boarded the *Miriam Strong*.

Hands clasped behind his back, Tom waited apprehensively for the question he knew was coming. How would he answer? What good things could he say?

'I'd like to know how my mother is faring, sir.'

The question was just as expected. Tom would have loved to tell him that his mother's health had improved and that she'd moved in with her sister at Portishead, but he'd be lying. There was no good news to tell on that front, but he knew it was desperately important to give the boy something positive from the mess that was his mother's life.

He tossed his unruly hair back from his face and kept his gaze fixed beyond the boy to the old warehouses on the opposite quay. 'I saw her recently. She's proud of you, glad you're going to make a new life for yourself.'

The boy sniffed derisively. Tom guessed he had not been fooled. 'Glad I'm off her hands, I'll bet. But never mind.' He saluted again. 'All I want is to leave this dirty place and see the prow feathering the water.'

Another of Jimmy's sayings. Tom smiled. 'I'm happy to hear it, though you may need to grow a little older before that happens.'

Clarence almost stood on tiptoe as he made the effort to look bigger than he was. 'I think I'm about eleven, sir. My mother thinks I am too.'

The predictable news that Clarence did not know his correct age stabbed at Tom's heart because he wasn't entirely sure of his own and had settled on being thirty out of simple expediency. He kept his own counsel and spoke to the boy like a captain would a time-served seaman. 'Not long before you get a berth then.'

Clarence nodded, but the shine of his eyes turned suddenly dull as if some inner cloud had passed through his soul. 'If you see my mother on her deathbed, tell her I'll always remember her in the yellow shawl.' Tom saw the boy swallow what might have been sobs. 'Men don't cry, do they, sir?'

Painful memories came to mind. Tom hesitated before answering, remembering the cold doorways and the gnawing ache of starvation. He also recalled the brutality of some men towards women who had nothing except their bodies to sell.

'They do sometimes,' he said.

With Edith and her charges in tow, having eaten their picnic and thrown the crusts to the ducks and gulls that frequented Redcliffe Back, he left the ship a few minutes later.

He tried to focus on Clarence's enthusiasm, rather than his painful childhood. Jimmy Palmer had taken the boy under his wing, judging by the ditty the boy had recited. Jimmy missed the sea and in his more thoughtful moments spoke eloquently of the way the waves broke before the prow, 'Like feathers falling into the sea.' On a day when the wind rattled the halyards and jeers against the folded sails and stout masts, Tom found himself also missing the salt air and heaving deck. If he was truly honest, he'd never stopped missing it.

'She's a lovely old ship,' said Rupert, as Edith and the other children climbed aboard the governess cart.

Tom agreed, holding the horse in check at the side of the Hole in the Wall as he gazed at the tall masts and the closed gun ports. He could almost imagine the cannon snouts sticking out and men behind them waiting for the order to fire. She was a good ship; Jeb was right on that count. It didn't matter what her name was, and Tom hoped the day would never come when Jeb told him her true name, because that would mean his death was close at hand.

Tom flicked the reins and urged the horse on.

Young George looked at him searchingly. 'Are we going to see Edith's brother? He's got dogs. Lots of dogs.'

Tom was in no mood to go visiting another part of the city. Perhaps if Blanche had come too, it might have been different. He wondered what she was up to back at Marstone Court. And what was Nelson up to. He couldn't bear the thought that they might be together. He had to get back.

'It's a fine day. Let's go home through the village. Ned Bramble's got a bitch terrier with puppies. Perhaps he'd let you see them.'

He fancied Edith looked disappointed, but it couldn't be helped.

The day stayed warm and bright. On the way back, the three eldest children played games – I spy and Spot the Cow. The youngest curled up in a ball on the floor and slept soundly. Tom wished Edith would do the same. She sat beside him again and didn't stop talking.

Ned Bramble kept and bred terriers for hunting rodents and rabbits. He lived in a cottage built of lime-washed cobble beneath a thatched roof. On the first floor, small windows squeezed tightly against the eaves. The door was solid and low.

'Just cropped and docked,' said Ned as he led them round the back of the house to a three-sided shed with a roof of woven willow that just about kept the worst of the weather at bay.

Tom winced at the news, thought about curtailing the children's visit, but they'd already heard the squealing puppies and got there before him.

The ears of week-old terriers were regularly cropped, the soft flaps of the ears cut off leaving the remainder standing erect. As with spaniels, the tails were docked, leaving no more than a stump. Most countrymen did this with their teeth, though some had a special pair of shears for the purpose. Tom didn't know much about the reasons for carrying out such a barbarous act, and found it distasteful.

The puppies' mother looked warily up at them as they entered, alert in case they should inflict more pain on her troubled offspring.

Caroline gasped. 'Poor things! Look at their ears. And their tails.'

Rupert was more curious. 'They're covered in blood. Why is that?'

Ned sucked on his pipe. 'Makes 'em look more alert and saves 'em breaking their tails when they're down 'ole after a rabbit. Fierce like 'er there.' Ned nodded at the black and white terrier bitch, whose ears were like neat triangles perched on top of her head.

'Must be frightening for the rabbits,' Tom said.

Ned was too wrapped up in his puppies and the children's reaction to notice Tom's sarcasm.

Rupert was about to ask more questions, but Tom could feel young George slowly sliding behind him, before flying into the folds of Edith's skirt where he hid his face and began to wail.

Tom hustled everyone out and didn't look back. 'Let's get home.'

'They've cut the puppies' ears and tails,' said an incredulous Caroline, as they all climbed back into the cart. 'I think it's cruel.'

'It's to make them look fierce and brave,' said an adamant Arthur, who seemed to like being privy to the harsher facts of the adult world, though only from a distance.

'Right,' said Caroline. 'When we get home, I'll take my needlework scissors and snip off your ears. Let's see how brave that makes you!'

Weakening beneath his sister's glare, Arthur clapped his hands over his ears.

Edith continued her chattering, though Tom hardly noticed what she was saying. It was like the wind in the trees, it was just there and not very noticeable after a while, which was why at first he failed to hear her question.

The children had heard what she'd said. 'Can we?' they all cried in unison.

He shook himself back to reality. 'Of course we can. What is it you want?'

Caroline's voice was almost as strident of that of her stepsister, Horatia. 'It's the market today! We want to go to the market.'

Tom composed his expression and smiled, though his face felt it would crack with the effort. Much as he wanted to get back to Marstone Court, he'd already said yes and the clamouring of the children and Edith's accusing countenance were too much to ignore.

Perhaps Blanche was in the village, taking the air and wandering around the market where farmers' wives sold homemade jams, eggs, spring vegetables and truckles of Cheddar cheese. Some also sold homemade remedies, mostly made from mutton fat and elderflower, or goose grease and rosehip. The former was recommended for chapped lips and sore feet, the latter for glossy hair and the treatment of boils. He knew Blanche was interested in things like that. The more he thought about it, the more he convinced himself that she'd be there.

'It's a fine day,' he exclaimed. 'Too nice a day to be indoors.'

He took it easy around the edge of the market, which was crowded with people, even though it was way past noon. People were enjoying the sunshine as much as they were the temptation of fresh food straight from the farm. At dawn today, the cabbages on sale would have still been in the ground.

He looked for Blanche in the crowds that loitered around the market stalls. She wasn't to be seen, but there were ample-hipped country girls galore. He smiled. They smiled back. In the past he would have lingered with a view to keeping company with them for the rest of the afternoon, but he had the children with him and, besides, his taste had changed.

A flurry of hawthorn blossom billowed from the churchyard to the south of the market place. Drawn by the shower of whiteness, Tom eased the horse in that direction. It would take no longer to skirt the churchyard than it would the market. There was a back way that wound around the edge of the birch trees. He knew it well from his youth. It was where he used to hide rather than sit through the hour-long sermon.

The children squealed with delight as they bumped along the track. Low-hanging branches flipped at their heads.

'Go faster,' Rupert urged and George giggled the whole time, his cheeks red as apples because he'd just woken up.

Just when Edith had turned her back, laughing at something the children had said, Tom spotted another low-hanging branch, and shouted, 'Look out!'

Edith ducked, but it was too late. The fake cherries on her hat caught on a branch.

'It's me best one,' she screeched. 'Don't lose me cherries!'

Tom checked the horse while Caroline unhitched Edith's hat. That was when he spotted them; two figures among the white trunks of lacy-leaved birch trees. Sunlight dappled her lemon dress and his dark green painting smock. Blanche and Nelson.

Tom drove back to Marstone Court in silence, Edith filling the vacant air with her continuous talk about her family and newly created stories of their exploits. For the most part the details went in one ear and out of the other – except one.

'Course, my Cousin Fenwick's done a lot of travelling. All round the world in fact. Started in Australia, he did, then went off to everywhere you could think of, Africa, Italy, Sicily...'

Fenwick? Wasn't that the name of the farm boy who'd helped the poacher at the time of Jasper's disappearance?

'What did you say your cousin's name was?'

Edith had obviously been trying to rouse him from his mood. His sudden interest made her beam with pleasure, oblivious to the tightening of his features and the sudden pallor of his face.

'Fenwick. Fenwick Clements.'

His throat felt dry. It wasn't a common name. Here at last there might be a chance to find out exactly what had happened to Jasper Strong. Everyone from the gardener to the scullery maids, to the stable lads had been in the ballroom listening to Emmanuel that day. Only the poacher – whom Emmanuel had shot dead the following day – and the farm boy – who'd been transported to Australia – had been out and about on the estate. They could have seen something.

Tom's voice almost cracked when he said, 'And you say he's been to Australia?'

There were a number of reasons a man might go to Australia: on a wool clipper, for instance. They were as good on that route as they were on the run back from China carrying a hold full of tea.

'Yes,' Edith said brightly, her smile hesitant as she concocted her next lie. She explained that Fenwick had gone out to make his fortune in beaver skins for top hats, but had decided the heat was too much and had come home.

Tom grinned. Edith's lies rolled off her tongue without any regard to truth. So far as Tom knew, there were no beavers in Australia.

'So where is he now? Still travelling?' Tom asked.

'Oh no!' she exclaimed. 'He came back and Ma took him in 'cos his mother had died. He's there now, complete with his own top hat and the ways of a toff. You'd never think he'd been brought up in the country, just down here in the village as a matter of fact.'

Tom had never been a devious person, and tried to do as well by others as Jeb Strong had done for him. He assured himself that the end justified the means and asked Edith to tell him exactly where her mother lived. 'I never got to visit,' he added, as though he'd had every intention of doing so.

To his great satisfaction – and shame – Edith told him.

Tonight, he decided, he would saddle up and ride back into the city. No one in their right mind would venture into the Pithay late at night, and besides, it wouldn't be fair to disturb Edith's mother at such a late hour. A bed above one of his favourite taverns would suffice for the night. In the morning he would seek out Fenwick Clements, and the sooner the better. Once the matter of Jasper was cleared up, he could concentrate on Blanche. Tonight he would lie in a bed in Bristol, but his thoughts would be with her.

## Chapter Twenty-Two

Alone with his thoughts, Tom didn't notice that he was being watched.

In the black shadows thrown by the Dutch-style frontages of the old buildings lining the quay, Reuben Trout skulked and watched, his pipe clenched in blackened teeth, his breath more fetid than the black shag in the pipe.

He had a boil on the side of his nose, a red bulbous thing that seeped a thick yellow liquid, which sometimes got in the way of his vision. In a drunken moment in a dockside tavern, he'd allowed some old witch of a woman to spread zopissa – the scrapings of tar from the bottom of an old boat – on it. It had done no good. If he concentrated too hard ahead then glanced quickly to the side, it almost seemed as if a pink, blurred presence – like a small devil or a loathsome imp – was on his shoulder watching him. That's how it was now as he sought a hiding place in Denmark Street, somewhere to scurry into should Tom Strong glance round and see him. But the only suitable doorway was already occupied. Pale and poorly dressed, he judged her just a whore out to make a shilling before midday, though in Trout's opinion she looked unlikely to make that in a week. Dark lines circled her eyes, which stared from deep sockets. It was when she glanced at Tom and then back at him, that he realized she'd cottoned on to what he was doing. And wasn't she the same whore he'd seen Tom drinking with and giving money to?

Digging deeply into the dusty pocket of his canvas coat, which was smeared with dirt and waterproofed on the shoulders with a few brush strokes of tar, he adopted a knowing sneer. An empty belly took priority over a curious mind, he thought as he held aloft a shiny shilling. The woman lifted her head and fixed her gaze on the coin. Unseen by Tom, he crossed over to the dark doorway.

In the morning, Tom made his way up Steep Street. First he would ride out to Durdham Downs, breathe the clean air and look down into the gorge and think of the sea. The tide was coming in. By the time he got there he might see a ship being rowed upstream, her sails furled, dependent on a mass of rowers to get her the seven miles of mud-packed bends and into the floating harbour. If she was small enough, she might make her way up into the heart of the city, but such ships were becoming fewer. The floating harbour was as far as most could go, and even that was a struggle, which brought his thoughts back to whoever wanted to buy the *Miriam Strong's* mooring.

Durdham Downs it would be. Decision made, he went back to where he'd left his horse, untied her and mounted up. Taking the climb up Steep Street on foot, he remounted before doubling back at the top and heading for Clifton where fine houses with high ceilings looked out to the Avon Gorge and the city beyond.

At last he could breathe and his head felt clearer. Clouds and sky seemed closer up there. He could almost believe that if he stretched he could touch them, pull them down and lay down in their softness. He urged his horse into a canter, greeted other riders – some just matrons or children on donkeys.

On the thin road that wound between the stretches of grass and trees, carriages drawn by matching pairs with cropped tails and arched necks sallied forth. He slowed to a trot, meaning to swerve back and head full pelt across the grass for the Gorge and its unparalleled view, but one particular carriage caught his eye. Black and shiny, and drawn by a matching pair of chestnuts, its blinds were closed against prying eyes, but a problem was brewing. One of the horses was foaming at the mouth and doing its best to toss its head free of the bit. The driver shouted, 'Steady there. Steady there!' and raised his whip, bringing it down on the horse's back. Matters worsened. The carriage began to rock and the horse reared, one of its front legs coming down over the centre shaft to which both animals were attached.

The carriage rocked more violently as the animal panicked, and someone inside screamed.

Tom urged his mount forward, hurtling headlong across the grass.

The coachman was stout and red-faced. His whip had fallen to the ground and one of his reins dangled among the horses' legs.

'Get down, man,' Tom shouted as he vaulted from his horse.

'The animal's gone mad. I'll have him shot! Shot, I tell you.'

Tom stayed calm. Quickly but methodically, he tied the reins of his own horse to a handy tree; there was no point everyone losing control.

He glanced at the closed blinds. Ladies and gentlemen of the highest order did not always act as honourably as they should. An errant wife or philandering husband, perhaps? Well, they'd have bruises to show if something wasn't done quickly. 'Get down,' he shouted again to the coachman.

The man hesitated still, the reins hanging loosely from his hands before he came to his senses, put the brake on and wound the reins in their proper place.

'And get your passengers out.'

'But they do not wish to be seen——'

'It is preferable to being dead. Get them out!'

He was vaguely aware there were two passengers, a man and a woman. Well, he'd not spoil their fun. Secrecy and the close confines of a carriage spurred passion to enormous heights, and he knew this from experience.

Not wishing to waste time on niceties, he went to the head of the upset horse, noted the panic in the animal's eyes, the foaming mouth and the sweat staining its neck and chest.

'Easy,' he said softly to the creature, and began to whistle. The horse breathed heavily, though still agitated that its leg was still over the wrong side of the shaft. Tom unbuckled the offside rein from the bit and threaded it back through the curb, a circle of metal protruding from the horse collar. He did the same to the other rein. The horse jerked his head and stretched his neck, glad to be free of the curb's tight control that forced its neck into such an exaggerated arch.

The coachman, a fat man in a green frock coat and a black top hat, came to Tom's side smelling of sweat and red in the gills. 'Why are you whistling? What are you going to do?'

'Whistling settles them. A Spanish gypsy told me that. Now I'm going to give the horse a hand getting his leg back and you're going to release the other animal's head.'

The coachman protested. 'But this is a brand-new harness, and people like to see my horses looking fashionable.'

'And what good's that if the animal has to pull with his neck muscles instead of his back? Broad backs were made for pulling. Necks stuck in the same position for hours at a time result in cramp. Wouldn't you want to stretch your neck?'

The coachman stared at him open-mouthed and rubbed at his own neck. Tom glared. 'Well, get to it, man! Put the animal out of its misery.'

The fat little man almost jumped out of his boots as he scurried to obey.

Still whistling, Tom bent down beneath the horse's chest, pressed the carriage shaft down, heaved his shoulder beneath the horse and lifted gently, just enough so the animal could right itself.

Instinctively, the horse brought its leg back over the shaft.

'There, there, boy,' he said, stroking the animal's pulsating cheek. The horse blew heavily and approvingly through its flared, pink nostrils.

It was only after the horses had been released from their bondage that the middle-aged man who had alighted from the coach approached him. He wore good clothes and an air of impatience. 'Is everything all right now, Sperry?'

The coachman touched his forelock and confirmed that it was.

'Thank you,' the man said to Tom, and pressed a shilling into his hand before turning his back.

'Thank you, Josiah.'

The man spun round, his nose held high and his cheeks trembling with pomp. 'Do I know you, sir?'

Tom didn't bother to answer. He was looking at Horatia, a picture of womanly elegance in dark purple, her skirt tiered in deep frills edged with black velvet, and her bonnet big with feathers of black, mauve and purple.

'My lips are sealed,' Tom said before she had chance to make her excuses.

Horatia's cheeks turned pink. 'This is not what you think!'

'How dare you address this lady in such a familiar tone,' said Josiah Benson. 'Apologize at once!'

Tom's smile froze, his anger still with him. He stepped towards the man, who took a pace back and another as Tom came forward, until his back was against the carriage and Tom was towering over him. 'Will you make me apologize, sir?'

'How dare you...'

Tom could smell his fear; sweat mixed with a large splash of eau de cologne. His hat fell off and he made the mistake of bringing a silver-topped cane up between them. Tom slowly wound his fingers about the cane, brought it up higher with one hand, and pushed the man's face down, forcing the silver top between his lips.

'Tom! Stop it!'

Horatia's gloved hand was warm through the fabric of his shirt. He smelled her perfume, felt the warmth of her breath on his neck.

Sweat trickled down the face and ran into the collar of the man he held against the carriage.

Though Horatia's fingers dug painfully into his arm, Tom did not let go. It was as if all the anger he felt about Blanche, about Jasper, and about the Strong family was encapsulated in this extremely wealthy, pompous man.

'Tom! Please. Please, Tom. For me.'

He looked down into Horatia's face. It was funny, but he'd never seen her plead for anything. And it was genuine. Her eyes were an incandescent blue.

Slowly, he let the cane slide from the man's mouth. What was the point in taking out his anger on him anyway? For God's sake, the man was dribbling on to his cravat!

With fear-filled eyes, Josiah Benson looked from Tom to Horatia for an explanation.

'My cousin,' said Horatia in a reluctant tone of voice. 'Captain Tom Strong. You have met before.' She looked Tom up and down. 'In a ballroom and wearing respectable attire,' she said.

Tom squirmed beneath her gaze. Even after all this time, she still made him feel as if he were a boy from the back streets.

She took Tom to one side, lay her hand on his arm and spoke sweetly. 'It's not what you think.'

He looked into her face, trying, as ever, to work her out.

'Is he going to marry you?'

'I've just told you, it's nothing like that.'

Tom shook his head and tried to clear his mind again. It had seemed so fresh up here earlier. 'I don't think I really want to know.'

He started to turn away. Horatia grabbed his arm. 'Please, Tom. Trust me. It's a business matter, and I don't want Father finding out about it.' She hesitated, as if she were fighting an inner battle before giving him an excuse or telling him the truth. 'I do need to speak to you, Tom. It does concern you. I tried to tell you before, if you remember rightly. But you're so forgetful, so embroiled in your own masculine thoughts. What chance does a weak and feeble woman like me have of getting through to a man like you?' She gave a laugh, the sort women use when they want to appear defenceless, though Horatia could never be that.

Josiah interrupted. 'Horatia, my dear. Do come along. We have business to attend to.'

Horatia paid him no mind. 'You could come with us,' Horatia whispered close to his ear. 'Josiah won't object, not if I insist. He's easily placated; a sweet smile, a stroke of my hand and, if all else fails, a vaguely positive answer to his hints of marriage.'

She smiled and stroked his hand too, but Tom turned away. 'I have to go,' he said, already striding away, his thoughts returning now to *his* day's business, finding Fenwick Clements.

She looked disappointed.

Josiah called to her again. 'My dear...'

The coachman was already up in his seat and the horses were standing in silence, their heads drooping gratefully. Horatia watched Tom mount his horse, acknowledge her politely and ride away.

He looked more sullen than usual. She wondered what had upset him, hoped he hadn't discovered too much about her plans for expanding the Strong family business interests. If she'd been braver, she would have insisted he listen to what she had to say, but he hadn't wanted to. I always meant to tell him, she told herself, but it was a lie. The truth was that his lack of interest had suited her because she'd feared his reaction. But soon he would find out. All she could hope was that he wouldn't be too angry.

–

No one in their right mind rode a horse into the Pithay. For one thing, the alleys and lanes were so narrow, the upper storeys almost meeting in the middle, that there was little room to pass. There was also the problem of what to do with his horse while he went into the Clements household to confront Fenwick Clements. Even if he paid a street urchin to look after it, there was a very good chance it wouldn't be there when he came out; sold on to a haulier or a butcher for a fraction of its true worth.

Ignoring the curious looks of residents peering out from dark doorways and windows, he strode almost unmolested to the crumbling building in Cock and Bottle Lane. Even though it was just after midday, little sunlight penetrated the standing gloom.

Striding over muddy puddles and what was left of wooden cobbles, he smelled the house before he got to the door, which was little more than a few planks nailed together. Rapping on it with his fist sent it crashing inwards against a wall where it remained, having slid off its hinges.

A small dog yapped. A larger one barked. The room was cold and dark. A chair and a table stood in the middle of the room and a bed was pushed against one wall piled with mildewed blankets. Cold ashes flowed in a silver heap from an open hearth. A pot the size of a cauldron was being offered to a third dog, just like one would offer a nosebag to a hungry horse. The woman offering it looked up as he entered the room.

'Yer in the wrong place,' she shouted, her pock-marked face blazing with anger. 'If you wants the trollops, they're in the 'ouse further down.' She waved a meaty arm in the general direction.

'Are you Edith's mother?'

The question took her completely off-guard. She blinked rapidly as she straightened, as though the sight of him was too bright for her eyes.

'Who are you?'

'Tom Strong. Captain Tom Strong.'

'Ooow,' she said, putting the pot down and smoothing her wool-covered hips. 'We're honoured, ain't we?'

'I want to speak to your nephew.'

Her expression seemed to grow cautious. 'What for?'

Edith was the one who made up stories. Tom decided he could make one up too. 'As I said, I'm a sea captain. I understand your nephew, Fenwick, isn't it...?'

She nodded. 'That's right,' she said, a wary crease puckering her face.

'Mistress Clements, I understand that Fenwick hasn't long come back from Australia. I'm thinking of travelling there myself. I wanted to talk to him about it.'

Preening a little at being called Mistress, her wariness vanished. 'Well,' she began, 'he is busy, you know. And time is money, so I've 'eard say...'

Tom fished a gold coin from his pocket. 'I understand.'

'Ooow!' she said, sniffing as she wiped her nose with the back of her hand before reaching for the coin. 'Is that a sovereign?'

'Pleased to help, Cap'n!' A tall, thin and fully dressed man leapt from beneath the pile of mildewed blankets, paused, stepped back to the bundle and pulled a battered top hat from a dusty corner.

Fenwick's pale eyes fixed determinedly on the coin and long fingers unfurled from his grimy palm. 'Anything you want to know about Australia, from Botany Bay to the back of beyond, I'm yer man!'

In one swift movement, Tom enfolded the gold coin back into his own palm.

'I lied,' he said, a determined look in his eyes and a firmness to his chin that Fenwick Clements immediately interpreted as meaning he was in trouble.

'I didn't 'ave nothin' to do with that dog scam. It was Spike and Edith. Tell 'er ladyship that. Not me, honest. Not me!'

Tom grabbed one of the man's lapels. The rotten material ripped easily, leaving Tom with nothing but a strip of it hanging from his hand. As Fenwick tried to rush for the door, Tom stuck out a boot. Fenwick went flying face down on the floor while his aunt, Edith's mother, screamed blue murder.

Tom shouted over his shoulder at her. 'Shut up if you want Edith to keep earning a wage.'

Mrs Clements stopped screaming instantly.

Tom bent over Fenwick, his knee resting on the thin chest. 'Never mind Australia. Let me tell you a story. There was a poor boy starving around the sugar barrels on the wharves where the ships bring in the produce of the Strong plantation. And one night a guardian angel came along and took him under his wing, thanks to the fact that this guardian angel had lost a son. And the adopted boy felt he owed a debt to that boy all his life, and then the chance came for him to pay back that debt by telling the truth about how he died. The beloved son I replaced was named Jasper Strong and I think you know what happened to him.'

'He was drowned!' Fenwick blurted, his eyes wide with fear.

Tom shook his head. 'The truth. Tell me the truth.'

Fenwick shuddered and his breathing became laboured. Tom pressed his knee more keenly into his chest.

'Tell. Me.'

'All... all... right.'

Recognizing that the man was having difficulty breathing, Tom eased the pressure on his chest.

'Tell me. Now!'

Gasping for breath, Fenwick began.

'Abraham Green, the poacher, was drunk when I called with the vegetable cart the day after the boy disappeared to collect the deer he'd nabbed. I got him to his feet and asked him where he'd got the drink. He said he'd got it in the house. There'd been no one about for a while, so he'd taken what he wanted. He said he had a headache and couldn't remember exactly what had happened, but he kind of remembered chasing a boy. Ran like a rabbit, he said, and laughed. Said he ran after him, just to frighten him like, so's he wouldn't tell.'

Fenwick licked his lips, his eyes rolling in his head as he tried to catch his breath. 'I can't... breathe,' he muttered. 'Please, give me water.'

Mrs Clements shoved a pewter mug under his nose as Tom got him to a sitting position. It looked like water, but smelled like gin.

Fenwick gulped it down. Some trickled down his chin and seeped on to his ragged clothes.

Impatient, Tom grabbed the empty mug and handed it back to Mrs Clements.

'Go on.'

'Abe liked frightening children. Did it in the village all the time. Said the boy ran into a room at the top of the house and hid. Saw his footsteps in the dust, he said, so knew he'd hid up the chimney. Thought that would frighten him enough. T'weren't till the next day that I heard about the boy drowning. We was dragging the deer up to the cart when they caught us. There was people everywhere. We never expected that. And Abe panicked, then ran. That was when he got shot.'

Fenwick seemed suddenly to notice Tom's stillness and the faraway look in his eyes.

'Was that the boy you was on about? The boy that drowned?'

Tom got to his feet and headed out of the door. He'd discovered the truth. He could now tell Jeb exactly how and why his son had died. But was that the reason he'd wanted to know in the first place, just so he could tell Jeb the truth?

On reflection it was the last thing he could do, especially now. The shock would kill Jeb. But what about when Jeb was close to dying, when there was no doubt that tomorrow would never come, could he tell him then?

Striding back along the dirty alleys, where bawds fought over the right to approach him, and children ran barefoot through the grime and stagnant puddles, he felt oddly lighter because *he* knew the truth. For the first time since being taken in by the Strong family, he felt worthy of their respect, if not their trust.

He collected the rangy chestnut from the livery where he'd temporarily left it, and turned its head towards Conrad Heinkel's refinery.

Conrad was in a reflective mood when he got there. 'I wanted to speak to you on a very serious matter,' he said over his shoulder as he led Tom into his office.

'Our scheme's worked, hasn't it?' said Tom, slumping into one of the comfortable armchairs with which Conrad thought an office should be furnished.

'Oh yes,' said Conrad, nodding affably over the bowl of his burning pipe. 'The sugar from Barbados has been successfully routed by way of the other refiners and into my yard. And beet from the continent is also keeping me running at close to full capacity.' He beamed gratefully. 'I thank you, Tom. I thank you from the bottom of my heart.'

Tom grinned. 'If Emmanuel knew I was involved, he'd shoot me.'

'Let us hope not,' said Conrad. His smile diminished as his expression turned serious. And was that a bashful blush on his big, friendly face? Tom wondered what it was Conrad believed to be more serious than sugar.

'Blanche,' said Conrad. 'She is of good family?'

Tom controlled his shock. Hopefully it did not register on his face.

'I do not know,' he lied.

'No matter,' said Conrad with a careless twitch of his pipe. 'She is very nice to look at, very nice to people, and very nice to my children. Do you think that if I asked her to marry me, she would accept?'

Tom felt his stomach churn. Without saying so, Blanche had more or less turned him down, simply because her head was bewitched by the vision of an evening gone.

'I think that is something you have to find out for yourself,' Tom answered.

Conrad nodded resignedly. 'I suppose you are right. But you know, Tom, I can order men to do this and that out there in that refinery, but when it comes to asking a woman a question like that, my wits become soup and I am a boy again, a stupid, bashful boy.'

'You're too big to be a boy, Conrad.'

It was all Tom could think to say. He was still smarting from seeing Blanche with Nelson in the woods near the village. And now here was another man who wanted her.

They talked some more about how best to fend off Emmanuel Strong and his designs on sugar refining. Tom told Conrad to be alert. Conrad told Tom to watch his back. Emmanuel burned with ambition, and would destroy anyone to get what he wanted.

He would have gone straight back to Marstone Court, but as he drew close to Corn Street, he spotted Aggie Pike waving her hands at him furiously.

Easing his horse through the throng of market stalls and corn dealers, he dismounted and asked her what she wanted.

Aggie looked worried. 'Have you seen Sally?'

'Not for a few days.'

It was true, and he'd thought it strange. A few days, and Sally would have been after some money. But he hadn't seen her.

'She owed me some money. She'd arranged to pay me.'

Ah, thought Tom. Besides being a bargee, a fence and an arm-wrestler, Aggie was also a money lender. Now Tom knew where his money had been going.

Aggie explained. 'I should 'ave known better than to let 'er 'ave the money. But it was Stoke!' She spat at the effort of having to say his name. 'Bastard!' she swore, then genuflected.

God, thought Tom, she's a Catholic.

'She weren't up to working the streets an' all, but Stoke was after her for the money. She borrowed it off me to give to 'im so 'e'd think she was working, though 'course, she weren't. How could she the state she's in? Trouble is, last time she said she was too ill to work, 'e beat 'er black and blue.' Aggie laid a hand on his arm. 'I wouldn't 'ave taken the money off 'er, Tom. Wouldn't 'ave lent it 'er in the first place, but she kept on, and I didn't want to see 'er hurt again. And I didn't 'ave too much money anyways. But she promised to be here, and Sally always keeps a promise.'

He couldn't ignore the worry in Aggie's well-creased face. He'd meant to get back at Marstone Court in time to see Jeb before he fell asleep. He visited him at the same time in the evening and hated missing, knowing Jeb looked forward to his company, but in the circumstances...

Sally was the modern-day equivalent of his own mother, and Clarence was the boy he'd once been. He had to know what had happened to her.

His first port of call was Cuthbert Stoke.

By the time he got to the Fourteen Stars, night was drawing in and a thick mist was rolling in off the river.

'Take care of my horse,' he said, passing the reins to a stable lad. 'A good rub down, a mound of hay and only a handful of oats.'

The stable lad, a cheeky chap with ginger hair and a sunburst of freckles across his nose, looked surprised. 'Is that all he can have?'

Despite his grim mood, Tom shook a warning finger. 'Any more than that and he'll be mounting every filly in the stable.'

The boy grinned. 'We ain't got no fillies, only old mares.'

Tom grinned back and flicked the boy a coin. 'Same in these stables as inside the Fourteen Stars then,' he said and disappeared.

The air inside the tavern was as thick with smoke as ever, though unlike the Druid Arms, it was uncut with the mouth-watering odour of fresh fish smoking and sizzling.

Stoke spotted him through the milky haze and sidled over, thought about sitting himself on the bench next to him, but stopped when he saw the unwelcome look on Tom's face. He made a big show of lighting his pipe and nodding at a few of the regulars while studying Tom, trying to gauge his mood and considering whether he could take advantage. Tom wasn't usually that easy to read, but tonight something bordering on anger – frustration perhaps – was obvious.

Although his gaze appeared to be elsewhere, Tom knew that Stoke had noticed his frame of mind and would have presumed he was in a fighting mood. Vengeful would have been a better description, but Tom wasn't letting on. Hitting Stoke in retribution for beating Sally was an option he discarded. Best, he decided, to hurt Stoke where it hurt most – his purse.

Stoke acted amiably. He always did when he wanted something. 'Care for another match? I've got a bloke come up from Devon called Simmons. Folks down that way tell me he's a battler.'

Tom barely glanced at him. 'How about tonight?'

Stoke looked surprised but knew Tom was serious because he had been about to down his drink and had stopped the moment a fight was mentioned. Unlike some bare-knuckle fighters, Tom drank little before a fight. 'Blimey! Who's upset you then?'

'Never you mind.'

Stoke knew better than to push it. Tom's scowl was enough to turn porter to vinegar.

'Mind if I take a pew?' Stoke asked, taking a three-legged stool from beneath the table, which meant he was close but not too close.

Tom said nothing.

'A fight's already been arranged for tonight, but I think I can fit you in if you don't mind hanging around. Rough sort, mind. Comes in with the blokes he works with. Hard drinkers, the lot of them.'

Tom nodded and fingered the tot of rum, leaving marks on the pewter tankard. The latter were used for everything because the Fourteen Stars owned few glasses. Most had ended up in bits in the sawdust on the floor.

'Do it.'

Tom pushed his drink to one side. If there was a fight in the offing, he needed a clear head.

Stoke eyed him warily before asking his next question. 'Seen Sally lately?'

Surprised by the question, Tom shook his head, reluctant to look into Stoke's face and see the satisfaction of a pimp who knows where his next meal is coming from. Judging by what Aggie had told him, it seemed a strange question to ask, implying, as it did, that Stoke hadn't seen Sally either, though it might not necessarily be the truth.

Stoke pulled a well-polished watch of sterling silver from his waistcoat pocket. 'You'll see her soon, no doubt. I told her to be up and about early. Just 'cos she's sick ain't no reason to—'

It was the worst thing Stoke could have said. Tom grabbed him by the lapels of his coat, causing the watch to swing from its chain and hit the table. Stoke almost choked.

'Let her go, Stoke. Can't you see the woman's dying?'

'I know that.' Stoke pawed at Tom's hands. 'But you can't stop her, Tom.'

Tom held on. The low hum of conversation, bawdy laughter and drunken shouting ceased. Everyone there watched, waiting with baited breath to see if Cuthbert Stoke was at long last about to receive what he justly deserved.

'Let her be!' Tom snarled, holding Stoke's face close to his so that their noses almost touched and the spittle of Tom's anger sprayed Stoke's face.

Stoke played the only winning card he could think of and trusted he'd correctly assessed Tom's mood. 'Tom, think. You likes fighting. She likes what she does.' He shook his head, his eyes never leaving Tom's face. 'God knows you've tried, Tom. God knows you have.'

In his heart of hearts, Tom knew Stoke was speaking the truth. The only thing you couldn't save Sally from was herself, but Stoke was also to blame. Tom forced himself to calm down. He'd have him yet. Slowly, he relinquished his hold.

The one-time ostler, sometime fence, and part-time pimp, rubbed at his neck and put his watch back into his waistcoat. The sound within the Fourteen Stars returned to a grumbling hum. Stoke took a deep breath, glad he could still do so and wondering just how close he'd come to receiving a knock-out blow from Tom Strong's powerful right fist.

Stoke collected his wits and his words. 'She won't go quietly, will our Sally. Thinks she's indispensable, that one. So long as she thinks she's useful, she'll keep going till she drops and nothing I says is going to change that. So let her be. She was born a whore and she'll die a whore.'

Tom smashed his fist down on the table.

Stoke sent the stool falling backwards as he leapt clear. 'Hitting me won't make things any different,' he said.

Tom thought about it. He was right. Squashing Stoke's nose all over his face would do little good, in fact, Sally, the silly cow, would probably come over all sympathetic for the nasty little toad.

Stokes licked his flaccid lips, which were already wet and shiny. 'You do this fight tonight and we split the purse sixty forty. The man's no pushover mind. Body like a bull and hands like shovels. Just as you like 'em. I've got a good crowd coming in. There they were, swinging axes and shovels into the ground on the other side of town, and all I had to do was offer them one free drink. What do you say?'

Tom said yes.

The smell of horse manure and urine was as strong as ever in the neighbouring building that housed Bennetts Carriers and the fights. As before, a ring had been constructed from hay bales. Cuthbert Stoke was strutting around with a smile on his face, a pipe in his mouth and a bag of coins in his fist.

'Any more bets?' he was shouting.

Tom pushed his way through the press of men, most of whom were complete strangers to him. Just before the fight was set to begin, a swarm of ugly men with hard faces, sweat-soaked kerchiefs around thick necks, and clothes that reeked of mud and stale body fluids flooded like a sea of rocks into the Fourteen Stars.

Stoke pointed out the other pairs that were fighting.

Tom weighed them up. 'I take it my opponent is one of this ugly-looking crew. What Irish bog did you get them from?'

Stoke took it as a huge joke and roared with laughter. He leaned close, his voice dropping to little more than a whisper. 'Temple Meads Meadows, if you must know. They're building the station and laying the track for Mr Brunel's wonderful railway. And not all of them are from Ireland.'

Tom frowned. The men's origins were of no importance. It was the fact that they were working at Temple Meads Meadows that stuck in his mind. This was the second time in the last few days he'd heard it mentioned. Temple Meads Meadows was no more than a mile or so from the berth of the *Miriam Strong*. Was there a connection? And if so, who was behind it all?

As the first fight got under way, bets and encouragements were shouted in a variety of accents, some he'd never heard before. Stoke nudged his arm. 'They're from Kingswood,' he said. 'Hard to know what they'm on about, eh, Tom? Even Taff Jones over there don't understand what they're saying and he's Welsh!'

Stoke seemed to find this extremely funny and slapped his sides. Tom peeled off his shirt and used it to rub away the film of sweat from off his chest.

There were many coalmines at Kingswood and the surrounding areas, but there was none at Temple Meads Meadows. It was too close to the river and these men were building and laying track for a method of travel that was rumoured would replace the mail coach and the canals in no time at all. And Mr Brunel's *Great Western* had already proved that crossing the Atlantic was far quicker by steam than by sail. A link between the track-laying and someone wanting the *Miriam Strong*'s berth clicked in his mind…

Stoke was taking bets at a rate of knots, telling everyone that Tom was drinking too much to win and the big bruiser navvy would flatten him for sure. The navvy had got himself quite a reputation, but Stoke was secretly in no doubt that Tom would flatten him and therefore, Stoke would be in the money.

Aggie, the woman who plied her barge up and down the Severn, nodded a swift greeting before squatting herself next to Tom. Her clothes stunk of coal dust. Bad breath caused by her rotting teeth wafted up Tom's nostrils when she leaned close to his ear and said, 'I reckon Stoke's done fer Sally. What do you think?'

Tom turned cold. 'I can't say,' he said, shocked. Stoke had certainly beaten Sally, but would he have killed her? He couldn't believe that.

Disappointed by his response, Aggie moved away. Tom concentrated on the fights.

In the second fight a blacksmith from Bedminster was soundly beaten by one of the miners from Kingswood. A warehouseman from Brandon Hill, a lithe and lanky type with long arms and quick feet, brought a thickset man to his knees. And through it all, Cuthbert Stoke smiled and counted money from one hand into the other.

Tom tried to look through the crowd for some sign of Sally. At the sight of a cluster of ostrich feathers or the trill of feminine laughter, he turned his head, fully expecting to see her. Instead his eyes met those of another woman. Of course, she'd have that same quick smile, that pay-me look in her eyes. But there was no sign of Sally.

'Your turn,' Stoke shouted above the din.

A big bruiser of a man stepped into the ring. His legs were like tree trunks and his arms matched.

Stoke nudged him. 'Told you he was built like a bull, didn't I?'

The monster in the ring cracked his fingers and stood glaring at Tom. His underwear flopped over a thick leather belt like a skirt. And he stank.

Like hounds on the scent of blood, the crowd erupted, their excitement rousing the pigeons in the rafters. Feathers floated down and excrement dropped like rain as the birds left the area above the makeshift ring to find less noisy roosts.

The two men faced each other within the straw ring.

Tom held his fists high and his elbows close to his side. Light on his feet, he circled the other man without blinking. His opponent was heavily built, and therefore slow on his feet. But his fists were like anvils; one blow was likely to take Tom's head off if he wasn't careful. But he didn't watch the man's fists. He always looked at his opponent's eyes. A man's eyes changed just before a blow was delivered. Less than a blink, the change was almost imperceptible, more a quickening of the pupil preceding the movement of the fist.

Tom had heard long ago that you could smell fear, almost taste it. You could also, he thought, smell excitement. He could smell it in the crowd now, hear it in the pregnant silence before the fight started, and taste it on the wave of beer-fuelled breath that tainted the air.

Men thrived on violence in different ways. Some thrived on feeling the crunch of their own bones against the jaw of their opponent. Others thrived on watching violence, the fighters carrying out the spectators' aggression by proxy.

He circled warily. The crowd erupted with excitement as he jabbed a right to the man's jaw. His opponent looked surprised.

This was not a man used to being beaten. Fear of losing face among his peers was as bad, if not worse, than losing the fight. He would become obsessed with his need to win, and thus become rash with his fighting strategy.

The big man lunged, arms flailing, fists flying. The stout legs, unused to quick movement, stumbled slightly as he tried to charge, head down and fists lashing. One blow almost hit home, but Tom saw it coming, and danced away. Again and again the man tried the same thing. Sometimes he managed to land a punch, but not in the danger zones. Head, heart and guts, that's where he needed to hit, but Tom wouldn't give him the chance. He kept on his toes, dancing away from danger the moment a connection looked likely.

Again and again the big arms ranged outwards, fists swinging and meeting nothing but air. Sweat flew from his stinking body and ran in rivulets into his creased underwear, the sleeves of which flew about his body like broken wings.

Tom landed a right, then a left and a right again on the big man's chin. His head jerked back. Blood streamed with snot from a cracked nostril, but still the man did not go down.

The crowd were baying for blood and their mood didn't sound good. The noise was enough to burst eardrums. The men working Temple Meads Meadows had come in force to cheer on their champion and their mood was turning as ugly as their looks.

Out of the corner of his eye, Tom spotted Cuthbert Stoke, but could not read his expression. He could guess how many bets he'd taken and could almost recite word for word what Stoke might have told them about the match.

*Tom Strong is a gentleman with a gift for a fight, but not a man who toils with pick-axe or shovel. Bound to be softer, but skilled, mark you, skilled!*

They would have believed Stoke and decided he was soft, and Stoke would have let them think that. He would not have added that he was a sea captain at the age of twenty-three, had sailed all the oceans of the world by his late twenties and had brawled and broken heads from Marseilles to Madagascar. He also had a habit of changing strategy halfway through a fight once he saw which way the fight was going. Stoke had made the crowd believe that the bull man would win, when in fact he was sure he would lose, which also meant that the majority, who had betted on the navvy to win, would lose their stake. Stoke would have it all.

For the briefest of moments, he dropped his guard and a fist the size of a small anvil sent him reeling – just as he'd wanted it to.

Stoke looked panic stricken. There he stood, clutching the money, money he'd thought would be going straight into his pocket.

Once more a big fist grazed Tom's chin. He reeled again, legs crumpling under him as he slowly fell back against the bales of straw that would cushion his fall. Satisfied that he'd judged it right, he closed his eyes and let himself drop.

Stoke was livid.

The big bull from the railway gang was not so easily fooled. He sought Tom out where he was washing himself with ice-cold water from the spring at the rear of the premises.

He spoke in an accent that had its roots somewhere in Killarney. 'There was no call for you to do that, mister. The way you was dancin' around me, I couldn't catch you let alone hit you. Why'd ya stop?'

'I had my reasons.'

The man nodded as if Tom had uttered the wisest statement ever made. 'Will you let me buy you a beer?' he asked.

Tom shook his head. 'No. Thank you anyway, but I've got an errand to do.'

The man shrugged and turned away and the small yard that housed the spring smelled relatively fresh once more.

Stoke was waiting for him outside the Fourteen Stars. 'You lost! You bloody lost!'

Tom grabbed him by the throat. 'Where is she, Stoke?'

Stoke garbled an explanation, though the words were strangled by the tightness of Tom's hands around his throat.

Tom loosened his grip and repeated his question.

'I don't know!' Stoke stammered. 'Unless she's at home in bed. She is ill, you know.'

He crumpled as Tom landed a heavy fist in his guts.

Tom left him there. At that moment, he never wanted to see the Fourteen Stars again.

The smell of decay was as strong as ever in the small alley leading off the Christmas Steps. Flakes of wattle fallen from the crumbling walls crunched underfoot. Flies rose in a buzzing mass from a pile of human excrement, deposited there by people with no access to a privy and no regard for who might come there after them. For once he was thankful for flies. Rather them warn him of where it was than step in it.

He peered through Sally's window and saw only darkness. There was no fire in the grate and no sign of life. Perhaps she was already dead, lying in her filthy bed, no one knowing her state. The thought of it panicked him. The door rattled at his assault. He banged and slapped the splintered wood and shouted loud until heads poked out of upstairs windows.

'What's all that noise?' someone shouted.

'I'm looking for Sally.'

'She ain't 'ere.'

'Go away before I call the watch.'

'I will not go until I've seen Sally.'

'If you want the strumpet from down there, you're out of luck. You'll find more of 'er like down by the docks.'

The sweat of the fight turned cold on Tom's back. He managed to ask, 'Is she gone?' It sounded futile, stupid. Of course she was gone. That was what they were telling him.

'Oh she's gone all right. Fished her out of the river this afternoon. Had her throat cut. But there, that's life, ain't it?'

A casement slammed shut some way above him and left him frozen to the spot. The years rolled back and again he was that little boy given the news that his mother was dead. History had repeated itself.

He made his way out of the alley and back to Bennett's where he'd left his horse.

Stoke was in the Fourteen Stars next door, his face red from drink and his voice rising in song with the Irish navvies. Tom grabbed his arm and dragged him into the stables.

'Did you know Sally was dead?'

For a moment, Tom could almost believe that Stoke was shocked at the news, perhaps even sad at Sally's passing. He changed his mind when Stoke said, 'Well, that's the way most whores go.' He shrugged resignedly. 'That's the way it is.'

Tom couldn't stop his hands tightening around Stoke's throat. 'You bastard! You stinking bastard!'

Not until Stoke's face had turned purple and he was close to being choked to death, did Tom let go. With one mighty heave, he threw him into a vacant stall – one that hadn't been mucked out.

Spluttering for breath and holding his throat, Stoke was wise enough to stay put among the horse dung and urine-soaked straw.

'And that's where you belong,' Tom said.

Outside a star-filled sky roofed the city. His head began to clear, but the feeling that he was trapped by circumstance would not go away. Life was harsh at sea, but he'd much rather be there than have to tell Clarence that his mother was dead.

## Chapter Twenty-Three

Blanche had made up her mind to tell Nelson the truth regarding how she felt about him. True, she dreamed of the incident at the edge of the churchyard, the warmth of his body against hers, the flush of released energy, but then, as she gazed up breathless into his face... she saw Tom.

Why? She watched the children make a new tail for their kite, thanks to their mother's lap dog. Prince Charles had got out again. Yapping in wild excitement, he had leapt up at the kite tail. For a split second it had looked as though he would take off with it but, stuffed with sweetmeats by his indulgent owner, he'd come heavily down to earth, the kite tail chewed and tattered.

Tom was easy to talk to.

Whatever he said was the truth.

Whatever he did was honourable and he wasn't afraid to confront Sir Emmanuel Strong if he thought something was wrong.

At that moment Sir Emmanuel was ignoring him, something to do with Conrad Heinkel's sugar refinery so she'd heard. It was Tom who had suggested she speak to Lady Verity about Grainger's treatment of the children, including her liberal use of certain homemade remedies.

She promised herself that as soon as she'd seen Lady Verity, she would seek out Nelson and tell him exactly how she felt, that their evenings on the beach were long gone, that they were different people now. Making love at the edge of the churchyard was an event not to be repeated.

Lady Verity sat in the drawing room before midday, reading or attempting to write music, unless a morning soirée was arranged. The mayor's wife, the sheriff's wife, and as many titled people as possible, resplendent in silks and lace, and smelling of violets, usually attended.

From what Blanche had heard, they talked mostly about fashion, furnishings and social indiscretions. They rarely, if ever, discussed their children, unless they were of an age to be married off and therefore interesting.

Happily, Blanche had chosen a morning when Lady Verity was alone in the drawing room.

She told Soames, Lady Verity's personal maid, that she wanted to see Lady Verity about the children's welfare.

Soames, iron-grey hair ballooning around her face and stuffed into a fat bun at the nape of her neck, had been with Lady Verity's family for years. When 'her darling Verity' had married, Soames had come too. There was nothing else so important in her life as being of service to her mistress. She never gossiped, never socialized with the rest of the household in the servants' hall and always took her mistress's part.

'Wait there,' she ordered Blanche, when it seemed she might cross the threshold without either permission or introduction.

She came out imperiously, as though she was as important a messenger as Moses bringing the Ten Commandments from on high.

'She can't possibly see you at the moment.'

'Did you tell her the matter concerns her children's welfare?'

Soames glared. 'Prince Charles is asleep on her lap and she doesn't want him disturbed.'

Blanche kept her temper – just. 'I would have thought her children were more important than a dog.'

Soames pursed her lips, deep hollows forming beneath her cheekbones. 'You are not here to think, merely to serve.'

It was no use arguing. Soames would be unmoved by allusions to the children. The only thing to unnerve her would be perceived danger to 'her darling Verity'.

Blanche feigned concern. 'Goodness!' she gasped, her hand clapping against her open mouth. 'Should she really be doing that? The fleas were popping and jumping all over the little creature when I saw him last, and he's got a dirty backside. It's those treats she keeps giving him.'

Soames took a sharp intake of breath as her jaw dropped. Hopeful, though not convinced that this piece of information would reach Lady Verity, Blanche went looking for Nelson. She bumped into Edith on the back stairs, a bundle of ironed baby linens in her arms.

'Blanche,' she said, her eyes brightening, 'I thought you might want to know that the Reverend has been asking for you.'

Edith was back to her old self following her visit to Bristol with Tom, his marriage proposal forgotten. It appeared that Tom might have forgotten too. Blanche hadn't seen him in days. And now Jeb Strong was asking for her, and Edith was allowing her to see him.

'I'll be along as soon as I can,' she said, throwing Edith a friendly smile. Nelson was first on her list of priorities. Asking a servant his whereabouts would only give rise to gossip, but Edith knew her secret.

'Have you seen Nelson?' she whispered.

Edith screwed up her face in thought. 'Might be out in the garden. Bin painting out there a lot lately.'

Marstone Court boasted a rose garden adjacent to the terrace, a water garden, an expanse of lawns, hedges, waterfalls and ponds that vaguely resembled Versailles, besides three separate vegetable gardens, a walled garden enclosing cherries, raspberries, gooseberries and other soft fruits, and an expansive orchard containing apple and plum trees.

Blanche started in the rose garden. The air smelled fresh, untainted as yet by the roses, which were still tightly in bud. She sniffed. Another scent permeated the crisp air. She smelled tobacco, sweeter yet more subtle than that of a pipe or cigar.

A cloud of smoke enticed her to a secluded arbour where yellow points of colour speared through the green of this year's buds.

Heart pounding as she rehearsed what she had to say, Blanche clenched her fists and told herself to be brave.

'Nelson...' she began, then stopped dead.

In pale blue silk with cream collar and cuffs, every inch the wealthy lady with her lily-white hands and creamy complexion, Horatia was sitting, scribbling at a mass of papers. Reddening, she tucked the papers beneath the folds of her skirt and threw the unsmoked cheroot into the bushes.

'What do you want?' she snapped.

'I'm sorry,' said Blanche, backtracking immediately. 'I was hoping—'

'To find my brother? You were looking for Nelson?'

Blanche took in the cool beauty of the woman, the strength of her face and the brave look in her eyes. In some odd way, she found herself thinking that something of the way she herself felt was reflected in Horatia's eyes, as though they were both leading lives to which neither of them was suited.

She couldn't possibly tell her the real reason she was looking for Nelson. It was too intimate, too likely to attract disdain and condemnation from his sister. Taking an unblemished leaf from Edith's book, she swiftly concocted a suitable explanation.

'I wanted to talk to someone regarding the children.'

Horatia frowned. 'Why Nelson? What have they got to do with him — or me for that matter?'

Blanche chose her words carefully. 'Sir Emmanuel is away on business. I have tried to see Lady Verity, but she...' Blanche decided Horatia might possibly stand the truth. 'Her maid, Soames, said that the dog was asleep on Lady Verity's lap. She couldn't possibly disturb him just to see me.'

Horatia's face softened. She raised her fingers in front of her mouth and laughed as lightly as the breeze disturbing the tangled briars above her head.

'The woman's more fond of that dog than she is of her children. What do you think of that, Blanche?'

For a moment Blanche was taken aback. Only Nelson and Tom had ever called her by her first name. It was almost friendly, but Blanche judged it unwise to be too friendly back or to criticize Verity openly. After all, she was still only regarded as a servant here. 'I felt it my duty to make someone in this house aware of the damage being done to the children.'

'And the someone you chose to confide in was Nelson,' said Horatia, her look a mix of disbelief and cunning. She never let an opportunity pass to demean her stepmother in her father's eyes. So far as she was concerned, Verity was no different than the host of whores he'd set up as mistresses in houses he owned in Kings Square, Royal York Crescent, and Cornwallis Crescent when her mother was alive. If she could make use of Verity's neglect to undermine their marriage, she would do so. She had a little time to spare before Josiah Benson arrived that day.

Horatia made room on the bench and invited Blanche to sit down.

'You have ten minutes,' she said, reverting to her usual abruptness.

Blanche explained about how Mrs Grainger used the cane, the attic and even composed songs for the children to sing praising their love for her, which never had and never would exist.

If she expected support, Horatia disappointed her. 'We had the cane when we were children, though I don't remember being locked up in the attic.'

Blanche shook her head in exasperation. Mrs Grainger was more damaging than that.

'This is much worse. It's as though she's trying to control their minds, to mould them to fear her, not for their own good, but for her satisfaction. She takes pleasure from punishing them, especially George. She enjoys being cruel.'

Horatia raised one eyebrow. 'I've heard of people like her – both men and women.' She gave it further thought. 'And Lady Verity takes no interest in their plight?'

Blanche shook her head, amazed to discover a different Horatia beneath the haughty veneer she habitually presented to the world. She'd had little to do with her in the past. Even when passing in the house, Horatia had never regarded her, hardly seemed to notice her. Now she seemed to have her full attention.

'I also think she's giving them certain tinctures,' Blanche added.

'Tinctures?'

'Laudanum. Opium. That sort of thing.'

Horatia cut her dead. 'But those things are hardly harmful. In fact, I know people who favour taking a little laudanum instead of brandy. My brother, for instance, is an artist and poet. I understand such a habit heightens awareness and creativity and that Mr Samuel Taylor Coleridge used opiates when he wrote his wonderful "Kubla Khan". All the poets use it.'

'That's not true!' Blanche told her about the warning she'd had from Miss Pinkerty when her mother had fallen ill. She also told her about certain houses in Barbados – and Bristol too, she'd no doubt – where men and women lay comatose under the influence of such tinctures. 'Their minds are destroyed,' she said finally.

Her eyes met those of Horatia. It was almost like looking into Nelson's, though without the languid other-worldliness. The expression in Horatia's eyes took on a sudden intensity, as if she were seeing someone other than Blanche. 'Obsession with the exotic,' Horatia said. Blanche wasn't sure whether she was referring to the opiates, to her or to something or someone else.

Horatia sprung to her feet, the papers she'd been hiding clenched tightly in her hand. 'Bring me proof,' she said, 'and I will deal with it!'

–

Blanche made up her mind to warn the children not to take any more tinctures unless they checked with her first. It seemed highhanded though; who was she to give orders? Her interview with Horatia over, she headed for the nursery.

As she burst into the room, she saw Mrs Grainger holding George by his shoulder and forcing him to drink something from a small glass. Was it laudanum? Blanche hit the glass and its contents to the floor. 'Stop giving them that stuff,' she shouted, her eyes blazing.

Mrs Grainger raised her sooty eyebrows. 'Dandelion milk? And what might be wrong with that, Miss High and Mighty?'

'Dandelion milk?' repeated Blanche.

'For George's chest,' said Mrs Grainger with a smug smile. 'And you, you darkie bitch, aren't going to get away with this. I'm going to see Lady Verity and have you sent from here!'

Skirts rustling and face red, Mrs Grainger made a melodramatic exit, her skirt filling the door and her voice cracking like a sail in a storm.

Darkie. It was amazing how much it hurt to be called that. In the privacy of her room, she checked her reflection in the mirror, half afraid in case she'd turned as black as the coal in the unlit grate.

It felt as though she were wearing Marstone Court around her neck. Tired and despairing, Blanche sat on the bed, her head in her hands, thinking that perhaps she should marry Tom, or reconsider running away with Nelson. She didn't raise it until Edith entered.

'You've missed tea,' she said brightly. 'It was your favourite. Mutton pie and raspberry jelly. And I promised to take you along to see the Reverend when you'd finished it.'

Blanche sighed and told her what had happened.

Edith's round, pink face expanded in amazement. 'The old cow! What use is dandelion milk for a bad chest? No wonder poor little George pees the bed. Me mum always told us not to pick dandelions 'cos they makes you wet yourself. And they do. I know they do.'

Her visit to the Reverend Strong forgotten, Blanche almost flew at the door. 'Come on. Let's do something about this.'

Edith followed, her feet thudding like rubber mallets as she thundered along the landing. 'Like what?'

'I don't quite know yet. I'll think of something.'

Horatia stood perfectly still, her features silhouetted against the window. The view was beautiful, though she was not really seeing it.

'Any news from Mr Trout?' she asked without turning her head.

Duncan looked disdainful. He hated dealing with Reuben Trout. 'He's been keeping an eye on the ship and on Captain Strong. He says the captain has not visited the ship as much as he usually does when he's in port.'

'Understandable. He has other obligations.'

'Yes, Miss Horatia. One of those *obligations* is a woman named Sally, a known whore on the waterfront. The other is Brown – Blanche Bianca as she prefers to be called – the nurse from Barbados. He's even been out and about with Edith, though in the company of the children.'

Duncan knew how Horatia felt about Tom and it gave him great pleasure to undermine her natural coolness. Her response made him feel powerful, more like a man who might – just might – get her to see that Tom did not desire her. But *he* did. Very much so.

Horatia did not see his smirk. The grass and trees outside the window had nothing to do with the green mist that swam before her eyes. The mere thought of Tom with another woman made her heart beat faster. Her jaw ached as she fought to control her surging emotions.

'Edith Clements looks like a pig. Blanche is merely a servant concerned about my half-brothers and sisters. It is only natural that Captain Tom should sometimes be in their company.' Her comment about Edith was unnecessarily cruel, but she couldn't help it. And Blanche *had* spoken to her about the children.

Duncan noticed Horatia's rigid back and trembling hands. He said, 'They – Captain Tom and the nurse – stayed overnight at the house of Conrad Heinkel.'

Horatia felt as though she'd been consumed by fire. Imagining Tom and Blanche together was unbearable. Through clenched teeth she said, 'And no progress has been made regarding that berth?'

'Mr Benson did mention that if there was no ship there, the berth would be free anyway.'

'Then we have to get rid of it!'

Horatia rarely let anger cloud her judgement or her actions, but the vision of Tom and Blanche together swam before her eyes and she only half considered the impact of what she was saying.

Like a puppeteer pleased to have pulled the right strings, Duncan felt bigger and better than he'd ever felt in his life. 'I will tell Mr Benson,' he said.

Horatia seemed not to hear him. 'Tomorrow you may take a message to Mr Benson regarding the matter of the *Miriam Strong* to that effect. Just tell him that I rely on his good judgement.'

After her most loyal footman had left, Horatia looked at the open page of a book Nelson had taken from the bookcase earlier entitled, *A Thorough Study and Pictorial History of the Sugar Islands.*

Sugar and the West Indies had been part of her family's history for a long time. The city of Bristol had grown far beyond its medieval confines as a direct result of the plantations and the triangular trade.

At least Josiah Benson understood her ambition. He had advised her on investment in railways, shipyards and a study of the mail system between Britain and North America. He also wanted to marry her, but her heart ached for Tom.

If Mrs Grainger hadn't rapped at the door, Horatia would perhaps have saved her anger for Tom, or more likely, Blanche. But Horatia's dislike for her stepmother was just as strong and with a greater history than her jealousy of Blanche.

Mrs Grainger's lips were pursed. 'Begging your pardon, Miss Horatia, but Lady Verity is bathing her little dog and can't see me just now, but I wonder—'

'Certainly.'

They stood, Horatia a whole head taller than the bulkier frame of Mrs Grainger.

'I have long been in this house—' Mrs Grainger began with a superior expression.

'Get to the point.'

Thrown for a moment, Mrs Grainger swiftly recovered. 'I've been giving Master George dandelion juice for his chest. Now, that young woman from Barbados has told me that it's my fault he wets the bed, that dandelion juice makes him do that. I feel under the circumstances—'

'She's right!' Horatia remembered as a child picking armfuls of the bright yellow flowers for feeding to the rabbits the gamekeeper kept for cooking. Their nanny at the time, one of the many Peters, had told her to wash her hands before eating because they were indeed a natural diuretic.

Mrs Grainger looked devastated. Blanche and that wretched Edith had come breezing into the nursery and laid down the law as if she had no status in this house, no power.

'Never in all my years—' she said.

'That's enough!'

Horatia turned on her heel and went back to looking out of the window, even though she'd tired of the view. She didn't want Mrs Grainger to see the turmoil in her eyes, the hurt, the anger, and the utter dejection. 'No more dandelion juice! Less laundry, though perhaps more coughing.'

Mrs Grainger was dismissed, but not before Horatia had thrown her one last question.

'How old are you, Mrs Grainger?'

Realizing the significance of the question and afraid to answer, Mrs Grainger's eyes darted swiftly around the room as if she were looking for the answer in the bookcase, behind the mantel clock or hanging from the tapestry face screen that sat before the fire.

'Sixty-two,' she said at last.

By this time, Horatia was sitting at her desk, running her eyes over the papers regarding the granting of Royal Mail contracts. She looked up from her paperwork. 'Goodness. I don't suppose you're likely to be around when Alicia May is ready for the nursery.'

She didn't see the look of terror on Mrs Grainger's face, but knew it was there. Smarting from Duncan's news regarding Tom and Blanche, Horatia had needed to lash out at someone. Mrs Grainger had chosen the wrong moment.

Still sick at heart after seeing Blanche with Nelson, and then having to tell Clarence that his mother was dead, Tom had stayed with Conrad rather than going back to Marstone Court or to the *Miriam Strong*.

A new centrifugal filtering system was being installed, and Tom assisted. Using his hands and working out what pipe work and machinery went where helped occupy his mind and keep darker thoughts at bay.

Conrad's shadow fell over him just as he was fixing the central balance of the system. The big German jerked his head casually as he slid his pipe into the corner of his mouth. 'We have a spy. I have seen a man hiding outside and he is watching us.'

Disturbed, Tom turned back to the job in hand to gather his thoughts. The spy couldn't possibly be informing on Conrad. Emmanuel had given that job to him, not that he'd actually done any. He liked Conrad too much for that and had ended up helping him, much to Emmanuel's displeasure.

'I hadn't noticed him,' said Tom, 'though I will keep an eye out in future.'

'You think he is watching you, not me?' asked Conrad.

Tom laughed, rubbed the grease from his hands on to his trousers, and shouted at the foreman to oversee the fixing of pipes to the new system now that the main tank was in place. He turned with Conrad towards the pleasant little office, which was painted green with windows that looked out over the river.

Conrad walked with head bowed, hands buried deep in his pockets, a habit common in tall men who wished to appear shorter.

'We will see if this man is following me or you,' said Conrad after the door to the office he shared with Tom was firmly closed. 'I have to go somewhere with my colleagues.' He patted his broad waistline and smiled in a satisfied manner, opened a drawer and brought out a big book, the same book Tom had seen beneath his arm before.

'You are wondering?' Conrad asked, his bright eyes sparkling with barely suppressed amusement, or so it seemed to Tom, who slumped into a chair and shook his head.

'Not really.'

Conrad's smile almost split his face in two. 'Your uncle thinks I am making covenants with my compatriots in the Sugar Bakers Association. He does not trust us because most of us are Germans.'

Conrad was an instinctive man and was not easily fooled.

'I trust you.'

'I know you do. But your uncle does not. Perhaps he has sent another spy because his first one failed him?'

Tom smiled at the inference and shook his head. Conrad had known from the start that he'd been placed in the refinery for more than one reason.

'But you do attend a lot of meetings, Conrad.'

Conrad placed the book on the desk and pushed it towards him. 'The Bible. We are Lutherans and have been holding services at each other's houses. Now we are going to build our own church. We have been making plans, meeting, pooling our resources in order to purchase a piece of land. Tell that to your uncle. He is invited to attend once we have built it.'

Tom rested his head on his hand. 'Sir Emmanuel's ambitions are confined to this life rather than the hereafter. No doubt he's depending on bluffing his way into heaven when the time comes.'

'He will fail. He looks less than an angel,' Conrad said with a laugh.

'Not pretty enough,' remarked Tom with a smile, thought of Blanche and fell into silence.

Conrad too fell silent with his own thoughts, which turned out to be much the same as Tom's.

'And how is the girl who makes kites and likes chocolate?' he asked. 'Miss Blanche Bianca.'

Tom remembered the way Conrad had looked at Blanche and felt a pang of jealousy. 'Half thinking of going back to Barbados,' he said as if it were the honest truth, though he knew full well that Blanche had changed her mind.

'That would be a very great shame,' said Conrad. He took a sheaf of paper from his desk. 'Will you give this to her?'

Tom took it. It was a sealed letter.

'I would like to make a contract with her to look after my children. As I said to you, it's clear she loves children and I think it would be good – for us and for her,' said Conrad, his blue eyes thoughtful behind the plume of smoke that rose from his pipe.

'Yes,' said Tom, envisaging Blanche employed as a governess in the Heinkel household, which was less demanding that the Strong family and without the autocratic atmosphere of Marstone Court. He'd avoided her since witnessing the scene among the silver birch trees. However, he took the letter and slid it into his belt.

'So, who do you think this man is?' asked Conrad, reverting to their initial subject of discussion.

Thoughtfully, Tom flicked his fingers at the chair arm. 'Is he out there now?'

Conrad sighed and nodded. 'I think so.'

Tom followed him to the second floor of the refinery. Rows of windows let in plenty of light by which to work. The building had been so constructed because unshielded candle flames were too much of a hazard. Even now, sugar refineries were notoriously difficult to insure. Pressed tightly into one of these windows, Tom and Conrad gazed at the scene on the ground without being seen themselves.

Like a dockside rat, the spy lurked between a mountain of barrels and bales of charcoal.

'Do you know him?' Conrad asked.

'Oh yes,' said Tom grimly. 'That's Reuben Trout.'

'He is not a friend?'

Tom shook his head. 'No. He is not a friend.'

—

Jimmy Palmer had drunk too much. In his fuddled brain he dreamed he was hot and that someone was pressing a blanket over his head. He couldn't breathe. If he could just get the blanket away from his mouth…

He pushed at it. The blanket disappeared and still he couldn't breathe. Shedding the euphoric comfort of dreams, he blinked his eyes open, but saw nothing. The pungency of burning caulk assaulted his nostrils like grains of hot sand. Just a dream, he thought, as his eyelids got heavy and began to close. Just a dream…

'Mr Palmer! Mr Palmer!'

With great difficulty, he blinked his eyes open again. Someone was calling him and hammering on the cabin door… Smoke was pouring under the door and the first flames were licking at its base. Coughing and spluttering, he roused himself to the point of one foot landing on the floor. If he hadn't been drunk, perhaps he'd have been quicker, but just as he managed to put his second foot on the floor, someone outside shouted, 'Clarence! Get out!'

Jimmy heard no more. A wall of flame spread like an opening fan from the door and along the walls. The force threw him back on to his bed and this time he would not wake up.

# Chapter Twenty-Four

The *Miriam Strong* was no more. Tom was on his way home from the refinery when he saw the flames rising above the roof of the Hole in the Wall.

Dreading what he would find, he spurred his horse through the narrow streets, street vendors, urchins, sailors and packmen diving out of his way.

The boys, black with soot and shivering in their nightshirts, huddled in a group against the tavern wall, staring with unblinking eyes at the remains of the ship. For most of them, it was the only home they'd ever known.

Mirrored reflections of the flames skidded over adjacent windows and highlighted the terror in the boys' faces.

'Is everyone safe?' he shouted. 'Is anyone still on her?'

No one answered. Dumb with fear, the boys stared up at him. Tom didn't hesitate.

He organized a human chain, pails of water passed hand to hand. The ship was insured, but there was no time to knock the men of the insurance company's pumping engine out of bed. Help was needed now, and although there were onlookers, men used to working as a team would be best.

Slipping from his horse, he passed its reins to a sailor he recognized as having once served under him. 'Ride to Heinkel's Refinery. Ask for help. Tell them I sent you.'

By the time help came from the refinery, Tom's muscles were aching with the effort of passing pails of water, hoping there was no one left on board, but having no time to count the boys or rouse them from their terrified stupor.

The men from the sugar refinery automatically formed long lines, working in unison. Conrad was there too, towering above everyone, barking orders one minute, and saying prayers the next.

Tom sent the sailor and a gang of men to the shed where the insurance company kept their horses and pumping engine, though

in his heart of hearts he already knew it was too late. He instructed an innkeeper to give the boys food and drink.

'I'll stomach the costs,' he added.

Shortly before dawn, the charred timbers of the *Miriam Strong* crashed into the water, sending up a great plume of spray. Slowly she sank, steam mixing with smoke as she finally came to rest.

Exhausted with the effort of it all, Tom stared, his arms hanging lifeless at his sides.

Like the skeleton of an upturned beetle, the ship's ribs stuck up through the muddied water, unrecognizable objects floating like digested food in between them.

Face caked with soot and hair singed by falling sparks, he turned away from the ship. Conrad Heinkel put a hand on his back. 'I am sorry for this, Tom.'

Tom's throat was too dry to speak, burned up with the dry air and thick smoke. 'I have to tell Jeb. It was his ship. He got her years ago...'

His voice faded. What a sorry sight he must look, his hair and eyebrows singed; even his eyes felt blistered by the heat.

Conrad thrust a jug of water in front of his face and bade him drink. 'Never mind the ship,' he said.

Tom swallowed and looked at the boys, who had declined the innkeeper's offer to sleep in his very comfortable rooms. They looked back at him expectantly.

'Are you all here?'

He began counting.

One of the older boys said, 'Mr Palmer's not here.'

He knew already. Jimmy was the reason he'd attempted to put the fire out, even when he realized it was impossible. If Jimmy had been alive, he would have been out here, standing side by side with his boys.

Tom had known Jimmy Palmer since the minute he'd first set foot on a deck. The flat-bottomed decanter was never empty and Jimmy was a serious drinker. Tom guessed Jimmy had drunk enough of it last night to send him into a deep sleep. He had been a sea-going man, so Tom thought no less of him for it. He'd been a hard man who'd led a hard life. And he'd been a friend. Tom would miss him.

'Are they all here?' Conrad asked.

Tom shook his head. 'All but one.'

He scoured the dirty faces that looked up at him, searching for one face above all others and not finding it. 'Where's Clarence?'

The same boy who'd answered his earlier question, spoke up now. 'I think he got off. Don't know fer sure though.'

Fear made Tom suddenly angry. 'Did you see him get off the ship, or didn't you?' he shouted.

The boy winced.

'The boy is frightened. Please. Be gentle.' He could not resist Conrad's strength and soft voice. His anger, at least towards the boys, died.

'I saw someone,' said a small boy with dribble hanging from the corner of his mouth. 'Don't fink it was 'im though. Looked like a man.'

'A man?'

Tom and Conrad exchanged looks.

Tom asked, 'Who was this man?'

The boy shrugged. 'Don't know. Just a man. Seen 'im about though.'

Tom sank slowly to his knees until his face was level with that of the boy. 'What did he look like?'

'Well, he didn't have much hair, and 'ad a boil as big as an onion growing out of 'is nose.'

—

Lady Verity Strong bundled the baby back to Blanche and refastened her dress. 'Take her away.' She'd been in a mood all morning. According to Edith, her husband had stormed out of the house the night before, after she'd accused him of neglecting her. Obviously he hadn't come home and Lady Verity suspected the worst.

Rumour below stairs was that he had another woman who was young, possibly foreign, named Susannah, information gleaned by way of the coachman whose job it was to take Sir Emmanuel into the city and wait around till all hours of the night. Rarely did he get back in time for breakfast nowadays.

Still hungry, the baby began to mew, her face screwed up in protest. Blanche tried to soothe the child, jiggling her about in her arms, but to no avail.

'She hasn't had enough,' she protested.

Verity snapped her gaze away from the brimming breakfast tray Soames had deposited on the bedside table and glared at her.

'How dare you! The child is mine, not yours. Now take her away. I've given her enough.' She rubbed at her nipples with her fingers. 'Besides, she hurts me. Now, where's Prince Charles?'

The little dog leapt on to his mistress's lap, licking slyly at her hand, which Verity interpreted as affection. It was more likely the dog could smell spilled milk, Blanche thought.

'But if you use the lanolin—' Blanche began.

Lady Verity's small blue eyes were like stone above her round cheeks. 'Mutton fat, no matter what fancy name you may give it! It may have escaped your notice, Brown, but *I* am the mistress here and *I* give the orders. Take her away. Now!'

Clenching her jaw so she wouldn't say the things on the tip of her tongue, Blanche retreated. Leaving the baby hungry was cruel but her opinion would count for nothing. I'm getting to know my place here, she thought grimly, and I don't like it.

Alicia May wriggled with vexation all the way along the landing. 'Sshh,' said Blanche, and wondered whether she dared give the child cow's milk. So long as it was boiled first, it should be all right.

Back in the nursery, Blanche put Alicia down in her crib. She glanced at the clock, wondering if she had enough time to visit Reverend Strong. He'd been ill for the past few days, though Edith said he was a little better now.

The door swung open just as she was about to open it and make her way to the Reverend's room.

Tom filled the doorway, and although she smiled warmly at him in welcome, his face was like stone.

'Captain,' she said, thinking it might be appropriate to address him formally. 'I haven't seen you in days.'

He clenched his jaw so hard that slight hollows appeared beneath his cheeks. 'I have had no occasion to seek you out until now.'

'I'm sorry about Saturday—' she began.

'So am I,' he said coldly. 'Here,' he said, handing her the letter from Conrad. 'This is for you.'

Whatever was eating at Tom? Was it because she had not been able to accompany him to Bristol with the children and Edith?

Faced with the sudden possibility that he'd seen her with Nelson, she felt her face burning with shame. She shouldn't have done it. Holding the letter with both hands against her chest, she could hardly bear to ask.

For a moment it looked as though he was going to say something, his mouth moving, almost forming words, then straightening in a tight, hard line.

She watched him stalk off, his image flicking from mirror to mirror all along the landing. It was like watching ripples on a lake. It hurt to see him go and she felt bereft.

For a while she stared at the letter, presuming it was a goodbye note from Tom. When she opened it she found it was not.

Dear Miss Bianca,

My children were full of praise for your advice on making a kite. They have not stopped talking about you. Rarely have I seen them happier since their mother died. I ask you to consider taking her place and therefore a marriage between us. You need time to think about this, I know, and should give me your answer when you have considered the advantages of such a match.

Respectfully yours,
Conrad Johann Heinkel

A marriage proposal!

Taken completely by surprise, Blanche sunk into a chair, the letter fluttering from her hand.

The words were touching. Hardly a love letter, almost a contract, based on her instruction to his children on how best to make a kite!

She had no doubt that Conrad was a good man and she'd have a comfortable life, with the security and comfort most women only dreamed of.

Carefully, she picked up the letter, refolded it and put it into her trinket box. She'd just closed the lid when Edith barged in.

'Mrs Grainger's put George up in the attic, Blanche! Do something, please do something,' Edith wailed.

'Look after the baby,' said Blanche immediately.

'What are you going to do?' Edith asked.

Blanche set her mouth in a straight line. 'Get him down, of course.'

If she'd been less upset about Alicia May being hungry, less angry about George being locked in the attic, she might have seen from Edith's eyes that she was lying. But she did not, and rushed headlong for the narrow staircase that led to the attic.

The marks of many footprints left a trail through the dust. Ahead of her, a thin sliver of light fell from a door that was slightly ajar. Blanche crept forward on tiptoe and did her best to ignore her thudding heart.

Old boards untrodden for years creaked beneath her feet. There were ghosts up here, according to Edith, and all the servants agreed. Blanche didn't need to believe in ghosts purely on their say-so. She'd seen enough in Barbados to scare her into believing that this world was not the only one.

'Might be a mad relative hid up there,' Edith had said, and Blanche had laughed. But what if Edith was right? She shivered and told herself not to be a fool. Shabby, dull and dreary, but no sign of mad relatives. I've seen stone shacks kept better than this, she said to herself. The paint on the walls was dull. Dust lay on the window ledge to her left and the door ahead looked dry and narrow, untouched for some time. It squeaked like a dying mouse as she pushed it open. Before her courage failed her, she stepped into the attic.

'George?'

Her voice echoed among the dust-covered furniture, discarded portraits and leather-bound chests.

Not a sob. Not a murmur.

A flurry of wings against a shuttered window made her jump.

'Just a bird,' she said, her hand against her heart as she waited for it to stop racing.

'Silly,' she said, clicking her tongue at her foolishness. 'There's no one up here.'

Saying it out loud reinforced her courage. And then it was gone. Her heart almost stopped, or at least it felt that way, as she saw a figure standing silhouetted against a large, round window.

She gasped, half expecting it to be the mad relative Edith had insisted was imprisoned up here. She stepped backwards and bumped into the door.

The figure stepped away from the window, features forming as he stepped into the light.

'Blanche?'

Nelson held out his arms.

'Blanche,' he said again. 'I'm sorry I got Edith to lie, but I thought you wouldn't see me otherwise. I get the impression you've been avoiding me, but I don't understand why. And I want us to be friends again. I want us to lie on the beach in Barbados and make love in the sun.'

Shaking her head, she knew without a doubt that the magic of those evenings in Barbados was gone for ever. The man who'd made love to her in the churchyard was different from the man who'd made love to her in Barbados. This man before her was different again. His eyes stared. His skin glistened and was pale. Purple rings circled his eyes and his voice was strange, as if he no longer owned it. Apollo, her golden god, had become Pan her demon lover.

'The doctor told you not to take opium,' she said softly.

He laughed. 'Cook's biscuits, the special ones she makes for me. It's the leaves, you see. She thinks they're sage or caraway seeds.' He pulled her close, laughing at her struggles, saying something about taking her to paradise, lying naked beneath silken sheets, tented roofs, and seas of midnight stars.

'You're mad,' she said, still struggling and dragging herself to the door. She thought she was getting the better of him, was almost there, until he kicked it shut behind her.

He knocked her arm as she reached for the handle. 'I'm not mad! I'm sane. *You're* mad for not wanting to be with me in Barbados. Who else would you want to be with? Tom?' He laughed. 'You can't have Tom. My sister wants Tom. Don't you know that?'

She decided to humour him. 'I'll go with you to Barbados in time.'

'In time?'

'Not yet,' she said, smiling up at him as if she really meant to reconsider. 'Besides, we don't need to be in Barbados, do we? We can be together here.'

He gathered her close, his lips brushing her hair. 'We could indeed,' he said dreamily, his eyes closing. 'And I could paint you and write poems to you – with the help of Cook's wonderful biscuits. "Through caverns measureless to man / Down to a sunless sea." '

'Those aren't your words. That's not your poem.'

Nelson laughed. 'That's not the point. I can write poetry as visionary, by smoking or chewing a little hashish, just as Coleridge did.'

Blanche backed away, shaking her head, and feeling foolish that she'd let him make love to her. 'No,' she said, now flat against the door. 'No.'

'Blanche, if we don't run away to Barbados, I will have to marry my lacklustre cousin, whose mother dictates everything she does?'

Blanche almost laughed. 'Everything?'

Nelson made a po-face. 'Imagine the honeymoon!'

It was hard not to be amused, but the look in Tom's eyes haunted her. She'd hurt him, she could see that now. He'd been to Bristol that day, and she'd been with Nelson. He must have seen them. He must have.

As she was distracted by her thoughts, Nelson took advantage and dragged her back towards him, pulling her dress from her shoulder and exposing one nipple. The sight of it seemed to inflame him. She twisted away, but he spun her round and tried to knock her legs from under her as he rained kisses upon her neck and shoulders. If he hadn't stepped on a loose dustsheet and revealed a painting, she would have continued to struggle. Instead she froze. If she hadn't known she was looking at a painting, she would have thought she was looking into a mirror. The woman looking out at her had her own grey eyes, the same dark hair and even the same mole under her right eye, but her clothes dated from years before. It wasn't her but someone who looked like her.

Nelson's head fell on her shoulder, but somehow she found the strength to push him away.

'Who is it? Who is that woman? Is it me?' she asked, her voice trembling as she pointed at the painting.

Nelson blinked away his blurred vision and stared. 'She looks very much like you, doesn't she?'

'Who is she?' Blanche shouted, curtailing the urge to slap him.

Nelson looked shocked. 'I'm trying to remember...' He tugged the painting forward. 'Verity had a lot of family portraits removed and replaced with mirrors, but I believe Father insisted they were all catalogued and notes made of their identity on the reverse of each painting, though this one looks as if it's been up here a lot longer than the ones she had removed.'

Apprehensive, but also excited, Blanche stared at the painting.

Nelson's face became still as he noted whatever was on the reverse. 'It seems that Verity was not the only second wife to remove family portraits.'

All passion gone from his face, Nelson's gaze flitted nervously between Blanche and the painting.

'This lady is our grandmother.'

Amazed that her parentage was at last confirmed, Blanche exclaimed, 'So I *am* Otis Strong's daughter.'

Nelson shook his head. 'No. You're not.'

She looked down at the painting, the clear eyes, the tumbling hair. It was her and yet it wasn't her. The woman was paler skinned, but that was all. She was almost her double.

'Patience Strong,' Nelson read out.

'What is it?' Blanche asked, sensing that something about the painting was troubling Nelson.

In a wavering voice, he managed to say, 'Patience Strong was my father's mother. Samson Strong's first wife. Uncle Jeb and Uncle Otis were the children of his second marriage. Just like my father marrying Verity and having all those brats,' he added with a light laugh that almost seemed to choke him.

As her legs turned to jelly, Nelson looked at her, the same realization that had come to her reflected in his eyes.

Clutching at her stomach, Blanche backed towards the door shaking her head. Otis Strong was not her father. Emmanuel was. She and Nelson were brother and sister.

Suddenly, she wanted to be anywhere excepting here at Marstone Court. She ran from the room, the heels of her shoes clattering like pony hooves over the stairs and along the landing to her room.

'Blanche!' Nelson ran after her, but fell flat on his face before reaching the first landing.

Blanche heard the thud as he hit the floor, but didn't stop. She'd lain with her own brother, the ultimate sin. All this time she had believed that Otis Strong was her father and Nelson her cousin. Now she knew why Emmanuel had averted his eyes rather than look into her face; not just because she was a servant, but because he remembered his mother and knew that she was *his* daughter. Lady Verity knew it too. She'd known of the painting's existence when she'd first married Emmanuel and had replaced some of the Strong family portraits with mirrors. Deep down Verity hated the Strongs. Small acts of sabotage made her feel better, including smearing mud on the tomb.

And George had probably known too, sweet, lovable George who had loosened the sheet from the painting, recognized Patience as looking like Blanche, and perhaps cuddled up to it for comfort. Her mother, had she known? She remembered the perfume coming once a year on the Barbados packet from Bristol. She must have known. That was why Nelson had been sent away in the first place, though it seemed as though Viola and Otis had kept that particular secret to themselves. The Strongs would never have allowed her at Marstone Court if they'd known the truth about what had happened between Blanche and Nelson in Barbados.

As Blanche threw clothes and precious things back into the sea chest, and other more immediate needs into a leather bag, Edith's head appeared round the door, her face wreathed in smiles.

'Did you like the surprise?' she asked innocently.

Too troubled to say anything, Blanche continued packing.

Edith had obviously been expecting a thank you for having orchestrated the meeting on Nelson's behalf. Her face dropped. 'What are you doing?'

'I'm leaving,' Blanche said, as the last of her dresses were packed into her sea chest. 'I can only carry a small bag. I'll send word to you of where I am. Perhaps you could arrange for my things to be delivered once I've got an address? I might take passage to Australia.'

Edith shook her head. 'I don't understand. "E didn't 'urt you, did 'e? I wouldn't 'ave followed his orders if I'd thought he was goin' to 'urt you.'

'It wasn't your fault.'

She didn't look at Edith, and she didn't stop packing. Her jaw hurt with the effort of keeping her mouth shut, just in case she shouted out the truth, and she couldn't admit to that, never in a million years.

Edith looked hopelessly lost. 'I thought you loved Nelson.' She sounded on the verge of tears.

*As a brother.* Blanche was devastated.

'Leave that to one of the men,' Edith said, as Blanche pulled on the leather straps that fastened the wooden chest.

'I can do it.' She gave one final tug, and the strap slid from around the chest. With a surprised yell, Blanche fell back against Edith, knocking her over like a skittle, Blanche sitting in Edith's lap.

It was all too much. Blanche began to cry. Edith let out a loud moan. 'I've broken something.'

Concerned for her friend, Blanche wiped her eyes. 'Where does it hurt?'

'It doesn't. I've busted me corset. Just look where it's pushed me bosoms.'

Blanche twisted round. Edith's corset had moved up with the impact of falling. The top of her ample bosoms wobbled like half-set jellies above her bodice. Blanche couldn't help but laugh through her tears. Edith was a character, far from perfect in looks or deeds, but good all the same.

Edith's laughter gradually subsided. 'Don't go,' she said. Her concern was genuine, her eyes sadder than Lady Verity's spoilt spaniel.

Blanche got to her feet. 'I have to.' She kissed Edith on the cheek. 'And thank you for being a friend.'

Edith looked perplexed.

'Remember my clothes when I first arrived? If it hadn't been for you I would have frozen to death – and looked a fright.'

Edith shrugged. 'Even though a woman's only got the purse of a pauper and the taste of a toff, she should still do 'er best to follow fashion.'

Blanche unfastened the shell-studded jewellery box that now contained the money received from Aggie Pike and Tom. She sighed. 'I hope this is enough to get me a passage back to Barbados. If it's not, I might have to sell the earrings.'

'Fen could sell them for you,' Edith said brightly, 'but if you want a bit to tide you over...'

She lifted her dress and fumbled in the folds of her calico petticoat and pantalets.

'Here,' she said, handing Blanche four warm guineas. 'I was savin'' 'em for me bottom drawer, which is why I kept them in me drawers...' She giggled.

'Most apt,' said Blanche.

'Most apt,' Edith repeated. In awe of Blanche since the day they'd met, Edith had taken to copying some of the 'posher' things she said.

With a guilty expression, Edith fell to silence. 'Blanche, do you really have to? Is it my fault?'

Blanche shook her head. Her instinct was to run away. It didn't matter that both Tom and Conrad had asked to marry her. She had been familiar with her own brother and felt eternally damned for it.

She fled the Strong house, her shame giving wings to her feet, her small leather bag banging against her side.

-

Blanche stopped running when she reached the riverbank, out of sight of Marstone Court. A sloop was leaving on the tide along a golden path thrown by the setting sun. Her gaze strayed from the ship to the cliffs of the Avon Gorge. 'Women wounded by love throw themselves over they cliffs,' Edith had told her. The sloop seemed a preferable alternative. She watched the unfurled sails fall from its mast. Better to leave on a ship than leap off a cliff.

By the time she got to the city, she'd long ceased running. Her legs ached and her arms felt heavy. Wisps of hair strayed from beneath her bonnet and blew across her face. The evening breeze whipped at her shawl. Tired after such a long walk, the weight of her bag wearied her further, even though she'd only packed the minimum of clothing. The rest would be sent for, she'd told a distraught Edith, but she didn't know when, mostly because she didn't know where she was going. Getting a ship seemed the best thing to do, and she didn't really care where the ship was going.

Lights came on in the windows of houses and inns as she entered the city. Shouts, singing and laughter poured from the doors of dockside taverns. She wished she could be merry too, but didn't think she'd ever be so again.

Still clutching her bag, she paused on the cobbled quay and studied the names of the ships berthed there, hoping to recognize one she'd seen in Barbados.

Suddenly she felt terribly homesick and missed her mother as never before. Then the raucous shouts of drunken men roused her from her thoughts and three sailors fell from a tavern door, their pigtails askew and their faces red. One of them spotted her and staggered forward.

'What price for a little dockside doxy?' he shouted, his hand shovelling in his pocket. 'If she wants money to fill that bag she's carrying, she'll take all three of us.'

His friends laughed. He reached for her, and Blanche ran. Swifter than any of them, she ran blindly away from the quayside, the drunken men and the tarts, their grubby breasts on view, and their hands on their hips.

Breathing heavily, she ran into alleys that smelled of mould, maggots and urine. So long as she could see the masts of ships, she kept running until she found herself entering alleys that seemed vaguely familiar. She was in the Pithay where Edith's family lived. Dire as it was, she had to have somewhere to sleep tonight, and Edith's family were all she had. And Fen might be of help to her.

As she approached what she thought was the right house – one hovel looked much like another in the unrelenting darkness – the door flew open. The meagre light shining from within lit a man's sharp features, natty clothes and short stature. She thought she recognized him, and he seemed to know her.

'Now then,' he said, pulling up sharply, his goatee beard quivering and pointed like the tip of a sword. 'What have we here?' She'd seen him – somewhere. In any case, there was no one else around, just smells and emptiness, and he was all she had.

'I've come to see if Mrs Clements can give me a bed for the night,' she said in as confident a voice as she could muster. 'I'm taking a ship for Australia before the end of the week.'

She didn't know why she didn't say Barbados, or even whether there was a ship in harbour actually going to Australia, but she knew convicts were sent there, and the jails were full so she reckoned it had to be a regular run.

The nattily dressed little man eyed her appraisingly, then smiled and jerked his head towards the open door, which was swaying slightly on its hinges. The smell of dirt seeped into the night air. 'Could you put up with that stink for long?'

The smell was noxious, and somehow different than the last time she'd visited. And there was no barking.

'Are the dogs gone?' she asked. Perhaps Spike had stopped stealing dogs in order to claim rewards.

Right on cue, the sound of a braying donkey broke the silence. 'He's branched out, you might say,' said the man, grinning broadly. 'Some rich brat's pet donkey that got lost, you might say, up on the Downs. Takes up a bit more room than dogs did.'

Blanche tried to peer past him, looking for some sign that Mrs Clements was there.

'She's at home,' said the man, 'though not quite with us.' He pushed the door open.

Edith's mother was sprawled on the only chair she owned, her legs and mouth wide open, a tin mug and a cracked jug within inches of her meaty hand.

'Drunk,' said the man.

Blanche winced as the disgusting stink of the place hit her full in the face. She covered her mouth and nose with her hand, though it gave little respite.

The man, whose identity she still couldn't quite recall, nudged her with his elbow. 'Stinks somethink 'orrible, don't it?'

One look conveyed her agreement.

'Come on,' he said, taking hold of her elbow and guiding her back down the steps, 'I know a place you can stay. T'aint nothink posh, mind, but it's a bit cleaner than this place.'

Blanche let herself be led. Anything, she decided, was better than spending the night with a braying donkey and a gin-sodden woman.

That was before Stoke took her to stay with Mrs Harkness, who was a little cleaner, but a lot more dangerous.

## Chapter Twenty-Five

As Blanche bumped into Cuthbert Stoke, Mrs Grainger was taking the children downstairs to have tea with their parents at Marstone Court.

The governess greeted her master then her mistress with a curt nod and a sharply announced, 'Good evening.'

The atmosphere in the dining room seemed more formal than usual, but she gave it not great regard. The room was big, the marble fireplace ostentatiously elaborate, and the gleaming furniture reflecting the light of a hundred candles.

It then occurred to her that neither parent had returned her greeting. How terribly impolite, she thought, swallowed her ire, but promised herself to take it out on whoever she could before the night was out.

'The children have learned a charming little poem for you,' she exclaimed, her lips stretching thinly across her small, yellow teeth. 'Come along, children,' she said, pushing each one into their place beside each other.

Sir Emmanuel's voice boomed out, 'That won't be necessary.'

Not easily deterred from her objectives, even by her employers or the lack of moral fibre in others, Mrs Grainger chose to believe that she had misheard, and repeated again that the children had learned a poem especially for them.

Sir Emmanuel got to his feet and, for the first time since entering the room, she saw the coldness in his eyes. At the same time, she heard the crockery rattling in Lady Verity's hands, and noticed then that the mistress's hands were shaking and she was not looking in her direction as she usually did.

Seemingly prearranged, Duncan appeared.

'Have you found Miss Horatia?' Emmanuel asked him.

'Yes, sir.'

'Bring her here.'

Mrs Grainger had never been so flummoxed. Her sooty eyebrows furrowed and she suddenly sensed, instinctively, that her reign was at an end. But she was not a woman who took kindly to being dismissed. Making an instant decision, she said, 'I do apologize for any inconvenience, but I have received a message to say that my mother is sick. She's very old. I have to go to her.'

The fact that her mother was long dead and would have been around ninety-eight if she were still alive was not the point. She had not given the Strongs chance to sack her. She had resigned.

'I'm sure you'll understand,' she said, with a tight smile, her surprisingly spindly fingers clasped before her.

'Yes,' said Sir Emmanuel, and as she didn't mention a pension or references, neither did he.

Horatia entered, dressed in green velvet, a crochet-work collar gracing her shoulders and framing her face.

'See that Mrs Grainger packs and leaves the premises, my dear.' He glanced disdainfully at Lady Verity. 'I don't think my wife is up to it.'

Horatia smiled triumphantly. In one fell swoop she had brought her stepmother low and had gained the ear of her father. Perhaps soon he would be favourable to her having as much input in Strong business affairs as Nelson.

'This way, Mrs Grainger,' said a gloating Horatia.

Although Mrs Grainger's back was ramrod straight, she didn't seem as tall. Losing her job had left her looking squashed and small.

Before they got out the door, Nelson came flying into the room, his face white and his blue eyes big as saucers. He looked into the faces of all of them, as if seeking help in saying what he had to say.

'It's the ship, Uncle Jeb's ship. It went up in flames last night.'

Emmanuel looked shocked. 'Good God!' he exclaimed and with genuine cause. Lost ships meant lost money. Had Jeb insured the *Miriam Strong*?

'Was anyone hurt?' asked Horatia, immediately thinking of Tom.

Nelson nodded, glanced at his sister, and noted she was as white as death. 'The captain.'

Horatia's hand flew to her chest.

'Jimmy Palmer, I think his name was,' said Nelson. 'But that's not all. Someone was stupid enough to tell Uncle Jeb. His heart's giving out. I've taken the liberty of sending for the doctor.'

—

Tom couldn't find Clarence and now there was no time to look. A stable boy had been sent from Marstone Court with a message. Jeb was sinking fast and news had reached him about the fire. He had no choice but to return there as quickly as he could.

As usual, the room smelt of lavender. Tom decided he would always hate the smell of this inconsequential plant.

Jeb lay silently against his pillows because he could no longer do anything else. There was no respite now from being turned to one side or the other. The rattling of his chest echoed around the room in the same way as the ticking of a clock, each sound representing the relentless passing of time.

The doctor silently shook his head. Emmanuel stood with pursed lips, hands behind his back and a worried frown creasing his forehead. Nelson and Horatia stood side by side at the window but apart from their father.

Tom sat with head bowed, aware he still stunk of charred wood and singed hair. He was afraid to look into Jeb's eyes.

Edith, usually so blustery and busy, moved like a shadow as she wiped Jeb's dribbling mouth, rinsed the cloth in a china bowl, then gently bathed his face. Once she'd finished, she left the family gathering and moved away into an adjoining room.

Tom clasped his hands tightly together. 'The *Miriam Strong* went up in flames last night,' he said, though he knew that Jeb had already been told the news. He hung his head, not able to look into the eyes of the man whom he truly wished was his real father. 'I'm sorry,' he muttered and stared down at his knees. 'If I could have prevented it...' He stopped. He couldn't think of anything else to say.

Jeb began to speak, his words slurred and accompanied by more dribble. Tom strained to hear.

The doctor fluttered closer. 'He shouldn't be talking,' he said to Tom as though it were his fault. 'It will drain his energy.'

The doctor retreated before Tom's frozen glare. 'And he'll live perhaps an hour longer? Let the man speak!'

343

Jeb spoke more clearly than he had for months. 'Like me, her time's done. Atonement. We both sinned. Both killed... Her... the ship... more... honourably... than I did.'

Tom stared, not understanding, not wanting to hear. 'You're sick. You don't know what you're saying.'

He heard Emmanuel clear his throat and shuffle his feet. 'I'll see you out, Doctor.'

The door opened and closed. Horatia and Nelson moved closer, their expressions confirming that they had no intention of leaving Jeb and Tom to face this alone.

Jeb shook his head and weakly raised a hand, the veins blue and pulsating against the slack, pale skin. 'I must... confess,' Jeb began.

Tom shook his head. 'No. There's no need.'

'Every need!'

The old man turned red in the face as he raised himself up off his pillows. Tom considered calling for Edith. Jeb had barely raised his head for weeks.

'The ship...' said Jeb, and pride came to his eyes, 'old ship... fighting ship. More prizes than *Victory*.'

Jeb spluttered. Tom raised the pillows behind his head so he could bring up the phlegm from his congested lungs. He held the bowl. Jeb spat out what was left of his lungs. Horatia swallowed her revulsion and dabbed at his face with a cloth. Nelson stood on the opposite side of the bed to Tom.

'I have... to... tell.'

Horatia leaned across and mopped Jeb's brow. 'You don't have to tell anything,' she said softly.

Nelson frowned questioningly at Tom. 'What's he talking about?'

Jeb's eyes glittered with amusement as Tom finally guessed Jeb's long-held secret. 'He's talking about the *Miriam Strong*. Under her former name, she took more prizes than *Victory*.'

Still not understanding, Nelson shook his head.

'*Temeraire*?' ventured Horatia, sounding and looking astonished.

A fleeting smile crossed Jeb's face.

'Turner's *The Fighting Temeraire*?' said Nelson. 'I still don't understand. He painted her on her way to being decommissioned. Is he saying she never got there? That he bought her?'

Tom smiled. 'Just a few years after Trafalgar.'

Suddenly Jeb's deathbed seemed less fearsome or sad.

'Had... to... have... her,' said Jeb, his weak mouth seeming to catch somewhere between a smile and a grimace.

The Battle of Trafalgar, the *Temeraire*. A veil seemed to lift in Tom's mind. It all happened years ago, long before Jasper was born. Setting up the training ship had been one of many good works Jeb Strong had undertaken *before* his son's birth. Could it be that Jeb might have adopted him anyway? And if that was the case, what was the atonement he'd referred to?

Tom was startled when Horatia touched him on the shoulder. 'I'm sorry about the ship,' she said, and he fancied she was crying.

He didn't look up at her, just mumbled a grateful acceptance.

'I'd like to kill those responsible,' he added, but didn't see Horatia's hand tremble as it left his shoulder.

Jeb turned piteous eyes on his beloved adopted son. 'No... killing... sin... stays with you... atonement.' He raised a fragile hand and tapped his chest.

Did he mean that *he'd* killed? Tom found it hard to believe. Jeb was a religious man, known for his good works, his amiable attitude, his adoration of his deceased wife and family. The next slurred statement turned him cold.

'I... killed...' He sighed, threw his head back and closed his eyes.

Tom exchanged swift glances with Nelson and Horatia. The former looked calm though concerned; the latter seemed agitated, almost beside herself with grief.

'Take her out of here,' Tom said to Nelson.

'Come along, Horatia,' said Nelson, placing his arm around her shoulder and guiding her to the door.

Jeb seemed relieved when they'd gone. He took a huge breath, as though what he had to say could not be said in the halting manner he'd adopted so far. Resolve stiffened his body and held his head erect as he said, 'I was young. In Barbados. My brothers and I had been drinking... There was a mulatto slave. Pretty. Brought to us... naked.'

In the oppressive heat of his heavily draped sick room, Jeb's few words painted a picture of rich young men out from England, the heat of the tropics, the strong, brown-skinned women and the plentiful supply of rum. Between deep breaths, he described waking to see a man spitting into his brother's face, fearing the worse and bringing a candlestick crashing on to the man's head. 'I killed him,' he said quietly and coughed so badly, it seemed his lungs might collapse there and then.

Sensing he had more to say, Tom remained silent, and kept his gaze fixed on Jeb's face as he waited for him to continue.

'She conceived,' Jeb said. The regret he obviously felt seemed to pull at the loose flesh of his face, almost as if it were likely to slide off his skull. Tears poured from his eyes. 'Otis looked after her... and the child.'

'Blanche,' said Tom. He wished she were here. She'd been so sure that Otis was her father. Was Jeb admitting this? He looked down at the floor. 'Blanche suspected Otis was her father, but he'd never admitted it.'

Jeb shook his head. 'Otis and I... had drunk too much.' He pushed on, determined to finish. 'Patience. Samson's first wife... Emmanuel's mother,' said Jeb sadly. 'Otis and I...' He patted his chest as he coughed and fought for his words. 'Second marriage.' *Patience.* The name etched in one of the panels at the mausoleum and splattered with mud. Like a dreadful spectre, the scene he'd witnessed in the churchyard between Nelson and Blanche drifted into his mind. 'God, no!' he groaned, his head sinking into his hands.

'Lord's name... vain...' slurred Jeb.

'The Lord's gone deaf,' Tom said bitterly. 'Didn't hear Jimmy Palmer shouting for help, did he?'

'Patience...?' Jeb said, his power of speech receding, now. 'Blanche...'

Sick as he was, Jeb sensed that something more than the burnt-out ship was troubling Tom.

'I have to see Nelson,' he said, getting up and turning towards the door. 'I'll come back.'

Before he got there, it was opened from the outside by Duncan, the footman, his face shiny as a conker, his powdered wig as white as snow. Horatia brushed past him without a second glance. The door closed. Horatia stood alone, her face flushed, her hands tugging nervously at the braided loops that fastened her bodice.

With ill-disguised revulsion, she glanced at her uncle's pallor, the stained bib and the rolling eyes. 'Tom, I have to speak to you about the fire. Is it true that no one was hurt?'

'One man's dead.'

'And the children?'

'Safe except for one who is unaccounted for.'

She sighed. 'Thank goodness. When Benson told me—'

'How did Benson know?'

'Because... I heard... be... be...'

Her hesitation worried Tom, though he couldn't exactly say why. Perhaps it was because Horatia never got flustered or stuck for words, yet here she was stammering.

At last she managed to say, 'He was brought news, and rushed straight out to see me.'

Tom knitted his eyebrows and stepped closer to her. 'Why would he do that? What's it to him? What's it to you, for that matter?' Horatia nervous? He couldn't remember ever seeing her look like this before, excepting close to Clifton Gate when the carriage horse had reared and come down on the wrong side of the shaft. She'd been in the company of Benson then.

'He takes care of my investments,' she said using a small voice, as if she were weak or a child. 'He advises me on business matters, and we wanted the berth because the mail to North America—' She didn't need to go on.

Incidents that had seemed unconnected suddenly clicked into place. It was Benson that had gone to see the port authorities about paying more for the *Miriam Strong*'s berth. Someone had mentioned that you see the tower of St Mary Redcliffe church from her decks, and Temple Meads Meadows beyond that, where the navvies were building a station. The *Miriam Strong*'s berth was close to Temple Meads Meadows and big enough for an ocean-going vessel of the sort developed by Mr Brunel. All in all, it was the ideal place for the mail carried from London to Bristol by steam train, on to a ship and across the Atlantic.

'The berth was closest to Temple Meads Meadows...'

'It was a golden opportunity!' Her eyes shone with excitement. 'You must see that, Tom. The railway bringing mail from all over the country for onward passage to America, Africa and all the far-flung places where British people are leaving their mark. Wasn't it worth transferring the training school ship to another berth?' Tom looked at her lovely face, her shining hair and wished she were a man so he could land his fist on her chin.

'Was it worth setting light to her? Was it worth a man's life and the homelessness of orphans?' His tone was bitter and there was hatred in his heart.

Too angry to move lest he forget she was a woman, Tom stood like a rock, studying her expression. A torrent of emotions showed in her eyes, echoing the speed of her thoughts. He guessed she was tumbling from guilt to guile, from shame to ambition.

'Darling, Tom,' she purred, and tried to stroke his arm.

He hit her hand away, saw the hurt in her eyes and felt no regret. His gaze held steady.

Then she threw her hands over her face. 'Oh, Tom! I'm so sorry.' She was crying. He'd never seen Horatia cry before. It surprised him even more when she sank down on her knees before him, her hooped skirt spreading out around her like a blue silk tent. 'Please forgive me.'

'Who did it?'

She raised her tear-stained face and for a moment he allowed himself to believe that she was regretful, really contrite. 'I didn't mean for that to happen. That wasn't what I asked for.'

A sudden movement from the bed caught his attention. 'Sinners, Tom. We're all sinners.' He spluttered.

Tom rushed to him, eased him forward. 'Get that bowl,' he shouted at Horatia.

She looked confused but got to her feet and found the bowl. It pleased Tom to see her wince, as Jeb brought up a mix of porridge and bread.

Tom laid Jeb back on the pillows. Horatia's complexion turned daisy white as she set down the bowl and covered it with a piece of red flannel.

'Tom...' said Jeb, his voice as weak as his body.

Tom shook with anger and indicated with a wave of his hand for Jeb to be silent. Hair tumbling over his forehead in casual disarray, he glared at Horatia, his deep blue eyes as unfathomable as his heart. 'I'm going to see Benson,' he said and attempted to remove Jeb's hand from his arm. Surprisingly enough, it wasn't easy. Somehow and from somewhere, Jeb found the strength to grip and he was shaking his head, his eyes big with pleading.

Tom looked down at him. 'I'm in no mood to forgive and forget, Jeb.' He shook his head forlornly. 'I can't.'

348

Horatia looked desperate. 'I didn't actually set fire to the ship, and neither did Josiah, Tom. He just misunderstood my instructions. It was another man, whom everyone in the family has used at some time or another.'

Tom grabbed Horatia's shoulders.

'What man?' he asked.

'Reuben Trout.'

He might have known.

'Please forgive me, Tom,' she said, wheedling like an errant child that wants to be loved.

Tom studied her. Horatia was cleverer than her brother. There was much she knew, much she kept to herself.

Jeb's body was again racked with the fierceness of his coughing. 'Blan… che!'

'Edith! Fetch Blanche! Now,' Tom shouted, leaning over the bed, trying hard to catch the words that Jeb was hardly able to whisper.

A red-faced Edith rushed in from the other room. No doubt she'd heard everything that had gone on between him and Horatia.

Fidgeting and hesitant, she at last blurted, 'Blanche is gone.'

Tom felt his knees go weak, and his expression turned to thunder. 'When?'

Jeb began to splutter again.

'Yesterday!'

Tom grabbed her arm. First the ship going up in flames, Jimmy dead, Clarence missing and now this. 'Blanche went yesterday?'

Her shoulders stiffened. 'Yes.'

Tom glared at Horatia who shook her head. 'I know nothing about it.'

The room echoed to the sound of Jeb's lungs as Dr Langdon entered. Never a man to rush, he placed his bag on the top of a glass-fronted credenza and blew his nose loudly into a lace-edged handkerchief before approaching the bed.

'Well?' snapped Tom, as the doctor laid his palm on Jeb's chest.

Casually, as though, like Pontius Pilate, he had washed his hands of the whole affair, Dr Langdon shook his head and turned away.

Tom would have hit him there and then, but Jeb's gasping breath suddenly became a loud rattle interspersed with half-formed words as his cold fingers reached for Tom's hand. His voice broke through the ugly sounds. 'Tom.'

Tom dropped his head close so he could hear better, uncaring how bad Jeb smelled and that the spittle from his cracked lips was dribbling down his chin and saturating his nightgown.

'You... are... a... good... son.'

Tom squeezed his eyes shut, but it failed to stop the tears.

When he opened them again, he knew that something had changed. Jeb sighed, just once. There was no more rasping breath, no more rattling lungs. Jeb Strong was dead.

The room remained silent, Tom sitting on the side of the bed, the doctor standing by the window, not sure what to do or what Tom would do if he dared to abscond before Tom gave him leave.

'I never told him,' Tom said softly.

The doctor asked nervously, 'Told him what, sir?'

With finger and thumb, Tom closed Jeb's eyes.

'How much his son loved him,' he whispered, referring to himself, not some angelic boy who'd died through misadventure. Whether by drowning or suffocation, Jasper was long gone. It would have done no good to tell Jeb what had truly happened. Anyway, they were together now.

## Chapter Twenty-Six

Mrs Harkness wore a cotton bonnet with red strings. Every so often, she used the latter to swipe at the streaks of snuff that ran from her nostrils and into her mouth. Her eyebrows were like hairy caterpillars, forever on the move, each seemingly independent of the other. Stiff hairs bristled from her upper lip, and her breath smelled of stale liver.

Her eyes didn't seem to move, but Blanche knew a bawd when she saw one. She was in a house of ill-repute, and wasn't sure how easy it would be to get out again. She should have known better. If she hadn't been so tired, she would not have gone along with the man who called himself Cuthbert Stoke. She recalled now that Fen and Edith had said something about him, a comment in passing. It hadn't seemed important at the time.

At present he was standing between her and the door, leaning on a walking stick and eyeing her speculatively, no doubt calculating her worth and his profit.

As he watched her, he spoke to Mrs Harkness about the weather, the ships in port and the flood of navvies earning good money for digging tunnels and laying rails.

Mrs Harkness was a woman of few words.

'Spain and Portugal,' she said.

'No. I'm from—'

Stoke interrupted. 'I think Mrs Harkness is referring to the seamen at present in port.'

'Oranges, wine and sherry,' said Mrs Harkness, her gaze never shifting from Blanche's face.

'You're probably right,' said Stoke. 'There's a few fast-sailing barques up from Jerez. Plenty of sailors with money in their pockets.'

'Rough navvies,' said Mrs Harkness.

'Big men,' said Stoke. 'From all over, I hear tell. Some are wearing boots for the first time in their lives and proud of 'em. Only wear them fer working and hang them around their necks the rest of the time.'

Blanche was amazed at the one-sided conversation. Mrs Harkness uttered a few seemingly unconnected words, and Stoke replied. He obviously knew her well.

She was tired and trapped, but her mind was working fast. If she made a run for it right away, he'd stop her. Best to appear docile, she told herself. Bide your time. Wait and run for it when you can.

'It's very kind of you to put me up,' she said in the manner of a demur maiden with no idea of who and what this woman was. 'A little rest, a little food and I'll be on my way in the morning.'

'Eat, drink, sleep,' said the woman, her smile revealing few teeth but plenty of gum. She went to the door, leaned past Stoke and shouted, 'Mary! Now!'

Within seconds, a pale girl in a blue dress and a less than clean white apron limped into the room. Mousy locks fell from beneath a mop cap and completely obscured one eye. She was thin, though not necessarily poorly nourished. Tall and gangly, her arms were long and her neck seemed to jut forward, which gave her a curious look, as though she were looking for what lay around the next corner.

Mrs Harkness barked out her orders. 'Special broth, special drink, special guest room.'

Mary limped off. Blanche turned cold at the thought of how the girl had come to be limping, why her hair fell over only one side of her face. She'd heard tales in Bridgetown of bawds breaking runaways' legs, damaging their looks.

'Ladylike,' said Mrs Harkness, looking her up and down and assuming – wrongly – that Blanche knew nothing about whores, bawdy houses and rough waterfronts. And that's the way it would stay, Blanche decided. For now she would play the part and she could do with some food and rest.

Stoke was telling her that she'd be right as rain in the morning, and that he was sure he could help her get to where she wanted to go–

Mrs Harkness suddenly reached out and ran her finger down Blanche's cheek.

Stoke explained. 'She's just checking that you really are that colour. Amazin' it is, how some people try to pretend they're exotic when they ain't. Now you, my dear girl, are exotic and I don't think yer name should be Blanche.'

Mrs Harkness frowned and nodded in agreement.

'So how about calling you Sharitari? How's about that for a name, eh, Mrs Harkness?'

'Sharitari,' repeated Mrs Harkness, and her frown disappeared.

'No, ma'am. My name's Blanche.' She clutched her bag tightly against her, a nervous little virgin lost and all alone. Inside she felt angry and determined to get the better of them. Why did everyone in this country want to call her by anything but her own name?

'A white dress,' said Mrs Harkness, looking her up and down as if she'd made a decision.

Out of the corner of her eye, Blanche saw Stoke straighten, his eyes full of interest. 'Innocent and exotic,' he said thoughtfully.

'If you could tell me how much my bed and board will cost,' she began, 'I'm sure I can pay you before very long.' She was wise enough not to admit she carried money or valuables.

'Mrs Harkness will be fair with you,' said Stoke. 'Just as I shall be for the rendering of my services.'

She wondered at the relationship between him and Mrs Harkness and who actually owned the house. Stoke most likely. Mrs Harkness merely ran it for him.

Before Mary came back, a clattering of feminine footsteps came from the stairs. A dark-haired woman, then a redhead, glanced her way. She saw the pitying look in one set of eyes, the warning in the other.

Mrs Harkness was making small talk. 'Fans. If you come across one, Mr Stoke. I like fans.'

Stoke smiled and said, 'I expect you like fans too, don't you, Blanche? Shall I get one for you too?'

Blanche smiled bashfully and pretended that she was too overcome with nerves to speak.

When Mary came back, Mrs Harkness put her arms around Blanche's shoulders and guided her towards the stairs. 'Up with Mary.' She reached for the leather bag that Blanche still clutched tightly to her chest. 'I'll take care of your bag.'

Blanche smiled, shook her head and held it more tightly. Once her bag got into the bawd's grubby hands, she'd never see it again.

Mary led her up a narrow staircase that wound left at the top into a narrow, dark passage. About halfway along, Mary kicked at a door. The noise of her kicking bounded off the musty smelling walls. The door refused to budge. After kicking it a few more times, it opened, groaning like an old man with stiff knees.

The room smelled of lavender. A generous bunch was strung in front of the window, though it wasn't quite enough to keep out the miasma wafting up from the city sewers. The room had chalky walls and bare boards. A length of green tartan served as a curtain to one side of the window. Two bolster pillows lay at one end of the bed, tubes of fine lace falling from the ends of each.

Mary put the tray down on a table with thin legs, which wobbled slightly as if the weight was too much to bear.

Her task done, Mary hobbled towards the door.

'The tartan's nice,' said Blanche.

Mary paused, looked at the door as if preferring to go through it rather than speak. At the last moment she looked back at Blanche. 'A Scotsman left it. He used to wear it, so he said.'

Blanche touched the lace trim on one of the bolsters. 'And this? It's very fine.'

Mary's taut expression relaxed a little and one side of her face rose in a smile. 'They were pantaloons that got ripped at the waist. I used the legs to make them. That's why there's only lace at one end.'

'They look very grand.'

Mary looked around the room as if it held memories that were hers and hers alone. 'This used to be my room. I wanted it to look pretty.'

Blanche tried not to stare at the half of her face hidden by the fall of hair. There were too many cruelties in the world, and Mary seemed to have her fair share of them.

After she'd gone, Blanche ate the broth, the bread and the unexpected piece of cheese. There were two cups on the tray. One held milk and the other was undoubtedly gin judging by its smell. Blanche chose to drink the milk.

Although the bed linen seemed clean enough, she did not undress and willed herself to rise before dawn. She wanted to be out of the house before Mrs Harkness arose and demanded she pay for her board, though – she suspected – not in cash. And Cuthbert Stoke would be right behind her.

It pained her to think of what she and Nelson had done. She also felt a fool for believing all this time that Otis Strong was her father. Why hadn't her mother told her the truth? At least then she would have directed her attentions elsewhere, perhaps responded more warmly to Tom's affection.

As her eyes began to close, the advice her mother had consistently given her, slid into her mind.

*In this world, security matters above all else. While your looks last, grab the first man who offers you security. That way you don't starve and don't keep house or do laundry for no other woman.*

Ma was right. My, but she'd be pleased to know that I've had two marriage proposals, she thought, as she began to drift into sleep, the leg of cotton pantaloon soft against her face. Despair was not far away. Marriage had been a viable option before she'd made love with Nelson, before she'd found out he was her brother. How could she face either Tom or Conrad, let alone accept one of them as a husband, especially if... Her hand automatically went to her stomach. Please God, no, she pleaded as she fell swiftly and suddenly asleep.

She slept deeply, hardly aware of sound or movement, mostly due to the fact that the milk she had consumed – liberally laced with something ground from fungus – was more liable to make her sleep than the gin she had left alone.

As she slept, two shadows fell over her. The first was that of Mrs Harkness. The second was of a middle-aged gentleman with white side-whiskers and a portly waistline.

Mrs Harkness said nothing, but her eyes saw everything. Like maybugs, they danced between her companion and Blanche.

The man used his walking stick to lift the single blanket covering Blanche. 'She's still dressed,' he said in a disconsolate manner.

'Five guineas!'

'For flesh I cannot see?'

'Five guineas.'

He let the blanket fall back onto the bed, and tutted. 'I hope she's worth it.'

Blanche did not wake before dawn. When she did at last open her eyes, the sun was streaming through the window. Outside, people were shouting and laughing and someone or something was squealing in terror.

She struggled to her feet, staggered to the window and looked out. Below her ragged children were chasing a pig towards a narrow alley where a broad-chested man stood hugging a meat cleaver to his chest.

Blanche covered her eyes against the sight of blood and the glare of the sun. Her head hurt. She guessed the reason why and dipped her face into a bowl of water that someone had thought to leave there. She couldn't remember seeing it the night before.

She put her ear to the door, listening for any sign that Mrs Harkness or Cuthbert Stoke were coming up to claim her. She heard nothing, but even before she tried the door handle, she guessed it wouldn't be too easy to leave. The door refused to budge, and no amount of kicking would open it. Sometime in the night, a key had been turned and even before she looked for it, she knew her bag had been taken.

'Let me out of here,' she shouted and banged her clenched fists on the door. No one came.

Tears of frustration welled up in her eyes. How dare these people take her belongings, her mother's earrings and the money for a passage home! How dare they imprison her!

She hammered on the door until her wrists were sore. Despair mixed with anger as she slid to the floor, tears escaping from the corner of her eyes and running down her cheeks. Never had her life seemed so bleak. She was now trapped, compromised by her own half-brother, and penniless.

Eventually, she wiped her face on the hem of her dress and blew her nose. Crying was not going to solve anything. Blanche contemplated what to do next. Sometime during the day, food would be brought, though it was unlikely that Mary would come alone.

She cursed herself for being so stupid. Acting innocent had been her undoing. Drinking the milk and avoiding the gin had also proved a mistake. Both had been drugged no doubt.

Then the tartan drape at the window caught her eyes. It was long and strong, and although the window was small, there just might be a chance...

There was no time to waste. She bent down, pulled the back of her skirt through her legs and tied it at the front. The old style dress gave her freedom of movement, unrestrained by corsets and hoops. Thank goodness for that, she thought, and blessed her mother's inclination for the tried and tested and the fact that Barbados had been way behind when it came to fashion.

The grey slate roof outside the window looked safe enough, though it was wet with moss and copper nails stood exposed where slates had cracked and fallen into the dark abyss that was Cock and Bottle Lane. Blanche eyed an open window in the house directly opposite and calculated that it was no more than a broom handle distant. She didn't have a broom. A breeze stirred her hair and the tartan drape brushed against her face. Strongly woven, she decided, and gave it a tug. It was long but not wide, and looked as though it had been cut in half along its length in order not to swamp the small window.

'If I tie this around here... ' she muttered to herself as she tied it around the middle upright of the window, and used a bowline, a loop with tightened ends.

She was pleased with the knot and it gave her great satisfaction to throw the tartan out of the window and watch it dangle – but too far from the ground.

She groaned. Building a new life for herself after Barbados, after Nelson and Marstone Court, was not going to be easy. Prostituting herself for the likes of Cuthbert Stoke and Mrs Harkness would not bring her security, just looking at Mary was enough to tell her that.

She looked into the alley below. Two mongrel dogs were mating on the cobbles and a fat woman smoking a pipe watched with bemused interest while a small girl of about seven kicked at them.

Blanche tried waving, the only way she could possibly attract someone's attention. She feared shouting would only bring her to the attention of Mrs Harkness.

'Leave the poor creatures alone,' shouted the woman.

'Mind yer own fuckin' business,' the child shouted back.

Shaking her head, the fat woman disappeared into the doorway behind her.

A chimney sweep entered from one end, brushes carried over his shoulder like a military man about to do battle. A small boy followed.

The small girl ran towards him. 'Fancy a bit of slap and tickle? I know a tart who's willing.'

'No I don't. I got work to do.'

The child's attention was drawn to a sudden noise at the other end of the alley.

A pedlar bustled through, brushing her aside none too gently. A pair of beggars followed him arguing as to who was going to be the blind man that day, and who would be the nigger. Their voices ricocheted around the narrow alley so she heard everything twice. The sound of their voices was replaced by the trundling of cartwheels. A man appeared pushing a handbarrow on which lay two rough wooden boxes.

The young girl rushed up to him, saw what was on the cart and asked, 'Is they dead uns?'

He nodded. 'Yes.'

'Fancy a live un?'

'Off with ya,' he shouted, and lashed out at her with one hand. The cart toppled slightly. One wheel hit a rut displacing the lid of one box and revealing a small corpse wrapped in a scrap of old blanket. The man cursed, adjusted the lid and hit it shut with a clenched fist. The other box was even smaller. There were no mourners to follow the dead children to their grave.

Blanche watched silently, wished she were home, wished she were anywhere rather than in this grey city in this grey country with these grim people.

A movement in the window opposite drew her attention. At first she thought she was looking at a bundle of rags, then she saw the pale face, the white hair and the thickly knitted shawl drawn tightly around stooped shoulders. The woman was waving at her and her mouth was opening and closing as if she were saying something.

Blanche decided she was mad, then realized that she wasn't. The woman didn't want to be heard. She was mouthing, 'Throw it over here,' and signalling that she would tie the other end around the centre frame of her window.

Blanche looked down again. It was a long way down, too far to jump. She looked across at the woman. The distance across was just as frightening, but staying where she was would mean the end of her life.

With careful precision, she flung the piece of cloth across the gap – and missed.

A loose slate slid on its nail. Blanche sucked in her breath. If it fell, someone down below might look up and see her. Leaning as far out of the window as possible, she threw again. This time the woman caught it, pulled it tight before tying it.

'Come on,' she mouthed, crooking her finger.

Blanche tied on her bonnet but the brim was wider than the window and too stiff to bend. Off it came, and carefully, but quickly, she climbed out of the window, hooked her leg over the cloth – and heard it rip.

Just as carefully as she'd climbed out, she backed herself up against the side of the dormer window and felt her way around its side and on to the roof.

Her heart was in her mouth. Each time she moved, bits of slate and loose rendering broke off and slithered down the roof. If she weren't careful, it would seem as if it were raining slates. Heart beating wildly, she eased herself into a gully between her building and the one next door. Plans about what to do next whirled in her mind. Hopefully, her captors would think she had indeed clambered along the tartan to the building opposite – unless the old woman, who had now disappeared, had untied her end. Then they might think she'd dropped to the ground and run off – if she hadn't broken her legs. After that, they'd be sure to open the door, wouldn't they? What would be the point of locking a bedroom door if no one was in there? If she waited long enough, she could creep back, find it unlocked, and creep out.

That would have been her one and only plan if she hadn't seen the cockerel. He came up behind her, scraping and scratching at the dirt and debris that had gathered in the gully, his head ducking and dipping among the weeds, grass and windblown seeds. Blanche wondered exactly how he'd got up there.

Turning and crawling on all fours, she edged towards him as he clucked and scraped his way along the gully, his red comb quivering with indignation, one yellow-rimmed eye watching her as he backed off the way he'd come.

Blanche got closer still, sure now that the cockerel knew of a way down, one that wasn't too far from the ground.

The roofs to either side of the gully eventually ended. Another roof sloped off at a right angle, steeper than the others and running straight in to – a garden! At some time in its history, the building had been extended, a task that had entailed digging out the higher ground at the back of the house, though not all of it.

Once a grassy bank but now bare earth, the ground sloped up away from the house where hens clucked and scratched in the dirt, and washing was spread over the bushes to dry.

The roof at the back of the house did not exactly go into the ground but stopped about three feet short. Between the wall of the house and one built to retain the higher level, was a narrow alley.

Careful not to startle the cockerel or dislodge more tiles, Blanche peered into the rear courtyard. Rows of other backyards went off to either side. To her left was a woman using a washing dolly. Half hidden by her skirt sat a cat chewing on a mouse.

She eased back and thought about things. Such a small gap between her and freedom, but she didn't want the woman to hear or see her.

Making sure the woman wasn't looking, she got to her feet, quickly assessed the distance and launched herself into space.

All would have been well, but she'd forgotten that the back hem of her dress was still knotted to the front. Her skirt curtailed her leap. At the same time, the cockerel decided to move right into her path, and clucked and crowed angrily as he tangled with her feet. She barely made the jump, one foot slipping out behind her and causing her to fall headlong into the dirt, scattering the hens and hurting her nose.

Hearing the commotion, the woman stopped pounding the washing dolly and turned her head. Blanche glanced at her momentarily, just long enough to see the tangle of hair hiding one eye.

'Wah! Wah!' screamed Mary.

The dolly fell on to the cat. The cat yowled, dropped its catch and ran. So did Mary. Limping as fast as she could, she ran through an open door, screaming for Mrs Harkness.

'The minx!' A man's voice.

'Out of my way.' Mrs Harkness, followed by a thump and a squeal of pain from Mary.

Blanche got to her feet and, without undoing her skirts, ran as fast as she could. Laundry fell from bushes as she pushed herself through a gap and found herself in the yard of another house. Fortunately, this one had a door in the wall. Struggling at first, she pushed at the rusted catch. It was stiff, probably unused for years, but eventually it sprung upwards.

Blanche ran, not stopping until Cock and Bottle Lane was behind her and she was by the river, looking down on to the water, panting, desperate and almost feeling like throwing herself in.

'You are in some kind of trouble?'

Blanche lifted her head and fell into the arms of Conrad Heinkel.

## Chapter Twenty-Seven

Jimmy Palmer was dead, Jeb was dead, and thirty orphaned boys had been given temporary shelter in a disused warehouse directly opposite where their training ship had been berthed.

Bespectacled and a confirmed landlubber as well as a Wesleyan, the rotund Mr Trinder had encouraged members of his church to donate food, money, blankets and other necessities so that the orphan boys wouldn't be forced to return to their lives on the streets. Tom was grateful that someone else was doing something. There were too many other things he had to deal with at present. Firstly, there was Jeb's funeral, which was carried out in accordance with the family's wishes rather than Jeb's. Although a confirmed Wesleyan, the service was to be at St Michael's, internment to follow in the family mausoleum.

A host of relatives, noticeably absent during Jeb's years of illness, arrived en masse. Most carefully avoided Tom.

'The adopted son... a bare-knuckle fighter... a mere sea captain... drink and whoring...' Like a never-ending litany, his exploits were whispered from one 'mourner' to another. He ignored the disdain in alien eyes and sought those he knew. If Jeb had been present, they would at least have been civil. Now he was gone, they saw no reason to be.

His eyes met those of Jeb's eldest remaining daughter Rachel. At first she beamed, glad to see him, but her husband intervened before she could approach him.

He reached for a glass of Madeira. He might as well live up to his reputation.

Ruth and Leah, the two other remaining daughters, did approach him. Ruth was kind, smiling gently and touching his arm as she said, 'Thank goodness he had you, Tom.'

Leah, as dark and pink-cheeked as her mother and just returned from China, threw her arms around his neck and kissed his chin.

'Leah. People are looking. You're being unseemly,' said Ruth reproach-fully.

Leah blinked back her tears and held Tom at arm's length. 'They may think it's unseemly. Our father wouldn't.'

'And that's the truth,' said Tom.

Leah stayed close to him. They both watched as the black-plumed horses pulling the hearse made their way down the drive followed by the mourners, some in carriages and some on foot.

'Aren't you coming?' Leah asked him.

Tom shook his head, took off his hat and fingered its brim. 'No.'

Leah's husband called her, but she was slow to obey. 'You're going away, aren't you?' she said.

Tom didn't answer. He didn't need to.

She patted his arm. 'You filled a gap in his life, Tom. I'm grateful you did, and so was he.'

He did not tell them about Jasper. What good would it do? Father and son were at rest in the same churchyard. He watched them go and felt no guilt about not going himself. He'd stayed close to Jeb in life, and that was all that mattered.

'Will you go back to sea?'

'I'm not sure. I have some questions to ask and answers to find.'

By the time the funeral party had returned like a flock of carrion, he'd gone. His adopted sisters were disappointed not to see him there. Horatia was beside herself, running through the house, searching his room, Jeb's old room, the library, anywhere he might be hiding. At last she found her way into the attic, stared at the portrait of her grandmother and sunk to her knees. She hadn't seen it since she was a child. The skin was lighter, but the eyes were the same grey, and the mole... there was no doubt about it. Blanche too was a granddaughter of Patience Strong.

—

Reuben Trout had disappeared. A constant shadow, he'd followed Tom around for months, unseen until Conrad Heinkel had pointed out his presence. Tom was in no mood for forgiveness.

As darkness descended, the sights, sounds and smells of St Augustine's Quay altered. The stench of strong beer, sweaty bodies and rat droppings overpowered the daytime smells of ships' tar, tobacco and hot metallic smoke from the refineries and the glass kilns.

Tom searched and asked questions in dockside taverns, even hid in corners and doorways hoping to catch a glimpse of Trout. The only word he got was from Aggie Pike.

Her little eyes gleamed as she said, 'Heard yer after 'im, Tom. Heard yer out to kill 'im, old butt!'

Tom sipped at his rum, no longer keen on either its taste or the burning sensation it left at the back of his throat. 'He deserves killing,' he muttered grimly.

Aggie's pipe jiggled at the corner of her mouth as she nodded. 'Agree with 'e there. Never was a man that needed killing as much as 'im.'

'When was the last time you saw him?'

She closed one eye as she considered the question, wrinkles radiating out like spokes on a wheel. 'Weeks ago now. Didn't see me, though. Too busy offering a shillin' or somethin' to your friend Sally.'

Mention of Sally chilled him to the bone. It was as though there was nothing left in his stomach but a big, blank space.

Aggie went on talking. 'Her boy came in here a few days back asking 'bout his mother. I told 'im the same. Can't remember the date. Just knows that nobody saw Sal after that till she was pulled from the river with 'er throat cut.'

At the mention of Clarence, Tom grabbed her arm. 'When did you see her boy?'

Aggie eyed him quizzically. 'Just a few days ago.'

It had been two weeks since the *Miriam Strong* had gone up in flames. Clarence was alive.

'Thank God,' Tom said, throwing back his head and closing his eyes.

Aggie added, 'Can't tell you where 'e is though.'

'Never mind,' said Tom, rising from the high-backed settle from where he could see the door, the quay and the nightlife drifting by. 'I know someone who might.'

—

Conrad Heinkel and his family had moved from the house next to the refinery to a newer property on Redcliffe Parade. The house faced Dundry

Ridge at the front and Redcliffe wharf at the rear. The windows were large and let in ample light, and the furnishings, although of heavy design, appeared lighter in the brightness.

Big as he was, Conrad Heinkel had the gentlest touch. He personally bathed Blanche's scratched nose and gave orders to his servants to fill a bathtub and get his wife's clothes from the chest in which they were stored while hers were laundered. After that she slept.

In the days that followed, he left her very much to her own devices and did not press her as to how she came to be at the river. Life became normal, more so than she'd ever known it.

His children's governess had left to marry. Two weeks after Conrad had rescued her, Blanche found herself giving them lessons in reading, writing, drawing and arithmetic, sometimes in the big room that looked over the city through finely arched windows. On one particular day, they did their lessons on the grass at the edge of Gallows Lane where, young Hans informed her, the gallows really used to be.

'Then we'll go further up,' she said, disguising a shiver. They resettled themselves further along, close to the observatory at the top of the Avon Gorge.

Conrad Heinkel had clever children. They asked questions, talked about subjects the Strong children were not allowed to study. History seemed to be their favourite, though Hans was good at maths, better than she was. Most of all, they struck her as being uncommonly happy, and she put that down as their father's doing. Parent and children were uncommonly close. They were rarely out of each other's sight. Unlike mealtime arrangements at Marstone Court, the children ate with their father. At Conrad's request, Blanche joined them.

Every so often, she caught him looking at her and knew that it was only a matter of time before he asked her if she'd read the letter and asked for her answer. She had no intention of raising the subject herself just in case he also asked her why she had been distraught and dishevelled on the riverbank that night.

On a lovely evening in early September after she'd seen the children to bed, and the servants were clearing the table, Blanche wandered in the garden. Roses of every colour imaginable grew in the Heinkel garden and the air was heavy with their scent.

Blanche followed the redbrick path that led away from the house and through the rose beds to a trellised arbour with a grass-covered seat and a yellow rambler growing over it.

The arbour was positioned in such a way that anyone seated there could not be seen by anyone approaching. By the time she smelled tobacco, it was too late to turn back.

'I knew you would come here,' he said, his face openly congenial and a bright expectancy in his eyes. He patted the clipped grass beside him. 'Please. We must talk. There is something I want to ask you.'

Sensing that the moment had at last come when he'd refer to the letter, she sat down. Explanation was preferable to questions, she felt, and said quickly, 'There are so many things you don't know about me, so many things I didn't know about myself until recently. I've always known I was a bastard.' She thought it better to be frank from the start and to use honest words rather than try to be prim and proper. 'My mother was a kept woman, mistress to Otis Strong whom I had assumed to be my father, though now I find that is not so. I had a good life back home in Barbados and was waited on by servants, whom I should point out were also my relatives. I came to England fully expecting to be taken in as a true daughter by the household. Instead I found I was to be a children's nurse. My background, you see, was not deemed fit enough to be a lady, only a servant. Then I found out that Sir Emmanuel was my father and... there was a man... I might be having a baby.'

Conrad showed no sign of surprise. 'Go on,' he said.

She paused, rethinking what she wanted to say. 'So I had to get away, but unfortunately I ran in the wrong direction and almost ended up a dockside doxy, but I escaped.' She looked at him sidelong. He was staring at her, his mouth open slightly, the tip of his pipe resting on his tongue. 'I didn't know what to do next. They stole my bag, you see. Everything of value was in there. Then you came along.'

Conrad didn't move. She guessed it was taking some time to digest all that she'd told him.

'So now you know, without having to ask me,' she said, getting to her feet. 'And if you want me to leave...' She bit her lip, hoping and praying he would at least keep her on as a servant until the baby was born, for her body was telling her it would indeed be so.

Conrad shifted, his broad body almost taking up one third of the available space. He rested one hand on a meaty knee and sighed resignedly. 'An interesting story, though it does not answer the question I was going to ask you.'

Blanche looked at him with tear-filled eyes, and he looked right back, smiling gently and nodding his head as if he'd known all about her all along. He had such honest eyes.

'You never answered my letter,' he said.

She gazed transfixed, amazed by what he implied. 'You still want to marry me?'

He nodded slowly. 'Yes. I do.'

'And the things I've just told you… don't they matter?'

He shrugged and puffed on his pipe. 'I like you. The children like you. And you like me. I think these things matter. They are good things on which to base a marriage. And your baby needs a father.'

Blanche stared at him open-mouthed. Everything her mother had said about the world and women belonging to men came back to her. Without a man, preferably a husband, there was no security. And she had lost everything she'd had in the world. Where would she end up if she didn't take up his offer? The gutter, she thought, and shivered at the thought of Mrs Harkness, Cuthbert Stoke and Tom's mother who'd been pulled dead from the river. Conrad was the only option she had left.

–

Later she sat in the rose arbour telling the children a story. Conrad's proposal was still on her mind.

'…after the giant Goram died, his friend, the giant Ghyston, travelled to Salisbury Plain and erected a great monument to his friend, Goram. After that, he went to Ireland and built a causeway to the north of that land. Eventually he grew old and tired, came back to his beloved Avon Gorge, which he and Goram had cleaved from the rock with their great axes. He saw how pretty it was and tears sprang to his eyes. When he died, he fell into the river, which carried him out into the Severn where it deposited him midstream. Silt came down from the Welsh mountains and covered him, and at sunset when the tide is running low, you can still see his great burial mound dividing the river in two between the English and Welsh coasts...'

The two children were mesmerized. Mouths open and unblinking, they continued to stare up at her as if awaiting a sequel, the girl with plaited hair the colour of corn, and the boy with a freckled face and broken front tooth.

Were the giants bigger than my father?' asked Hans.

'Much bigger.'

'It must have taken a very long time to cut a gorge for the river to run through,' added Lisel, her stiff plaits remaining still though her head moved with each word she said.

'I hear you can see Goram's footprint in Blaise Woods,' said Blanche. She remembered Edith had told her that, and felt a sudden pang of loss. Rough and ready as she was, Edith had a heart of gold, and Blanche even missed her homespun wisdom and outright lies.

'A girl's got to be a bit respectable if she's gonna get 'erself a husband,' Edith had said. 'What kind of life can I have if I ain't got a bloke to look after me?'

Like my mother, thought Blanche. And also like Horatia, though the latter could afford to kick over the traces and be independent if she wished. Wealth made all the difference.

Hans suddenly asked, 'Are you going to be our mother?'

The question took her by surprise, although she'd been giving serious consideration to the matter. Conrad was a kind man and would make a good husband. She liked him and his children and felt warm in his company. Perhaps in time she might love him, but for now she considered they had enough in common with which to build a happy marriage. She smiled. 'I expect so.'

'When?' asked Lisel.

'Whenever your father wishes,' she said.

'The sooner the better,' said Hans and threw his arms around her.

Lisel followed where her brother led. 'I think it's the best idea in the world.'

'So do I,' said Blanche. It was the only course open to her. Only the night before she'd woken in a sweat, reached for the chamber and a strip of linen with which she wiped between her legs. There was no sign of her monthly flow.

The Fourteen Stars smelled of stale sweat, disturbed earth, and the sour grubbiness of men who worked, played and slept too close for comfort in hastily erected shacks. The navvies from the railway had arrived en masse.

Tom pushed his way through them, looking for the pock-marked face of Reuben Trout. News must have got out that he was hunting for him, thought Tom. He'd searched all his regular haunts, but without luck. If anyone in the shadowy underworld around the docks knew his whereabouts, it would be Cuthbert Stoke, but he too seemed to be lying low.

The landlord of the Fourteen Stars was a man named Herbert Champion, almost six feet tall with a mass of black hair and a plaited beard to match. Some said he was a direct descendant of Bristol's most infamous pirate, Captain Teach, better known as Blackbeard. Herbert exaggerated his appearance, sometimes sticking lighted candles in his hair just as his supposed ancestor had done.

Tom grabbed Herbert's shoulder. 'I'm looking for crew,' he said as if he really meant it. 'How do you feel about a passage round the Horn, Herbert?'

Herbert shook his head vigorously. 'You know me, Tom. Ain't never been to sea in me life.' He laughed as though fully expecting Tom to do the same. Instead of laughing, Tom's look darkened. 'Then tell me where I can find Cuthbert Stoke.'

'Well, I don't really—'

Tom bent Herbert's arm up behind his back. 'Tell me where he is, or you'll find yourself halfway across the Atlantic and living on salt beef and biscuits.'

'Mrs Harkness,' Herbert spouted, his face paling behind the black beard at the thought of actually going to sea. 'She keeps a house, if you know what I mean, down in Cock and Bottle Lane.'

The navvies, who had been keeping their own company up until now, heard the raised voices. Crazed eyes in weather-beaten faces turned in their direction. Those braver or less drunk than the rest, rose to their feet and rolled up their sleeves.

Tom attempted to push past, but they barred his way. They wanted to fight. They wanted him to fight. Drink had made them brave. Tom clenched his fists and prepared himself, though he had little chance of battling this many at once.

'Got problems, Tom?'

The navvy Tom had been matched against in his last fight raised a beefy arm before the human barrier, pushing them aside so that Tom could get through.

'Plenty,' said Tom, nodded his thanks, and made for the door.

Red for port. Green for starboard. That's what it was on ships, but every sailor in any port in the world knew what a red light hanging above a lone doorway meant. Chinks of light showed around shuttered windows, but neither they nor the red lantern of the brothel did much to alleviate the matt blackness of Cock and Bottle Lane.

Stumbling and slipping on the unseen cobbles, Tom headed straight for the red light, wrinkling his nose as the familiar smells of human dirt and despondency rose like a fog to meet him.

The brothel door opened with hesitant squeaks, as though someone had seen him and changed their mind about closing it again. Meagre light from within touched the hard features and light hair of a small person, a child.

'All right, mate? Want a good time, do you?' The child hung on to the door handle with one hand and perched her other hand on her hip. 'Got all sorts we 'ave. Milk white, mud brown and matt black. Some with teeth and some without – depending on what you want, if you know what I mean.'

Tom could hardly believe his ears. He'd been in many ports around the world, but had never come across a child as worldly wise as this. She was chirpy and cheeky, but God, he thought, once he'd looked into her eyes, she's a hard one.

'I'm looking for a man,' he said once he'd drawn level with her.

She sniffed and shook her head. 'We ain't got none of that kind of thing 'ere. Get yerself down to Sunshine's. He's probably got what yer lookin' for.'

'I want Cuthbert Stoke,' he said as he pushed past her.

'Oh! That's different,' she said, and slammed the door behind them both.

A Chinese woman wearing a muslin chemise floated down the stairs, her black hair writhing around her shoulders like a nest of dark snakes.

The woman halted. So did Tom.

'That's Chinese Dora,' said the small girl. 'Half a crown and she's yours.'

'Stoke,' he said adamantly, 'I want Stoke.'

The child shrugged. 'Your choice, chum.'

An effort had been made to make the interior of the house presentable. The walls were painted pale green, their plainness presently being transformed by a bent figure with a full beard and a palette of oils. Clusters of red and yellow pears, apples and other fruit decorated the walls above paintings of salacious ladies with plump thighs, tight smiles and no clothes.

The artist nodded a silent greeting and turned back to his work. Tom pushed at a door.

Lit by a central candle, Cuthbert Stoke and a woman with sharp features and black eyes, sat across a table from each other, coins and valuables piled up between them.

The woman leapt to her feet. 'Out!'

Stoke merely looked nervous. 'Tom!' He managed to smile, but his face was ghostly white. 'What can I do for you? Need a fight?'

Tom grabbed Stoke by the neck of his waistcoat and heaved him to his feet. 'Where's Reuben Trout?'

To Tom's surprise, Stoke seemed relieved. His expression softened. 'What do you want 'im for?'

Tom glared and said nothing. Stoke's eyes said it all. He knew why he wanted him.

'An eye for an eye, Stoke.'

Tom waved a broad fist in front of his nose and saw him swallow.

'What do I care about Reuben Trout?' said Stoke. 'I'll tell you where he is.'

—

Bennetts Carriers was a different place when it was empty, though it was always warm, even in the middle of the night. The heat of the horses' bodies saw to that.

Reuben Trout felt warm and safe beneath the loose straw he'd pulled over himself in the empty stall. To either side of him, horses snuffled at maize and oats, or pulled hay from iron mangers. Trout cursed himself for being so careless as to let himself be seen – and by Sally's brat no less.

Must be getting old, he thought, his joints creaking as he brought his knees up under the straw. He'd had no choice but to abandon the small room in the ramshackle boarding house owned by Cuthbert Stoke. Tomorrow he'd leave the city for good, sadly so, but he had no choice. The moment Clarence had seen him, he'd known it would be no time before Tom Strong was told and came baying for his blood.

Luckily, that bloke Benson had paid him well for getting rid of the *Miriam Strong*. And Cuthbert Stoke had been ready and willing – for a price, of course – to hide him prior to getting him out of the city.

He swigged the last drop of beer, then buried the empty stone bottle beneath the straw. Snuffling like drunks do as he settled himself, he closed his eyes, content that he'd be out of the city soon and safe in Ireland or some other haven Stoke had arranged for him.

He would have dozed off right away, but a slight sound that was not a horse or a rat or a mouse or a bat eased like a squeaking door out of the darkness.

Opening his eyes, he lay completely still, waiting to hear the sound again before putting it down to imagination. There was silence for a while, but just as his eyelids flickered with tiredness, he heard it again.

Slowly, so as not to make a sound, he rose up from the hay and listened. There it was. A footstep.

Suddenly he felt vulnerable. His heart began to hammer in his chest. If Tom Strong caught him, he'd be dead.

Cunning and lying had always got Trout out of tight corners up until now. Although he was getting old, these attributes still served him well. Keeping very still, he felt for the stone beer bottle, his fingers barely disturbing the straw. The stone was cold. Slowly, he wound his fingers around the bottle's neck as the pus from his boil seeped down the side of his nose. He couldn't hope to outfight Tom Strong, but whatever happened, he vowed he would not go down without a struggle.

The footsteps came closer. A long shadow fell in front of him. Distorted by the light behind, it was hard to judge who it was, but Reuben Trout was taking no chances. When flesh and blood replaced shadow, he hurled himself forward.

Whoever it was struck at him first. He heard his head crack as something heavy smashed down on it. Blood blinded him and mixed with the pus from his boil, seeping into his mouth and over his chin.

He might have choked on it, but another blow landed on his head, and this one was fatal.

'That's for my mother,' said Clarence, breathless from his exertion with the ironworker's mallet.

Footsteps sounded behind him and he turned.

'What have you done?' Tom could hardly believe what he was seeing. Clarence had taken the revenge that should have been his.

'I had to,' said the boy, his eyes wide and bright in his dirty face.

'Get out of here!' He snatched the mallet from the boy's hand and pushed him towards the door. 'Get out of here. Go down to the old warehouse opposite where the ship used to be.'

Tom felt the stickiness of blood on the hand with which he'd pushed the boy. 'But clean yourself up first. Get rid of that blood or they'll be hanging you.'

Clarence looked puzzled. Tom didn't have much time to explain. 'You've had enough problems in your life. Get out of here. I'll deal with this.'

The boy obeyed, though hesitated at the door. Then he asked, 'Are you my father?'

The question took Tom by surprise. It also clutched at his heart. He shook his head. 'No, son. But I wish I was.'

'So do I,' said the boy, and was gone.

Tom stared down at the grim corpse. This was murder and he'd taken the boy's guilt upon himself. Once his debt to Reuben Trout was paid, he'd had every intention of seeking out Blanche, of asking at every ship on the quay to see if she'd booked a passage back to Barbados. Failing that, he would have enquired at every inn, every boarding house along the quay. Clarence had changed all that.

He could not allow the boy to take the blame. He would have killed Trout anyway and hadn't really considered what he would do after that. Now he had only one option. He had to take berth on a ship, even if only as an able seaman. The Americas or Australia would be the best bet. Perhaps Boston, perhaps Botany Bay. The only thing that would stop him going would be if he found Blanche. He could protest his innocence. After all, Trout was a well-known ruffian. Anyone could have done it. But Tom had been asking questions and there were many who'd bear witness to that, especially Cuthbert Stoke, who must be aching for revenge after losing money on his last fight.

Leaving Trout to the devil and the darkness, Tom made his way to the quay and immediately found a ship needing a captain, the last having dropped dead after forty years at sea. From there he made his way to Somerset Parade. He had to get a message to Blanche.

Hammering at Conrad Heinkel's front door in the middle of the night would attract the attention of neighbours. He didn't want to be seen, or have Conrad implicated.

A high wall surrounded the garden at the rear of Conrad's new house in Redcliffe Parade. He remembered an arched door of stout oak set into the wall, mostly used by servants.

The access lane at the rear of the properties was dark and narrow. Tom felt his way along the wall, glad there was no moon, though the darkness impaired his progress. At last his fingers touched the gate handle, an iron ring hanging like the nose ring of a giant bull. He twisted it and pushed at the gate and found it locked.

He felt the stones of the wall. Unlike the house, which was built of smoothly finished Bath stone, it was rough, uneven and had useful footholds. Always good at climbing trees at Marstone Court, Tom used that skill now. His muscles further strengthened by the physical demands of a sailing ship, he clambered up and over the wall.

When he got to the back door, he stopped. Hammering at the back door was as bad as hammering at the front. Even if the neighbours weren't disturbed, the servants would be.

Looking up at the windows of the first floor, he calculated the exact position of Conrad's bedroom. He knew it was at the back of the house overlooking the garden, because he knew that Conrad didn't sleep well at times. After lighting his pipe, he sometimes stood at his bedroom window remembering his wife and how they used to walk together in the moonlight. Just as he thought that, the moon came out from behind the clouds making the garden seem as if it were covered in a silver cobweb.

It was luck, pure luck! He heard a window being opened, then smelt the aroma of good, strong Virginia. He stepped back and looked up.

'Conrad,' he whispered.

Conrad's head appeared out of the window. He wore no nightcap and no nightshirt either as far as Tom could tell.

'Tom?'

'I need to talk to you. It's important.'

Conrad nodded.

A minute later a flickering candle bobbed behind the scullery window and Conrad, dressed in a red quilted dressing gown, opened the door. He appeared apprehensive. Not surprising, thought Tom, being disturbed at this time of night.

For a moment, it seemed as though he wasn't going to invite him in, but then thought better of it. The candle was balanced on the edge of the copper, a scoop of a thing where Mrs Porter, the laundress, beat and boiled the family's laundry. Conrad closed the door a fraction, though not entirely. It was as if he was leaving Tom room to escape, as if he knew...

Quieter than usual, Conrad sucked on his pipe.

'I'm going away,' said Tom. 'I'm skippering the *Dominion* to Boston tomorrow – or perhaps I should say today.' He smiled, though inside he hurt.

'I will miss you. The refinery will miss you. But I understand.' Tom presumed he was referring to Jeb's recent death and that he understood how difficult it was for him at Marstone Court. But he couldn't leave it at that. He had to tell Conrad the truth.

He shook his head. 'You don't understand. Tonight a man was killed.' He went on to tell him about finding young Clarence standing over the body of Reuben Trout. 'Some may suspect me, but I want you to know the truth. I also want to give young Clarence a chance to get on with his life. Jeb gave me that chance. I feel obliged to do the same for Clarence.'

Conrad sunk down on to a chair, shook his head and rubbed at his face with his big, meaty hands. 'I thought you came here because...' He sighed and chose not to finish the sentence. He looked up at him. 'I will keep your secret, Tom.' He got to his feet and held out his hand. As they shook, Conrad smiled and looked suddenly sheepish. 'I thought you had come to see Blanche and to tell her not to marry me.'

Tom was stunned. 'You've seen her?'

'She is here. At present she is governess to my children. But I have asked her to marry me. It was in the letter you delivered for me?'

It was damned hard to hide his jealousy, but he did the best he could. 'Forgive me, Conrad. I forgot. Is she well?'

Conrad told him how distraught Blanche had been when he'd found her, and how even now she was asleep upstairs. 'In a separate bedroom, of course, until we are married,' he said. 'She has too much fire to be a servant, but she will make a good wife, one that will suit Conrad Heinkel anyway. We marry the day after tomorrow. Quick, yes? Tongues will wag!'

Tom didn't ask whether the Strong family would be informed or invited to the wedding. Social niceties meant nothing to Conrad. He did what he deemed right and as he pleased.

He thought about demanding to see her, but what did he have to offer? Word would spread that he'd killed Rueben Trout. He certainly couldn't deny wanting to, and he couldn't let Clarence take the blame. Just as he'd taken advantage of Jasper's death, so Clarence could build a new life if Tom took the blame overseas with him.

'I'm glad for you,' he said, though it pained him to say it.

'Good voyages, Tom.'

'Good voyages,' Tom repeated, the tightness in his chest seeming to prevent him from saying anything more. Although he wanted to leave a message for Blanche, telling her that his feelings had not changed, regardless of everything, what right did he have to come between them now? What could he give her compared with Conrad?

They parted, and although Tom knew that Conrad watched him until he disappeared through the arched doorway, he never looked back.

–

The breakfast table was set with the prettiest china that Blanche had ever seen in her life and every morning since moving in at Redcliffe, she'd taken great pride in helping the maid lay it out the way she liked it. Conrad had told her it was called Dresden and his wife had liked it just as much as she did.

Realizing it meant a lot to him, she always made a point after breakfast of helping to take it to the kitchen. Both the parlour and kitchen servants had been bemused, eyeing her warily as though trying to work out her motive. Although she tried to make friends with them, to put them at their ease, she found the task impossible. The moment she entered the kitchen, their gossiping stopped, except for this particular morning when she caught the tail end of the conversation.

One of the scullery maids was saying, 'I couldn't sleep, so I opened the window and looked out. That man was out there, the one who works with the master at the refinery but used to be a sea captain.'

'You mean Tom Strong?' said the cook with a frown. 'Now what would he be doing here in the middle of the night?'

'I couldn't hear what was said, but…'

The moment they realized that Blanche was in the doorway, the conversation ceased.

She must have looked like a ghost to them. Her hands shook so much that the china tinkled like broken glass on the tea tray. She wanted to ask them more, to shake it out of the scullery maid if necessary. Tom had clearly come to see Conrad, so she'd ask him why Tom had come here and why he hadn't told her.

Conrad's valet was brushing the shoulders of his favourite frock-tailed coat. It was green with black trim around the collars and cuffs, a little ostentatious for wearing to the refinery, but he liked it.

Blanche stood in the doorway, her fingers locking and unlocking with agitation.

Conrad smiled at her. 'Is something the matter, my dear?'

'Yes.'

Sensing her mood, Conrad ordered his valet to leave.

Blanche closed the door behind him. She hardly gave Conrad chance to cross the room before she said, 'What was Tom doing here last night?'

'Ah!'

'Did he come to see me?'

Conrad thought about it then shook his head. 'No.'

'So why was he here?'

As he always did when truth seemed the only course, Conrad sank into a chair and rubbed his cheeks with both hands. 'He is going back to sea.'

Blanche was thunderstruck. She'd never see him again. 'Did he mention me?'

Conrad thought about it. 'You were mentioned. I told him we were to be married.'

Her bosoms heaved. It felt as though her heart was trying to escape from her chest.

Conrad Heinkel was not a hard man. He was also extremely honest and would not force a woman into marriage if she had the least doubt about doing so. 'Look,' he said, 'I wish you to become my wife, but I will not drag you to the altar. Say your goodbyes to Tom before he sails. I understand that you must. And if afterwards you feel you do not wish to marry me, I will understand.'

He refused the presence of the coachman and drove her himself to St Augustine's Quay, but before they'd even got to St Augustine's Bridge, more commonly known as the drawbridge, they could see that the tide was in and the ship had sailed.

'We will still try,' said Conrad calmly and whipped the horses into a canter, dust flying as they headed towards Rownham Landing.

The ship slid like a spoon over milk, pulled by one of the new steam tugs.

Hooves slid on the shiny cobbles as Blanche and Conrad followed the ship and the tide out of the floating harbour and towards Windmill Hill. By the time they'd traversed the narrow country lane that led up the hill, they were slightly ahead of the ship, but not by much.

Blanche leaped out of the carriage before Conrad had chance to help her out. The wind caught at her bonnet. It was almost warmer now, not cold as on the day she'd first arrived in Bristol.

Conrad stayed by the carriage. She was grateful for that, though she had no idea what Tom would do when and if he saw her. Leap over the side and swim ashore?

Men were climbing in the ship's rigging, tying off sheets and making ready the sails for when they dropped the pilot, and slid out from the Avon into the Severn, the Bristol Channel and the open sea.

As the ship drew level, she saw a lone figure standing close to the helm. She could tell by the way he moved that he was giving orders, overseeing whatever was going on. When he shouted orders up into the rigging, she saw his head turn, his body stilled. He had seen her.

For one incredible instant they were alone together, confiding their innermost thoughts to each other, their regrets and their fears.

As the ship slid slowly by, he raised his hand in one final salute and Blanche raised hers. He was going where he had to be, and she was staying where she was needed.

She stood for a while until the ship had passed from view and the wind felt colder.

She'd brushed the tears from her eyes by the time she got back to Conrad who looked at her with concern.

'Are you better now?'

'Yes,' she said, and managed to smile. 'I'm better now.' And she really thought she was.

## Acknowledgements

My grateful thanks to everyone at Bristol Records Office who allowed me access to some very useful material indeed. And to Mary, my most loyal reader, and Darleen who started it all.